"HI" IN THE SKY

Up in the balloon, Frank nudged him. "Co—co—, uh." He seemed unable to finish his sentence.

"Hmmm?" Keith inquired, glancing up, and froze.

"Company," Frank choked out at last.

Keith found himself gazing into a pair of round, sky-blue eyes, but they weren't Frank's. In fact, the body they were attached to was hovering under its own power outside the balloon's basket.

The creature was about a foot high, and the cloudy blue-white of glacial snow. Below the translucent torso its substance thinned down to pale, insubstantial streamers. It had delicate, attenuated wings, and its face was like that of an owl, but where Keith would have expected to see a beak there was nothing at all. It tilted its inverted-wedge of a head at Keith. The being nodded.

"What are you?" Keith asked, awed.

The light creature recoiled from his outrush of breath and then swam closer to him.

A vision intruded itself into his sight . . .

"An exceptionally entertaining and unusual contemporary fantasy."
—*Locus* on *Mythology 101*

"Quite successful . . . Nye's prose style captures that sense of fun with just a touch of drama very effectively."
—**Charles de Lint** on *Mythology 101*

Also by Jody Lynn Nye

Mythology 101
Mythology Abroad

Published by
WARNER BOOKS

HIGHER MYTHOLOGY

JODY LYNN NYE

WARNER BOOKS

A Time Warner Company

WARNER BOOKS EDITION

Questar® is a registered trademark of Warner Books, Inc.

Cover design by Don Puckey

Warner Books, Inc.
1271 Avenue of the Americas
New York, NY 10020

 A Time Warner Company

Printed in the United States of America

First Printing: January, 1993

10 9 8 7 6 5 4 3 2 1

To Keith Doyle's 'godparents,'
Sue Stone and Brian Thomsen

Prologue

"I always cry at weddings," Diane Londen said, snuffling noisily into her handkerchief. "Oh, God, I only brought one hanky! I'll be a mess by the time the bride comes out."

Without looking up from his viewfinder, Keith Doyle reached into his pocket and passed her his own square of cotton. "Here. I can always grab a napkin off the table if I need one."

"Don't you dare!" Diane admonished him, refraining from shoving his shoulder only because it might knock over the video camera he was adjusting. His face was invisible, leaving only a thatch of wavy red hair showing over the body of the camera. She directed her remarks to that. "It looks too nice to disturb."

Freeing his eye from the rubber focusing ring, Keith glanced over at the huge buffet table laden with a feast of good-looking dishes that lined one entire length of the Little Folk's great room. Well, the concept of huge was relative. The tabletop hit him just above knee height, as he had found out to his agony when he had arrived and tripped over it, and the bowls and platters were small compared to what graced the Doyle family table on major holidays. But the feast itself, for pure variety and quantity, was nothing less than spectacular.

The Hollow Tree farmhouse had been transformed fantastically in the few weeks since he and Holl had returned from their transatlantic trip; almost more than it had since the Little Folk had moved in at the beginning of the summer. With a special

impetus urging them on, the Folk had worked wonders. In one
month flat, the house had gone from being a pretty ordinary
building where people lived and worked and repaired the neglect
of decades, to a fanciful bower, complete with braided arches of
vine and flowers over every door, and 3-D pictures in wood,
glittering stone, and colorful woven tapestry on nearly every
wall.

All the Little Folk were already in the big room. It just about
held the eighty-some of them, with a little space left over for the
handful of Big Folk visiting for the wedding. Midriff high to a
medium-sized human adult, the Little Folk resembled the Big
Ones in nearly every way. They were proportioned just like
humans, with the notable exception of tall, elegantly pointed ears
and faces that looked young, almost childlike, even on those
with beards or gray hair. And they could do magic. They assured
Keith time and again there was nothing about the wonders they
worked that he couldn't do himself with practice and patience,
but he still held them in awe.

Not enough awe to quench his delight that his best friend
among them, Holl, was marrying his ladylove Maura, and that
he, Keith, was here to witness the event, not to mention record
it for posterity. This gave him a rare chance to see his mysterious
friends at their best. Keith knew that this was to be the first
wedding among the Folk in over forty years—the first since they
had come to the midwestern United States—and the first real
celebration of any kind in who knew how long.

Out of pure excitement, not to mention a little pride, everyone
had gone all out to deck the house in beauty for the occasion.
Flowers festooned every vertical surface, leaving one to perch
well forward on the chair seats lest a casual move crush a careful
arrangement and dust the unwary sitter with pollen and petals.
The blossoms' scents filled the air. Living vines had been en-
twined with streamers to arch across the ceiling and doorways.
Each one of the Folk, large and small, had on new clothes,
specially made for the occasion. Keith surveyed the range of
costumes that embraced styles from a nod to ancient Greece to
a whimsical interpretation of modern metalhead.

And there was the feast yet to come. Among the Little Folk
there were some notable cooks. After years of school food, any
meal actually prepared for less than a hundred tasted pretty good

to Keith. Add skill and time to improvise and season, and the results were actually ambrosial. Keith's belly rumbled in anticipation. On the table, plates of cold meats, cheese, and fruit were arranged around big empty spaces awaiting the arrival of the hot dishes, which Keith could smell cooking just beyond the doorway. Big bowls, carved beautifully in some of the elves' favorite designs, ivy and honeysuckle, held their quivering cargo of creamy yellow or ruby red confections ever so slightly out of reach of the flies that circled hopefully overhead. No pest alighted on the food or dishes. There was a distance beneath which the insects couldn't go, though they kept on noisily trying. Keith sensed a benevolent buffer layer of magic that protected the picnic from the ants. He wondered if it would keep out the questing fingers of a hungry college student hoping to extract an olive from the crudités tray.

To Keith's delight, in the center of the table was a broad, flattened bowl filled with unsliced loaves of fresh bread. He didn't need to see the look of pride on the face of Holl's sister Keva when she caught him eyeing it hungrily. Keva made the best bread in the world. Keith had eaten enough of it to give it his wholehearted approval. To make his joy complete, he spotted butter and fruit preserves in wooden dishes nearby.

Though pastries and other goodies abounded, there was no wedding cake as Big Folk were accustomed to seeing, so he suspected the ornately-fashioned braided bread at the nearest edge of the table would serve much the same purpose. The wooden-staved keg at the other end, seeming a little self-conscious under its crown of vine-leaves and larkspur, had to be full of home-made brew. Elven hooch sneaked up on you, Keith recalled. It had to be magic, because although it packed a good kick, it didn't leave behind hangovers as a lasting memento. The wallop happened all at once, and got the punishment over with.

Holl and Maura had kindly waited for the fall class session at Midwestern University to begin before celebrating their nuptials, so their classmates could join them. That consideration told the Big friends that they were as valued as much by the bride and groom as the folk of their own size. Keith thought this was a terrific way to begin his junior year.

A peep through his viewfinder framed some of the Big guests arriving. Keith waved over the camera's top at Teri Knox, a

pretty girl who'd been in the secret classes taught by the Elf
Master. She graduated this summer. Her honey-blond hair was
almost hidden by a wreath of silk flowers, a medieval accompaniment to her modern, sleeveless, soft jersey dress. Teri spotted
him and waved, making a deliberate face for the camera. Barry
Goodman, next in the door, echoed the expression. Teri caught
Lee Eisley's sleeve and pointed toward Keith. Lee shook his
head with a pained, pitying look on his dark bronze face. Keith
grinned. This was going to be a great tape.

Lee was the first Big pupil the Elf Master had ever taught.
He'd been out of college for over a year now. Though he was a
quiet man, Lee's high GPA in journalism had helped him to get
a foot in the door at the Indianapolis daily paper. Hard work and
talent got him the occasional featured article, each of which
Catra, the archivist, had carefully preserved in a scrapbook. The
Elf Master was proud of his oldest pupil and was glad that the
young man made time to keep in touch. Contrarywise, Keith
knew Lee would rather lose his byline and five or six teeth than
miss an event like this. All of them had reason to be grateful to
the Little Folk for helping them to master difficult academic
subjects but, before Keith came along, had never had much social
interaction with their small benefactors.

Dunn Jackson was the newest keeper of the secret. He was
Diane's addition to the class, as Diane had been Keith's. The
three of them shared an Introduction to Philosophy course that
threatened to swamp them all in a wave of gibberish. If the
Master hadn't begun a parallel tutorial in the basics of philosophi-
cal thought, Keith could have kissed goodbye his consistent B
average. Dunn's cheeks were flushed red under his light coffee-
colored skin. He was excited to be here, too. His eyes were
wide, moving here and there, trying to take in everything at
once. Keith liked him. Dunn had an enquiring mind that ran
along some of Keith's favorite channels. He and Keith had gotten
together over speculations that if Little Folk of the Caucasian
persuasion existed, there might be some of his own color out
there somewhere. It was a concept worth exploring one day.

The other newcomer was an elf from the Old Country. In
Keith's opinion, Tiron felt at a disadvantage in a new country
among seven dozen new Folk, and it came across as an attitude
problem. One facet of his real personality was as clear as the

blue sky: Tiron was a womanizer. Without having to ask for details, Keith could tell Tiron had set the sisters Catra and Candlepat against one another—not too difficult a thing to do—for the prize of his affections. But his direct challenge of Holl's position as acknowledged future leader was going nowhere; Holl was too popular. Pity would have been out of place for the newcomer, though. Tiron wasn't suffering for lack of attention. The older Folk sought him out as a tie to the old country, and the younger ones as a curiosity, someone like them with whom they hadn't grown up. His skill in woodworking was also great, putting him immediately into the first rank of craftsmen and craftswomen at Hollow Tree Industries. Keith was sure Tiron would relax in time. If he didn't, some of the fathers of daughters would take turns decking him until he did.

Things were different now that the Folk had a place of their own. The first change Keith noticed was sound. When they were living beneath the Midwestern University library, everyone had been quiet, listening all the time for footsteps, fearful that they would be discovered by the terrible Big Ones. They were liberated now. The twenty acres of thickets and meadows around the house echoed with the more normal hubbub of eighty or ninety beings, plus farm animals, plus pets. Out in the small Near Meadow, just beyond the kitchen door, were a handful of sheep and a dog barking at them. And there was music. Tuning up in a corner was a small band consisting of a harp, two wooden flutes, an ancient fiddle, a guitar, and a gadget that looked like a combination of the last two. The guitar player, Marcy Collier, was a Big Person, a friend and former object of Keith's unrequited affection. She smiled at him shyly and bent her head to tune a string. Her thick, black hair was crowned with ivy and roses, like those of the Little People around her. Unlike most Big Folk, Marcy belonged here, on Hollow Tree Farm. She and Enoch, the Elf Master's son, were an "item." Marcy took a lot of good-natured razzing on the topic from her friends, but she was learning to defend herself and her choices. In Keith's opinion, the Constitutionally-guaranteed pursuit of happiness included dating someone half one's height. He applauded anything that made Marcy happy. With love and support, she was blossoming into a capable, confident woman.

The music and the noise in the room died away suddenly as

Curran, Holl's clan chief, appeared at the door. For once, the sour old elf had a smile on his face. By contrast, Holl, behind him, looked solemn and nervous. His usually pink cheeks were pale. He was dressed in new clothes of russet and dark green that were cut to unfamiliar pattern that made him look as if he had stepped out of a long gone time. His dark blond hair was slightly damp and curled up at the ends, as if it had been wet-combed just moments ago. On his head he wore a woven circlet of white bellflowers. The magic blossoms gave off a white light visible to those who could see that kind of thing, gathering strength from and giving strength to Holl. Keith regretted that the video camera didn't have second sight to catch the almost perceptible pulsations of mystic energy. Beside him, Diane sighed. In the corner, the harp player began a soft, winding melody like the memory of a forgotten dream.

There was a whisper of sound from the opposite side of the room. The Elf Master stepped into the doorway leading from the kitchen, his head held high and proud. Maura held his arm. Her rich hair, a deep auburn almost the color of carnelians, was braided into complicated patterns and crowned with bellflowers, the blossoms nodding with every step she took. Embroidery ran down the bodice of her dress and around the long sleeves, blending the green and gray ivy pattern favored by Holl's clan with the green and yellow honeysuckle motif of her own. In her hand she clutched a bunch of the white flowers, their energy gleaming and spilling over her fingers like water. Maura's lips were trembling, caught between a smile and tears. She stepped toward Holl with a look of love and anticipation burning in her deep green eyes that made Keith catch his breath. The Little Folk were so childlike in appearance that sometimes he forgot that they were mature adults, far older and wiser than he. That brief flash reminded him. Holl came forward to meet her, his right hand outstretched.

Candlepat broke through the ring of witnesses and hurried to Holl, clutching his arm and turning him away from his bride. Keith was shocked. The blond elf, a pixie carved by Playboy, had lost her usual self-assurance, and looked pathetic, even woeful.

"Holl, don't go to her. I care for you, too. What about me?" she begged, her eyes gleaming with tears.

Keith was horrified. Blindly, he felt his way around the camera and edged forward. Candlepat was such an all-round flirt, even vamping him sometimes, he'd never suspected she had an honest attachment to Holl. This was no time for her to bring it up. He couldn't let her interrupt the ceremony. She probably needed a good heart-to-heart talk with someone. If he got her outside, the wedding could proceed uninterrupted.

Steel-strong fingers gripped his forearm and dragged him back. Keith glanced down. Maura's black-haired brother was holding on to him with all the natural strength of a full-time carpenter. Did he want his sister's wedding disturbed? What was going on here?

"It's part of the custom," Enoch growled under his breath. "Explanations later."

Arrested, Keith nodded, his eyes fixed on the figures in the center of the room. "All right," he whispered. Carefully, he edged back to his post, hoping he hadn't gotten in the way of the lens.

Holl put the girl gently aside, with a tender touch on the cheek.

"I want only Maura," Holl answered her softly. His hand came away wet with her tears. "You'll find someone, lass. But not me." Candlepat withdrew to the edge of the ring, and her sister enfolded her in a comforting arm. Keith couldn't see Candlepat's face, but she was too proud to show disappointment in her posture. He wondered how much of her performance had been sincere.

The couple took a few more steps toward one another, and Enoch shoved forward, moving between his sister and Holl.

"Think, sister," he said, almost hoarsely. "You're too young to make a life's commitment."

Smiling, Maura touched his hand with her fingertips, then clasped it briefly in her own. "Thank you, but I made my choice long ago." She leaned to kiss him.

Enoch nodded, and eyes down, moved out of the way. As he returned to his place, Keith could see him smile. The two pairs met in the center of the circle and the clan leaders put the marrying couple's hands together. Curran and the Master shook hands—the white head and the red nodding politely to one another—and stepped away, leaving Maura and Holl alone together, joined.

Holl smiled at Maura. "Before our friends, I swear that I will be a good husband to you, support you, and provide for you. Not only a lover I'd be, but a friend and partner in all things. No other will ever supplant you in my heart. I promise to treat your dreams as dearly as my own, to enjoy and suffer life along-side you all the days of our lives.''

"Since we were children, I knew we were meant to be to-gether," Maura replied. Her voice trembled as if she might burst into tears. "I've never wanted another for my lifemate, and I come to you with joy.''

The audience sighed with pleasure as Holl bent his head and kissed Maura gently. Keith waited, but the embrace deepened, went on and on. The Elf Master cleared his throat. After a long moment, the couple broke their kiss and came up for air. Maura's cheeks were rose-pink.

The Master held out his hands to them. "As you haf claimed one another, none of us shall stand between you or compel you apart. I offer my congratulations and good wishes.'' Beaming, Holl and Maura moved to embrace him, then turned to enfold Curran. The crowd converged on the couple, shouting well wishes. No longer constrained to silence, Diane honked loudly into Keith's handkerchief.

"You'd think I'd learn to buy waterproof mascara," she said, smiling. Her eyes were rimmed with soggy black. She dabbed it away. "Oh, I'm so happy.''

"Me, too," said Keith.

He couldn't stop grinning. Happiness seemed to be conta-gious, because the foolishly indulgent smile he wore was on every set of lips in the room.

"And now the feast begins," curly-haired Rose called out cheerfully. Like a flock of pigeons abandoning one old lady with a bag of crumbs on a park bench for another, the crowd reversed and made toward the feast table. Keith managed to barge through the throng to Holl and Maura. He knelt to kiss the bride on the cheek and gave Holl a strong embrace and a hearty slap on the back.

He tried to find something deep and profound to say, but all that came out was, "Congratulations and good luck.''

Maura squeezed his hand. "It could not have happened with-out you," she said.

"It was nothing, Maura. I'm a sucker for a happy ending," Keith said, feeling his cheeks burn. "Hey, what was all that about a challenge tradition? For a moment there I thought the whole thing would stop."

"It is one of our oldest traditions, ye ignorant infant," a gruff voice said from behind him. Enoch stepped over Keith's ankle to get to his sister. He embraced her and his new brother-in-law. "I'd never have kept Maura from claiming this grinning oaf if she truly wanted him," he aimed a warning scowl toward Holl, "nor would I have let him take a step nearer her if she looked at all unhappy about it." The rough edge in his voice was undoubtedly connected to the bright gleam in his eyes. Keith's mouth was open as he considered the delightful revelation: Enoch was sentimental. When the black-haired elf turned back to him with a suspicious glare, Keith's mouth snapped shut like a trap. "I'll explain it all to you in words of one syllable. Come with me, and listen."

While they stood in line for the buffet, Enoch explained the custom of the challenge. "It's to ensure that each of the pair loves the other without doubt. In the face of the challenge, either is entitled to turn away if they feel they're being coerced into the match or making a hasty decision. We like to take our time to decide things, as well you know. There might be hurt feelings this way, but no lifelong mistakes are likely to be made, and we live long lives."

"I like that a lot," Keith said, nodding approval. "To win your ladylove, you have to be proof against temptations or threats."

"So pretty a custom," said a voice at Keith's elbow, making him start. He looked into the twinkling blue eyes of the elderly woman beside him. Ludmilla Hempert must have been standing beside him the whole time, listening to Enoch talk. She patted Keith on the arm with a somewhat large and surprisingly strong hand. "I surprised you? I have been resting in one of these so fine rooms. Ah, my little ones! A feeble, old lady like me, and they must have me by them when they bless the young."

Ludmilla was a retired cleaning woman who had been working for the University at the time the Little Folk had taken refuge there. She was the first benevolent Big Person the Little Folk had ever encountered, and they treated her like a guardian angel. As for her protests as to being a feeble old lady, Keith wouldn't have bet against her bench-pressing her weight in grandchildren.

"It wouldn't have been the same without you. Can I make you a copy of the videotape?" Keith asked, politely.

Ludmilla beamed. "Oh, yes, I would enjoy it. But how would I explain to my family when they visit?" she asked, with a sly quirk of her mouth.

Keith grinned back. "I'll put opening credits on it. You can tell them it's a Hollywood short subject called 'A Mid-Autumn's Afternoon Dream.' "

Beer would make him too drowsy to enjoy the dancing, so he wandered into the kitchen to find a glass of water instead. There were clean cups on the table, but when he reached for the tap, Shelogh called out to him.

"The purified water's in the jug. Have all you want of that. We've a cisternful down below. Don't bother with the tap. The water stinks."

"What's wrong with it?" Keith asked.

"Oh, nicht much," Shelogh said, mixing midwestern English with the Germanic accent the middle-aged Folk had picked up from Ludmilla Hempert. "Just some nasties, smells like it seeped out of a barn instead of from between limestone sheets."

"Bizarre," Keith said, pouring out water from the jug and tasting it: pure, clear, invigorating as wine. "Should I start looking for a water-purifier for you?"

"Oh, no," she cried, "when we can do it ourselves? Ach, Keith Doyle. We haf energy to spare now that it's our own home. Have you not noticed?"

"Oh, yes," Keith said, with a grin. "I have. It's terrific."

Holl came through with a stack of dirty plates and put them up on the drainboard.

"Hey, it's a rotten thing to mention on your wedding day, but what's wrong with the water supply? It smells like runoff from a feedlot, but there's no feedlot within miles. One cow and seven sheep couldn't do that much damage, not to the underground water table."

"Oh, that," Holl said. "Olanda has listened to the water's

heart. She said it isn't natural. Someone is pouring an evil smelling mess into it.''

Keith's brows drew down over his thin nose. ''That sounds like deliberate contamination of the groundwater. That shouldn't be going on down here. You ought to try to arouse some local action to look into it. You should write letters to the editor, or something.''

''Of that wee paper that comes out once a week?'' Holl asked, astonished.

''Come on, Holl, you live in a small community yourself. Everyone reads *The Central Illinois Farmer* because it's more personalized to them than, say, the *Chicago Tribune* or *The New York Times*. You could write really stirring letters if you put your mind to it. You're the most environmentally aware people I know. You can *hear* streams and trees complain. You waste nothing. I know your homes in the library were built with scrap, and you use everything to death.''

Holl stroked his chin. ''Then the ones to blame might be more apt to pay attention to a well-written plaint, eh?''

''Right,'' Keith said.

''Would they listen to the cries of a mythical person, then?'' Holl spluttered.

''No one who can mail a letter is mythical. If it goes that far, I'll come down here when they check out the groundwater on the farm,'' Keith said. ''But hey! I didn't mean to get you off on a tangent. This is your wedding day. Have a blast!'' The band in the corner began to play. ''Dance with your wife,'' Keith finished, with a grin.

''Just the thing I was about to suggest to him,'' Maura said, coming up to claim her bridegroom. She tucked her hand into the crook of his arm and drew him out onto the floor. Keith watched them swirl away to the merry beat of the dance band.

With all their friends and relatives clapping the beat, the bride and groom circled the room. The music had as much magic in it as the crowns of flowers they wore. Keith found himself tapping his toes with the rhythm, and longing to get out and do the modified polka which was his standard for weddings and other festive occasions.

Pat Morgan, Keith's former dorm mate with whom he was

currently sharing a cheap student apartment just off the Midwest-ern campus, came over to poke him in the ribs with the handle of his dessert fork. "Look at this," Pat said, gesturing around him with a sweep of his arm. "It's like a Shakespearean pageant, with all the elements of traditional drama—love, suspense, happy ending." He sighed. "It would never make it in the theater today." Pat had a melancholy bent that went with his Ricardian looks.

Breathless, the bridal couple broke apart though the music was still playing. Each ran to the sidelines and joined hands with the parent-in-law of the opposite sex. Then those couples parted to bring others onto the floor one by one. Maura's tiny hands seized Keith's, and pulled him out to dance. His partner looked like the bride on the top of a traditional wedding cake, and was almost small enough to fit. He felt like an uncle escorting a five-year-old niece.

"You look beautiful. Could you possibly be that happy?" he asked, feeling indulgent.

"More so, Keith Doyle," Maura said, her skin fresh and pink, her eyes like firelit emeralds. "I feel I owe you much."

"Holl did it," Keith said, hastily, turning away in embar-rassment but making it look as if he was making sure they weren't going to bash into the next set of dancers. "Holl did it all. He saved my neck, too, you know."

"He learns quickly, but he had a good example set him," Maura said, not letting him off the hook. "Well, when will we see you as happy as we are? When will you ask the pretty Diane to wed with you?"

"Uh, not yet," Keith said, feeling his cheeks flush. "At least let me get out of school first and find a decent job! Love in a student-grade apartment isn't all that romantic."

"When you're in love, any bower is a palace," the elf lass reminded him. She fixed him with a searching gaze. "You didn't gainsay me. So you'd actually do it, would you? She's the one of your heart?"

"Uh," Keith said, feeling the floor drop out from under him. He looked around wildly, wondering if anyone was in a position to overhear them. Thankfully, the music was pretty loud. "Come on, Maura, have mercy! I want to do things in the right time. Don't tell her."

"*I* don't have to," the girl said, coyly. With a gay smile, she spun away from him and chose another partner. Inspired by Maura's last teasing words, Keith turned to find Diane and draw her into the dance, but to his amazement, the Elf Master had already asked her.

"Claim-jumper," Keith muttered. He turned and bowed to Ludmilla Hempert and assisted her gallantly to the floor.

In the second set, he managed to secure a dance with Diane. She was breathless and flushed.

"Isn't this wonderful?" she asked. "I'm so happy for them, Keith."

"Keith Doyle!" Dennet, Holl's father, waved to them from the side of the room. "There's been a package for you, by the by. Did Rose give it to you?"

"Uh, no," Keith said, puzzled.

"Oh, I'll find it. There's been enough of a stir these last days, so there has." He bustled away and returned with a flat box covered with brown paper and tied with waxed string. "From Ireland, it is. Have you friends called Skylark, then?"

"Mailed from a pub of that name," Keith explained, unwrapping the brown paper. He grinned, and showed the contents to Diane and Dennet. The flabby rectangle wrapped up in fine embroidered cloth had a fancy lettered card tucked under the ribbon. "It's not for me. It's for Holl. A wedding present. From the Niall."

Dennet's eyes twinkled. He looked like a teenager letting them in on a prank, in spite of his white hair. It was disconcerting, considering how old Keith suspected he was. "There's the name of a man whose face I've not seen these, oh, well, how long has it been? Your photographs were like a work of wonder, lad. I thought never to see those likenesses again in life. What's in the package, then? Ah, gifting time won't be far off. I'll have to hold my curiosity 'til then."

"How long *has* it been?" Keith asked, pointedly. He had never managed to learn how long ago the Little Folk had made their way to the New World, nor how old they grew to be. Curiosity made his invisible whiskers twitch.

"Oh, a long time," Dennet said. He smiled conspiratorially at Keith. Maybe he thinks I already know, Keith thought, dismayed. "Gifting time's coming soon, after Holl and Maura have

broken their fast together as husband and wife. My son's eaten
nary a thing all day, though he's been up since sunrise, he's that
nervous.''

"I can't blame him," Keith said, and recoiled as Diane socked
him on the arm. "Ouch!"

"Well, go and enjoy the feast," Dennet said hospitably. He
turned to follow his own advice.

Keith went back to his camera and filmed some of the guests
eating, talking, dancing, and eating some more, then turned his
lens and hastily focused on a full plate moving toward him.

"There," Diane said, putting her hand over the lens. He
lowered the camera and she handed him the plate. "Stay out of
trouble."

Keith dug in to his second helping. His anticipation had in no
way been exceeded by the reality. The food was terrific. Meat
dishes were few, with a more significant presence by savories
that got their proteins from nuts and beans. The vegetables were
as ornate as the room's decor: carrots were cut into corkscrews,
celery shredded into small replicas of wheatsheaves, relishes
and salads appeared as colorful as mosaics and stained glass
windows—and everything was delicious.

"Did you see the dessert?" Diane asked, pointing to the edge
of his plate with her fork.

Two half-blown rosebuds lay together near the salad. They
were nearly lifelike, except for the fact that they were larger and
transparent. "Those are amazing. What are they made of?"
Keith asked.

"Jell-O," Diane said, with an impish grin. She ticked the
plate rim with her fingernail, and the gelatin rosebuds quivered.
"When I asked how they did that, Calla said, 'Enhancing, lass,
enhancing!' " Diane mocked the Little Folk's teasing tone.

"That's all the answer you'll ever get out of them," Keith
said, with a grin.

After much of the feast was eaten, the newlyweds were en-
throned on the finest of the flower-strewn chairs. At their feet
the children placed the colorfully-wrapped packages entrusted to
them by the adults. The presents from other Little Folk were
few. The Big Folk proffered their large, and in Keith's case,
heavy, boxes with slight embarrassment.

"Oh, don't concern yourself," Holl assured them. "It's most generous of you to include us in your custom. Heart's generosity is always welcome. In our ways, which are a bit rusty, as you might guess from forty years' disuse, presents given to the newly-wed couple are mostly personal in nature, since everything else is shared for the good of all. But Maura and I are grateful for whatever inspiration you've been visited by. Be sure none are unwelcome. We'll open yours first, after a presentation of my own."

He turned to Maura and lightly held out his hand for hers. When she extended her palm, an inquiring expression on her face, he placed in it a tiny, carved wooden box.

"We work mostly in wood, but I wanted something a little thinner and stronger," Holl said. Maura pressed the minute button and lifted the box's lid. Inside was a ring made of braided silver and gold. In its center, glowing with the blue of a cloudless sky, was an oval sapphire. Keith and the others let out an appreciative gasp as Maura showed it around.

"But where did you find the stone?" she asked.

Tiron cleared his throat. "A heart's gift from me, cousin," Tiron said hoarsely. "I swear by the trees and the earth that there are no love spells on it to make you turn to me, nor any other influence that would lessen your joy." Surprised, Maura smiled warmly at him.

The sentimental, generous gesture showed a side of Tiron that surprised Keith. The strange elf seemed at times to be the greatest of egotists. He blushed when Maura rose from her throne to kiss him heartily on the cheek.

"We welcome you among us," Maura said, squeezing his hand. "I can't thank you enough."

"Well, it's nothing," Tiron said, blushing.

"But you're trying to belittle the gift," Holl protested. "He told me that the stone came from the hand of a king in days long gone. This king, a visitor from over the water, gave it to our people in Ireland and promised to keep faith with them, but he was killed soon after by traitors."

"Which king?" Keith asked eagerly. "How far over the water? England? Scotland? Denmark?"

Tiron shrugged. "I'm sure I didn't listen to the old stories," he said. "You can write to the Niall, for all the useless rambling you'll get out of him."

"Well, it's a mighty gift," Maura said. "Thank you. And thank you for the crafting of it into such a treasure," she said to her husband, bestowing a tender kiss on him. Holl reddened, beaming. "And now let us see what our other kindhearted friends have given."

"Uh," Keith said, flushing red while Maura circled around the box he offered with anticipation. "Since you have a working windmill for electricity, I thought this might come in handy. It's used, but I had it tuned up before I brought it down. I coated the wheel with urethane so you wouldn't get metal burns." He had prepared his speech ahead of time but it seemed silly and stilted now. "Um . . . don't lose the traditional skills you have just because technology makes it easier to perform your tasks."

"Vell put," said the Master, nodding, "and very true. I didn't think you had it in you, Meester Doyle."

"Uh, thanks. Just tear it, Maura," Keith suggested, watching the bride run her hands along the side looking for gaps in the cellophane-taped seams. "The suspense is getting painful."

"As you wish." Maura shredded the paper and tossed it aside. Together, she and Holl pried open the cardboard box. "It's a sewing machine," she said. With a good deal of assistance, she drew it out of its protective nest. "A fine one." The name was embossed on the black enamel of the steel body below the dials. At Holl's urging she flipped up the lid on top and read the small chart. "Look at all the stitches it will do!"

"Machine doings, huh!" Dierdre sneered. She was the oldest of the old women, a contemporary of Curran, and a clan leader in her own right. "It takes all the soul straight out of the work, so it does. That'll never make anything worth keeping."

"Oh, come, gran," Candlepat admonished her, with a cocky tilt to her head. "Do you truly enjoy hemming sheets and seaming curtains? I don't. The machine will leave your hands free for the fine work, which *is* worth keeping."

"That may be qvite true," Rose said, with a thoughtful expression. Though a Conservative, she was suspected of having Progressive leanings, and in any case trusted Keith Doyle absolutely. She and a few of the needlecraft workers examined the old Singer with pleasure.

"It'll come in most useful, you'll see," Tiron said. "Next year there'll be cloth from the backs of those sheep outside. The first of the looms will be ready by year's end."

Diane blew her nose as Maura undid the paper on the next present and lifted the esoteric-looking machine inside to her lap.

"It's a blender," Diane said, and burst into sputtering tears. Through her sobs, she explained. "I always give blenders for wedding presents. It does all kinds of things. You can return it if you've already got one, or you can exchange it for something else you'd like better. The receipt's in the bottom. Oh, I'm so happy for you!"

"There's never a thought of returning it. We're pleased to be part of your tradition," Holl accepted gravely, "as you are a part of ours. We will use it with joy in the generosity of the donor."

"It's not that big a deal," Diane said, sniffling, but she was pleased.

"The last one's a surprise," Keith said, handing over the cloth-wrapped bundle. "The Niall sent you something from the Old Country."

"Why did he not send it through me, then?" Tiron burst out, disappointed. "And me just lately departed from his domain?"

"You're illegal, remember?" Keith pointed out quickly. "No one is supposed to know you're here."

Tiron nodded, stroking his chin. "I'd forgotten. Ah, but forced anonymity is hard."

Holl pulled the ribbon off the cloth package, and it spilled open over Maura's lap, wave after wave of foamy lace escaping in folds down her knees to the floor. Laughing, the two of them knelt to gather it up. Holl threw a swag of it around his bride's shoulders, where it lay gleaming like joined snowflakes. She beamed and kissed him.

The others exclaimed over the fineness of the work. "How beautiful. Best I've ever seen. Probably very old, feel the texture and the quality."

"That wasn't finished in a day, nor from any hard, iron machine," said Dierdre smugly.

"No, from a small bone shuttle," scolded one of the other oldsters. "This is the work of years and many hands."

"The card says, 'with best regards and a thousand bless- ings,' " Orchadia said. "Well, that's very fine of them."

That was the last of the presents. Rose, Calla, and the other ladies serving, circulated with wooden cups, followed by their husbands with kegs of wine. They poured libations into larger goblets for their Big guests, who were touched by the special effort.

"The toast to the wedded couple," Dennet said, stilling Dunn's hand before he could drink. The newest student grinned, sharing a smile with Holl's father.

"Sorry. Guess I'm just a little too eager to wish them well."

The Master raised his hands for silence. "I haf vun more announcement before anyvun becomes too merry to compre- hend," the Elf Master said. "In three days, please, I vould like from each of my senior students an essay of four pages on the subject of the psychological impact of the Industrial Refolution on those already liffing in the great population centers of Europe at the time. That is all."

Keith, Dunn, and Diane groaned. As the Big students scram- bled for paper and pen to write down the assignments, Teri Knox and Lee Eisley exchanged relieved glances.

"Master, I miss you, but I sure am glad I don't have to do the homework anymore!" Lee said fervently. He raised his cup in salute to the little professor, who regarded him with austere complacence over the rims of his glasses.

Holding Maura firmly by the hand, Holl turned to Keith with his glass high.

"As the one who's most responsible for helping to facilitate the day's events, Keith Doyle, will you make the first toast?" Holl asked.

Keith flushed. "It'd be an honor." Thinking hard to come up with a toast that wouldn't be too long or too maudlin, he cleared his throat. The room stilled, and all his friends looked at him. He smiled.

"To my friends, Holl and Maura, I wish every happiness," Keith said, raising up his wooden cup. "Today is the first day of the rest of your lives. Make the best of it."

"That's lovely," Diane whispered, giving him a hug.

"Very profound," said Pat Morgan, dryly, eyebrows raised over the brim of his glass. "You ought to write greeting cards, Doyle."

"I like it," Holl said, decidedly, touching his winecup to his bride's. "To today, and every day hereafter."

Chapter
ONE

A year and a day later, Keith prepared to go calling on Holl.

From the basket of his conveyance, he leaned out and addressed the crowd gathered in the middle of the Midwestern University experimental farm. The handful of students, variously dressed in lab coats or filthy jeans, watched him with interest and thinly-disguised amusement. The ground crew, two men in blue jeans, jackets, goggles, and gloves, walked the balloon at shoulder height, as if carrying a sedan chair, to the designated launch point.

"To the Scarecrow, by virtue of his enormous brain," Keith said, gesturing grandly, "to the Tin Woodsman, by virtue of his Heart . . ." The rattan basket tipped slightly as he leaned over the side, and he stepped back in alarm.

"What are you doing?" demanded the other man in the balloon basket, turning away from the gas jet he was adjusting. Frank Winslow's vintage WWI flyer's helmet was jammed down over his head, pushing out the goggles standing on his forehead that made him look like he had four round and glassy blue eyes instead of two. "Are you weird, or something?"

"Nope," Keith replied cheerfully, turning away from his audience. "Just always wanted to do that." Deprived of their entertainment, many of them left. A few continued to gawk at the balloon. "Anything I can help with?"

"Nope. Just sit tight and stay out of the way. Let 'er go!"

The lanky pilot waved to his crew, and they loosed the balloon and stepped back. With a roar, the flames leaped up into the balloon's heart, and the Iris jumped up in response.

The Skyship Iris was an ovoid rainbow as it rose over the buildings of Midwestern University. Keith clung fast to the edge of the waist-high basket until he discovered that the motion was far less than he had expected, milder even than the college library's geriatric elevator. He felt almost as if the ground had dropped away and to the side beneath them, leaving him hovering in place, stuck fast in the sky while the world moved. There was no vibration but that caused by the thrum of the burners. Frank fed more propane in whooshing spurts. The remaining spectators dwindled in size until they resembled grains of rice in the midst of a vast plate of salad.

A ringing sound went off just behind Keith's back as the balloon gained altitude. There was a loud click, followed by the sound of Frank's recorded voice. "Hi. This is Skyship Iris. I'm tied up right now, so could you leave a message at the sound of the tone, and I'll get back to you as soon as I can. Bye." BWEEP!

"Good takeoff, Frank," said the voice of Randall Murphy, one of Winslow's ground crew. "See you at the other end." CLICK!

"You got a phone in this?" Keith asked, watching wide-eyed as the pilot, now with hands free, ran the tape back to the beginning.

"Sure," Frank said, leaning back against the frame that supported the twin burners. He looked like a skinny stevedore, a full head taller than Keith, and his grin popped out the corners of his narrow jaw. "Gotta keep in touch. Can't just land a balloon next to a phone booth. You figure you have to be self-sufficient in piloting one of these babies. There's a lot of Zen involved." He grinned again, showing broad white teeth. "Modern technology don't hurt, either. I figured out a new valve that makes my tanks last for six hours apiece. Walkie-talkie batteries don't hold a charge that long. Cell phone's easier."

"Great!" Keith exclaimed.

Frank had also brought along a sophisticated-looking but lightweight cooler. "For champagne," he explained. "Traditional.

Soda water today, too." Slung by a loop at the basket's lip was a crank-powered AM/FM radio.

In spite of its high-tech accoutrements, the balloon basket resembled a relic of a past century. It was made of woven rattan with a padded bumper and curved base of leather, a fragile-seeming craft in comparison with the metal-and-plastic jets and other small aircraft Keith was used to seeing. They were moving pretty fast, judging by the clip at which the ground was passing underneath them, but the basket, at one with the wind currents, remained seemingly motionless. It didn't even spin around, which surprised Keith.

The air was unexpectedly cold. Keith shrugged into his thin jacket, zipping it hastily up to his chin, and wrapped his arms around his ribs. The pilot grinned at him and fastened down the flaps of his aerialist's helmet.

"Need a blanket? There's one under the cooler."

"N-no, thanks," Keith said. In a few moments, he was acclimated, and his muscles relaxed. He nodded to Frank.

"Fine and dandy," Frank said. "Enjoy the ride!" The pilot perched on the basket's edge with his long legs up on the other side, and shifted his close-fitting helmet back to reveal his forehead. "Ahhh."

Keith, less daring, stayed by the metal frame and gazed at the scenery. It was still a long way down.

Frank seemed completely at home in the air. Nothing fazed him, not even floating around in a craft as fragile as an eggshell.

In just a short time, Keith had relaxed, too, and was enjoying the sensation of effortless floating. He leaned back and looked around. Everything looked so beautiful from here.

The day was fine and clear. For some this might have been a mere pleasure trip. For Keith, it was business. Emptying his mind of fear, excitement, and any extraneous thoughts that might interfere with his concentration, Keith closed his eyes. Somewhere out there, he was certain, were air sprites, Little People of the air. He tried to visualize what he thought would be out there in the sky. Did they look like dragons? Pixies? Airplanes? In such a formless environment, would they be able to take any shape they chose? He let his mind drift to catch the trail of any elusive magical creature that might happen by within range.

Notwithstanding the occasional strong-smelling fume from feed lots they passed over, the air tasted cleaner up there than it did nearer the ground. Keith reasoned that if he were a creature of the air, he wouldn't hang out so close to the ground, not with the whole sky to range. Holl and the Elf Master had scoffed at his theory, but they'd never checked, had they? The only one of the Little Folk to attain any altitude had been Holl, on his flights with Keith to and from Europe, but he'd been too preoccupied to sense anything outside his own concerns. Tiron, as a stowaway on the flight back, had been bent double in a suitcase, and would have remembered nothing but the difficulties he'd had in breathing and finding some measure of comfort among Keith's dirty clothes and souvenirs of Scotland and Ireland.

Still, even if there had been any air sprites around when the two of them had been traveling, they'd have fled screaming from the jet, which Keith felt was too noisy to get close to the sensitive creatures he pictured. He wanted not only to sense the air sprites, but to see them. To do that, he needed to achieve altitude, but in a quiet, nondisruptive fashion. Barring finding wings of his own somewhere, he'd looked for some suitable conveyance. Gliders were unpowered, and therefore silent, but uncontrollable and too dangerous for an amateur. Helicopters set up too much of a racket. None of the craft with which he was familiar would simply allow him to hang in the air and listen.

When Frank Winslow, a competition balloonist, came to speak at Midwestern, Keith felt a lightbulb go on over his head. A balloon was the perfect vehicle to test out his theories. It was almost completely silent, flew slowly and smoothly, hovering in the very wind currents sprites might live in. Keith was in a fever for the rest of the lecture, wondering how he would convince Winslow to go along with him. After the pilot's talk, Keith took him to a quiet corner of the Student Common Room and laid out his plan.

Upon hearing Keith's theories of mythological beings, Winslow had made it clear he thought Keith was nuts, but decided he liked his company and wouldn't mind giving him a chance to test out his ideas. Frank was preparing the Skyship Iris for a cross-country race. It cost little extra to have an extra body in the basket while he ran distances he would have covered anyway: he'd probably have a passenger along during his long-distance runs. All he asked for was a portion of his propane costs, like sharing gas money. Keith thought that was more than fair. The flat plains of Illinois were as good a place as any to practice skimming techniques, pretending the land was the surface of the Great Lakes.

As Keith opened up his senses, he felt disappointed. Both outer and inner sight told him that the sky was empty. The odd bird intruded its neutral presence on his mental radar. He ignored it, feeling farther out.

Something flared suddenly into his consciousness. Off in the distance to the north, he sensed tantalizing hints of a *presence*, a strong one. Tamping down his delight, he concentrated all his thoughts on following them, projecting as hard as he could thoughts that he was harmless and friendly.

The wave of his mental touch broke over the thing he sensed, and it scattered abruptly into countless alarmed fragments, losing power and definition as they dissipated, like the sparks from an exploding firecracker. They receded ever further into non-existence as if they could feel his pursuit. In a moment, there was nothing on which he could put a mental finger. Dismayed, Keith was left wondering if he had just imagined the contact. He sighed, planting his elbow on the edge of the basket and his chin on his hand. Another time. He sent his thoughts around, seeking other magical realities.

There were no more in the air. Below and ahead, the concentrated presence of the Little Folk at Hollow Tree Farm was the strongest magical thing he sensed. Everything else seemed unreal and insubstantial, as far as magical traces went. As he got more practice at inner sensing, all the natural things around him acquired a stronger aura of reality than he had ever known before. A few things just felt more real than others.

"Do you think there's anything out there?" Keith asked Winslow.

"All the time," Frank said. "Not sentient magical beings—well, not *secular* ones, anyway. Got my own ideas about the sky, Gods and elementals and stuff like that. Almost holy." He turned a suspicious eye toward Keith. "You don't want to hear it."

"Sure I do," Keith said. "I'm looking for any kind of clues I can find."

"Well . . ." Winslow began to explain haltingly. Soon, he

warmed to his subject and began babbling like a brook, defensively hurling forth ideas as if he expected Keith to refute them,
talking about gods and forces of nature and sentient spirits. Keith
pulled a tattered spiral notebook out of his pocket and began to
take notes. Frank's personal cosmology was as interesting as
anything he'd read in mythology books. Keith guessed that he
was the first person Winslow had ever opened up to about his
ideas. There was something useful in being known as the weirdest person on the block: it made other people feel that maybe
they weren't quite so off the wall when all they were was sensitive
or creative.

The sky above them was blue and daubed here and there with
cottony white clouds. In the distance, Keith saw birds doing
aerial acrobatics, and wondered if Little Folk of the sky would
sport like that. Below them, the flat, checkered, green expanse
of Illinois farmland stretched out to every horizon. Like a piece
on a game board, the miniature shadow of the balloon skimmed
from square to square. Winslow pulled the ring on the gas jet
for more altitude. The crosscurrent swept them slightly more
northeast than north.

"You sure you can find this farm?" Winslow shouted above
the roar of the flame. "I mean, most times I put down where
they've got landmarks."

"I can find it," Keith said, confidently, then felt a twinge of
worry. What if his inner radar suddenly ceased to operate?
Tensely, he closed his eyes for a second, then turned in, throwing
his sense outward toward Holl and his friends. There they were,
just where they'd been a minute ago. Keith let his shoulders sag
with relief.

"You feel sick, Keith?"

"Nope," Keith assured him, opening his eyes. "Just feeling
the basket sway."

"Won't fall," Frank promised him. "Never has yet. Want a
soda? Or some champagne? Traditional." The pilot popped open
the cooler at his feet and took out a frosted can of seltzer. Keith
shook his head. "Won't be through again for a couple weeks.
I'm on my way to Florida after today. There's a race over the
Everglades."

"Sounds great!" Keith said. "I want to stay in touch with

you, if you don't mind. I'd like to go up again when you get back."

"Oh, yeah, air sprites," Winslow said, with a grin. He jerked on the tether. The flames roared. "Well, any time I'm in the area, it's okay with me. You've got the number. Heading for South America in November, joining a rally over the Andes. Wind's too strong for ballooning around here after then."

Like a beacon, the presence of the Little Folk shone through strongly from one of the homesteads ahead. From above, Hollow Tree Farm looked exactly like all the other farms on the road. It was only Keith's inner sense that told him when to signal to Winslow to put down in the right meadow. Feeling a little tired by the effort, he turned off his second· sight. Immediately, the auras around everything faded to a nearly invisible glow.

The Iris lowered gently onto the grass between the barn and a field of standing crops. She curtseyed as Keith's weight left the gently swaying gondola. Immediately Winslow started to feed heat to the envelope.

"See you in a couple of hours," Frank called, his voice diminishing as the balloon rose. "Truck'll come and pick you up here!"

Keith waved, and walked off the meadow into the cornfield. The rainbow globe vanished behind the canopy of green leaves.

Corn stood over six feet high in the field behind the house, concealing the individual cottages he knew were standing there. The Little Folk had come up with an excellent system of camouflage. Since each of the little houses stood no higher than the wooden playhouse Keith and his siblings had had in their backyard while they were growing up, during the growing season the cottages were hidden by the tall stalks of grain. Even in the wintertime, after the corn was cut, the houses defied detection. Their outer walls were dark wood, carved into strandlike patterns and stained to blend in with the County Forest Preserve that stood behind them. Only someone with superior depth perception, who knew what to look for, could perceive the miniature village, and then only if they could see through the aversion charm the Little Folk had placed on each structure. Keith fairly admitted he couldn't do it. He relied instead on the white pebbled paths that led through the cornstalks from one doorstep to another, until he could make out each home by its shadow.

Despite the protective coloration, each home was very different. Most of the eight that were fully built were occupied by members of Holl's age group, the Progressives, who had quickly shed the fears of the last four decades and taken off to live in the open air, away from the larger community in the farmhouse itself. As was their thrifty custom, the Folk had used scrap wood of every size as well as whole boards to build, binding the resulting conglomeration with skill and magic. Glass windows, pieced together like stained glass, were backed by small, beautifully woven curtains that Keith guessed had been rags they'd unraveled and blended together again. Little details gave away clues to the identity of the occupants of each house. Marm, one of Holl's—and Keith's—best friends, had carved an ornamented trellis-work surrounded by the figures of animals on the wall that faced away from the road. This season, the trellis was covered by climbing green grapevines. Marm's wife, Ranna, was a celebrated wine-maker.

Without knowing Holl's personal taste, or Maura's skill with a garden, Keith would still have picked out the sixth cottage as theirs. Neat as hospital corners, the little borders around the edges of the tiny house glowed with beauty. Garnet tea roses, proportionately accurate for the Little Folk, grew closest to the house, bracketing the dark walls with spots of rich color. Autumn flowers were just coming into bloom. Hummocks of blue autumn asters dotted the dark beds. Most particularly, on either side of the doorposts grew a handful of white bellflowers, a token and a tribute to Holl's difficult journey overseas to win the right to offer for his lady's hand. Keith grinned as he rapped on the roof's edge with his knuckles.

Inside, he heard hubbub, and Holl, his cheeks red, peered out the curtained window.

"It's you, then," Holl said, pulling the door open. "Miss here won't take her sleep. I've been walking her up and down for an hour. I think she knew there was company coming." Without shifting the bundle in his arms, he rolled his shoulders to ease them. "Will you take her so I can stretch a bit?"

"Boy, she's grown, hasn't she?" Keith said, accepting his "niece" in his two hands. The baby, still hairless and toothless, looked like any baby he'd ever seen, except that her eyes were already turning green to match her mother's, and no Big baby ever sprouted those ornately-whorled ears. The points were just a little softer than an adult's, the way a kitten's ears were rounder than a cat's. Asrai recognized Keith and cooed at him before her attention wandered off again after the next pretty shadow. He cradled her on one elbow and felt around in his pocket.

"Asrai?" he said softly. "Hey, baldy, I'm talking to you."

The baby's cloudy eyes wandered up to his face, and focused just for a second. With surprising speed, her tiny fist shot up, and grabbed. She pulled down, trying to get her captured handful into her mouth.

"Aaagh," Keith breathed, trying not to yell. He put his hand up to get between the baby and his cheek. "Holl, help. She's got my whiskers." Keith's whiskers, a magical Christmas present from the Little Folk some three years before, were tangible, but invisible to the average eye.

Holl sprang forward to undo Asrai's fist, and picked the invisible strands by touch, one by one from between her fingers. "There, there. Well, there's no doubt now she's got the second sight, is there?"

"You sound pleased," Keith said, rubbing the sore place where his offended vibrissae were rooted. "Why didn't you tell me she'd grab?"

"My apologies. She's always taking handfuls of her mother's hair," Holl explained, a little embarrassed, "but yours was too short to catch. I didn't think of the whiskers. We don't know what she can see, if you follow. We're new at being parents. Any fresh discovery is as if it's the first time it's ever happened in the world. Is it all right?"

"No problem," Keith said. "I guess they can't be pulled out, can they?" He glanced down at the baby, who wasn't upset at having her new discovery taken away from her. He put his hand back into his pocket. "Hey, kid, you know I brought you something for yourself." The baby's eyes fixed on his hand as he waved a blue rubber ring at her. "Look. Teething toy."

"It's a little soon for that, Keith Doyle," Holl protested.

"Nope, my mom said teething always starts before you expect it." Keith fitted the tiny fingers around the ring. They barely closed on the other side. Asrai was so small she looked more like a baby doll than a baby. "Hmm. That was the smallest one I could find."

"She'll grow," Holl said, gruff with pride. The child immediately drew the vanilla-scented ring to her face and put her mouth to the edge. Her little pink tongue explored the bumps on the blue rubber surface, and she looked surprised.

Holl watched her adoringly.

Keith glanced up. In contrast to the flowerpetal complexion of his daughter, Holl's face seemed for the first time to be creased and tired. Keith was concerned for his friend, but he made light of it. "Fatherhood's made an older man of you, Holl."

"And it has," Holl said with a sigh. "For no reason at all the babe wakes in the night and cries. She isn't hungry, and she isn't wet, but she cries. It's amazing to me how loud she can get. I'm glad it's only Marm next door to us. He never minds a thing when he sleeps, and Ranna can ignore everything, but the wailing keeps *us* wide awake."

"Trouble," Keith said, shaking his head. His eyes danced with mischief. "What do your folk say when they're fed up with their kids? 'I wish the humans would come and take you away'?"

Holl favored him with a sour expression. "Very funny, Keith Doyle. May I offer you a snack? You've come a long way."

Keith looked around the interior of the cottage. The floor, covered with smooth tiles of wood, was well swept. There wasn't much in the way of furniture, except for a pair of chairs, a large table and a small one, and bookshelves built cunningly into the walls. Holl caught the sense of his gaze.

"Oh, the food's in the larder under a hatch in the floor. It's not too big, just enough for a pat of butter and a drop of milk, or what have you," Holl said, rising heavily to his feet. "There might be a heel of bread as well."

With concern, Keith watched him go. Holl looked genuinely tired. Keith's mother had said that the first six months after a birth were the hardest. At least Holl and Maura were in the back stretch, now that Asrai had hit the three-month mark. He couldn't believe that this tiny baby, who just barely overlapped his hands, could yell so loudly.

"Less insulation to hold down the sound, huh, punkin?" he asked her. The baby, wisely asleep with the ring clutched to her cheek, said nothing. Keith knew better than to trust Holl's assertion that there was no more food on hand than drops and heels. The Little Folk might eat less in proportion, but they liked plenty of good things to eat as much as their Big cousins. Holl returned with a handsomely carved wooden tray bearing a tall pitcher whose foaming, white contents slopped gently from side to side, and a basket of rolls with a good chunk of primrose-yellow butter on a small dish in the center.

"Keva's doing," Holl explained, at Keith's question. "They all knew you were coming for a visit, and she insisted on leaving these to break our fast."

Keith's own particular mug, a long-ago present from the Little Folk, was here on a framed shelf beside those belonging to Holl and Maura. He accepted milk and a handful of rolls. "What, no beer?" he asked, impishly.

"Not when I'm on nursery duty, if you please," Holl said, grimacing. "Whew! It was a long night last night down here. A good thing we're out as we are in the middle of the sky. Under the library, she'd have shouted the stacks down. They'd have thought there was a banshee trapped in the steam tunnels! Maura and I share duties. It's my shift with the babe. She's inside the big house helping prepare the lunch before class."

"She's not having to cut short her education because of the baby, is she?" Keith asked.

"Oh, no, don't you fear it," Holl said easily. "You don't know the benefits of communal living. We don't lack for volunteer child care. If no other adult has extra time to help us care for the little one, Dola or some of the other medium-sized children help out. She'll be here soon, and glad to see you, I won't doubt."

Keith smiled. Dola was Tay's daughter, a sweet, blond child who had a strangling crush on him. She'd accepted Diane's pre-eminence with Keith only under protest, and had often expressed herself willing to step in as a substitute should Diane be unable to continue as Keith's girlfriend. Dola had a special talent for forming illusions on a length of thin cloth. Keith decided that as a babysitter, that wasn't a half bad knack to have.

"So this is a different thing for you," Holl said, pouring a mugful of milk for himself. "You're not in classes, but you're still earning a grade?"

"It's called an internship," Keith explained, "and they're actually paying me, too. I'm working in the Chicago office of

Perkins Delaney Queen, the advertising agency. They're shuffling me and three other students around the departments until we find the ones that will take us for the rest of the semester. I was interested in the business office at first, and then there was research, but I'm having more fun in the design department. If they like me, they'll let me stay on for the spring term, and maybe there'll even be a job opening after graduation."

"I am sure you are well liked," Holl said, the corner of his mouth going up in a wry smile. "You have a way of worming yourself into good regard."

"I hope I can make it." Keith sighed. "But it's a tough business. I miss college. I called Pat to see how it's going, and he said it's been a lot quieter without me." He pulled a face, and Holl laughed.

"They don't let you live on the premises?"

"Heck, no," Keith said, shaking his head. "It's an office building."

"Don't act as if I ought to know that," Holl admonished him. "We lived in an office building."

Keith shrugged. "Well, usually people don't," he said. "I'm back in my old room at home. I miss living with Pat Morgan. We got along really well, all things considered. My brother Jeff resents like hell having me back. He had our whole room to himself for three years, and now he's got to deal with having me crowding him for an entire year, if not for good. Jeff's done everything but draw a line down the middle of the room to mark his territory. I'm glad we don't have a sink in the corner, like we did in the dorm. I'd end up with half the basin and one tap. If the soap's on the wrong side, forget it. Laser beam time." Keith's finger drilled an imaginary hole into his chest. Holl tilted his head to one side.

"Not literally, I hope. It sounds as if it's nearly time for you to have a nest of your own, Keith Doyle," Holl said, nodding. "If you chose, you know you'd always be welcome here, permanently, or whenever you dropped in from above." Holl pointed toward the ceiling.

Keith smiled, genuinely pleased and touched. "That'd be great, but it depends on what I'll be doing after graduation. It's a real temptation. You've sure done a lot with the property. It's shaped up incredibly since last summer. I may take you up on your offer so I can live in a country manor with all the amenities instead of a dinky apartment.''

Holl scowled. ''Your 'dinky' accommodations might have more to offer you. It is not easy being homeowners. Everything constantly needs repairs. The water continues bad. We collected a sample of the stinking mess we were filtering out, and matched it to the seepage from Gilbreth Feed and Fertilizer Company.''

''What, that place across town?'' Keith asked. ''How's their runoff getting over here?''

''We've written to ask how it's possible that we're getting pollutants from their factory,'' Holl said. ''But there's no doubt it's theirs. Tay and Olanda went over there one night to compare.''

''They must be dumping,'' Keith said, frowning darkly. ''I wish I could be here to help handle it. Complain. If they don't respond to you, you can write private letters threatening them with the Environmental Protection Agency.''

''Oh, we're sending appropriate letters to the editor, and having a fine extended argument with the owner of the company on the side. But let us put such gloomy matters away. The Master would like to see you, if you please.''

Keith felt a momentary surge of guilt at the thought of being called before the formidable little teacher. He was up to date on his mail-in essays; what could the Master want him for? ''He would?''

Holl must have guessed his thoughts, because he laughed heartily. ''A visit, you impossible infant! You're not behind on any assignment for him, unless it's to show your face and be welcomed more often than you are. As soon as Dola comes to look after the babe, we'll go up to the barn.''

A shy tapping at the door heralded Dola's arrival. The elf child, now twelve, was on the threshold of young womanhood. Slim and blond, with her elegant ears poking out through her shining tresses, she would have made a good model for the flower fairies in the books Keith's mother had read to him as a child. In the hot weather, she wore only a knee-length green shift that softly outlined her body. Keith surreptitiously took note of the subtle changes in her figure, but she noticed. Comfortable though she was with Holl, Dola was self-conscious around him.

''How do I look, then?'' she demanded boldly, then blushed at her own forwardness.

"All you need is lacy wings," Keith said, gravely. The compliment pleased Dola. She beamed, the long dimples in her cheeks throwing her high cheekbones and pointed chin into relief. Feathery wings of dragonfly diaphanousness sprang out of her shoulder blades. The illusion was perfect. "That's it." Keith chuckled and reached out to tweak a lock of her hair.

Suddenly shy, Dola dodged away coyly. She pirouetted lightly on her toes, coming to rest before Holl, who gently placed the baby in her arms. The wings vanished as quickly as they had appeared.

"Dola's been the most zealous caretaker we could ask for," Holl said, over the girl's head. "She practically attended Maura at the birth. She'll only share responsibilities with Ludmilla, my babe's unofficial grandmother, and that not often."

Dola stuck out her chin defiantly, to show that even that sharing was unwilling. She clasped the baby close to her. Asrai, half asleep, roused enough to coo at her babysitter. Dola bent to kiss her on the forehead.

"Well," Keith said, watching with delight, "even the best babysitters need a day off. They deserve a little spoiling of their own."

"I wouldn't mind *that* now and again," Dola agreed. She kicked off her socklike shoes and sat down in Holl's chair.

"I'll see what we can arrange," Keith promised. "Some weekend, okay?"

"Oh, yes! Okay!" Dola said, much gratified.

"We'll be at the barn, if there's any need for us," Holl said.

"There'll be no need," Dola assured him. She began rocking. On her lap, the child's eyes drifted closed, and her breathing slowed. Keith waved at them through the window, and followed Holl down the pebbled path toward the barn.

Chapter
TWO

"**S**o what do you do in the meantime?" Holl asked over his shoulder, as he stumped down the narrow, sloping path toward the dull-red, painted barn. "I can't imagine you with only one activity to siphon off all your energies."

"Oh, I'm pursuing my old interests," Keith said casually. "Remember my theory? Air sprites?"

Holl sighed. "And how could I not?"

"The guy who flew me here is training for a cross-country balloon marathon. He said he'd take me up whenever he's around," Keith said, ignoring his friend's amused expression. "If there's anyone to be found in the upper atmosphere, I'll find them."

"If anyone will," Holl agreed, "you will."

From the outside, it looked like a barn Keith might have passed on any of the county highways. Inside, it had been transformed into a combination school, workshop, and living quarters. Little Folk hurried around like so many of Santa's elves, carrying from here to there wooden handcrafts in varying stages of completion.

The old barn had been converted nearly as much as the house had. Between the rafters, its high ceiling was lined with the same fuzzy rows of light that had illuminated the Little Folk's home beneath Gillington Library. The tiniest children dashed in and out of the old stalls where their elders worked, each on his or her own particular task. The building still smelled pleasantly of hay, though its concrete floor was swept clean. Added to that scent was the spicy blended aroma of fresh sawdust, oil, and paint. Under a window with its shutters thrown fully back to let in the morning's light, Enoch threw them a salute with his wood plane, then went back to smoothing the board he had propped on two saw horses. Keith thought it looked like he was making a new door. When Enoch upended his work on the sawhorses, Keith noticed that the door was constructed, as usual for the Little Folk's woodcrafts, of assorted scrap culled from other projects. They wasted nothing, lending the dignity of utility to even the most hopeless leftovers, even bits of rubber or cloth scrap. Some of the wooden jewelry he'd been selling to the boutiques on behalf of Hollow Tree Industries featured beads laminated with ancient bits of calico and gingham. They had a neat antique-y look that went well with the natural luster of wood. Ms. Voordman, their most assiduous customer, had been pleased by the hit the necklaces had made.

It was the proudest accomplishment of his life that he had been able to be of service to the Little Folk, helping them to get on their feet. He wasn't vain enough to think that he'd been responsible for their success, but if he hadn't come along and helped to find them a home when they needed one, they might have been discovered. It frightened him to think of his friends swept helplessly away to one of those secret government facilities that the tabloids liked to crow about, for potentially-fatal testing, or whatever it was they did there. Or they might have ended up homeless after the library's destruction. A chilling picture crept into his mind of the Folk scattered along the roadway, terrified and starving during the cold Illinois winters, ducking into the nearly bare fields to escape notice whenever cars passed. The dream passed, and Keith laughed, only a little uncomfortably. It was a warm September afternoon, and this house and barn, though they were bought in his name, belonged most definitely to the Little Folk.

He was only willing to take credit for facilitating matters. Kudos for the overwhelming success they'd achieved belonged strictly to them. Their skills had been passed down for centuries and honed with love, and they had learned quickly what else they needed to know. Sometimes he felt like he was protecting an endangered species.

He was warmed by the mere fact of their existence, and their regard for him was an added bonus. It gave him great satisfaction to share as much of their lives as they'd allow.

As Holl and Keith approached, a handful of children sprang off their benches, and ran toward them, shouting. They had interrupted the junior literature class. The Master in shirtsleeves, standing before a chalkboard on an easel, peered over his glasses disapprovingly until his gaze came to rest on Keith. Then he nodded austerely.

Keith shot him an apologetic smile and a 'what can I do?' expression.

"You came from the sky," Borget cried. The nine-year-old, a pudgy-cheeked imp with bronze curls. "Didn't you? You flew in the rainbow balloon! We saw you."

"I sure did," Keith said, crouching down to Borget's level, where he was immediately surrounded by the crowd of children. The boy immediately turned on his smaller companions.

"I told you he came from the sky," he said, with an air of one-upmanship. "I told you!"

"Can we try it?" Moira asked. She had striking dark blue eyes that contrasted richly with her magnolia-blossom skin. "Mother might say yes since it's you."

Keith thought of Moira's mother, an arch-ultra-Conservative, and privately doubted the girl's optimism. "I'll ask," he promised.

"Will you take us to the amusement park?" Anet begged. She had flaming carrot-colored hair and brilliant green eyes. "I read an article about the great wooden roller coaster. I would love to ride it! The writer said the slope was a hundred and sixty feet at a fifty-five-degree incline!"

"Uh," Keith said, picturing the park full of Little People. He thought quickly. "Well, you know, coasters like that have a sign that says you can't ride if you're under this tall." He swung an arm out to one side at about the level of his chest. "See? Even Holl couldn't get on. The safety harnesses wouldn't hold him because they're made for really big people, and they're made of steel. You could get hurt."

"Aw," Anet said, sadly. "Is there nothing in the rest of the world made for children our size?"

"Not a lot," Keith admitted. "But you have a lot of advantages Big kids don't. None of them have magic lanterns and toys that run by themselves without batteries."

Since those were things the Little children saw every day, it was small consolation. With difficulty, he extracted himself and went to meet his former teacher.

"You are doing vell enough on your assignments," the Master acknowledged, when Keith asked about the subject troubling him, "though you might be spending more thought on them."

"I've been busy," Keith said, shamefacedly. Neither time nor distance had dimmed the small, red-haired professor's ability to make Keith feel like a little child called on the carpet. Whenever he was fixed by the bright blue eyes behind the gold frames of the Master's spectacles, he felt like digging his toe through the floor, with his tongue caught in the corner of his mouth, while he thought up an excuse why his homework wasn't done. "I'll do better on the next one. But what are you doing here? It's Tuesday. Aren't you teaching?"

"I no longer go in every day to the classroom," the Master said, laying down his pointer. "It is too much of an imposition on my kind volunteers. I vould rather they make only one trip to come here to me, vhere there is less difficulty and," an ironic glint flashed in the glass lenses, "less chance of a charge of illicit entry. Gradually but vith many regrets, ve leaf Gillington Library behind for gut. It is a wrench to many of us, but much safer."

"You stand less a chance of being detected if you don't keep going in and out," Keith said, nodding.

"It is true. Ve are already imposing enough upon our good friends that they must supply the book needs of such a large group as we," the Master said, smiling slightly. "Diane's good friend Dunn has shown much talent for extracting efen restricted volumes for our perusal."

"Well, he works in the library," Keith pointed out.

"He maintains a legitimate entree for us," the Master said. "And though, like you, he professes to owe us a debt of gratitude for his instruction, the debt is many times repaid by his services as our," the sapphire eyes glinted again, "bookvagon." Keith suspected that the term was Dunn's.

The Master stopped, as if a thought had come to him, and rummaged in his pocket. "One of the benefits of staying in vun place and hafing vun's own mailing address is to be able to maintain personal correspondence vith professional colleagues. I haf had a letter from Professor Parker," he said, extending a much-creased envelope to Keith.

"Hey, great!" Keith said, running an eye down the page. The archaeologist was traveling in the United States with exhibits from his dig in the Hebrides. He invited the Master, in his guise as the noted researcher, Dr. Friedrich Alfheim, to come and visit the display when it came to the Field Museum in Chicago. "Well, you ought to go. Are you interested? I'll drive you. He'd really enjoy seeing you."

"And I him," the Master said. "He has a fine mind." From the Master, that was the height of compliment. Keith retained considerable respect for Professor Parker. It took brains and imagination to see a thriving civilization in burned-off stumps and buried heaps of animal bones. "If it is possible to go, I vould be grateful for the opportunity."

"Consider it done!" Keith said, cheerfully. He sketched a bow to the Master. Holl, rolling his eyes skyward, nudged him in the kidneys with an elbow.

"Come, then," he said. "We can't interrupt the class forever, for all the children would like it, and there're others waiting to see you."

Marcy Collier was among them. Keith greeted her as she came over from the sawyer's table, where Enoch was working over a mitre box with a hand saw.

"So how's the romance going?" Keith asked, playfully.

"All right," Marcy said, sighing. "I tried to talk to my mother about Enoch. You know what she said? 'Tell me again, Marcy. I want to hear it from your own lips. Your fiancé is an *elf*, and he makes *toys*. Have you told your father yet?' "

Keith laughed, but immediately composed his face to rueful. "Gee, I'm sorry."

Marcy gave him a tiny smile. "Yeah, it's funny. I just don't know how I'll get past that."

"Not to mention your fiancé's family connection with the supernatural," Keith said, glancing quickly over his shoulder to make sure none of the Folk were listening to him. To them, all the wonders that they worked were strictly natural. "I know! We'll fix you up with a big biker guy who spits on furniture. Tattoos that say 'I love torture' and 'Blow up the world, starting with . . .' what suburb do you live in?" Keith drew an imaginary picture on the air.

"You should be in advertising, Keith," Marcy said, shaking her head.

"I'm working on it," Keith said cheerfully.

"And there you are, Keith Doyle!" Tiron called out. The Irish elf urged Keith to come to his workspace. "Behold," he said, gesturing at the loom, his pride and joy. "And now do you think it was worth the time and trouble to bring me to America?" He handed Keith a length of cloth. The fabric was like the beautiful Scottish tweeds he had seen overseas, but this had a life and a magic which reflected the nature of its weavers.

"It's fantastic," he said. Holl, hanging back out of Tiron's way, nodded his approval, too.

"Keith Doyle, there you are!" Catra called, waving a handful of papers at him from a carrel against the far wall. "Come and see!"

"I'm in demand today," Keith said, excusing himself.

As nearly as possible, the Archivist had re-created her favorite perch from Gillington Library. From somewhere, the Little Folk had provided polished walnut rails that surrounded a neat little area filled with polished wood bookshelves and drawers. The only untidiness in the office was the top of Catra's desk. It was scattered with daily newspapers, letters, scraps of paper, books, and scrapbooks. One vast specimen, nearly the height of the elf woman, was open across the top of it all. They had caught her in the act of pasting a clipping onto one of the pages.

"Here, read it, do," she said, offering Keith a letter she snatched from its position half hidden underneath the big book's spine. "Here's the latest sally we've composed to do public battle against the polluters."

Grinning, Keith took the letter. "So you're really writing letters to the editor. How's it going?"

Catra's eyes gleamed. "We're doing well enough, to be sure. We have joined the lobbyists for a cleaner environment. Now that we're part of a community, however covertly, we want to aid in improving it."

Keith knew about some of their good works. Over the last year, they had been using their talents to fix things around town, repairing pipes and ductwork, just like they had in his college library.

On half of the desk, her sister Candlepat was paying the farm's bills. Using her talent, she was lifting Keith's signature, from a sheet filled with examples that he had provided for them, onto a blank check. That way he didn't have to be present every time the Little Folk needed to endorse a check. There were also two examples of "For Deposit Only, Hollow Tree Industries, account 2X-3B-3485" in his script.

"Nice," Keith complimented her. "Couldn't tell the difference myself. You're not thinking of taking up a life of crime, I hope?"

The blond girl pursed her lips playfully. "Catra wanted to use these to sign the letters to the editor as well," she explained, "but Holl said he'd rather not have you have to explain words you hadn't written. I write the text out myself. Tell me why, Keith Doyle, that the letters on a typewriter do not go in the order of the alphabet?"

"I'm not sure," Keith said. "I bet Catra can find out faster than I can."

"Oh, she! She's all taken up in this environment issue," the girl pouted. "She's nearly no time for anything else."

"Okay. I'll look it up for you myself," Keith said, placatingly. "What's the latest?"

"I'm sure it's around," Catra said, when consulted. "It was read aloud with great glee at breakfast time."

They tracked down the letter to Marm, who had spread out blueprints and tools over it. Spotting the stationery by a characteristic corner, Holl yanked it free.

"There you are." The letter suggested that Gilbreth had no real regard for future generations, since it wouldn't take care to evolve a waste-disposal program that could solve today's problems today.

"Wow," Keith said. "Inflammatory. That ought to curl someone's hair."

"We're not doing it for cosmetic reasons, Keith Doyle. There's a higher purpose to it as well. If the land is to remain habitable for long, it must be brought out into the open and

resolved as to what is to be done with waste, and whether the
gains justify the end product. At present, I do not think you trust
your leaders, nor do I think you can. We all read newspapers.
The special interests whose matters are taken before yours remind
me of Orwell's Animal Farm, in which some animals are more
equal than others.''

"Quiet," Keith said, "or the Master will hear you. You don't
think becoming a father makes you exempt from those surprise
essays.''

"Would that it did, at least for a time." Holl sighed. "The
little one spat up across my geology text two nights back. I
cannot think what the university bookstore will assume has happened when we return it quietly to their stock.''

Keith laughed. "Ever been in a frat house? Considering what
else happens to those books, baby drool won't stand out much.
This mudslinging in print will stand out a lot more.''

Holl nodded. "That's good to know. We're grateful for the
loans, authorized or not, and try to be good stewards for that
which we borrow. It's different, doing all this at long distance.
We're relying heavily upon the good will of the Master's Big
students. So far, they've been most helpful.''

"I'm sorry I'm not there to help," said Keith. "You sure you
don't miss me?''

"Haven't we had enough excitement in the last year?" Holl
asked. Keith raised his hands in helpless agreement.

"Can Hollow Tree Industries manage without me?''

"What do you think? Our work gets done. Deliveries go out.
Our income matches well with our expenses. Our goods continue
popular. I've a new line of jewelry that your Ms. Voordman
wants to see offered to the department stores. We're surviving.
Why do you ask?" Holl inquired.

"Well," Keith said, lamely, "I like to feel needed.''

"Then feel needed, you widdy, but go ahead and have your
job. I'm sure it'll be more interesting than hanging about watching me change diapers.''

"Oh, no," Keith said. "That'd be very interesting. In fact, I
ought to make a complete photo record. That way, you'll remember this time of her life long after she's grown up and has
boyfriends.''

Holl gaped at him, openmouthed and speechless. Keith was delighted.

"Quoth the Maven, nevermore," Keith said, with glee.

"Will you let me worry about one year at a time, without raising the specter of times to come?" Holl demanded, when he had recovered his voice. "Isn't it enough . . ."

Holl's reply was cut off by staccato tooting. The Little Folk looked around curiously for its source. Keith stood up hastily.

"Thanks for the hospitality, Holl. I've got to go. That's my ride!"

Chapter
THREE

T he next morning, Mona Gilbreth opened to the editorial page of *The Central Illinois Farmer* with a mixture of dread and disgust. The ongoing battle between environmental interests and business—her business—had become an embarrassment. She hadn't even known there *were* environmentalists in Sullivan before the paperborne tirade had begun, about a year back. It had started with a letter about dumping of industrial waste in the local watershed, and gone on from there to veiled and then not so veiled suggestions of guilt. Customers were asking pointed questions about whether the allegations against Gilbreth concerning unsafe dumping and toxic waste were true. This wasn't national politics, where the querents were reporters she'd never see again who could be put off with a press release from one of her assistants. If she was forced to make expensive changes in her business practices, it would take money she could hardly spare from her campaign funds. She had won the nomination for representative, but it would take careful management and a lot of fundraising to see her all the way through the November election. There was a chronic shortage of donations for the smaller candidacies. Mona Gilbreth yearned for the day when her political dreams would be realized, she would be elected to her House seat in Washington, and she could shake off the stinking dust of her father's business and her home town. After she left, she could safely disavow any knowledge of how the business was being run.

At first she had wondered if her political opponent was behind the mudslinging. Nastier people were beginning to call them Kill-breath Feed. It was hard to get a stereotype out of people's minds once it was set. Small towns had long memories, she thought, remembering her grammar school nickname of 'Treetop.' Once a year, someone from her year at Sullivan High School was sure to bring that up again. It wasn't her fault she'd grown taller than anyone else in fifth grade, finishing up at a quarter inch short of six feet before her thirteenth birthday. It was enough to make any sane person take to the top of a church steeple with an M-16.

"Has anyone in the plant been talking to anyone from Hollow Tree Farm?" Mona asked her manager, Jake Williamson.

"You know us," Williamson assured her, leaning back with his thumbs in his hip pockets. The khaki overalls that the company used as a uniform made him look like a prison guard. "We don't talk to strangers."

"Then how are they so sure the stuff's coming from here?" Mona wondered, folding over the page and creasing it with her fingernail. She was comfortable with Williamson because he was one of the few people at the plant who was taller than she was.

"It is, isn't it?" Williamson asked, showing his teeth in amusement.

She ignored him. "These results couldn't have come from an EPA analysis, because we'd have been notified, and that would have meant reporters all over the place. Are they following our trucks?"

"Couldn't be. Some of them county routes are as flat as an ironing board. We'd have seen anybody. What's wrong? This H. Doyle write another letter full of insults to the editor?"

Without looking up, Mona nodded. She crumpled the edge with her fingertips, began to tear scraps of paper loose and scoot them around the desktop. She hated keeping up the public front. It was an effort, protesting that Gilbreth was innocent of any wrongdoing, that the management was interested and involved in environmental issues. But she still needed grassroots support to keep her campaign alive.

In the meantime, the business was running badly without her continuous intervention. She wished again her father hadn't died. His timing was so inconvenient. The last thing she needed was

to be personally involved with a business whose waste products
pushed so many buttons among her constituency. There were
loud supporters on both sides of the issue, pro-farm and pro-
environment, and sometimes they were the same people, but
silence was better than noisy debate any time.

She ran her finger down the page to the end of the letter. There
was the signature Mona had been dreading: H. Doyle. The gist
of the letter above it was typical and predictable. Unnatural
growths of algae had been observed in artesian ponds and marsh-
water, suggesting that phosphates and other organics had been
dumped in the sensitive headwaters, giving rise to explosive and
unwanted growth. H. Doyle was angry about the pollution of the
groundwater, suggesting that if organic pollutants were disposed
of with so much secrecy, might not PCBs and dioxins have
been dumped as well? Didn't the name Times Beach render any
reaction?

Mona ground her teeth. It did. It was true, Gilbreth Feed and
Fertilizer had dumped a lot of its waste on abandoned property.
Money was the problem. If for no other reason than to keep her
nose clean for the inspection of her political foes, she would
cheerfully have paid for proper dumping sites and disposal. But,
as it was, the Gilbreth Company couldn't afford it and still take
care of payroll, advertising, and all the other expenses it took to
run the company. H. Doyle of Hollow Tree was exacerbating
her troubles by humiliating her in public. Mona could feel her
temper rising, getting her dander up, as her old grandmother
used to say.

"We've got a load of stuff, and the bills aren't paid yet,"
Williamson said, almost as if he could read her mind. "Got to
get rid of it. There's no more room in the tanks, and Browning-
Ferris won't make a pickup until we pay."

"Empty the tanks into our trucks. There's a dumping site I
want you to use," Ms. Gilbreth said, without looking up from
the Op-ed page.

Dola appeared at the door of Holl and Maura's cottage. "*There*
now," she said, disapprovingly, drowning out the unhappy cries.
Holl turned toward her, his face full of undisguised relief, his
arms full of wet, bare-bottomed baby. "You can hear her nearly
all the way to the barn!"

"Bless you, lass, can you do something with her? She's soaked through, I've got a full day of tasks to finish, and I can't put her down!"

The girl's hands were on her hips, and the expression on her face was an echo of her great-grandmother Keva's. "She's all to pieces, and you're no help, are you?" she asked. She took the wailing baby in her arms, and whispered a little song to her. Asrai, recognizing Dola's voice, stopped crying and gurgled. Holl, amused, stood back from the powder-strewn changing table, and let the girl take charge.

"Well, you know me, don't you?" Dola asked, her tone softening as she laid the child down. With deft hands, she cleaned up the spilled powder, swabbed Asrai clean with a moist cloth from the bowl on the table's edge, and dried her. She straightened out a fresh diaper, the loose edges smoothing into a snug fit around Asrai's waist as if it had always been thus. "It's easy to see you need me," Dola said, holding Asrai up against her shoulder and regarding Holl fiercely over the infant's head as she wrestled Asrai into a loose, lightweight smock of fading red-flowered cloth.

"We rely upon you absolutely," Holl told her gravely, with a little bow. "I've promised to help Tiron and Enoch repair the big loom today, and there's a handful of other things that need looking into. Maura has promised that if the weaving turns out well, she'll make you a new winter coat with the first lengths on her sewing machine. Tiron and the Master agree you deserve it."

Dola seemed placated by Holl's adult regard of her. Her small chin relaxed, and she smiled up at him. "It's no worry to me. I'll take care of her as long as I'm needed. Only, Mama wanted me to help with the vegetables for dinner."

"One of us will be back here long before that," Holl promised. He checked his toolbox to be sure his good working tools were inside, and picked it up. "She's just been fed, so she won't need feeding for a while. You grant us a few hours of needed respite every day, and we're not forgetting that. We're grateful to you, Dola. If you get tired, find us in the house or the barn," he said from the door. "There's sweet cake in the cupboard."

Acknowledging his last statement with a bare nod, Dola was already seated comfortably with the baby beside the unlit fire-

place, making pictures in the light for Asrai's amusement. Holl
smiled at his daughter's happy coo and glided away between the
cornstalks.

It was not as satisfactory as it might have been to have such
important employment, Dola found herself thinking as the baby
dozed on her knee. It was a fine day, what she could see of it.
The sun was warm and golden. Anyone could tell the corn crop
was a fine, thick one. Her mother, who had a way with green
and growing things, was well pleased. Dola herself was glad that
their first real summer's planting would feed them easily during
the winter to come, but it did block out the scenery so completely.
How hard it was to think of the winter, months and months away,
new woven coat or no! It was boring to stare out at the crops,
and she had not brought a book along. The only books she could
find in the cottage were on the bedside shelves, and those did
not interest her. Holl favored technical manuals of Big Folk
science, and Maura's stack had novels, but in foreign languages.
There was not even tidying up to be done to keep her mind
occupied. A pity Asrai's screaming made her unwelcome in the
general household. She might have been kin, but their clan-
leader Curran had a minimal tolerance for noise. It came of
spending too many years in enforced silence.

"You'd think we were a lot of Trappist Monks! Well, he
didn't say we might not go elsewhere, did he?" she said out
loud. "Just to be back before time to make supper."

On a hook next to the baby's cot was a sling woven like a
fisherman's net. Made for fullgrown Folk like Maura or Holl, it
was too big for Dola when she first tried it on. She tied the top
fold in a square knot. It stood upon her thin shoulder like a fist,
but the carrier now lay correctly with its bulge upon her hip.
Dola fitted the sleeping baby into the sling and arranged her so
that her head was supported by the upward curve of cloth against
Dola's side. It felt sufficiently secure. Dola tucked her illusion
cloth into her waist-pouch chatelaine, and they went outside into
the sun.

The rhythmic disturbance of moving from one place to another
woke the baby to dreaming wonder. Dola caught sight of her
gentle blue-green eyes wandering from one bright spot to another

in the gardens. For a moment, she was afraid the baby might start crying. Asrai started when a crow burst like black cannonfire from between two stalks of corn, and Dola held her breath, but Asrai laughed out loud. Dola explained to her very carefully what it was she was seeing.

"Maybe you'll remember some of this when you're grown," Dola said, thoughtfully. "I wonder just how much it is babies can understand."

Birds sang and swooped overhead in the bright sky. Dola followed their song out of the cornfield and into the meadow behind it. She hopped across the narrow cut of the stream, and followed the curve of the earth uphill. There was a good spot just over the crest of the gentle rise that was always sheltered from the wind, like the palm of a cupped hand. The two of them were completely alone there. The great farmhouse and barn were out of sight behind a stand of trees, as the cottages were concealed among the corn. No habitation, for Big or Small Folk, lay within sight. All around the edge of the meadow was a curtain of trees. Most of it belonged to the Forest Preserve owned by the state, so Keith Doyle explained to them. It meant that never would a house be built there. The Folk's privacy would remain absolute as long as they lived in this place. That knowledge gave her a feeling of hitherto unimaginable freedom. It was glorious.

She sank into the tall, cool grass and spread out a soft blanket for Asrai to lie upon, face up. The infant, her face protected from the sun by an overhanging dock leaf, inspected the nearby weeds and pulled a handful of plant stems toward her toothless mouth. Dola glanced at them to make certain none of them were harmful or poisonous, then let her taste them. She looked around at the splendor of the day.

Only a few feathered clouds streaked the sky, far above her. It would be bitterly cold when night fell. Aylmer, who read the weather better than anyone else, said rain wouldn't fall for several days. Dola was glad. She'd give all she had for more golden days like this. The privilege of sitting out in the sun seemed an unimaginable gift. She shut her eyes and breathed in the heady scent of growing corn, grass, flowers, trees, and listened to the quiet whisper of the stream.

How life had changed. Before last year, she had never seen

an open field. Now she and her people owned this fine stretch of land—owned it safe and secure, thanks to Keith Doyle. Dola sighed. If only he were not quite so Big, nor so old. She was his favorite among her people, she knew, but if they were more on a level, he would act less like a kindly uncle toward her and more like a—what? A boyfriend? Dola felt her cheeks burn. Such things were beginning to intrude themselves on her consciousness as stealthily as the growing changes in her body. Her mother smiled indulgently at her when they had little, private discussions. Why were her own feelings always in such a turmoil these days?

She knew the time had come to turn her back on childhood, but it was such a long, long path to becoming a woman. One day, she'd have a babe of her own. For the meanwhile, it was good practice for her to care for one like Asrai, who was so good.

The baby, fistful of hay stuffed into her mouth, was watching her.

"Well, what are you staring at, then?" she asked, her voice caressing and indulgent. For a moment, Dola heard the echo of her own mother asking the same thing. Perhaps she was further along the path than she thought. Would it really be so hard a journey? "Little one, look at this!"

Dola spread out the vision cloth between her two hands. The scrap of cotton was growing ragged after many years' washing and folding. Now that the loom was assembled, she might have a new cloth woven to her taste. She wanted a piece of white percale, just like the soft, old sheets Keith Doyle had once given the Folk. Or perhaps she would have a brocade, with a white on white pattern and a looser weave to let the dreams through. In the end, it wouldn't matter what it was, or how it was made, so long as the cloth fit between her two hands.

The scant, thready weave disappeared in the heart of the vision she imagined. White was the sum of all colors, the Master had told her, so she was merely separating out each from the others when she made her illusions. It was a talent, he explained, like the ability to paint. Practice would give her more scope for her visions.

Asrai only seemed to see bright colors, so the image of flowers and horses Dola created was exaggeratedly brilliant. A hot, red blossom, then one of deep violet, and one each of sun-yellow and orange-yellow spun in the center of the cloth, surrounded by green leaves and small royal blue blooms. The baby's eyes flitted from one image to another, her damp, rosebud mouth tilting up in the corners. Dola made a shocking-pink horse dash from one edge of the cloth to the other, scattering the flowers, eliciting a shriek from her enchanted audience. The horse's image grew in the center of the cloth until only its head was visible, its huge, long-lashed eyes blinking soulfully at Asrai.

"I saw that pony on the television when we lived beneath the library, before you were born," Dola said, delighted. "Perhaps by the time you're grown, we'll have a horse like that here on the farm."

The horse shrank and began to run across and back on the white field of cloth. Asrai's wide eyes followed every passage. Orange and sea-blue horses followed the pink one onto the insubstantial track, legs floating in rhythmic sequence like the beating of a heart. When the baby kicked her small legs and gurgled happily, Dola brought all three horses together and made them race around in a circle. She gave them wings, and they began to glide. Asrai let out a happy shriek.

Movement among the trees at the edge of the Folk's land distracted Dola. Concentration broken, she let the veil fall to her lap. Deprived of her entertainment, Asrai exclaimed her protest.

"Hush, little one!" Dola whispered suddenly, putting a gentle hand on the baby's chest. She peered down the hill into the trees.

She couldn't discern shapes through the thick stands of pines, but a metallic boom told her it couldn't be animals crashing about back there. Big Folk did sometimes drive up and down in the roads of the Forest Preserve, but the predominant sounds were almost always engines running. This was different. The baby cooed again, demanding attention.

"Be silent, little one," Dola begged Asrai, and gathered her into her lap.

A big brown truck with a cylindrical tank backed out of the forest and onto the land at the top of the meadow, just beyond the Hollow Tree property line, not far from the head of the marsh waters. Dola stared at it as a Big man climbed out of the passenger seat. He walked around to the back and opened a pipe that began to dribble dark liquid underneath the body of the truck. Dola sat frozen, clutching the baby in her arms. Suddenly, she realized she was visible to him. Her eyes and the eyes of the man met.

Chapter
FOUR

Grant Pilton squinted up at the hilltop and put a hand over his eyes to shield them from the light.

"There's a kid up there, watching us," he called to Jake Williamson. "A little girl."

"What?" Williamson climbed down from the truck cab. "Ms. Gilbreth's not gonna like that. She don't want witnesses. Where is she?"

Pilton pointed. "Right up there."

Williamson squinted. The little girl up there looked about five or six years old. "Maybe she don't know what she's seeing. Let's talk to her."

They walked toward her. The little girl sat frozen in place, her wide blue eyes fixed on them like those of a deer caught in the headlights of an oncoming car. They noticed that she was clutching something to her chest. It writhed, and she spoke to it, too low for them to hear her.

"She's got her baby brother or sister with her," Williamson said. "Let's just go up and make friends, and I'll give her a buck or something to go back in the house."

Suddenly, the child sprang to her feet, and ran up the side of the hill.

"There she goes!" Pilton exclaimed. The two men broke into a run, jumping over the shallow stream and charging up the slope.

"Why are we chasing her?" Williamson asked suddenly, stopping on his heels.

Pilton paused only for a heartbeat. "Well, we don't want her to tell anyone we're here. She knows somethin's wrong now. We gotta catch up with her."

"We don't want to get the sheriff out here," Williamson agreed. It would be a bad idea to have anyone investigating their presence in the forest preserve at this time, for whatever reason. Williamson poured on the speed, and outdistanced his companion.

With their long strides, they crested the hill in no time. The girl was just a few lengths ahead of them, the soft soles of her green-shod feet flashing down the hill. Pilton shouted, "Hey!"

The running girl looked back at him over her shoulder. All at once, she dropped to her knees. Suddenly, for no really good reason Pilton could detect, she vanished from sight.

"Where'd she go?" he yelled. Williamson dashed to where the girl had last been visible.

So far as Pilton could tell, Williamson was reaching for a handful of empty air, but he came up with the little girl's upper arm clasped in his big fist. She reappeared as if a curtain was being drawn away from her, then Pilton could see there was a white scarf or something like it on the ground around her feet. The little girl wrenched her arm free to support the bundle in her other arm, and Williamson took hold of her long blond hair instead.

"Right here, you idiot. Can't you see her?"

"I can now, but she was invisible before," Pilton insisted. "How'd she do that?"

"She wasn't invisible," Williamson said, his voice scornful. "She's wearing green, and you've got the sun in your eyes."

"No, she's magic," Pilton said. "She disappeared, like in a trick."

"You're just blind, that's your problem."

"What do you want of me?" the girl demanded, clutching the baby protectively to her chest.

Pilton and Williamson inspected their prisoners. The girl stood about three feet high, with long, silky blond hair that was now tangled and festooned with pieces of weed. She wasn't as young as they'd first suspected. The summing up look she fixed upon them wasn't just that of a hyperintelligent six-year-old. If she hadn't been so small of stature, Pilton would have thought she was just on the early side of teenage.

"Why did you run away?" Jake asked her.

"Well, you were chasing me," she said, her chin stuck out. She looked as though she might cry, and Pilton felt sorry for her. "Let me go. I want to go home."

"What do you want to do, Jake?" he asked, staring at the child. She was a pretty little thing, and scared to pieces.

"No names," Williamson snapped back, looking alarmed.

"Let her go, huh?"

"Shut up! I got to think!" The harshness of his voice alarmed the girl, who tried to take a step away. Williamson tightened his hold on her hair, and she whimpered. The baby, catching her alarm, burst out crying.

"My God, that kid has lungs!" Pilton said, taken aback by the sheer volume of noise the minute baby produced.

"Quiet! Shut it up!" Williamson thundered over the shrieking.

"I can't!" Dola said, stamping her foot. Tears began to track down her cheeks. "You frightened her!"

"Shut her up or I'll wallop you! Dammit, I can't think with all this screaming going on. Put her in the truck," Williamson said.

The girl's eyes went big, and she attempted to struggle free. Her efforts had no more effect than if she had been held in the grip of a stone statue. With a gesture of impatience, Williamson thrust her toward Pilton, who wrapped his hand around her upper arm and steered her over the hilltop toward the tanker. Her bones felt as small as a bird's. He sneaked a glance sideways at her. Through the tresses of her hair, the tip of her left ear peeked out. It was pointed, like a cat's. The girl caught him looking, and tossed her head back. The ear was hidden again, but Pilton was certain he'd seen what he'd seen. She bent her head over the baby, talking in a low, soothing voice. The infant's shrill cries abated about a yard from the truck, and settled into low, frightened sobbing. Her little nose was red.

Pilton relaxed as soon as the noise stopped. It had to be a very new baby. Both of his kids had sounded like that for the first few months of life.

"We've caught a fairy woman," he told Williamson, when

they'd stowed the girl and baby in the truck cab. The seats were so deep that only the heads of the two children were visible over the side. Both faces were streaky with tears and huge-eyed with terror.

"Don't talk crazy," Williamson said, turning his back on them. "She's a midget, like those Munchkins in the Wizard of Oz movie."

"I think there's something weird about her," Pilton insisted. The girl stared at them through the truck window, her expression half defiance, half mute appeal.

"Dammit!" Williamson swore, pounding his fist on the tank wall. Pilton saw the girl jump, and set her jaw. "We can't just trust her to keep her mouth shut, not when we've scared the heck out of her like this. We better take her back and let Ms. Gilbreth figure out what to do with her."

Dola was frightened. She wanted to get out of this evil-smelling vehicle and away, but there was so much metal around her that the very air burned. The Big Folk had bundled her in here, without so much thought for her feelings as they'd give to a package. She curled in on herself, wishing the world would go away. The only thing preventing her from becoming a little knot of self-pity and fear was her concern for the baby.

Thankfully, Asrai had stopped crying the moment the truck door slammed shut on them, or she'd have deafened Dola completely. It must have been the presence of all that cold metal that shocked her silent. This was the first time in her young life that she'd been in a hostile environment. Dola liked it no more than Asrai, but she knew such things existed, and was better prepared.

"I'm with you, little one," she whispered. "I'll protect you, I swear it." Though how she was to accomplish her vow, she had no idea.

Who could these men be? They were dressed identically in button-up coveralls of a drab color and sturdy construction. The outfit looked better on the bigger man. The other one was so skinny that only his shoulders filled out the uniform. The two men seemed to be disagreeing on what to do. Meanwhile they were fiddling with the hose running from the truck's tank, which had been spewing foul-smelling liquid onto the ground near the source of her drinking water. The elders would need to be told at once, so they could contain the contamination.

When both the cab doors opened at once, Dola put the baby across her shoulder and prepared to climb down, but the two men got in, one on either side, leaving no room for her to pass. By the set of their jaws, there was no room for argument, either. She was a prisoner.

What's going to become of us? she thought despairingly.

Without a word, the one called Jake started the engine. The skinny one with hair the soft brown color of river clay kept glancing at her sideways. Jake, driving, didn't look at them once, but Dola could tell he was acutely aware of them. She peeked up at him through her hair, trying to study his face. He didn't look like a bad man, but he was scared, too.

"I tell you, this must be a fairy woman and her baby," the skinny one said, talking over her head, when the truck had passed out of the Forest Preserve and onto the main road.

"C'mon, you idiot," said Jake, "there's no such thing as fairies."

"Well, what do you call her?" Skinny poked at Dola's ear.

She was shocked. Incarceration was one thing, but personal assaults were another. Dola turned her head and bit him on the hand. He yelled, and she recoiled, spitting out the taste of his skin.

"Ugh, do you never wash your hands?" she asked boldly. "And it's not my baby, it's my cousins' baby. You'd better let us go home, or they'll be upset."

It was the wrong thing to say. All of a sudden, both men grew quiet. They didn't say another word to her. She looked from one to another, hoping for some sign of kindness or mercy, and found none. Dola felt a cold wash of terror slide down the middle of her back. These weren't Keith Doyle and his harmless Big friends whom she knew and trusted. They were strangers, who might mean to do her harm. She might never see home again.

Dola tightened her arms around the baby and stared out the windshield at the road, trying to memorize the sights they passed. She had to be brave, for Asrai.

In the early twilight, Maura peered into her cottage. It was silent within, and none of the lanterns had been lit. She found the one closest to the doorway and blew on the pointed cotton wick mounted in the scrolled wooden candle between the carved screens. The cotton began to blaze with its bright, unconsuming fire.

There was still no sound. "Dola? Where are you, child?"

Maura checked Asrai's cot. It was empty, and cool to the touch. Perhaps both girl and baby were asleep in the master bed. She smiled. That would explain why Dola hadn't reported for kitchen duty. The day had tired them both out. Maura started putting on the other lights in the small cottage.

"Dola?" she said, her voice gently chiding, as she leaned into the bedroom. "Lass, it's nearly dinnertime." She was astonished that Asrai wasn't awake already. Maura was more than ready to feed the baby, and their physical alarms seemed to go off at the same time.

The cottage was empty. Well, no harm. Perhaps Dola was in the barn or the main house and their paths had crossed, each seeking the other. Maura went out to seek baby and babysitter.

They were not to be found. By full dark, Maura was beside herself with worry. She had covered nearly all the farm property, calling. The girls weren't in the fields, nor the workshop, nor visiting other children in the clan rooms of the main house. Maura had even knocked on the door of each of the cottages to ask her neighbors if the girls were with them. No one had seen either child for hours.

"Where can she be?" she asked Holl. "I've been listening for them, but I can't hear them."

"I am sure they are here somewhere," Holl said, trying to be reassuring. He knew Dola to be responsible. Wherever they were, he was certain that they were safe. "Probably Dola became interested in some small project, or reading a book, and she lost track of the time."

Maura favored him with a look full of exasperation. She crossed her arms gingerly over her chest. "But *Asrai* would not forget. She must be very hungry. A babe's stomach can only hold enough food for two or three hours. We ought to be able to hear her crying by now."

"Aye, that we should," said Ranna, not unkindly. "If we could train the babe to rise at dawn we wouldn't need a rooster."

"Dola wouldn't have wandered away," Shelogh said, reasonably. "That child is responsible."

The thought, so far kept at bay, rose inexorably, that Dola and Asrai were gone from the Farm itself. At once, the elder Folk began to suggest alternatives to the unthinkable.

"Could vun of our Big friends have come to visit and taken them away?" Rose suggested. "The good Ludmilla has said often that she vould like to treat Dola for the good work she does in caring for your babe."

"She might have walked into town," Marcy suggested, crouching down beside the Little Folk. She had just returned from a class at Midwestern, and was concerned when the situation had been explained to her. "With all the Big People going home over these roads at this hour, she's probably hiding out. And I'm sure she's sorry. Holding on to an unhappy baby when you've missed feeding time is its own punishment."

"Or it might be they've gone on a wee adventure," Marm said, his foolish, bearded face concerned but smiling. "It's a long way back to the Library, but she knows how to get there. Perhaps she ran out of books to read!"

Immediately, Holl wanted to dismiss Marm's idea as foolish, but who knew what ran through the minds of almost-teenaged children? It was true. All of them did know the way back to their old home. The distance was too great to walk, but there were buses that stopped at the county road intersection only one mile away. If that were the case, she'd have arrived at the Midwestern campus within the last twenty minutes.

"But it is dark now," the Master reasoned. "She will have taken shelter somewhere for the night. Dola has learned basic survival. All vill be vell."

"But Asrai needs to feed," Maura exclaimed. "What will they do?"

"Peace, daughter," the Master said, patting her hand. "Undoubtedly she has found that her adventure has placed her too far away at a critical point. Ve vill telephone to Ludmilla and see if she has seen them. Our good friend will aid Dola in dealing with an infant who has missed a meal. Our needs are similar, though our sizes differ. It is too late to bring her here before she is fed, but no doubt some Big Folk equivalent vill be made to suffice."

The suggestion made good sense, and served to calm Maura and Siobhan somewhat. Concentrating on eluding detection by either mother, Holl extended a wisp of sense, feeling outward for his daughter.

"They'll be with her, won't they?" Maura asked, bravely, looking up at Holl for support.

"Aye," he said, distracted. If she'd seen him concentrating, she'd know what he'd been trying to do, and worry all the more. "They won't leave her."

"It is I who speak, old friend," the Master said into the telephone receiver. All the Folk who could fit into the farmhouse kitchen were crowded around. "It vould be very good to see you at the veekend, should you care to visit. No, I call for another purpose. Two of our children have gone wandering. Have they come to you? My daughter's child, and young Dola, her caretaker." Holl watched with dismay as the small muscles in the Master's cheek tightened. He was disappointed. "Vill you keep watch for them, and summon us vhen they appear? I thank you." He cradled the phone and shook his head.

"The Library," said Siobhan desperately.

"Do you want me to go?" Marcy asked.

"It vould take too long," the Master said. "I will ask one who is closer by." He put in another call. Everyone held their breath while the Master counted the rings until the receiver was picked up. "Mees Londen, I haf a favor to ask of you."

Holl was waiting by the telephone when it rang, half an hour later.

"Nothing," Diane said. "I went through the whole village with a lantern. I checked every house, and every level of the library stacks. They aren't there. I left a note on the wall with my phone number. If Dola goes down there, she'll call you or me when she arrives."

"Thank you," Holl said.

"Dunn and Barry are going over the rest of the campus on foot. They'll call you direct if they find her." Diane's voice was hesitant. "I'm sure they're all right. Probably they're just lost. Can I do anything else to help?"

"You are doing a great deal. Just keep your eyes open for them," Holl said.

"Please keep me posted," Diane begged. "I'd better go. She might be trying to call you."

"That's right," Holl said, and hastily hung up. He waited, hoping that the telephone would ring as soon as he put down the receiver. He stood with his hand on the handset, ready to snatch it up, waiting for the bell. His eyes met Maura's. Her lips quivered slightly, then tears overspilled her lashes and streamed down her cheeks. Holl opened his arms. She moved close and put her head on his shoulder, closing her arms tightly against his back. Throat tight, he clasped her to his chest, his lips touching her hair. He was glad for the feeling of being enfolded. The close contact gave him a sense of security which he sorely needed.

No time for subtlety. He let his mind clear to do a full finding. His sense tripped lightly out, touching all the places on the farm that Dola liked to frequent. It met the edges of the property, feeling gently along the forest paths, and into the small pockets of air under the greater tree roots that the children liked to hide in when they played their games. His sense ranged further and further afield, touching the minds of Big Folk drivers in their cars, the metal of which burned him slightly. Dola and his baby were nowhere nearby. He knew in his heart that they lived, but he couldn't find them. Enoch burst into the kitchen. Holl, his concentration broken again, turned to his brother-in-law.

"We've been out in the field. Strange Big Folk were there today," Enoch said, his distaste evident. His face was drawn and angry. He ran a dirty hand through his touseled black hair. "Their footprints and Dola's overlap. Bracey did a sniffing, and he says there was a scuffle, and she left with them in a truck. He can't figure out who they are. They drove through a puddle of that muck that those fertilizer people have been dumping on our land."

"My baby's been taken away by the Big Ones!" Siobhan burst into hysterical tears. Tay gathered her into his arms, and sympathetic friends surrounded her.

"Hush, woman," Tay said hoarsely. "Screeching won't bring them back. The girl will come back if she can. All we can do is continue to look."

Siobhan's panic was nothing compared to the agony Maura suddenly experienced as she realized her baby was gone. She began to cry, silently, with more and more force until she was gasping uncontrollably. Her father stepped forward and clapped a hard hand over her mouth and nose.

"Calm. Gain control. Your next breath vill be a calm one. Concentrate." Above his hand, her eyes cleared, and she nodded. Her mother put an arm around her shoulder, and more friends and relatives gathered close to lend their comfort.

"We must call Keith Doyle," Holl said, holding Maura close. Both their faces were pale and drawn. "He'll know what to do."

The Master nodded assent. Catra snatched up the phone and began to dial.

Chapter
FIVE

" ' **A**ll rise,' " Paul Meier said, and snickered. He turned to squint at Keith, his thin, curved nose wrinkling with good humor. "Great stuff, Keith. Pithy, and a neat play on words. The client might actually want to use it. I love the concept illo, too." He held up the white rectangle of pasteboard to study. It showed a courtroom scene. There were no human beings in the illustration. All the participants in the trial were baked goods. The jury was twelve muffins in a two-row pan, and in the witness box was an angel food cake with a piece of black veil on its top and a hanky folded into the front curve at one side. In the presiding seat, surrounded by satin bunting, was a yellow, black, and red packet labeled "Judge Yeast." The caption, which Meier underlined again with a fingernail, was "All rise."

"Angel food cakes don't use yeast," Sean Lopez pointed out, disdainfully. His black brows lowered over his pugnaciously snubbed nose.

"So what?" Meier said cheerfully. He grinned, white teeth brilliant against his olive skin. "She's only a witness. It makes a great image, Sean, and it makes you remember the product. If the client wants to change the angel food cake for a loaf of challah, he will. They always want to change something. We often leave something in deliberately for them to pull out."

"You go to all the trouble of putting something in you know the client will want to kill?" asked Dorothy Scott, tapping one

63

smooth, walnut-hued cheek with the charcoal pencil she held between her elegantly manicured nails.

"Whatever works," Meier said. "You have to understand what you're dealing with here, kids. It's not an easy business. This is Hollywood East. There's a lot of ad firms out there, and a finite amount of money. We're here to make sure the most money possible falls into our pockets—that is to say PDQ Advertising's pockets. The way we do that is not just through clever ad campaigns, but by making the client feel more special here than anywhere else."

"You mean make him feel like he's our only client?" suggested Brendan Martwick. Keith studied the pen he was rolling between his fingers. Brendan was one world-class brown-noser. He and Brendan had already decided they didn't like each other. Keith believed in group efforts, and Martwick believed wholeheartedly in all for one and every man for himself. He was a snooty north-sider. If he ever broke down and called Keith 'common' or 'vulgar,' Keith wouldn't be surprised. He sounded like a barely-updated character out of a Victorian novel, and dressed like a Polo mannequin. Whatever young and wealthy J. Bennett Throgmorton-Snipe III was doing taking an ill-paid internship when he could have lounged at a desk in Daddy's stockbrokerage firm, Keith couldn't guess. Maybe someone had told him advertising was easy. It wasn't.

"You've got it," Meier agreed. "Our time is flexible, as far as they're concerned, because they're paying. You've got to psych out their likes and dislikes, and avoid the buzzwords and shibboleths of their particular industry or product. Not easy sometimes, which is why we have a research department that I think rivals the FBI's."

Keith and the others nodded, grinning. The creative director's department was the second department the interns had been assigned to for orientation. Research had been the first. Keith had been impressed by the resources the ad company had at its fingertips.

"Will we really get our names on the presentation?" Keith asked, tapping the matte. "Dorothy did the artwork and lettering."

"Yeah? Nice job, Dorothy," Meier said, flashing a half grin at her. "I'll have to check out the client's feelings on having internship students working on his campaign—y'know, if inexperienced kids came up with this hot slogan and ad, why is he paying PDQ the big bucks for professional creative teams? I'll get back to you. No promises, now.''

Keith and Dorothy nodded, and exchanged a quick glance. Whether they got outside credit for the idea or not, this would be like really working for an ad agency. No experience was wasted, as Meier was fond of saying, but Keith would have been upset if Dorothy's careful penwork had gone unrecognized. She was really good. All he had done was blab out his idea, and she'd put it on paper—really brought the images to life.

A pity they couldn't form a firm alliance. She was less concerned about him getting equal credit than he was on her behalf. The way the internship program was set up, the students were frequently pitted against one another, striving for the best assignments and the few advantages that would put them before the eyes of PDQ's management to secure the single job offer that would be made at the end of the term. Each of the current students started out approximately equal. They'd each fought their way through four interviews and a written essay detailing why they'd be of value to PDQ's internship program. They'd been chosen from among eight hundred applicants, half from state universities, half from private schools. Each had some personal business background, plus artistic or creative talent, as well as a high grade point average, appealing personality, and a declared major in business. They had each had to self-promote so fiercely it had become part of their everyday behavior. Keith was disappointed that even after each had secured one of the coveted internship spots they couldn't seem to put aside the competition. Even he had to fight down suspicious tendencies, and he didn't like it.

Keith recognized there was nothing personal in the imposed animosity, but after studying the way things worked at PDQ, he saw how small, core groups of individuals could consistently come up with good, marketable ideas. They weren't in constant fear of being shot down by the other people in their department. For the items, everyone's ego was on the line all the time. It would have been a more realistic experience if they'd been treated more like a creative team, though even the teams had some internal competition.

Keith shifted his copy of *In Search of Excellence* further underneath his notebook, where it couldn't be noticed, and decided to can his ideas on cooperation for the time being. The competition would never end, not with PDQ's policy of offering the best student in any year a position in the company. That plum could represent a five- to ten-year leap in one's career. Instead of having to shine year after year in a small company, it would be possible to come straight to one of the majors.

PDQ would be a terrific place to work. Keith already knew he loved dreaming up campaigns, making up slogans that tickled people but had the heart of the product represented in a few words. If he got the job, so much the better for him, but his usual cooperative soul might cheat him out of it, encouraging PDQ to hire Dorothy or one of the others instead. Sean Lopez was the most jumpy of the group. He was nearing the end of his MBA program, and was actively seeking a position to slide into after graduation in June. Brendan already acted as if the job would be his by right. Maybe his attitude would be a factor in the management's eventual choice, but it was sure a pain in the neck for the duration.

As a supervisor, Meier was the best possible choice. He'd gotten his job from a good review during an internship just like theirs, and was actively on their side, a fact that made him different from 85% of the other people working in advertising in general. He warned them about the competition, the cutthroat techniques, the downright theft of ideas, and the destruction of careers. He kept bringing in phrases like 'dog eat dog,' and 'every man for himself.' Maybe it was the mark of a good ad campaigner to think in cliches. Keith respected the hard work he put in, maintaining his own job while shepherding and acting as father-confessor to the four interns.

At the very beginning, Meier had read them a lecture. "I don't care where you're from, what kind of background you've got, who your daddy knows. This is another world. Nothing's real here; we make our own reality. If it looks like someone's ripping you off, it's nothing personal. The only job we have is to impress the client first, then all of that client's customers with the sheer fabulousness of that client's product or service. If somebody has to use your ideas to do it, he probably will. Someone might actually come up with an idea that sounds exactly like yours. It's possible; there's only so many ideas out there. There's plenty of ego-tripping here. Ignore it. There's a lot of politically incorrect 'isms.' Ignore them. Do your job, and don't get lost in the office politics. Like I said, in the end none of it's real. It doesn't affect you after you go home.

"This is the most rotten business in the world. You can't trust anyone. No one gives you credit for your work or your ideas. Your suggestions get ignored, then you get blamed when things are screwed up because no one paid attention to your recommendations. Everything costs money. You work late hours for months on a project that's cancelled without notice. And the client is never happy with anything you do. Other than that, it's a great job. I want you to know that."

Brendan was still muttering about Judge Yeast. Meier shuffled a handful of papers on the table, and cleared his throat. Martwick instantly turned a respectful and attentive face toward him. Keith resisted the urge to kick him under the table.

"Okay," Meier said. "I'm going to throw out some product names and concepts. Some of them are real, some aren't. Each of you take a few. I want some creative thinking about these by tomorrow. No need to knock yourself out on the artwork yet, Dorothy," he nodded at the young woman, "unless that's the way you think best. We'll brainstorm on all of them over the next few days. Not every one will come up strong, so I don't want anybody shooting themselves if they don't get the next Clio winner. We need all the grist we can get, and out of that we may get some goodies. Got that?"

"Yessir," Sean muttered, flipping open his notebook.

"Ready," Keith said. Meier shot him a look full of humor. Keith grinned back. He felt that he and Meier had 'clicked,' getting along instantly from day one, but he understood that there could be no favoritism shown. Still, win or lose, Keith promised himself he'd look Meier up for lunch after the internship was over. They could be good friends.

Meier showed them stat sheets and photographs of a new luxury car, details about a new breakfast cereal, a new soft drink, ground plans for a theme amusement park currently under construction. "These are the real ones, kids. You've signed secrecy agreements, so leak these, and you're through. I mean it. Oh, and just for the hell of it, I'm throwing in some ordinary, everyday items: flower pots, potatoes, uh, brown paper bags, and carrots. Let's see if you can give me some new thoughts on them, too. Pick one.''

"Potatoes," Keith said, quickly.

"Oh, I'll take carrots," Dorothy said. "They're healthy!"

"Brown paper bags," Sean said.

"That leaves flower pots," Brendan said, with an eternally world-weary air. "I can handle it."

"I'm sure you can," Meier said without expression, jotting down names next to the categories. "Okay, folks, that's all. See you tomorrow. Don't forget to clean up in here, okay?"

"Clean up the coffee," Dorothy said, dejectedly, wiping the table with a paper towel. "And we end up making it most of the time, too. I hate to be made to feel like a secretary."

"Not secretaries," Keith said, cheerfully. "We're flunkies!" The interns, when not working directly under Paul, spent their day doing errands for the rest of the staff, pulling files in research, running files back to research, taking messages, running layouts from one department to another. They certainly were learning every facet of the business from the bottom up.

"Why potatoes?" Sean asked Keith on the way out after they'd grabbed their coats out of the conference room closet and taken the used coffee cups back to the employee dining room. "Why'd you look so excited about that?"

"Inspiration," Keith said, grinning, tapping the side of his skull with a forefinger. "You know how much vitamin C there is in your average potato? You could start your day with a big helping of potatoes with C. Sunrise Spuds," he said, painting an imaginary banner on the sky. "They're not just for dinner anymore."

Sean laughed. "You're nuts."

"The trouble with you," Keith said, "is that you have to learn to let your hair down more."

"The trouble with you," Brendan said disdainfully, pointing at Keith with his briefcase, "is that your hair is already hanging around your knees."

Keith gave him a big smile as he slipped into the only space left in a crowded elevator, and watched Brendan's annoyed expression narrow and vanish between the closing doors.

Keith spent his commuter train trip drumming on the seat between his knees, smiling at passersby who met his eyes. He drove home from the station with all the windows of his old, black Mustang wide open to let the wind cool him down while inspiration cooked. If the competitiveness didn't kill them first, there were opportunities galore for creativity and experimentation at PDQ. While Keith's tensed muscles wound down, his active brain was spinning on product ideas. Maybe some of them were way out, but that was half the fun.

In a way, being an intern was better than working for the company, because he could play around with suggestions without the possibility of being fired if the ideas turned out to be clunkers or money pits. Keith had purposely let some of the others pass on some of the silly-sounding names so he could have them. He let Brendan take Rad Sportswear in exchange for Appalachi-Cola. None of the others wanted a soft drink with such a weird name, and they couldn't understand why Keith's eyes had gleamed at the sound of it. He could picture more scope for Appalachi-Cola. It suggested wonderful images to him.

"As refreshing as a Florida vacation," he murmured to himself, peering out over the steering wheel at the usual afternoon backup. Sounded good to him. Chicago in September was steamy and hot, without the promise of white sand beaches to relieve the gasping atmospheric inversion. Keith swerved through the lanes of traffic making notes on a legal pad splayed out on the passenger seat. Who knew? Maybe one of his ideas would be a winner, and he'd have the joy of seeing a campaign designed around it.

Through the kitchen curtains, he could see his mother taking something out of the refrigerator. He grinned. With a gusty sigh, he threw open the door. His mother turned, wide-eyed, as he staggered in, wrenching his tie loose from his throat, and plopped down in a chair, limbs splayed limply.

"Very dramatic," his mother said ironically, applauding. "You win the Academy Award for best performance by an actor getting home from work. Please don't leave your briefcase in the door, honey." She hooked the slim leather case with one finger and extended it to him.

"Sorry, Mom," Keith said, springing up like a Jack-in-the-box for a kiss on the cheek. His mother eyed him.

"In spite of the Sarah Bernhardt routine, you do look tired," Mrs. Doyle said, handing over the case. "Have a good day?"

"Great!" Keith said, enthusiastically. "No more orientation. We're working on formulating ad campaigns for new products. This department's a lot more interesting than Research. We can really use our imaginations. Our supervisor, Paul Meier, said this is just what a real creative team does during 'ideation.' I like Paul. He's trying to treat us like regular employees, while still leaving us room to make mistakes."

"Too bad all life experiences aren't so forgiving," Mrs. Doyle said, glancing down the hall opposite. It led to the family bed-rooms. Keith caught the meaning of her expression, and pulled a long-suffering expression.

"Jeff's home, huh?"

"Yup. Dinner in half an hour, sweetie," Mrs. Doyle said. "You can make the salad after you change."

The battle of the day was fought, but the battle of the evening was just beginning. Keith got more tired out in four hours arguing with his younger brother than he did in the ten hours of commuting and working downtown.

The younger Doyle was on the floor of their shared room with his back against the bed. After a short glance to make sure it wasn't anyone important who had entered, he returned his attention to the small electronic game propped on his hunched knees. Jeffrey Doyle had almost a movie star's good looks. He had much the same shaped jaw as Keith, but it had more squared bone and a little more muscle. His hair was red, too, but deeper, with bronze in it, and his eyes were an olivine green, instead of changeable hazel like Keith's. His skin never freckled; it wouldn't dare. He tanned smoothly in the earliest spring sun. In him, the Doyle intensity fueled his emotions. He never forgave a slight, and Keith returning home to stay in the room he had staked out as his own was a personal affront.

"There's a message for you," Jeff said tersely.

It was almost the most civil pronouncement Keith had heard from Jeff in a month. "Thanks. Where is it?"

Without looking up, Jeff gestured toward Keith's bed.

On the pillow was a scrap of paper torn from the corner of a junk mail flyer. In the corner, under the paste-on address label, was a scrawl in Jeff's seismic handwriting. Keith scanned it. "Catra called? When? 'Check the front page of the paper,' " he read. "What's that mean?"

Jeff raised resentful eyes to him. "Couldn't tell. She had a weird way of talking. She said something valuable was stolen. Your strange friends." He went back to his game, glowering at the miniature screen.

"Today's paper?" Keith asked.

"She didn't say," Jeff said shortly, and set himself to ignore any further questions Keith asked.

His audience obviously at an end, Keith went to find out for himself. "Mysterious," he said, as he hurried out of the room to find the daily paper. For one of the Folk to telephone long distance generally meant that something was very wrong.

It had already been consigned to the recycling bin. Keith pulled section one from the heap and straightened it out. At first he didn't see anything that related to the Little Folk, until he noticed the boxed reference in the upper left hand corner under the daily weather report.

"Archaeological display at Field Museum!" Keith breathed. He felt his invisible whiskers twitch. Surely that was what Catra meant him to read. He flipped through the pages to the main body of the article. There, as the Elf Master had predicted, was the display of Bronze Age artifacts brought to the United States by Professor Parker. The photograph that accompanied the article showed the comb Keith himself had unearthed in Scotland.

"It must have been stolen," Keith said to himself. So that was the problem. You just couldn't have a magic comb bouncing around the city. He picked up the phone and dialed Hollow Tree Farm. The line was busy.

Never mind. He'd go and investigate for himself. Thankfully, the Field Museum had late hours. Keith snatched the family membership card from the niche in the desk where his parents kept it, and hopped into the Mustang. The traffic outbound from the heart of the city was thick, but inbound, he had reasonably clear sailing.

The museum's ornamented portico had shadows across it already as the daylight dwindled. Keith shot up the flight of shallow steps to the grand entrance.

"Good evening," Keith said to the woman behind the marble counter just inside the doors. "I'm a friend of Professor Parker." The woman gave him a noncommittal smile, as if uncertain of the significance of his statement. "The English archaeologist who's visiting with the Bronze Age stuff from the Hebrides? Is he here?" The woman still looked blank. Keith glanced confidentially from side to side and leaned closer. "The short one?"

"Oh, yes!" the woman exclaimed, her face lightening, then looking a little self-conscious.

"I'd like to see him, if that's possible."

"Sorry. He's busy this evening."

"How do you know that, when a second ago you didn't know who he was?" Keith asked, plastering a foolish grin on his face to soften the question.

Flushing, the woman countered with another question. "Did you want to visit the museum this evening, sir?"

"Uh, yeah." Keith plunged a finger and a thumb into his shirt pocket for the membership card.

The woman beamed to acknowledge a museum supporter. The young man might be strange, but he was a patron. "Thank you, sir. Would you like a map?"

"Will it help me find the professor?" Keith asked, full of innocence, as he took the pamphlet.

"I can't help you with that, sir," the woman explained patiently. Their voices had gotten louder, echoing off the polished walls. A security guard on watch near the entrance started forward, hand on radio, but she waved him back. "I can direct you to the Bronze Age exhibit. Second floor."

Using the map, Keith had no trouble finding Parker's display in the upstairs gallery, sandwiched between another small visiting exhibit and the museum's huge Oriental collection. Four or five showcases were dedicated to the finds, which combined the discoveries of two or three groups of archaeologists working in the same region of the Hebridean northwest. Keith felt a surge of pride when he found the case that contained the round clay bottle and the string of amber trading beads that he and his Scottish friend Matthew had unearthed together a little over a year ago. Moreover, their names were typed on the little identification tag pinned in front of it. Parker was generous in giving credit. Keith was delighted. He wished that someone he knew was there, so he could show them his name.

Most of the artifacts were of the shard and fragment variety, with carefully-made mockups of how the pieces were assumed to have looked when they were in use. Once again, Keith was impressed by the way the scientists had extrapolated the shape of the whole items from formless fragments found out of context in three thousand years' worth of dirt. Previously discovered examples were used as templates, but it took a good eye to tell the difference between the potential fracture zones of the neck of a jar from its similarly-formed pedestal. Bone pins, small toys, glass beads and the like were all that remained fully intact after the passing millennia.

Keith surveyed the display. Each of these pieces was as ordinary as it looked. None of them aroused that tingle of second sight, making his whiskers twitch the way the wood-and-bone comb had. Catra's elliptical message had been correct. The comb was not where it belonged. In the next to last case, he saw the little label designating where the comb belonged. A little bar labeled "REMOVED" lay in most of the empty spots where artifacts had been taken out, but none marked this particular absence. His invisible whiskers sprang erect in alarm.

He dropped to his knees in front of the case, his nose almost pressed against the glass. Keith felt a lead weight drop into the pit of his stomach. He stared into the heart of the case, hoping for a clue. Had someone else latched on to the fact that there was something extraordinary about that one piece, and stolen it? The Little Folk would want to avoid letting any artifact that could be traced back to them wander loose. It had been safe with Parker. Keith knew he had to find it and get it back here where it belonged. He suddenly felt someone's eyes upon him, and looked around.

A uniformed security guard stood against a pillar, peering obliquely at him, clearly wondering why a young man in suspenders was getting so worked up about Bronze Age antiques. It was the same guard who had been near the front door. Keith gave him a huge, mindless smile. The guard scowled, and looked away.

Keith sighed. It would be harder to investigate the comb's disappearance with a tail following him all over the museum. Nonchalantly, Keith backed away from the case and stared up at the large map suspended above it, showing the locations in Scotland where the various artifacts had been found. A light sound came from behind him, as if the guard had shifted a foot on the polished floor.

Without haste, though his nerves were going bonkers, Keith sidled away from the Parker display, and ambled toward the nearest stairwell.

Was there any way to trace the comb, using its previous presence in the cases as a thread? Keith threw a mental glance over his shoulder, hoping the guard wouldn't notice. The case didn't emit any perceptible energies pointing one way or the other. There wasn't enough magical oomph in the comb to have left a trail. As a psychic detective, he was on his own.

Keith started walking down the stairs. The guard sauntered behind him, the radio on his hip emitting whispering sibilants. Keith looked up and smiled at the man, whose brows drew together in a scowl. He guessed that it hadn't been too smart to draw attention to himself at the museum entrance. Now the staff was suspicious. How could he get rid of his tail?

On the main floor of the museum were the famous dinosaurs, a Tyrannosaurus rex standing triumphant over the prone body of its prey. Keith stopped at the well-worn handrail and stared up at its toothy jaws. The guard paused about twenty feet away, arms folded, wearing a carefully neutral expression that made him look no less threatening than the giant dinosaur. Keith studied paleontology, wondering what to do.

There hadn't been a news report on the radio about the theft of the comb from the museum, so either the loss hadn't been discovered yet, or the museum staff was covering up. He wondered how the elves had gotten the word so quickly. Maybe Professor Parker himself had called the Master with the news.

It was likely to be an inside job, Keith reasoned. Those cases couldn't be opened easily without keys and, to judge by the persistence of the security staff around suspicious visitors, without being observed. If the comb remained on the premises, maybe he could find it. It gave off a recognizable auric energy that Keith had detected shortly after he'd found it. That process of investigation, as Holl and Enoch had been at pains to instruct him, took concentration. Keith stared up into the eye socket of the Tyrannosaurus, and looked past it, focusing his own inner eye.

Suddenly, he was surrounded by ghost-lights, as ordinarily-unseen energies pulsed at him, beckoning him toward a myriad of glass cases, visible in the large chambers that led off from all sides of the main hall. More energies thrummed at him through the floors from upstairs and downstairs.

Oh, great, Keith thought, overwhelmed, looking around at the display. He didn't know where to turn first. This place is *full* of magic artifacts.

Well, where better to hide a needle than in a haystack full of needles? Keith went from one source of energy to another, hoping that one of them belonged to the missing comb. Most of the Hopi kachinas glimmered at him in their case, creating a tremendous mass presence that was the most powerful thing for yards. A few of the Inuit household goods shone brightly against the dimness of the hall where they were displayed. Keith hurried through the aisles, eliminating one false lead after another. After the thirtieth false alarm on the ground floor drew him to yet another Native American display, he made a mental note to research those mystical traditions one day.

Slowly, he was able to fine-tune what he was looking for. While the Indian items had their own strong identity, they didn't match the sensation he had had when he'd handled the comb. Gradually, he began to sense that what he sought was not on this floor at all, but somewhere below.

A loudspeaker interrupted his thoughts with a pleasant chime, followed by a woman's voice that echoed through the big chamber, drowning out the identityless roar of human voices and footsteps. "The museum will be closing in twenty minutes."

Keith looked around him. A few of the other patrons stopped what they were doing and headed toward the main entrance or the gift shop. No one was paying attention to him. At long last, the guard who'd been tailing him had gotten bored with the seemingly-aimless tour of the Native American rooms, and abandoned him. Hands in pockets, Keith strolled along the inner wall of the museum, toward a down staircase.

Maybe before technology humankind knew more about the mystical side of life, but the Industrial Revolution had changed things. He'd read about a theory that suggested that people stopped believing in fairies after machines were invented that spun thread and made shoes, because then such tasks were no longer such hard work. Keith knew better. Humanity was just ignoring its closest neighbors. He smiled, a little smugly.

His new skill made the world look subtly different to him. His expanded perception gave him insights into other cultures in ways he had never dreamed of. He was grateful to his Little friends for making it possible. Running errands like this was one of the very minor ways he had to show thanks.

The Egyptian rooms were an unexpected ordeal. Definitely the ancient kingdom had a handle on unseen energies. Ever since he was a kid, the Field Museum displays of mummies and sarcophagi had given him a feeling of exciting and incomprehensible danger, like the chilling sensation aroused by hearing really good ghost stories around campfires, and now he knew why. Every mummy in the glass cases had a creepingly terrifying pseudopod of light coming from it that reached out to him, questing snakelike to investigate him, and as he shrank back from its touch, fell away. It seemed as if each mummy was looking for someone, someone particular—maybe the people who had defiled the tombs where they had once been buried— but was not interested in anyone else.

The keen thrill of terror made him shiver, wondering if he was in for the same kind of retribution for snooping through the remains of the Celtic villagers in Scotland. No, there'd been no sensation of evil or anger there. The priests and embalmers of Egypt had deliberately instilled malign influences that reached out long after the body was inert matter, to avenge the departed Pharaohs against the despoilers of their graves.

Lessons in countering the Little Folk's talent for misdirection brought his attention obliquely to an unmarked steel door at the end of the corridor at the opposite end of the hall from the exhibits. It had been painted the same color as the walls to make it unobtrusive. From the musty smell wafting gently underneath it, Keith guessed that the corridor beyond probably led to the archives and storage rooms.

The pulse he was following grew stronger and stronger the closer he got. He was more and more convinced that it was the Scottish comb he was tracing. It *was* still in the museum, but there was a sense of urgency about it. He was puzzled.

No security guards were in sight, but it wouldn't hurt to use a little misdirection of his own. After a moment of concentration, he observed happily that none of the museum visitors looked directly at him anymore. Under cover of a large crowd heading for the stairs, Keith slipped in the door, and closed it gently behind him.

He'd never been 'behind the scenes' in the museum before. It made him feel a little uneasy, as if now he'd see the fakery and animatronics that made the place run, but everything remained blessedly if not refreshingly real. The storage rooms at the end of the corridor reminded him strongly of the library stacks at college. They consisted of numbered shelves along narrow aisles, but instead of holding books they held antiquities of every description, smelling of spice, dust, and time. There wasn't much light, but it was sufficient to navigate by, using his whiskers to keep from bumping into outthrust objects. And besides, he wouldn't need to see the comb with his normal vision to find it.

Echoing eerily down the clay-scented corridor came the voice of the public address system. "The museum is now closed. Will you please make your way immediately to the exits. Thank you for visiting the Field Museum." That was it. Keith was now on the premises illegally. He hoped he could get the comb back where it belonged and get out of the building without causing a fuss.

The sensation that he was being watched by someone smiling made him turn slowly around to see who was there. He jumped in surprise. The empty eyeholes of a mask from the South Pacific stared at him blankly, the shards of polished shell, jade, and bone set into its face gleaming softly, like milky jewels.

Hand on his chest, Keith leaned against the shelf opposite while his heart stopped pounding basso staccato.

"Whew," he whispered.

As in the outer museum, there were plenty of artifacts in storage that provided their own illumination. Keith was able to pass most of them by without even looking at them.

The feeling that the comb was very near persisted. On the other side of the second huge room of shelves were several small doors. Offices, Keith guessed.

A yawn erupted suddenly. He stifled it with difficulty. Using his second sight so much was making him tired. He hoped his energy would last until he solved his mystery and got out of the museum. He wasn't so nimble at making excuses when his wits were fuddled with fatigue.

The first few offices were dark. Each was small, every available corner and every flat surface crammed with books, papers, small artifacts, stones, and assorted impedimenta. A quick glance into each office was enough to tell Keith that what he sought wasn't there. The yearning cry of the Scottish artifact was still up ahead.

The tingly glow summoned him to the last room on the left. It was larger than the other offices, with an extra door standing ajar in the right hand wall. Beyond that door, Keith could hear someone with an English accent and pedantic cadence lecturing. Good. If everyone was occupied, no one would notice him while he investigated.

To his great relief, the comb was in the glass case across from the inner door. The moment he came around the corner he was washed with a sensation of relief and comfort, like meeting an old friend. Whatever had been the purpose of its magical enhancement in the Bronze Age, the comb gave off a soothing radiation that calmed anyone in close proximity. Not a bad survival trait for something so fragile.

Keith stood back to think, eying the case. The object was in plain sight. No attempt had been made to disguise it, so there was no question that it was down here deliberately, with the blessing and knowledge of the museum. He wondered why the Little Folk had been concerned about it.

Maybe their real reason for sending him was feedback from the artifact next to the comb, which was putting out a louder and more insistent signal. It was a thumb-sized baked clay figurine, made to be strung on a necklace, shaped like a stylized human child except for—Keith had to lean down closely to make certain—the pointed ears.

"Oh, my God," Keith breathed. He wondered who else was aware of the charm's special characteristics, and what conclusions they'd drawn from it. He wasn't sure why the Folk were worried that they might be at risk for discovery from the display of a Bronze Age clay fetish in Chicago. Maybe it was something that belonged to them that got lost. Well, if that was the case, he was going to make sure they got it back. But how to 'liberate' it? He hunkered down in front of the glass door to see if there were alarm wires or anything that would be triggered when he opened it. He put his hands flat against one of the panes and started to slide it slowly left.

Suddenly, the voices behind him got louder, and the door at his back was flung open. Keith turned around, blinking with terror at a group of knees mostly wearing suits or neutral skirts, and the person at their head, an adult human male who was currently at eye level with Keith. Professor Parker, researcher and lecturer, was a dwarf.

"As I live and breathe, Keith Doyle!" exclaimed Parker, coming forward with his sailor's gait. He extended a cordial hand to Keith. "How very nice to see you! This *is* an unexpected pleasure."

"Professor," Keith said weakly, putting out his own hand.

Parker shook it vigorously. "Well, well, well, what have you been doing with yourself?"

"Oh," Keith replied, smiling up at the small researcher's companions. They didn't seem as pleased to see him as Parker was. He glanced back. His handprints were clearly visible on the front of the display case. "Uh, hot air ballooning. Things like that."

Parker's face lit up with childlike delight. "Really? Very different from the last time I saw you, young man. Above the ground is undoubtedly better for you than below it, eh?" Parker chuckled heartily. Keith joined in, sounding like a sick engine valve.

"Well, Keith Doyle, what a businesslike dash you cut!" The small professor looked him up and down. Keith was suddenly acutely aware of his fashionable short haircut, and the fact that he hadn't changed out of the white button-down shirt, with the fatuous patterned suspenders holding up his trousers, he'd worn to the office that day. The outfit looked silly next to the conservative autumn-weight suits on all the men in the room. Suddenly he was aware also that there were a lot of them, and some austerely dressed women, too. Though Parker was happy to see Keith, he'd obviously interrupted a presentation of some kind.

"Uh, thanks."

"And how is my good friend Professor Alfheim? Although it is not uncommon for people our size to have children *your* size, you're not really his son, are you?" Parker asked conspiratorially.

"No, sir," Keith admitted, a little shamefacedly, remembering the subterfuge the Master had employed to have an excuse others would accept for why he was helping Keith. "But we are distantly related. There was a good reason why he said so, really."

"Ah." Parker nodded. "I rather thought so. There is a fairly strong resemblance. And how is your cousin Holl?"

"Married," Keith said, with a grin. "And . . ."

"What? Surely not. He's just a boy. Must be about sixteen by now, what?"

Keith backpedaled furiously, clamping his mouth closed on the phrase 'and they have a baby girl.' "I mean as good as married. He's got a girlfriend, Maura. They're really serious about each other."

He dug into his back pocket for his wallet and pulled out a picture he'd taken of the two of them at the wedding supper, wearing their flower wreaths. Keith was certain those hid the points of their ears, but there wasn't time to check before Parker seized the picture and admired it.

"Very pretty. Very pretty. What interesting clothes. Lovely embroidery. Almost medieval. Could it be some kind of Renaissance Festival?"

"Uh, kind of," Keith said weakly.

"What a lot of varied interests you American youths have. I hope you haven't lost interest in the study of past cultures. I thought you showed a lot of promise. Young Matthew is doing very well, by the way. Came to admire your addition to the display, did you?"

"Well, yeah," Keith said, struggling to turn the conversation his way. He pointed at the case behind him. "You know, Dr. Alfheim would really like to see that little figure. That's really unusual. That kind of thing is his specialty. Really." He was suddenly aware of how silly he sounded, and swallowed. Parker didn't appear to notice.

"Forgive me, Professor," one of the curators interrupted. "But may we get on with the lecture?"

"Oh, yes, forgive me. Forget my own head, that's what I'll do," Parker said, apologetically, smacking a hand to the side of his head. "Ladies and gentlemen, this is the young man who discovered the comb. He was one of my assistants that summer. And what a fruitful summer it was, I must add.''

"So we are finding out," the curator said, pointedly. Parker took the cue a trifle sheepishly, and returned his attention to Keith.

"It was very nice seeing you, Keith. Please give my best to Dr. Alfheim. I hope to see him some time soon. Perhaps we can all have a little time together then. I would be delighted to show him the clay pendant and give him all the details of its discovery. Oh, and you, too," he added.

It was a dismissal. Keith had no choice but to accede. He stood up, feeling awkward to be taller than the professor. Parker didn't appear to notice. "Uh, I'll tell him."

Keith took another glance at the glass case. The small clay figure continued its insistent psychic wail; so insistent that it made him wonder if he could use the elves' invisibility-avoidance technique to divert everyone's attention away while he took it out. But with another glance at the curator, Keith saw that his chances of staying in that room would increase only if he was in another glass case, preferably stuffed and mounted.

"Um, could I stay and hear the lecture?" he asked, hopefully.

Chapter
SIX

The same security guard who'd been following Keith around was summoned to escort him out of the building. Keith thought that the guard was enjoying himself just a little too much, hustling him through the echoingly empty chambers to the front door. With a thrust reminiscent of a garbage collector shooting a barrelful of trash into the back of his truck, the guard shoved Keith out into the warm autumn night.

Keith stumbled on the uneven threshold and rolled down a handful of stairs before he came to a halt on a landing. He rose to his feet and brushed himself off as the heavy bronze doors boomed shut above him.

At least, Keith consoled his bruised dignity, the comb was safe. He spent the walk to his car, and the long drive home, thinking up one plot after another for getting the little clay charm out of the museum without being detected. He had to let the Little Folk know that the original treasure was okay, and that the distress call they must have sensed was coming from something entirely new.

Although it was very late when he telephoned the farm, the other end was picked up on the first ring.

"Hello?" Catra answered, her voice sounding anxiously hollow.

"Hi, it's Keith. Mission accomplished. The mystery is solved. You've got nothing to worry about," he said, and it was on the tip of his tongue to tell her about the little female clay figurine when she interrupted him.

"Wonderful! Then you mean she's with you? Oh, I'm so glad, you cannot imagine. How did she get there? Why didn't you call us at once when she turned up?"

"You knew about it? Yeah, Parker had it himself," Keith said, remembering his embarrassment at blundering into the austere classroom in the museum basement. "He was using it for a lecture. I interrupted his presentation to the other researchers at the museum. He says 'hi' to the Master. If he wants to come up and see the exhibit, I can take him up this weekend. I'm free." Catra's words suddenly penetrated his consciousness, and he paused to let the outpouring of relief, unusual for the coolheaded Archivist, catch up with him. He blinked. "Who?" he demanded. "Which she? Who's supposed to have turned up?"

"Dola," Catra said pleadingly. "She's gone missing, and Holl's babe with her."

"What?" Keith yelped. Jeff, and Keith's younger sister, turned their heads away from the television to stare at him. He lowered his voice at once. "When did it happen? And how?"

Catra sounded ready to burst into tears. The words poured out in a tumult. "Dola was caring for the babe until dinner time. She didn't turn up to do her chores, and she wasn't in the cottage when Maura went looking for them. Holl and Maura are half mad with fear," Catra said, finally getting the sense that she and Keith had been talking at cross-purposes but were on the same wavelength at last.

Keith was horrified. "Did you call Ludmilla?"

"The first thing we thought of," Catra said, "and we've called upon Diane, who telephoned all the other Big Folk. With the evening's delay while we were waiting to hear from you, there would have been plenty of time for Dola to reach the Midwestern campus . . ." Her voice trailed off, leaving the phrase "if she was able" left unspoken but understood between them.

"I'm sure sorry I didn't understand," Keith said. "I should have waited until your line was clear to find out what your message meant, 'look on the front page of the newspaper.' "

"No harm done, Keith Doyle," Catra said. "No further harm done, that is. It's my fault. I was so upset I forgot you'd be looking at another paper. Our local had a story about a kidnaped child.''

"Look, I'll get down there right away— No, I can't,'' he said, tearing at his hair despairingly. "I've got to go to work in the morning. What can I do?''

"Stay there, for now. You must not toss aside your responsibilities. There are plenty of us here. Tell us what to do.''

"Why do you think she's been kidnaped?'' he asked.

Catra explained quickly about the Big Folk footprints, and the marks of truck tires.

"Okay,'' Keith said, thinking quickly. "If someone grabbed her, there'll be a ransom demand. That'll mean a call or a note. They'll probably tell you they don't want interference from the cops, but you can't call the police anyway.'' The idea passed through his mind of all the pictures of lost kids he'd seen on the backs of milk cartons, and the horrible things he had heard that sometimes happened to them. He'd seen too many true-life crime programs on television. Not to his little pet, Dola, and Holl's baby—it just couldn't happen.

Catra had a practical nature, and she read more newspapers than most of her Folk. She must have guessed what was going through his mind. "Aye,'' she agreed, speaking carefully. He knew then that there were people in the room around her. "We'll have a watch put on the telephone to wait for a call and trace its source when it comes.''

"Good,'' Keith said. "Gather up all the clues you can as to who might have taken her away. You want all the, er, *forensic* evidence you can find. The Farm is pretty well sheltered. Whoever did this was there on purpose.''

"I'd thought of that,'' Catra said grimly. "And we're not certain yet as to why. In the meantime, should we search?''

"You bet,'' Keith said. "If you can do it without being observed.''

"It's what we're best at, Keith Doyle, going unobserved. We'll do anything not to endanger the children.''

"Let me know what's going on,'' he said. Keith hung up and sat staring at the phone. For once, he was at a loss for what to do, and realized there was nothing immediate he *could* do. All he could think was that the real world had no business impinging on his friends. For a moment, he wished he'd never discovered them underneath the college library. They'd been better off when they were safely mythological. He felt helpless, and he hated feeling helpless.

He picked up the receiver and dialed Diane's number. If he couldn't be there in person, he could at least help her coordinate the search.

Mona Gilbreth glared at her employees. Pilton looked, as usual, slightly bemused. He was concentrating hard on keeping his eyes fixed on hers, as if enlightenment could be found through direct eye contact. Jake studied the floor. He seemed embarrassed. Mona didn't care about his feelings. She was so angry she didn't know what to yell about first.

"You two have really dumped me in it this time. Why did you bring those kids back here? What do I want with two little kids? I told you to dump that truck and get back here for the next load. Now these kids' folks will be on the lookout for us. You've involved this company in a felony . . . and for what?"

"She was watching us dump the tankerload in that sumphole," Williamson said defensively. "We couldn't tell what she'd seen, or how much she understood. She ran away, and we ran after her, and it just snowballed."

"Let me tell you about snowballs," Mona said angrily, poking a finger close to his eye. His gaze shifted nervously back and forth between her sharp red nail and her face. "What do you think this is going to do to my political career? Can you see the headline? 'Local business owner kidnaps two local children in waste dumping scandal.' How can we return them, just like that, and tell the parents, oh, sorry, it was just a mistake?"

"I dunno, Ma'am."

"This girl's uncanny," Pilton said, drawing his two superiors' attention away from their quarrel. "There's something strange about her. I think she's a fairy or something like that."

"She ain't no fairy," Williamson said, rolling his eyes. "Got no wings, Grant."

"Well, she's real small, and what about them ears?" Pilton wanted to know.

Williamson tried to explain. "It's a mutation, like those people in Spain who have ten fingers."

Pilton checked. "*I* got ten fingers."

"On each hand!"

Pilton was fascinated and delighted. "Weird!"

"If we've finished with the natural history lesson?" Mona asked, with heavy sarcasm. "You go keep an eye on them while I think what to do. Where are they?"

"I shut them in one of the offices in the back. It's only got a grille vent for a window. She can't get out that way."

Dola stared as the door slammed shut behind them. There was only one source of air and light in the room, and it was high and small. If she'd had only herself to think of, she'd have been through the frame and out, running for the nearest patch of green no matter how much skin it cost her. Beyond the room's edge, though, she could sense nothing but a sort of organic horror. The miasma tainted the intangible world as well as the purely physical. If her mind could wrinkle its nose, it would have. The comfortable sense of her family and people was hidden far behind that awful curtain. She was in the midst of an industrial complex of huge metal cylinders and bolted-together pipes, all emitting hollow and sinister noises.

Asrai whimpered softly in the cold room. It had been a hard and frightening ride for the infant, for all she'd ridden in a car once before. She was hungry. Dola knew that Asrai had nearly reached the end of her minute patience, and would be giving forth with a fierce and terrible yell at any time. Mother was nowhere nearby, and she doubted these two big men would let them go merely to fulfill the needs of a three-month-old infant.

As she had feared, the storm soon broke. Asrai started sobbing, catching her breath in short gasps. When Dola propped her over one shoulder, Asrai let out one of her famous banshee yells and began to shriek in earnest. Dola jogged her gently, talking in a smooth murmur, and hoped that one day her ear would cease ringing.

"Come on then, it isn't so bad," Dola crooned. "You'll dine soon, I promise you, if I have to cut my own veins for you. Calm, little one, please." She noticed an edge of panic in her own voice, and sought to calm herself. "Easy, Asrai. I love you. None will hurt you."

The door opened.

"Well, and not before time," Dola said. She glared at the men who regarded her from the doorway. They glanced impassively back. She held the baby up. "Her mother will be worried. We must go back."

Disturbed, Asrai's mournful cries grew louder. Her small face and the tips of her ears began to redden. The two men looked at each other, exchanging regretful glances, but when they turned back to her they had once more lost all expression. Dola's temper flared.

"Can't you see she's frightened and hungry?" she asked them. "Take us home! She's got to be fed. A mite like this has little time."

That worried them. They must never have thought a baby could starve to death in the arms of someone caring for her. Skinny looked uncomfortable.

"We can't," he said. "The boss-lady said we have to keep you here."

Dola stood up and stamped her foot. The movement startled the baby, who whimpered loudly. To those who knew Asrai, it was a warning signal.

"Then get her food, if you won't take her back to her mother!"

As if on cue, Asrai let out another wail. Both of the men jumped, just as if they were some of the Folk who had no children of their own. In unison, they turned and fled into the echoing hallway. They maintained enough presence of mind, Dola regretted, to shut and lock the door behind them.

The wait for milk was endless. Dola had to use every trick she had ever learned to distract Asrai from the growing void in her small stomach. Her own throat was dry from singing endless nursery rhymes and chanting the nonsense verses that babies didn't understand but loved because of the cadences. She joggled Asrai on her shoulder, and walked around the room, trying to amuse her by showing her Big Person things: the huge, oversized desk, the filing cabinet, the tall locker with its handle as high off the ground as Dola's head, the small washroom with toilet and sink and mirror. All those things were made with a great deal of metal in or about them, and served to make them both more uncomfortable. Dola winced as Asrai continued to shriek. The noise gathered in the tons of cold steel around them, and made it sing a high, frightening note that only made things worse.

Dola boosted herself up into the room's only chair, a petal-shaped extrusion of orange plastic with four tall spindly legs too high to let her feet touch the floor. Its cup-shaped bottom made it difficult to get leverage to rock the baby, but she managed a back and forth motion that soothed Asrai from her screaming rage into unhappy hiccups. By the time the Big Folk arrived with feeding supplies, Dola felt completely worn out, but at least Asrai was quiet.

Jake watched her from the door. She glanced at him distrustfully. The thin man came closer, and handed her a tall can, a plastic bottle, and rubber nipples which would have been good for feeding a cow. Dola held up the can to him.

"What is this?"

He seemed surprised she asked. "Formula. It's a substitute for mother's milk."

Dola tested the temperature of the can against her cheek. "I can't feed her this. It's cold."

The two men conferred and the skinny one left. He came back with a device Dola recognized as a coffee maker. There had been one in the staff room in the Library.

She watched closely as Skinny poured water into the screened top, and waited for it to dribble out into the glass carafe. Skinny broke open the top of the can with an attachment on his pocket knife, and filled the bottle partway, then put it in the steaming jug of water. While it was heating, Dola dealt with the delivery system. The bottle's capacity would have fed the child for days, but the nipple simply wouldn't fit into her small mouth. It would have to be adjusted.

Dola, shaking her head at the thoughtlessness of Big Folk, began to think about the lessons she'd been learning lately with others of her age group: how to enhance and move *with* the substance of what one sought to alter. She measured it. The broad end needed to remain intact so that it would fit between the plastic collar and the bottle top. In her hand she squeezed the rubber bulb, willing it smaller and smaller. Skinny shook his head when he realized what she was doing.

"Hey, that won't help. When you let go it'll just bounce back to its normal shape."

"No, it won't," Dola said. She opened her hand, and the altered nipple lay there, elongated to the shape of a stubby pencil.

"You must be strong," the man said, impressed.

"A trick my father taught me," Dola said, offhand. Let the Big Person think it was strength. He already suspected something of the truth about her. The less he knew for certain the better. The other man didn't believe what he saw, and that was all to the good. She did not want them thinking there was something uncanny about Hollow Tree Farm that bore closer investigation.

A dab of formula on the wrist, and she knew that it was drinking temperature. Fishing the bottle out of the coffeepot, she assembled the bottle and offered it to the unhappy child. Asrai refused it. She looked at the men, and at Dola, and sobbed weakly. Dola was furious.

"Well, you're scaring her!" she said fiercely. "Go off, then. I'm not going anywhere. Do you think we can sneak out through keyholes?"

They went. Dola had figured out what was wrong, and wanted privacy in which to resolve the problem. This was the first meal of her life Asrai was not to receive from her mother.

Glancing over her shoulder at the door to make certain the men weren't peeking in, Dola took the old gauze square out of her pocket and put it over her head. Willing it with her strongest thoughts, she caused Maura's face to superimpose over hers. Illusions were easy. The next part was hard. She used the enhancement to make her voice like Maura's as well.

"Hush, now, little love," she whispered. The baby stopped crying, alert, and looked up at Dola's face in surprise. "Well, are you hungry?" She put her arm behind Asrai's back and urged her to reach for the artificial nipple. She held the bottle close to her chest to simulate the placement of Maura's breast. Asrai latched on to it eagerly and began to suck. Then she made a little face and put out her tongue, rejecting it.

"Oh, come." Dola/Maura forced a chuckle, though she was worried that the unnatural mock-milk might do the baby harm. "That's no way to act. Feed, little one, then you shall sleep."

Mollified, the baby began to suckle, desperately at first, then slowing down. She drank half the bottle of formula, an incredible amount. Dola was relieved to watch the heavy-lidded eyes droop halfway, then close entirely.

"Oh, a blessing, a blessing," Dola whispered, wiping the milky lips and kissing the child on the head through her veil.

The door opened behind her. Dola had just enough time to

snatch the translucent cloth from her face before her captors could see.

"You're good with her," Skinny said in a very quiet, respectful tone.

Dola straightened her shoulders with some pride. "And so I should be, having helped with her care since her birth."

"I've got two kids of my own," Skinny offered.

"And what would you think if someone carried one of them off as you have done," Dola said, her eyes filling with tears. She was too proud to let them hear her voice quaver, but she was a child too.

"I brung you something else," Skinny said. The boxes he set down on the desk next to her were decorated with pictures of a plump, golden-haired baby, and were marked 'disposable diapers.'

"If she's had a bottle, you'll want this next."

"Well! Logic!" Dola exclaimed, gratefully. She raised an eyebrow at the man. "Thank you," she said, bobbing her head. Skinny seemed embarrassed but pleased.

He pulled a wadded pad out of the first box. They both saw immediately it was too big; it would have fit Dola herself. Skinny took a pad from the second box. It was about twice too big, but Dola could cut it in half lengthwise with the scissors from her chatelaine.

There was another box, made of thick blue plastic. "Cleaning cloths." Skinny pried open the half-lid and showed her one. It stank of some Big Person chemical antiseptic that made Dola cough.

"It's not a cloth, it's some kind of paper," she said, after a close look. "What a dreadful wasteful people you are, first diapers meant to be thrown away, then cloths that aren't really cloth."

The man shook his head, crouching beside her. "I suppose you're one of those green people," he said, amused.

"No, we're not," Dola said, with spirit. "That's a myth."

Skinny paused, as if about to deliver himself of a difficult query. "Do you grant wishes or something?"

"And what if I did?" Dola asked. "Would I do anything for those who've imprisoned me against my will, and endangered my charge?"

"I'll make things nice for you," the skinny man said. He rose and left the room.

Mona sat at her desk with her head in her hands, going over alternate wording for the apology she was going to have to make to those children's parents.

"I'm so sorry we accidentally kidnaped your daughter," she recited bitterly, practicing the sound of it. She shook her head. It wasn't going to be easy no matter how she phrased it. She was embarrassed. When every single instance of public exposure counted, this was going to be a huge demerit. Except for their problems with waste disposal, she had done all the right things to keep the public on her side. She had been responsible for beginning a town-wide recycling program for plastics. All the Gilbreth office stationery was made of recycled paper. Even the wooden desk in her office was made of wood from a replanted forest. That girl and baby were innocent bystanders, snatched up by her employees in the midst of an illegal act. Could she apologize to the parents and ask them not to inquire into what her men were doing there on their property?

Mona felt her ire rising. Yes, that was right. This girl came from Hollow Tree Farm. They were already trying to ruin her reputation in the community. Instead of feeling ashamed, she was getting angry.

"Miz Gilbreth," Pilton inquired, tapping on the door. "Are we gonna take the kids back?"

Mona looked up at him sharply. "Grant, go back and ask that girl if she's any relation to H. Doyle."

"Yes, ma'am," he said, backing out of the office obediently.

Pilton was back in a moment, looking more bemused than usual. "Miz Gilbreth, she says he's her uncle."

"My God!" she cried, throwing her head back. "I can't eat crow to him! It's the end of my career!"

Headlines danced before her eyes, worse than the ones she'd imagined before. She had to think. The national committee must never, never get to hear of this incident. Maybe she could negotiate with the man. If she could get the Doyles to agree that it was all a mistake, and promise not to press charges, she could still get out of this with a whole skin and an intact political career.

"Well, we can't have her going back to him and saying we

maltreated her," Mona said, half to herself. "We just can't let her go yet."

Pilton looked pleased. "I was just gonna say, ma'am, it's kind of cold in that office. If she's going to stay awhile, I thought I'd go home and bring her my daughter's sleeping bag. Would that be okay with you?"

"Give them anything they want," Mona snapped.

Pilton grunted under the weight of the cardboard carton he was carrying. He shifted it to rest between his hip and the wall as he reached into his pocket for the key to the office, kicked open the door, and backed into the room.

The little girl was just where she'd been sitting when he'd left. "I got some nice things for you," he said. She looked up at him with dull eyes. The baby was sleeping on her lap. It was a cute little thing; had the same kind of ears the girl did. He wondered if Jake was right, and the shape was just a mutation like her size. Maybe their folks had been drinking the water that was tainted with the runoff from the factory. Pilton himself had seen what too much of that nitrogen feed could do to plants. Just think what effect it might have on animals and people. And maybe he was right, and they'd captured a real live fairy girl.

"Here's a sleeping bag for you. It's my daughter's, but she won't need it back right away. It's just been washed, so it smells really good." He held up the quilted bag. Dola glanced at it, put her nose in the air, and turned away again.

"Got a few toys for you and the baby and a couple of books and magazines." He showed her colorful digest-sized periodicals. Dola tried not to look interested even though she'd never seen those titles before. "I brought you a portable TV, too. The reception's okay. Here's a TV guide. You want to try it out?"

Dola was very interested in trying the television, and in wrapping herself up in the warm-looking coverlet, but she didn't want to seem too eager to accept his offerings. She hadn't missed the query about her relation to Holl. It couldn't be mere accident that the very people who were ruining their water supply were the same ones who had kidnaped her in their haste. They must be very uneasy. Skinny wanted so badly to make friends, but did she dare to appear vulnerable? He and the other man were

responsible for bringing her here against her will. She had the
sudden urge to make him pay dearly for her incarceration.

"All right," she said, hopping down from the chair. The seat
was warm where her bottom had rested, so she set Asrai down
there. Skinny plugged the set in and unrolled a long wire from
the top and hooked it to the metal window frame.

"Got no antenna," he said. Dola watched carefully as he
switched the set on. A small dot appeared in the center of the
screen, unfolding outward toward the boundaries until the picture
could be distinguished. The sound warmed up just as slowly.
She disliked the electronic hum behind the music and voices.
Dola clapped her hands over her ears as the squeal grew louder
and began to eat into her consciousness. On the chair, Asrai
began to mutter and squirm in her sleep.

"For the love of nature, turn it off!" Dola exclaimed. Skinny
jumped for the controls and switched the set off. "Take it away.
It's so noisy I'd never enjoy a minute of it with all the terrible
squeals and hums it makes."

"I thought you'd like it," he said, hurt. "Look, here's a
program guide, and everything." He put the magazine down on
the desk and pushed it toward her. "My kids like the cartoons
in the morning."

"I don't watch cartoons," Dola said haughtily.

Skinny nodded knowingly, evidently remembering that she
was something special. "I guess you don't," he said. He un-
plugged the set. "I'll take it home."

"No, leave it," Dola said, suddenly curious what Big children's entertainment was like. Hollow Tree Farm had no television, and the sets at the library were not attached to antennas.
All she had ever seen on them were educational tapes.

"Can I get you something to eat?" Skinny asked.

Dola assessed the empty feeling in her stomach and judged
that her pride wouldn't hold out against a night of abstinence.
"Yes," she said. She thought longingly of a treat that was
forbidden at home by her Conservative relatives, and impetu-
ously burst out, "Pizza!"

"Sure," Skinny said, and started out the door.

"And it can't be just any pizza," she said, imperiously level-
ing a finger at him. "It must be in a proper box!"

"Gotcha," he said, shrugging into his coat.

* * *

Dola was watching the television when she heard the man coming back. Hastily, she switched it off, but was privately glad to do so. The evening news was scary. She was glad to be rid of it. No wonder the elders didn't let Keith Doyle bring them a television to keep! It was almost enough to make one fear living in the world.

Skinny's footsteps came all the way to the door, and stopped while keys jingled and entered the lock.

"Here you go!" he said, putting a large, flat box down on the table. "I brought you some soda, too."

Dola approached the box and gazed at it avidly. She only got pizza if Keith Doyle or one of their other Big friends was visiting. Great-gran Keva disliked it because the toppings hid the beauties of her prized bread, and most of the other elders hated it because it was so messy. Dola, like her friends Borget and Moira, loved it, and not just because Keith Doyle did, although that added to its attraction. The label attached to the box gave her pause at first. She sniffed carefully at the huge pizza, and tasted a bite with even greater care. She tried a larger bite of pizza, taking in a small, round slice of a green vegetable. It was very hot, but there was no doubt that it was fresh.

"Why is it called garbage pizza when all the ingredients are unspoiled?" she asked.

Skinny grinned, still watching her with open curiosity. "That's because they just dump tons of stuff on top of it. It's good. You like cola or lemon-lime?" He proffered two bottles with the tops twisted off.

Dola sampled one, then the other. Both contained fizzy drinks, the kind the Big Folk liked. She made a face. If this was the ale that custom demanded be served alongside pizza, she'd drink it, but it was a punishment in itself—gassy without substance.

"I'd rather have juice," she said, and eyed Skinny to see if he'd obey her.

He did. He went away and came back with orange juice, then went away again for freshly squeezed juice when Dola complained about the canned variety. She accorded him imperial nods of approval, instead of voicing her thanks, but he didn't seem to find her behavior out of the ordinary, probably since he thought she was some kind of supernatural being.

The pizza was very good, but Dola felt a little guilty enjoying it so much. She was being indulged more thoroughly because she was kidnaped than on the most sumptuous birthday she had ever had. It was turning out to be one of the best things that could have happened to her. She refused to think of what might happen to her hereafter, but her mother would be so glad to see her come home she'd surely forgive.

By now there were few other noises in the great buildings around them. Occasionally she heard the slow footsteps of a heavy man passing by under the window. It was beginning to impinge upon Dola that unless she could cudgel her wits into coming up with a plan she was going to have to sleep in this room, that she couldn't leave. One of her cousins was wise about locks, and could undo anything Big Folk could do up, but Dola's particular talent was for illusion. She could make the door seem to vanish, but such a vision wasn't enough to allow her to pass into the hallway beyond.

She was getting sleepy, and wagered that Skinny's wits were becoming muddled with exhaustion, too. Perhaps now was the time to try and make her escape. It was worth a try to see if he could be persuaded by the avoidance charm to miss seeing her, at least until she could sneak past him and away.

Concentrating on the TV program book, she willed the space around its surface to become slick so that all glances would slide immediately off toward something else. When she was having trouble keeping her eyes on it herself, she turned to Skinny.

"Where has that TV book gone?" she asked pleasantly, dandling the baby in her lap.

Skinny looked at the top of the desk, missing the book completely, and cast around. "Well, it was right here," he said. "I'll find it for you. Maybe it just slid off the desk." He started searching, even picking up the sleeping bag and shaking it out. He picked up the pizza box and looked underneath, almost touching the book when he put the box down. Dola nearly laughed. Slowly, surreptitiously, she started applying the technique to herself and Asrai.

Skinny, eager to please, was all but turning the office inside out in search of the book.

"Well, I know it was here a minute ago," he said, then turned around just as Dola sealed off the enhancement around herself. "Hey, little girl, where'd you go? Hey! This isn't funny. Don't hide on me. Come out this minute!"

Now he was actively searching the room. Dola had to keep dodging around to keep him from touching her. If once he made physical contact no amount of sight-avoidance would work to preserve the illusion.

A key jingled in the lock. Her opportunity was nearly there. Dola gathered herself for the dash. The door opened, and Jake stood in the doorway, a gun in his hand.

"What are you making all that noise for?" he demanded.

Skinny turned around, arms flailing and eyes wild. "She's gone! She just disappeared again, like she did this afternoon. She got away!"

"Crap. The door's been closed the whole time, right? Then she has to be in here somewhere," Jake said. Dola crept near him, waiting for him to move into the room to help Skinny search. He cocked the gun and held it up. She stopped, aghast.

"Okay, kid," he said, looking around at the empty air. "You come out right now or I'll start blasting everything in this room. You hear me? You show your face right *now* or you're gonna have a bullet in your gut!"

Swallowing, Dola went back by the tall locker and removed the avoidance charm. She stepped out, holding the baby protectively with her arms covering as much of Asrai's little back as she could. Incredibly, Asrai had slept through all the shouting.

"There," Jake said, "you see? She's still here. And she'd better still be here in the morning," he thundered threateningly down on her. "You got me?" Timidly, Dola nodded. "Good. Come on, Grant. You better get home. Your wife called looking for you."

"Right. Good night, little girl," Skinny said, with a friendly smile for her.

The door boomed shut and was locked tight. Dola stood staring at it for a moment, feeling more lonely and scared than ever. She heard the men's footsteps booming away down the hall and all the lights went out suddenly. Under the door, Dola could see the ghostly phosphorescence of emergency power lighting. She turned on the TV and tolerated its angry hissing for the light it provided. The room grew colder, and she drew near to the coffeemaker to warm her hands in the steam rising from the glass pot. Asrai still slept. Dola envied her the confidence of innocence.

Chapter
SEVEN

K eith spent the next day worrying and wondering about Dola and Asrai so much that he didn't hear what Paul Meier was telling him until the second time through. "I said, Judge Yeast likes your idea. They're crazy about it, in fact," Meier said, gleefully. "The clients don't mind that you're an amateur. They said you gotta get your creative people from somewhere—they don't drop out of the clouds, you know. So your names are on the layout."

Keith let the realization dawn with a sort of incredulous joy. A whoop wound its way up from the deepest part of his insides, until it burst out in a deafening crow of triumph. "Yahoo!"

Dorothy beamed, and the end of her pencil danced a happy rhythm.

"What did they like so much?" Brendan asked. He looked miffed, but was trying to pretend it didn't matter. "I thought it was stupid."

"Anthropomorphism," Paul replied, pronouncing each syllable with satisfied emphasis. "The client thought it brought to mind the Pillsbury Dough Boy and the Parkay margarine tubs all in one. No other yeast uses a character, and yet yeast is *the* ingredient in breads that makes it all happen. What with the growing surge in home baking, this is a big deal. They liked the connotation that if the package is a real judge, not just named for the Judge Company, it suggests that it's a wise choice for bakers. They want to see a whole campaign based on it."

"Great!" Keith said, his eyes aglow.

"Glad to hear you're happy about it," Meier said, with a sardonic tilt to his head. "Now here comes the work. You and Dorothy get to work on ideation. I want some more suggestions. You're now working parallel with the pro team. I expect you to come up with more good stuff than they do. Show me some ideas tomorrow." Dorothy perked up and nodded vigorously at Keith.

"Uh, Paul," Keith said, circling around the table and taking the supervisor aside confidentially, "could I maybe spend tomorrow doing some field research on, say, one of PDQ's downstate clients? I've just got to get down to the Midwestern campus. It's an emergency."

"Problem with your girlfriend?" Meier asked, suddenly skeptical.

"No!" Keith exclaimed, and lowered his voice to a whisper. "It's something else. It's really important, Paul. I wouldn't ask for any other reason. Would it be impossible to wait the brainstorm session just one day?"

Meier sighed, but lifted his shoulders helplessly. "Kid, this is a tough biz. All right. One day. Down by Midwestern, huh? You can go talk to Gilbreth Feed and Fertilizer, get a feel for what they're up to. They'll like that. We don't usually pay house calls."

"Gilbreth? In Sullivan?"

"You know them?"

"Sure do," Keith said, with emphasis. Meier gave him a curious look.

"Good. I'll give you a letter of introduction to the owner, Mona Gilbreth. You can go and get a feel for what they're up to. Ask questions. Look around. Maybe it'll give you some ideas for their account."

Keith already had an idea of what Gilbreth was up to, namely polluting on a large scale and hiding their tracks, but he agreed to visit the factory. An in-depth visit might provide him with some good dirt for the Folk to use in their next letter to the editor. If Mona Gilbreth strewed toxic waste all over the downstate area, her factory must be full of pollution violations.

He smiled at Paul. "I promise I'll take a really close look at everything that's going on at Gilbreth."

Late that night, the telephone on the kitchen wall rang at

Hollow Tree Farm. The circle of Folk gathered around it glanced
sidelong at one another, rolling their eyes like frightened horses.
Even Holl hesitated, wondering what to do. Marcy looked at all
of them, then snatched up the handset.

"Hello?" she said. She turned to Holl, and with a significant
look handed him the receiver. The other Folk tensed.

"Hello?" he said. "Yes, this is . . . Mr. Doyle."

The voice at the other end was male, deep and gravelly. "The
girl and the baby are safe. They're healthy—I mean okay."

Holl's eyes narrowed, and the others drew close around him.
He signaled wildly with one arm for them to attempt the trace.
The circle drew closer, and joined hands. Some of them closed
their eyes; others stared fixedly at Holl and the telephone. Marcy
stood outside the circle wringing her hands anxiously.

"I see," Holl said, trying to keep his voice from cracking.
"Am I to assume that since you've not brought them to the
telephone that there is a problem?"

"It was a mistake," the man said, after a brief hesitation.
"We don't want any repercussions. We want a guarantee from
you."

Holl's voice sharpened. "How can I know enough to give you
a guarantee. Is my daughter safe? Who are you? Hello? Hello?"
The phone clicked loudly in his ear. He spun, wild-eyed. "Did
you get a sense of the caller?"

"Not enough," Curran said, sadly, letting go the hands on
either side of him. "Only he's as scared as you."

"What did you do that for?" Mona demanded, staring at her
employee. They were sitting very close together behind her desk.
The telephone receiver had been cradled with a bang.

"The baby's his daughter!" Jake exclaimed.

Mona bit her fingers to keep from yelling. "Not H. Doyle!"
she whimpered, her teeth denting her knuckle. "Not the man
who has been singlehandedly ruining my business and my political career! Oh, no!" She passed her hands anxiously over her
face and dropped her fingertips to the desk, where they drummed
almost with a life of their own. "Now, what do I do?"

Jake stared at the wall, a curious expression growing on his
face. "Maybe you can make a good thing out of this," he said.

"A good thing?" she asked, bitterly. "What if I just turn the
two of you in and ask for arraignment as an accessory?"

"You know we're all in this together," the foreman said, shaking his head patiently at her raving. "You could work the situation to your advantage."

"What?" Mona asked, ashamed of herself. She realized that they were partners in crime, no matter how this one incident ended. Mona was glad Jake hadn't responded to her threat. She had a lot more to lose than he did. "Extortion? Money?"

"Well, a *donation*, maybe." Jake's stress on the word was careful. "He doesn't know about the dumping, not for sure. Maybe you could get him to lay off criticizing you in the papers until after the election."

"He doesn't have to know who we are," Mona said quickly.

"He'll find out. The kid knows. She wasn't blindfolded on the way here. You can ask for immunity from prosecution, and tell him to knock off writing to the papers."

"Well, maybe," Mona said, uncertainly, "but after the kids are back home all bets are off."

"Then get money," Jake said, reasonably.

Mona hesitantly dangled a pen over a pad. She certainly could use money for the campaign, and to pay for legitimate dump sites until her receivables picked up again. "Okay. Our demands. One, money. Two, immunity from prosecution. Three, no more letters to the editor. In exchange, the children will be returned safely."

"Give him a couple of days to stew about it, and we'll call back," Jake said. He grinned menacingly. "Just like in business. A little pressure, then back off a while to let him decide. He'll cooperate."

"Not a trace," Diane said to Keith when he stopped at her apartment near the college early the next morning. "I've been back to the library every day, hoping the kids would show up. Not a sound. Nothing. My footprints are the only ones in the dust down there."

She leaned toward the driver's side of the car, and Keith gave her a quick kiss.

"This wasn't the way I wanted to spend my days off down here with you," he said, helping her slide in, "but what else could I do?"

"Nothing," Diane agreed, settling herself against his right

arm as he pulled the car away from the curb. "It's horrible, and I'm glad you're here. I know the others feel that way, too."

The main room of the farmhouse was crowded. All the Folk, both Big and Little, chatted together in low murmurs until Keith and Diane appeared. They greeted the two students solemnly, and invited them to sit down in the center with the elders. Dunn and Marcy perched on small chairs among the throng of elves. Ludmilla was there on the old sofa between Lee Eisley and Maura. The young elf woman seemed to be at the center of a carefully made up support group. Maura looked not only tired, but haunted. Her usually pink complexion was dull white. She was trying to be brave, but everything reminded her of her missing infant. All her actions were jerky, uncoordinated, and she seemed constantly on the edge of tears. Catra had admitted over the phone to Keith that some of the others had had to lay charms on Maura in the evenings to make her sleep, or she'd wander around at all hours looking for her baby.

Keith was shocked to see how worn out Holl was. As the successor-apparent to the leadership of the village, everyone looked to Holl for strength and direction, and Keith could tell Holl was about out of both. It had only been two days since the disappearance.

"We had a call late last night," Holl said. "It was of too short a duration to give us any idea from where it came, or who the speaker was, but we were told the children live and are well. Still, the call did not serve to inform us how we may redeem Dola and Asrai, nor why they were taken away in the first place."

"This incident has affected us profoundly," the Master said. "In all the years past ve haf nefer had a crime committed against vun of our number. Vittingly or unvittingly, those who abducted the children haf intruded upon our peace."

"My poor little ones," Ludmilla said. The old woman held Maura's hand and patted it.

"We feel vulnerable," Candlepat said, glancing nervously around for agreement. Many of the others nodded their heads. "Much more so than when we lived in secret."

"We risked discovery then, but only when we set foot outside our fastness," Curran said, narrowing his eyes at Keith as if he had personally carried away the children.

"In a way I feel sort of responsible," Keith said. "If I hadn't butted into your lives, you wouldn't be in such trouble."

"You provided us with the means to find a new home," Holl said.

"Yeah, but not until I endangered the old one in the first place."

"Ve could not haf remained in the old place for long," Aylmer said, coming to Keith's rescue. "Ve are better off than effer ve ver. And ve are glad of your friendship."

"Do not take more upon yourself than you deserf," the Master said, closing the subject with an austere stare over the tops of his gold framed glasses. "You did not perpetrate this crime. Now it must be solfed."

"What can we do?" Maura asked, speaking for the first time. Her voice was thin and seemed to come from a long way off.

"This is impossible," Lee said, his brows drawn. He ticked off his points on his long fingers. "You can't call the police or the FBI. Advertising in the papers is out. You can't get a phone tap because that takes a court order. It would be great if we could use one of those crime-busting TV shows, but they'd laugh us off their hotlines if we told them we were looking for a couple of missing el—uh, Little Folk." He spread out his long hands. "Where do we start?"

"Can't you do fortune telling or something?" Diane asked hopefully. Curran glared, and started to stand up.

"That's nae the way our talents work," Dierdre said, carefully patient. She grabbed Curran's wrist and pulled him down again.

Holl shook his head. "The others call me the Maven, but I'm a novice at searching for the missing," he said, with a bitter laugh. "We're simply unused to being so far apart. I am the only one of us who has been separated any distance from the rest of us, and I was under my own power. I'm too close to this problem. I've no idea how to proceed."

Keith's eyebrows went up. "Maybe I do. Never mind trying to find the kidnapers. You remember teaching me how to see where the Folk were from Scotland," he said. "It was neat, Diane. In my mind's eye, I could see just a little light in the horizon, like a radar blip. Can you sense just one of your people like that, Holl?''

"It would be a very weak trace," Holl said, his eyebrows ascending, "but I can try it."

The others, especially the Big Folk, looked skeptical. "We've already searched the surrounding countryside in that fashion, Keith Doyle," Enoch said. "We found nothing."

Keith felt impatient at the quitter attitude everyone was displaying. "Well, send your radar out further. Holl saw you from half a world away. The girls couldn't be farther away than that. Pour on whatever power it takes!"

"We're not machines," Tiron grumbled. "I'm as far from my folk as Holl was from his last year, and I couldn't tell if there's one or fifty back along at home."

"Ve haf no proof that the children are still vithin the immediate area!" Aylmer broke in.

"It's still worth the attempt," Holl chided them. Keith gave him an encouraging nod. "Lend me your strength, friends." Tentatively, Maura stretched out her hand to her husband. Around the room, others joined hands, or touched in some other way, until all the Little Folk were making physical contact. The Big Folk, tentatively, sheepishly, joined hands and reached out to the others. Holl shut his eyes to concentrate. He was silent for a long time. "I see nothing so far—no! There's something. To the west of here."

"Is it Dola and Asrai?" Keith asked.

Holl shook his head. "It's so small and far away I'm getting no detail at all, just that there is one of us, or someone like us, off in that direction. It *feels* right. It's very hard, searching at such a distance for a pinpoint, instead of aiming in the direction I know it to be, as I did for the village from overseas."

"It *is* her!" Maura cried. "It's my babe."

"You cannot be sure," the Master said gently, "but I think there is something there vorth investigating."

Try as he might, Keith could get no sense of what Holl and the others were doing, beyond a slight perception of mental concentration. But now was not the time to ask for additional lessons in magic; he was going to have to trust the pros.

"Okay, what if we try looking out that way? Now that we have a general direction to work toward, what if you and me, and some of the others drive around until we can triangulate in on the girls' position.''

There were mutters of ''Progressive!'' and ''Big Folk talk,'' but Holl smiled wryly.

''Military tactics?'' he asked.

''Could work,'' Keith said, raising his hands palms up as if offering the idea.

The Master looked around at the faces of his family and friends. Many of them were bemused, and Tiron and some of the elders looked doubtful, but in some of them the light of hope was shining. ''In the absence of other suggestions, Keith Doyle, your motion is carried.''

Holl leaned over the rear seat of Keith's Mustang, prepared to dive underneath the folded tarpaulin beside him if any other driver should get close enough to the car to see him clearly. Hope had given him back a little of the elasticity of his normal nature. Keith kept an eye on him through the rearview mirror, prepared to stop instantly if Holl got a solid vector. Walls of tall, green corn and wheat on either side of the road prevented them from getting more than occasional views of the farm buildings.

''Drive slower,'' Holl said.

Keith eased off the gas, and glanced at the knot of farm buildings to their left. ''You still seeing their blip in the same place?''

''I *was* sure,'' Holl said, shaking his head and sinking back into the rear seat. ''It was very strong for a moment. Perhaps more over that way.'' He pointed westward.

Diane was charting their progress on a map of the state. She drew her pencil upward on the sheet. ''We're half a mile from the junction with the next county road. You can turn left there.''

Keith glanced around for other traffic as he slowed down for the intersection. They'd been on the road for hours, and had still not pinned down the girl's location within a hundred square miles. Every time Holl was certain he was on the correct tangent to find them, something interfered with his mental fix.

Somewhere out on the roads, three other cars—each containing one of the Little Folk and a volunteer Big Folk driver— were doing the same thing. As soon as Keith's suggestion was taken, Marcy and Enoch had immediately offered their services and Dunn and Marm had volunteered at once, planning to go off together in Dunn's little green Volvo. Lee had said he would take Tay in his car. Ludmilla, though she had driven in from Midwestern by herself, remained behind with Maura and Siobhan.

"How will we know who is who?" Marm had asked, reasonably, while they were coordinating their plans.

"You won't," Diane had said, "but if you find a fifth body out there broadcasting whatever it is you're looking for, then you've found her."

"Besides," Keith had added, "the chances are that their trace won't be moving, and all of us will. If things go right, we'll converge on the place where the girls are hidden."

"That's sense," Enoch had said, nodding. "Let's go."

"Meet at the Grandma's Kitchen diner at three," Keith had said, naming a family-style restaurant that was one of his favorite hangouts on the county road north of Midwestern University.

Except for confirming the existence of Holl's 'blip,' the day's search was largely unfruitful, so no one had much appetite for the enormous meals Grandma's Kitchen served. The baseball cap Holl wore to disguise his ears drooped low over his forehead as he picked at half of a turkey sandwich. Tay was exhausted, and sat with his head tilted backward, staring at the ceiling, ignoring the plate of fries he had ordered. Marm ate with the singleminded determination of a man who didn't know when he'd next get a meal. Both Tay and Marm must have put some kind of illusion on themselves, Keith decided, since they seemed to be bare-chinned now, but had had beards when they'd left the farm. No sense in attracting attention they didn't need. The lack of hirsute adornment made Tay look even younger than one of the Folk usually did. The waitress had brought all four elves crayons and placemats with black-and-white line drawings of farm animals to color.

"There's some kind of interference," Marcy complained as Enoch doodled with a red crayon on the picture of a cow. "We had a strong impulse to go eastward for about three seconds, then it was gone."

"At least we've eliminated part of the state," Dunn said, pursing his lips. He filched fries off Tay's plate and dunked them in the ketchup on Keith's. "It's still not going to be easy to pin down."

"Even if we are right, and the trace we've all been following is Dola and Asrai," Keith said, remembering his lengthy tramp through the Field Museum. "You know, there could be other beings out there."

"I'm sure this has the right sense to it," Holl declared strongly, but with more force than confidence. "I ought to know my own child's emanations."

"There's hope," Marm said. "The mystery trace is within this area." He spread out the driving map, and pointed to a square much smudged with pencil marks. "They're in here. They are." He offered a smile around the table. Keith couldn't help but return it.

"That's still a lot of square miles," Lee said, whistling.

"At least we know they're still in the county," Diane said. "We can cut that down in no time."

"Not today," said Enoch unexpectedly. The black-haired elf turned up a face that was woeful, but pinched-looking and pale around the mouth, with smudges of purple starting under the eyes. "I'm tired enough that any moment I'll start finding squirrels instead. I've only so much strength. I'd give up my last heartbeat to find my sister's child, but I can't guarantee accuracy from here on in. I need rest."

Reluctantly, one by one, the other Little Folk admitted to the same weakness. "Our strength's not an inexhaustible well," Holl said, sadly. "All the influence you can raise from an object, or a person, is that which is inherent in it."

"Then we need fresh scouts," Keith said, resignedly. "Tiron said he'd help. I can go on driving until I drop."

"I can, too," said Lee. "All I have to do to get tomorrow off is to call in and tell 'em I'm onto a story. I've never lied to them before, but this is a good cause."

"I appreciate all your help," Holl said, relieved. In spite of his exhaustion, he looked better than he had in the morning.

"I, too," Tay added. "Without you we'd not be able to cover this much physical distance in a summer, let alone an afternoon."

"Then we'll go back to the farm and ask for more volunteers," Keith said, raising his hand to wave at the waitress for the check.

* * *

At the farm, there was a telephone message waiting for Keith.

"It was your father," Catra explained. "He said he'd had a call," she looked at the wall clock, "an hour and a half ago now, that Ms. Mona Gilbreth will see you this afternoon, and also that Frank will be looking for you at Midwestern tonight. Your friend is a poet," Catra said, a wry half-smile lighting up her solemn face. "All the message he left for you was, 'cool, still sky.' A pretty image."

Keith looked shocked at himself for forgetting. He smacked himself in the head. "The ad firm! But I can't go," he said.

"But you must," the Master said at once.

"I can't," Keith insisted. "I ought to be here to help. I can call Frank. And I'll beg off from seeing Ms. Gilbreth. That was only an excuse to get down here. Paul won't be too mad."

"You cannot be here all the time. We did get along before you met us. It is time you learned to delegate, young man," the Master said, not unkindly. He shook a finger toward Keith's face. His straightbacked stance still made him no taller than Keith's middle shirt button. "You haf responsibilities of your own, Meester Doyle. Gif ofer to us. Mees Londen, Mees Collier and these others vill stay and assist. Tell us what should be done, and ve vill do it."

Keith looked at Holl and the others. He knew they counted on him. He thought of Dola and baby Asrai out there somewhere, scared and maybe in danger. He met the Master's eyes, and read there that the old elf knew the realities of the situation as well as he did himself. He knew what he was asking Keith to do.

Keith's shoulders slumped in resignation. "That's the hardest lesson you've ever given me," he said.

"I hope it is the only vun of its kind you must learn," the Master said, with a sad smile. Keith recalled suddenly that Asrai was the Master's granddaughter.

"I'm sorry," Keith said lamely.

The Master waved away his apology and nodded toward the door. "Nefer mind. Ve vill find them. Go. Perhaps you vill discofer information of interest to us."

Chapter
EIGHT

"**M**rs. Gilbreth is expecting me," Keith told the plain, cheerful girl sitting behind the combination reception/telephone switchboard desk. The young woman picked up the receiver and punched two numbers.

"Representative from PDQ is here to see you, Ms. Gilbreth," she said, smiling up at Keith. She nodded, replaced the handset, and gave him a coy glance. "If you'll just wait a minute, please."

Keith thanked her and stepped back to examine the walls of the reception area. Framed photographs of green cropfields hung against walls paneled in cheap brown wood. If he'd owned this place, he wouldn't have spent much money on expensive furnishings, either. The whole place exuded a choking, clinging miasma that had to go home on everyone's clothes, and out in every piece of mail sent from the office. Could that be useful in any way? Direct mail advertising to the discerning farmer? he thought with some amusement. The employees he saw were dressed in tan coveralls about the same color as the smell. He wondered how long it took to get used to it. Dust tickled his nose, and he sneezed. Surreptitiously, he took out a handkerchief and wiped the taste of airborne fertilizer off his tongue.

"You can go back now," the receptionist called out. "Second door on the right."

Keith thanked her. The gray-painted hallway had the same threatening anonymity as the corridors in the Death Star. No pictures interrupted the dullness of these walls. Did the proprietor match the unprepossessing aspect of her factory? He expected her to be funereal in aspect, or maybe hearty, like the stereotypical pictures of a farmwife.

Mona Gilbreth fit neither of his preconceptions. She was very tall, a few inches taller than Keith himself, and dressed in a neat and fashionable skirt suit that would have fit right in on Michigan Avenue. With her frizzy hair dyed a uniform rusty brown, and her large teeth which, though straight, gave her the appearance of a slight overbite, she was not very pretty, but rather determinedly attractive. Her makeup was very skillfully applied, playing up her better features, and her hair was firmly coiffed away from her face, to give her an open, approachable look. She gave him a strong, cordial handclasp that reminded him she was running for political office.

"How do you do," Ms. Gilbreth greeted him. "So you're from PDQ, Mr. . . . ?"

"Keith Doyle," he said, with a friendly smile.

She gave him a sharp glance. "Doyle? You don't have any relatives down here, do you?"

"No, Ma'am," Keith lied. "I'm from up near Chicago." He pulled Paul's letter out of his back pocket and unfolded it. She took it from him and read through it.

Ms. Gilbreth breathed a perceptible sigh of relief. Keith was secretly amused. He could almost hear her mental processes churning as she dismissed the suspicion that he was connected with those pesty Doyles at Hollow Tree Farm who'd been writing all those destructive letters to the editor. "So how can I help you, Keith?" she asked.

"I'm a college student working as an intern under Paul Meier at PDQ," he explained. "He wants us to learn everything we can about the ad business, and research is part of our job. I had to come down to, er, get an assignment from one of my other teachers, and Paul suggested I drop in on you and familiarize myself with your company. To bring our work on your ad campaign right up to the minute," he added helpfully.

Mona smiled. "That's very good of Mr. Meier. I'd be delighted to give you all the information you want. The most important thing I want you to stress right now is my candidacy for state representative. I hope he's continuing along the lines we set out the last time I was up there.''

"You bet," Keith said. "I'm sure you'll be impressed with what they're doing when you come up next. Say, while we're talking would you mind showing me around? I've never been in a place like this before."

"I'd be delighted," Mona repeated, seeming a little taken aback. After a moment's thought, she decided the request was reasonable. "Will you excuse me just a moment?"

Keith gave her a friendly grin as she sidestepped around the desk and out the door. He was pleased. There he sat, right in the enemy camp. He'd just have to keep his eyes wide open for any signs of offenses Kill-breath Gilbreth was getting away with.

With a glance over her shoulder to make certain Keith wasn't following her, Mona hurried up to the reception area. "Page Pilton," she told the receptionist. The girl picked up her handset and dialed.

Grant appeared, stupid and willing, in his dusty coveralls. "Yes'm?"

She took him aside. As yet neither the receptionist nor any of the office staff knew about their two detainees in the back office. It was a secret between her, Pilton, and Williamson. Until she could figure out how to get rid of them, she couldn't risk having to explain their presence to outsiders. "We've got a visitor on the premises. I'm going to take him on a tour. Go keep that child quiet. I don't want her making noise and attracting attention. Got it?"

"Yes'm," Grant said again, and headed at once down the corridor toward the office where the children were confined.

He unlocked the door and let himself in quietly. The little girl was sitting in her accustomed perch on the orange chair, reading aloud to the baby from a children's magazine. Without a TV or radio in the room, Grant guessed it was as much to hear a human voice as anything else. They made such a cute picture, like a toddler reading to her doll.

Both pairs of eyes glanced up from the colorfully illustrated page when he entered. The girl had been very quiet since the night Jake Williamson had threatened to shoot up the room. Now whenever Jake went in there with him, she shrank back, holding the infant protectively in her arms, and keeping real still. She was a lot more calm around Grant, which he hoped meant she liked him better. He'd sure done his best to make things nice for her.

Pilton's wife had accepted the excuse that there were a couple of kids visiting from out of town, and allowed him to bring over spare blankets and more toys. He'd replaced the single stained flour-sack towel in the bathroom with a couple of Disney character bathtowels. After the little blond girl had rejected the TV, he'd brought a radio and a night-light instead.

He knew it wasn't right to keep these kids away from their folks, but he accepted Ms. Gilbreth's reasoning that they had to bring them back at the right time, to minimize the trouble the company would be in for taking them. It was mostly his fault they were here in the first place, so he accepted his employer's excuse.

The blond child continued to stare at him silently. He sat down, crosslegged, on the floor and stared back. The child pursed her lips disapprovingly, probably in unconscious echoes of a similar gesture one of her parents or grandparents used.

"Hey," he said, grinning at her, "go on reading, huh?"

Mona took Keith Doyle around the factory complex, pointing out the tanks and piping systems that carried individual products. Each system was painted a different color, giving it an orderly appearance in spite of the tangle of conduits, catwalks, and s-bend pipes that snaked overhead. At first she was grateful that he didn't ask about waste, then she became suspicious that he was leading her on somehow. "You don't ask anything about environmental impact, young man. Don't you have any interest in that?"

"I do," Keith said, disarmingly, "but I'm not a scientist. I only know what I read in the papers. Besides, I'm here to get the scoop on *you*. I'm working for your hired gun, remember?"

"Oh, yes," Mona said. "Well, remember, I'm campaigning on a 'Preserve Our Environment' platform." She swung a hand up in a graceful gesture to encompass the vast, sea-green tank beside her. "This is one of the most modernized systems for liquid and powder fertilizer transport in the world.

I want other potential polluters to look to me for leadership in preserving—''

"But I'd like to know more about how your business runs," Keith interrupted. "More of how you do things here. Your voters will want to look at the way you operate, your sense of fairness, your history, to give them confidence in how you'll do things in Washington."

The last thing Mona wanted to do was expose her business practices to this nosy youth, but it wasn't good policy to offend anyone with access to the media, especially media she was paying for.

"Oh, but that's so boring," she said, smiling determinedly at him. "Wouldn't you rather hear about the political issues? You see," she said, straightening the shoulder pads on her jacket then touching a wave of her stiff hair with a coy hand, "I want to show an honest image of myself to the voters of Illinois."

Keith nodded politely. "Do you have any literature about Gilbreth Feed? Didn't I hear that the firm was founded by your grandfather?"

"Why, yes," Mona said, flattered. "You've certainly done your research, young man. There are some flyers in one of these offices. Let's see."

She led him up the hallway toward the comptroller's office, where she seemed to recall there was a supply of public relations literature. As they passed close to the office where Pilton and the children were, Mona trembled. If the baby let out one of its rebel yells now it was all up with her. With the room set up as an improvised nursery and bedroom, there'd be no way of disguising her motives in keeping them there as a benevolent or temporary gesture of any kind. She steeled herself not to look at the door at the end of the hall, so as not to draw attention to it, and ushered Keith into the accounting office.

Dola finished the story and went on to the next one in the magazine. Her voice automatically laid stress upon strings of prose, and quoted dialogue in humorous voices, without her having to think about it too much—no problem, since she was no longer drawing images in the air to go along with the narrative. The arrival of Skinny meant to Dola that there was something going on in the building that the boss-lady didn't want her to disturb. Dola was more than a little afraid of the boss-lady. The Big woman was formidable in appearance and so very tall. Dola felt intimidated by her size.

Holding her breath, she listened as keenly as she could. There were voices in the corridor, but so faint that they were indistinguishable. One of them belonged to an adult male. Dola was convinced that there was some reason that the Big Folk didn't want her to be seen or heard by the possessors of those voices. Perhaps it was a police officer, who would wonder what a child was doing at a factory. If she could get his attention, maybe he would take her and Asrai home.

Dola glanced at the skinny man. He watched her as if he expected her to perform some other wonder, like the disappearance she had attempted on the hilltop two days before. She was impatient with him and desperate to get out of the room. In spite of the daft way he talked, her jailor was too big and too canny to be tricked into letting her slip by him. She needed a distraction— something dangerous, so he'd have to remove them from there to save their lives.

Skinny got up on his knees beside her to coo at the baby. Asrai stared at him, her round, milky green eyes wandering across the big face without recognition, but luckily without fear. So long as he was occupied, Dola had time to come up with a really terrifying illusion. A spider. One at least a foot across, climbing up the wall behind him, but farther away from the door than they were. That way he'd *have* to get them out. The footsteps were coming closer to the door. They couldn't be more than a few yards away. Her chance was at hand.

She shaped the sending in her mind's eye, seeing it form from eight irregular points on the pocked wall, solidifying in the center into grotesque head and abdomen portions of black and shiny bronze, with hair the length and thickness of cat's whiskers sticking out of the joints of the legs and covering the base of the body near the spinnerets. She admired her work, and glanced down at Grant, choosing the moment. If she managed to scare the baby when she screamed, Asrai would lend her lung power to hers, and they'd be free in no time.

Letting her eyes go wide with feigned fear, she started to take in a huge breath, readying a really loud outcry.

Her gasp alarmed Pilton, who looked up. Guessing what she

was about to do, he fell forward onto one knee and clapped his hand over her mouth. Quickly he looked around to make sure no one was coming into the room, and saw the spider. Dola made it hiss, spreading its palps and front legs menacingly. With the greatest presence of mind, Pilton let Dola go and put himself between the children and the horrifying arachnid on the wall.

"Look at that sucker!" he cried. "Stay back, little lady. It might jump." The spider assumed an aggressive stance, waiting for its foe to approach. Without getting closer, Pilton leaned over the table, picked up a magazine, and threw it at the spider. Dola had no choice but to imagine the beast falling to the ground and scuttling into a corner. Grant followed it and smashed it into a pulp with his big boot. "Whew! I haven't seen a spider that big since I was in the Everglades. It's dead. You aren't scared, are you?"

"I'm all right," Dola said, in a very small voice. She sank back, thwarted and a little tired from the expenditure of energy. The illusion, hidden from view, faded into nothingness. It's a pity I can't like him, she thought, because he's brave.

To her dismay, she heard the footsteps receding in the hallway. She'd missed her chance at freedom once more. Pilton resumed his perch next to Asrai, and began babbling nonsense words at her in a silly falsetto.

"No, the big bad thing's all gone," he said, making the baby gurgle. "Yes, it is. It wasn't gonna hurt you, no. I wouldn't let it do that. No, I wouldn't."

Dola tried to lose herself in the baby's happy murmurs, because she herself was close to frustrated tears. I want to go home, she thought sadly. I wish someone was here to comfort me.

Mona saw Keith off with relief so great she worried that it might show.

"See you on Monday, ma'am," the young man called. He waved. Mona waved back.

"It'll be a pleasure," Mona assured him. As soon as he was gone, she plopped down on one of the chairs in reception and rubbed her feet. She was exhausted but happy. The youth had led her all over the factory, sticking his nose into all the departments, but he had asked a lot of intelligent questions. She knew about the job PDQ offered its most successful intern. With the kind of initiative he showed, she wouldn't be averse to recommending that very polite young man for the position, if he promised never to come back to her factory.

She went down the hall and tapped on the door at the end.

"He's gone," Mona said. "Thank God. Come on out of there and get back to work."

"Yes'm," Grant said, and looked back at the child. "I'll come back later and bring you some dinner, okay?"

"All right," the girl said very quietly. They closed the door on her.

Dola was doubly depressed to hear the locks clicking shut. By the boss-lady's relieved tone, she guessed she'd missed a very important chance at escape. She and Asrai were left alone again in their prison. Who knew how long it would be before she had another opportunity. And what did these Big Folk have in mind for her and Asrai? The man called Jake and the boss-lady treated them like a pair of inconvenient parcels. Would they dispose of them the same way?

She was glad neither of them spent much time with her. If they began to suspect, like Skinny did, that there was something strange about her, she and Asrai would never be free to go home again. Catra had passed around many articles from journals and magazines, talking about what scientists did to alien-seeming artifacts and remains. She shivered, and covered up Asrai, who was sleeping again on her lap.

Pulling in by a wayside phone booth, Keith called the farm to offer his help for the evening. He didn't feel much like ballooning, and Frank didn't really need him. He volunteered to forgo his lesson and come back. The Master thanked him for his concern, but said the others had elected to call off the search for the night.

"Go to your lesson," the Master added. "You haf vorked hard today, aiding us in our search. Let it be. Ve vill continue tomorrow, and velcome you back at the weekend. As I told you, you cannot continue to take all responsibility for us upon your shoulders."

What the little teacher said was true, but it made Keith feel unwanted and unneeded. He could have helped more. Discontented, he turned south and headed toward Midwestern.

Keith was too late to help inflate the great bag. The rainbow of Skyship Iris was already rising like a multicolored sun beyond the trees on the campus. One of Frank's crew waved him over as he hopped out of his car, and asked him to help walk the balloon to its launch point.

His heart wasn't really in it, but he pulled against the light wind, his back and arms straining against the thin fabric of his shirt. He couldn't stop thinking about Dola and the baby. He had the same feeling his friends had, that the girls were off in a northeasterly direction, but the trace was too vague to pin down. You'd think that a small, isolated target like a pair of elven children would be easy to locate, but other things kept getting in the way of a direct connection, as if they were anchored too tenuously in reality to be easily detected. Maura was handling things incredibly well, but he could tell that wasn't going to last if the baby wasn't found soon. He suspected some of the others were doing subtle enchantments on her to keep her from going over the edge.

"Hop in," Frank said, peering at him through his flight goggles. "Didn't think you were going to make it."

With the help of Murphy and the other ground crew member, Keith clambered over the leatherbound edge of the basket and dropped in. The Iris curtsied a little. Acknowledging Frank's hand signal to stay out of the way, he sat on the floor and watched while the pilot reached for the burner controls. The flames shot high into the balloon. Smoothly, the Skyship Iris rose into the air.

He was so busy moping that the balloon had risen above the trees before he'd even noticed it. Frank nudged him in the back with a foot.

"What's wrong?" the pilot shouted over the roar of the burner. They rose farther into the sky and caught an eastbound breeze.

Keith strained to stare out over the northern horizon toward where Hollow Tree Farm lay unseen in the distance. "Some of my friends are in trouble."

"What?"

"Some of my friends are in trouble!"

"Sorry," Frank said, in his telegraph-like style. "Beautiful day. Hang on, cheer up."

The suggestion began to take effect. It was not in Keith Emerson Doyle to remain depressed for long. The day was beautiful and warm. There was less than an hour of daylight left, and the shadows were growing dramatically long over the landscape, adding depth to its beauty. Keith felt the taut worry in his chest unlock and unfold until he breathed normally again. He let go a tremendous sigh.

Then he started worrying again. What if the children were in serious danger? He thought of Dola as he had last seen her, cute as a button, trying hard to be a grown-up but still full of childish spunk. He stared at the ground far below. Dola could be in any one of those houses, or among the crops in the fields that stretched endlessly out into the distance. He wished that he could just call out to her, wherever she was, so she would know that they were looking for her, and not to despair. Clumsily aping Holl's magical radar, his mind reached out, sought, touched nothing and kept going, leaving him feeling lost. He wondered if he had missed sensing Dola, and went over and over the same angles. No wonder Holl was pooped. Poor Dola, poor little pet! He remembered seeing her from far above, how she looked with her golden hair reflecting the morning sun as she bent over the baby in her lap.

Keith shook his head to clear it. He was imagining things. Dola had never been outside in the meadow when he'd arrived by balloon.

"Uh, Keith," Frank said, nudging him again. "Co— co—, uh." He seemed unable to finish his sentence.

"Hmmm?" Keith inquired, glancing up, and froze.

"Company," Frank choked out at last.

Keith found himself gazing into a pair of round, sky blue eyes, but they weren't Frank's. In fact, the body they were attached to was hovering under its own power outside of the basket. Keith's own eyes widened until he thought they might pop out.

The creature floating beside the Iris was about a foot high, the cloudy blue-white of shadows in glacial snow. Below the translucent torso, its substance thinned down to pale insubstantial streamers, barely solid enough to see. It had delicate, attenuated wings like a great bird, and its face was like that of an owl, but where Keith would have expected to see a beak there was nothing at all, a blank plane, as if the artist had neglected to finish roughing in the rest of a watercolor portrait done in blue-whites and pearl grays. Thin, filmy arms ended in long, delicate feathers instead of fingers. It tilted its inverted-wedge of a head at Keith. The image of Dola in his mind looked upward and smiled. The being nodded, waving its long fingers.

"So it was your memory I was seeing," Keith said, awed. "What *are* you?"

The light creature recoiled from his outrush of breath. He repeated his question, more quietly, and was rewarded when the being swam closer to him, bobbing in the eddies of the wind.

A vision intruded itself into his sight, an enforced daydream. Keith saw the same creature, with dozens more like it, in all sizes from tiny to elephantine, swirling around and playing in the wind high above the face of the earth.

"I'm a jerk." He laughed. "You're *yourselves*. I'd call you air sprites. Is that all right?"

The vision filled with warm, rosy light. "I guess that means yes, huh?" Keith asked, delighted.

Frank must have been seeing the same visions, because he gulped and clutched the hot air release of the balloon with both hands. He stared, unable to take his eyes off the strange visitor.

"Keith, we ought to go down," the pilot said, carefully so as not to offend, but awed and frightened.

"We don't have to," the young man said, in a quiet, caressing voice. It pleased his companion more than his first attempts had, and calmed the pilot a little. "It's harmless. Aren't you?" he asked the floating creature. "Say hello to Frank."

The huge blue eyes turned toward the balloonist, and the vision of a sunrise appeared in their minds.

"Uh . . . sunrise to you," Frank said, waving a feeble hand.

Keith 'translated' by thinking as hard as he could about sunrises. His unmuffled broadcast was so forceful that the air sprite was propelled backward again. It bobbed up, its large eyes reproachful.

"Sorry," Keith said, sheepishly. "I'll try to think softly. This is new to me."

The intelligent eyes focused on him. They were so clear he

could see individual rings of muscle constricting within the irises. He was aware of an expression of humor that fleetingly changed to one of sympathy.

Keith had a vision of a small girl sitting washed in sunlight on top of a green hill.

"That's Dola," he said, and the vision faded. "We're trying to find her. You mean you think you've seen her?"

Images of many little girls flicked before Keith's mind's eye, large, small, black, white, Hispanic, Oriental, alone, or with other humans or animals, on hillsides, beaches, in fields, jungle clearings, in the backyards of houses.

"No, you were right the first time, the first one you were thinking at me. She's the one." Keith tried to picture her.

The sprite picked up on his efforts right away. The image of Dola reappeared with more details, so that Keith could see the scuffed shoes, her bare knees stained with grass, the hammocklike shoulder harness in which she carried Asrai. "That's her. You really have seen her! Yahoo!" he shouted. Alarmed, the sprite dropped away beneath the edge of the basket, its tail whipping out of sight. Keith leaned over the edge, careless of his own safety. Frank dove forward to catch the back of his belt. "Where? Where is she?" Keith demanded.

The sprite returned to its former altitude, and the pilot yanked Keith firmly back into the gondola. Stumbling backward, he bumped against the control panel. The sprite circled around until it was hovering beside his head. Keith concentrated on the newest sending.

I will ask the others, it sent, showing itself flitting from one to another of the many like itself. Each cocked its head, filling the air with more images that overlapped, as if they shared their thoughts freely. The sun appeared at the edge of the dream and traveled rapidly across the sky, and the sprite fixed its eyes on Keith's.

"It could take time, I know," Keith said, "but it's important. She was kidnaped, and that baby with her."

"That's the trouble they're in?" Frank asked, his mouth agape. "Man, *say* so! I'd help."

"We can use all the help we can get," Keith said, and thought rapidly. "I think we're on to something with our new friend here. It says it'll go looking for her. If it finds anything, I'll need you to bring me up to talk with it again. Maybe when the others remember where they've seen her last they can lead us to her.'' He tried to imagine the sprite hovering in front of the balloon, looking over its wing joint at them as it flew along. The sprite's visions took on the rosy hue again. Keith smiled. "Great!"

"Any day the wind's not too strong," Frank promised, somewhat distracted. He was still staring at the sprite.

"Thanks," Keith said sincerely. He turned to the sprite. "Listen, well, look," he amended, noting the creature's lack of visible ears, "let me know when you've located her, okay? Or the closest to when your people remember seeing her last under the sky."

The sprite sent a vision of Dola in her green tunic with the baby on her lap, then of itself. *I recall seeing her last before the bad smell came, and I rose out and away from it.*

"The bad smell?" Keith asked, puzzled.

In the image, the air turned the sickly green he had always associated with tornado weather. The sprite blinked its eyes at him, and the vision changed again to the crowd of sprites. *I will ask the others.*

Frank checked the gauge on the tanks and tapped Keith on the shoulder. "We're going down now," the pilot said. He leaned over the side, looking for a good place to land. When he spotted an open field nearby, he started landing procedures, and used the cell phone to tell the chase crew where to find them.

The sprite circled, staying beside them as the balloon made its way toward the ground, exchanging visions with Keith. But the farther down they went, the more the little creature began to be horribly compressed and distorted. The hands blunted into crablike claws, and the wings stretched out into infinity then shrank to the size of a cherub's. It blinked regretful eyes at Keith.

I cannot go into the heavy air, it sent woefully.

"Go!" Keith exclaimed. "The last thing in the world I want is for you to get hurt. I'll see you up here the next time I can."

The filmy being shot upward with alacrity, vanishing among the streaks of cloud in the evening sky. Keith had a faint vision, the visual equivalent of shouting from a long distance away, of a sunset. He exchanged a quick glance with Frank.

"Their way of saying goodbye, I guess," he said with a grin. The pilot looked shaken. "What's the matter?"

"That . . . that thing was real!"

"The sky's a big place," Keith said, shrugging. "I bet the beings you're sure exist are out there, too."

"That's what worries me. Never thought I'd run into any in person," Frank said, the whites of his eyes showing all around his irises, magnified by his thick glasses. "All supernatural beings can't be so friendly."

"Nope, they're not," Keith assured him, running a tongue around the fillings in his back teeth, "but the nasty ones usually like to be left alone."

As soon as he got back to Midwestern, Keith ran to the nearest phone to tell Holl about the air sprites. He was full of plans.

"It made pictures in my mind," he raved, waving one arm up and down. A woman waiting to use the phone booth stared at him, then walked hastily away to find another booth. "It's seen Dola and Asrai. It promised to help us find them."

"And how do you know that?" Holl asked. "Is the language of the air English, too?"

"No, they talk through telepathy. It made pictures in my mind, and it understood what I thought at it. It'll help us. As soon as it finds them it'll contact me."

"One of your pipe dreams, is it?" Holl asked, drearily.

"Uh-uh! Frank saw it, too."

"I know you want to help, Keith Doyle, but mythical all-seeing sprites is a little too much for me when my troubles are all too real. Forgive me. You've been a great help to us, and I'm not ungrateful. I'm merely tired. I'd best clear the line, to be ready in case the kidnapers call again. We'll await you on Saturday."

Keith was disappointed, but he reasoned, as he hung up the phone, that Holl hadn't been there, hadn't seen. He'd prove it, as soon as the sprites came through. If they didn't, the little Folk were no worse off than before. It was funny, he thought, that his excitement in finding out about Dola had almost made him forget that he had achieved his aim of finding the air sprites. It was a great, important discovery.

In spite of his concern for the missing children, he couldn't help strutting a little as he walked across the campus, back to his car. He was probably the first human being to make contact with the ethereal creatures. As soon as this terrible business was cleared up, he vowed to find out everything he could about this new race of hitherto mythological creatures. *Doyle's Compendium of Magical Species* began to write itself in his mind.

"Okay," the hoarse voice said when Catra picked up the phone, "we've got three demands."

Catra put her hand over the receiver and relayed the message to Holl. "What shall we do?" she asked.

Holl steeled himself. "Keith Doyle said never to give in to a kidnaper, but we can't risk annoying them. Hear his requirements, but promise nothing."

"Go ahead," Catra said. Her hands trembled.

"Here's what we want: money, immunity from prosecution, and one other condition we'll let you know about later, when we deliver the children."

"We have very little. How much money do you want?" she asked.

"Twenty thousand dollars in small bills. Unmarked. No explosives, no dye packets."

"Aye," Catra said, noting the specifics down on a piece of paper. Her companions crowded around to read what she was writing. "Now," she said boldly, "we've a condition of our own. We want to hear the children's voices. Hello?" She turned a frightened face to the others. "He hung up."

Chapter
NINE

Meier cleared his throat and rustled his pages of notes. Keith gave him a brief glance and turned from staring out the window, to staring at his fingertips, then back out the window as if he was looking for something hovering just outside the twentieth floor.

"Today," Meier said, "I'm going to show you a few products that are so new that they haven't even got names yet. The client wants a snappy presentation for her products, and we've got diddly on 'em as yet. I'm showing you these raw, so you see what we have to start with. It's not pretty." The others chuckled.

Meier threw onto the table five small clear packets. "There you go. Becky Sarter grows and dries organic fruits. Dried apricots, dried sultanas, dried berries and cherries, mixed dried fruit. No added sugar or preservatives. Cellophane packaging. Upscale. No name. Demographics of her target market are male and female ages twenty-five to forty-five, income level upwards of thirty grand a year, college educated or better. Go for it."

Three of the four interns picked up the packets, turned them over in their hands, searching for inspiration.

"What's a sultana?" Sean asked, feeling the substance of a dried apricot through the wrapper. It was flabby and flexible, like a fleshy orange ear. He wrinkled his nose.

"One of the names for golden raisins," Dorothy said, holding up that package. "Doesn't it sound more elegant?"

"Paul, how about Oh, Gee Snacks?" Brendan suggested, then spelled it. "Stands for the OG abbreviation of 'organic'?"

"Maybe," Paul Meier said. "It's kind of cutesy. Run with it. Gimme some thoughts on a campaign." But Brendan had shot his bolt. He grinned and shrugged.

"Ug—*ly*," Sean said. "You weren't kidding about not pretty. How about 'Ugly fruit, beautiful vitamins'?"

"I approve of the product," Dorothy said. "Environmentally sound packaging, no pesticides. You can compost cellophane, you know. Becky Sarter? How's 'Sarter your day with good nutrition'?"

Everyone groaned.

"Nothing there to hang on to, really, Dorothy. Half a pun is NOT better than none. But you have a lot of basic knowledge there about the product. That's good. But we need a *name*. How about you, Keith?" Meier asked. "Keith? Earth to Keith." He rapped on Keith's notebook with his knuckles.

Keith came back from his musings with a start. "Uh, sorry. What?"

"Let's hear it. What can you do with Sarter organic dried fruits."

"Would the client get all bent up about changing the spelling of his name?"

"Her name, and I don't know. Why?"

"You can't ask a client to change his name!" Brendan exclaimed.

"Why not? They've done it themselves. I read that Chef Boy-ar-dee is really a man named Boiardi." Keith spelled it.

"So what have you got in mind?"

"How about spelling it Sartre, like the philosopher?" Keith asked, mentally thanking the Elf Master for the intensive course in philosophy he'd taught the last semester of Keith's junior year. "He's the one who said, I think, therefore I am. I think."

"Descartes said that," Brendan said in disgust.

"Okay, so what?" Keith snatched up a pen and drew a bag, splaying the letters out across the top. *Sartre Sultanas. The Raisin d'Être.*

"It means, the reason for being—I mean, the *raisin* for being."

"Not another pun!" Brendan exclaimed.

Meier stared at it for a second, a tiny grin growing in the corner of his mouth.

"That's funny. It's sly. Not bad for someone who's been staring out the window all day. It might appeal to the environmentally conscious intellectuals who buy organic stuff." He picked up Keith's caricature, and drummed on it with the cap end of his pen.

"Hey, we're not supposed to be pandering to intellectuals," Brendan protested.

Meier raised an eyebrow. "We pander, as you call it, to the people most likely to buy the product. The readers who don't get it will buy the product because it's something they perceive a need for. Those who get it will like it more because it's an in-joke aimed at them. That's not all bad, because although the market is small, the availability of the product is limited, too. Says here in the research that there's been less than ten thousand pounds of organic dried raspberries available each of the last four years. Even if that increases drastically, that's still nowhere near the amount of good old-fashioned, non-organic black raisins being sold every day."

"You could have pictures in the ads of famous philosophers eating the product," Dorothy suggested.

"Except for Albert Einstein, who the hell is going to know what a philosopher looks like?" Sean said, looking bored.

" 'Yum! Much tastier than hemlock,' says Socrates." Brendan snickered.

"Why not?" asked Meier. "Come on, this is what brainstorming is all about. You may not get the best ideas right away, but they'll come if you feel relaxed about what you're doing. Keith here may have looked like he was catatonic, but his mind was racing along."

"You're right about him looking catatonic," Sean said.

Keith made a good-natured face at him, too preoccupied to think of a retort. He'd been a million miles away, thinking of Dola and baby Asrai.

Meier still looked thoughtful. "Keith, I'm going to take this to the committee." The others looked dismayed. "Come on, guys, it couldn't hurt. The pros have flunked out on this one. We've gotten a lot of self-righteous claptrap about wholesomeness, a couple of environmental fire-eaters offering obscure suggestions, some overly cute b.s., and a lot of blank stares. The four of you have done better on Sarter Fruit in less time than anyone else to date. This could spark the right inspiration in someone's mind. If they don't want Sarter. The raisin d'être.'' He chuckled.

Brendan regarded Keith with a look of pure hatred. Keith smiled innocently at him, fanning the fury still higher. If you can't join 'em, he thought, annoy 'em. Keith turned to Meier. "Same understanding as before," he said.

Meier nodded. "I appreciate your trust, kid. I won't take advantage of you. If they'll take it with your name on it, it'll be there."

The door to the little conference room swung open, and a man leaned in. He was tall and slender, with dark, well-coiffed hair that had just the faintest suggestion of gray at the tips of the sideburns, and a health-club tan. He glanced at the young folks, and his face lit up. He turned to Meier.

"Paul! Here you are. I've been looking for you."

Meier made the introductions.

"Doug Constance, one of our creative directors," Meier said, sweeping a hand around the table. "Doug, this is Dorothy Scott, Brendan Martwick, Keith Doyle, and Sean Lopez. My latest crop of interns."

"I know! That's why I came in," Constance said, grinning at them.

The four students favored the newcomer with big, hopeful smiles. "What can we do for you, Doug?" Meier asked.

"Well, we've got a new client we're pitching coming in this afternoon," Constance said. "I thought one of your interns might like a chance to see how it's done, maybe throw in a few suggestions, be in right from the beginning. What do you think?"

Keith sat up straighter. It would be a great opportunity to show his stuff. He could see that all three of the others had the same thought. Without waving his hand and yelling, "Me! Me!" it was difficult to make himself stand out from the group. He concentrated on looking bright, alert and, he hoped, creative. He smiled at the account executive, trying to meet his gaze.

But Constance's eye lit on Dorothy and her ubiquitous sketchbook. "There she is. How about her? Paul, we'd like to borrow this very talented young lady for the afternoon. We'd appreciate her input on Natural-Look Hair Products, and maybe she could do some sketches for layouts. She'd enjoy it, wouldn't you, Dorothy? Could you lend her to us, Paul?''

Paul looked at Dorothy, whose eyes were glistening beacons. "Sure, if you want. Go ahead, honey."

Dorothy rose with alacrity, her sketchbook clutched to her chest, and headed out of the room. Constance held the door open for her, then shut it behind them, with a final wink at Meier. "See you later!"

Disappointed, Keith spared himself one uncharitable thought as he sank back into his chair, that Dorothy would undoubtedly use this opportunity to promote her chances at getting the PDQ job. Maybe he'd have done the same under similar circumstances, but he wasn't so sure.

"Now, knock it off," Meier said, breaking into his thoughts. "I can see what you three are thinking. *No* decision has been made yet on who's going to be picked for the job—if anyone—and you've still got to earn a grade out of this term, so give me your attention. Got it?"

The three young men eyed each other. "Yes, Paul," Keith said. The other two murmured their agreement.

"Sorry, Paul," said Sean, cocking his head sheepishly to one side.

"Good," Meier said firmly, spreading out a sheaf of photographs from a folder. "Now, I've got another product I want your best thoughts on. It's one of my new accounts. Listen up. I'm going to give you these to chew over, then I've got a couple of meetings of my own."

"Come on, Doyle, I know what bifurcated means, and you know what bifurcated means, but the average jerk on the streets is going to think it's something dirty." Brendan shook his head at the ad copy Keith had scribbled on a mock layout.

"Hey, sex sells," Sean said, laughing.

"It's got nothing to do with sex, and I think it sounds dumb. Just like everything he comes up with." Brendan threw an annoyed gesture toward Keith, who turned his hands palm upward in appeal.

"No, look, it'd make great copy. It's supposed to be obscure, then you come to the tagline, which would read," Keith held up his yellow pad and declaimed, " 'But instead of wading through our grandiose verbiage, why not come and see how our tire sails through water.' "

"Too wordy for anyone except *The New Yorker*," Brendan said, drumming his fingertips. Keith shrugged, and started drawing lines through his copy.

"When you're right, you're right," he conceded. Brendan looked surprised to have Keith agree with him, then sat back smugly. He put his heels on the table.

Meier opened the door. Brendan immediately swept his feet down and sat up straight. Teacher's pet, Keith thought in annoyance.

"Nice to see little birds in their nests agreeing for a change!" Meier said cheerfully. "Dorothy not back yet?"

"Nope," the three young men said in unison.

"Okay," Meier said. He flopped into his chair and sighed deeply. "What a day! Okay. What's Dunbar Tyres' PLC's new centrally-grooved aqua-handler tire going to be called?"

"The Brain," said Sean.

"The English Channel," said Keith and Brendan together.

"No consensus, eh?" Meier asked. "Typical. You sound like you work for an ad agency. All right, Sean, why 'The Brain'?"

Sean turned his photograph of the product and his rough sketches toward the instructor. "Because it looks like a brain, or the top of it does, if you see it straight on. I wrote, 'Your car is five times as smart when you add four Brains to the one behind the wheel.' "

"That's not bad," Meier said, nodding. "Doesn't hurt to flatter the customers."

"I looked at the *bottom* of the tire where it hits the pavement," Brendan said, "and to me it looked like the rear end of the girl on the beach in the Bahamas tourist commercials, but you don't see *me* suggesting we call it The Tush."

"Why The English Channel, then?"

"Because nothing handles water like the English Channel," Keith tossed off patly. "Dunbar's an English company."

"Americans like things that are English," Brendan added. "It makes you think of people swimming the Channel, which is a real accomplishment. We're riding on that," he finished, cocking a distrustful eye toward his erstwhile partner.

"Har, har," Keith said, obediently. Brendan looked surprised, but Keith smiled at him. "Cooperation, remember?"

"True, true," Meier agreed. He glanced at the clock, which showed 5:15. "Okay, you wanna leave me all of this stuff, and I'll look it over tonight? I'll give you my thoughts on it tomorrow, and you can let me know if you want me to propose your ideas or not. Good work, gentlemen."

Keith rose and gathered up his belongings. He realized guiltily that he hadn't thought about Dola's plight in hours. Still, there was nothing he could do for at least another twelve hours, and there was the chance that he could get a call any time that Holl and the others had found the kidnapers and managed to pull off a rescue without him. The important thing was that the children were alive and well.

He carried his coffee cup down the hall and into the employee lounge to wash it out. Only one light was on in the long, narrow room, over the sink at the far end. The flat-napped carpet swallowed up his footsteps, so that it seemed the only sounds were his breathing and the water running as he rinsed out his mug. Until he heard the sob.

"Who's there?" he asked gently into the gloom. He made out a shape at the table next to the window, and thought he recognized the outline. "Dorothy, is that you over there?" There was no answer. He turned off the water and put the cup down.

His eyes quickly became used to the gloom as he went to sit by her. Her makeup was smudged, leaving matte streaks on her skin, and she looked miserable. He scooted his chair close to hers.

"You were gone all afternoon. How'd it go?" he asked.

"Horrible!" Dorothy burst out, and her voice caught as she struggled not to cry. He could see that she was not only unhappy, but very angry. "Do you know what that big sell was all about? What they wanted me at that presentation for? A token! Natural-Look's president is an African-American woman. PDQ doesn't have any creative directors who're both female and African-American, so they pretended they needed me there to help with the presentation. I just sat there and nodded the whole time. They listened to my ideas once in a while, when I managed to speak up, but you could tell they weren't really paying any attention.

It was all phony! For looks! So *she* would think they were politically correct. She thought I was a staff artist. They never told her I was just an intern. I hate this place.''

"Whoa," Keith said. "Meier warned us that this business was tough and that practically everyone's a rat."

"I'm just here as a token," Dorothy said, her eyes burning with tears. As she scrabbled in her purse with one hand, Keith handed her his own handkerchief. After a second's hesitation, she took it and dabbed at her eyes and nose.

"Nope, you are not here as a token. You've got talent," Keith said firmly. "Come on, how many interviews did you go through to get in here? Same number I did. And you had to have the grades and the background even to be considered, right? After they offer you the job at the end of the year—"

"Hah!" Dorothy said, bitterly.

Keith waggled a finger at her. "Don't interrupt me when I'm complimenting you. —You can start making changes here. You can move up to where clients are asking for you."

"You just don't know what it's like." Dorothy turned her head to stare out the window at the dusk. Lights were coming on all over the city, little pinpoints of red, amber, and white.

Keith thought about it for a moment, and gave a half-grin. "You'd be surprised," he said. "Most of my best friends—"

"If you say they're black, I'm going to kill you," Dorothy snapped.

"Nope, only some of my friends are black. I was *going* to say most of them are elves," Keith said. Dorothy gestured disbelief, but the tension began to melt out of her face. "You know, being the only Big Person in the crowd makes it difficult for me, sometimes, especially when they speak their own language, but we have a great time learning from each other. I don't share their common background, so of course I feel left out a lot."

"Yeah, sure," she said, but she was diverted from her rage. "You're strange, Keith."

"My stock in trade," he said, grinning.

At that moment Meier appeared, silhouetted in the hall door. "What's the matter, kids?" He came to sit down at their table, shoulders hunched forward over his folded hands. "Come on, tell Papa."

Dorothy turned to stare out of the window, leaving Keith to explain what had happened to her. The lines of Meier's face deepened, and his lips pressed into a thin line.

"I'll take care of this," he said. His voice was calm, but the suppressed power in it told Keith how angry he was. "Dammit, they're supposed to keep their damned games off you students."

"Why, so you can grab our ideas for yourself? So you can use us yourself?" Dorothy snapped.

Meier turned his surprisingly calm eyes on her. "Dorothy. Ms. Scott. I always tell you when I'm taking your ideas, and when I'm not, and I tell you why. I am working for your best interests, although you might not believe me right now. You want the magic of seeing your ideas used by the clients? If not, tell me. I won't propose any of yours. I told you there's resistance to using unpaid interns' suggestions. You agreed to that at the beginning of this session. You want to take it back, you can. It doesn't make any difference to me. I've got my own ideas, and I get plenty from the rest of my creative staff. I don't need yours. I was doing you a favor. There's no reason for you to have to put anything else on the line. You can go on just learning from me about this business, and participating in the class. It won't affect your grade, because it really just doesn't matter to me. You can believe that or not. It's up to you."

Dorothy's gaze dropped. "I'm sorry, Paul," she said meekly. "I didn't mean that. I just feel used. Dirty."

Meier nodded kindly, and slid into a chair. "I apologize, too, Dorothy. I work with these yotzes every day, but sometimes they even fool me. Like today. It's my fault I let Doug get away with using you. And I do put your names on the proposals when I can, but you've got to understand how delicate the balance is we've got to maintain. We can't let the client feel at any time that we're incompetent. Okay, let's look at it from another angle. You were in on the initial meeting between a client and a creative team—a crucial moment in the relationship. Did you get anything out of that?"

Dorothy looked at him in surprise. Even the puffiness around her eyes was beginning to recede. "Well, yes, I felt them measuring out what she wanted. It wasn't easy. She had an image in her mind, and nothing we proposed seemed to match it. That was tough. She wasn't good at seeing the potential in rough sketches. She needs to see finished mockups."

"Good assessment. They work out how much she can spend?"

"Uh huh. I guess it wasn't much. She has to aim straight at her demographics without a lot left for general advertising, so it's up to us to figure out where her customers are and how to reach them. After being in research, I know how much it costs to put up certain kinds of ads, so I could see just what she could get for her money."

Meier nodded encouragingly. "And how far creativity, both in the ads and in the placement of those ads, can make that money go. Not easy, but you could begin to understand how we begin to form a campaign. You see? No experience is ever wasted, is it? You feel better?"

Dorothy gave him a look of gratitude. "Yes."

"Great," Meier said. He glanced at his watch. The shiny face picked up a few of the red and white points reflected in from the window. "Okay, I've gotta get out of here, kids. See you tomorrow." He rose, chucking a friendly fist into Keith's shoulder, and strode out.

"I like him," Keith said, watching the door swing shut.

"I do, too," Dorothy said. "And I like you. It was nice of you to come and sit down with me. How come you want to help me, when we're competing for the same spot? We can't both win, you know."

"Oh, I'll get along if I don't get the job," Keith said reassuringly. "I'm not a type-A personality. There'll be other opportunities for both of us, lots of them. Listen, want to grab a bite to eat? I just missed my train home, so I might as well have dinner down here."

"Sure," Dorothy said. The luster was back in her cheeks, and she smiled at him. "Let me clean up first. I must be a mess!"

The Chicago Loop empties out swiftly at the end of the workday. Most of the places the interns were accustomed to going for lunch were already closed. Keith and Dorothy found themselves on the uppermost floor of a shopping center, looking out the window at the city. Ribbons of red lights marked the outbound traffic on the expressways. The river, snaking between high-rises

and the Merchandise Mart, glistened with the colors of sunset
reflected from the sky. On the horizon, tiny planes to the west
and southwest appeared in the sky, rocketing along an upward
vector: the evening flights at O'Hare and Midway airports. The
sulphur yellow of sodium vapor lights made an eerie graph pattern of the streets to the north of the Loop. Keith and Dorothy
watched in companionable silence until their meals arrived.

"Paul was right," Dorothy admitted. After she had eaten a
few bites of food, she seemed restored to her usual competent
self. "This internship is doing me good, and I like it a lot more
than I thought I would."

"Me, too," Keith said. "Before, I sort of thought ads wrote
themselves. I mean I wasn't aware of the mechanism that creates
commercials and print ads. Now I go around making up slogans
and layouts for everything I see. Baloney Billboards," he
sketched across the sky, "for the biggest ideas around. Or the
watch ad I thought up that no one will ever use."

"Oh?" Dorothy asked encouragingly, amused.

"Yup. Shows a giant watch with its band fastened around the
Tower of Pisa. Slogan: if you have the inclination you might as
well—"

"—have the time," Dorothy finished with him. Her laugh, a
deep, throaty gurgle, was pretty. Keith beamed at her. "I should
have seen that one coming. I know what you mean," she said.
"I'm doing it, too. I love it. I draw storyboards and magazine
ads. I've got sketchbooks full of the weirdest stuff." She turned
serious for a moment. "I really want this job, Keith. It would
mean getting right into the big-time business, without starting
out in Podunkville."

"Great," Keith said, without a trace of jealousy. "And when
I graduate, you can hire me."

"I could use a good copywriter," she said, assessing him
mock-critically.

"Why, with your brains and my looks," he said, with a self-
deprecating grin, "we'll go places. You could have a great
career." He could picture her in an executive office putting
people like Doug Constance into line. He could picture her holding Asrai, being hustled along by two large men—no, that was
Dola being pushed, the baby clasped to her chest. Keith shook
his head to clear it. He looked up.

Outside of the window behind Dorothy's head, a knot of air sprites whisked and hovered. One of them flew forward, showing that the memory belonged to it. Insistent, the image replayed itself in his head. Dola and the baby, being escorted from a big tank truck into a brick and paneled building by two men, roughly sketched out in twilight. He struggled to continue the conversation, but knew immediately he was mouthing gibberish. Dorothy gave him a strange look. He smiled and asked her a question about art, but he wasn't sure exactly what. The sprites flew in irregular patterns, aping his agitation and excitement. They'd found her! They knew where the children were!

"Something wrong?" Dorothy asked. His face had gone pasty, then reddened until it was nearly the color of his hair.

"I just remembered something," Keith said, pushing back his chair and standing up. He grabbed the check. He hoped Dorothy wouldn't turn around and see what he had been staring at. "I'd better get out of here. I'm sorry. I just remembered something. See you Monday!"

With his jacket flung over his arm, he dashed out of the restaurant, stopping only to slap down the bill with some money at the register. Bemused, Dorothy picked up her fork and went back to her meal, neglected since the two of them had started building castles in the air. She shrugged. At least he'd been a gentleman about it. Since he had to run off, he had treated, but she was still puzzled why he'd left in such a hurry.

"Well, was it my breath?" she asked herself. The skyline was pretty tonight. When she finished eating, she was going to make a sketch of it.

Outside the window, four air sprites streaked away from the building and parted, taking off in four different directions, their filmy tails fluttering farewell, their thoughts full of sunsets.

Chapter
TEN

"I ain't happy about this, and I don't care who knows it," Pilton said moodily. He sat in the orange chair, elbows propped on his knees, and stared at the ground. "I'm not supposed to have to work Saturdays. I ain't on this shift."

"Nor do the baby and I want to be here," Dola said, without looking up. "If we weren't you wouldn't have to." She was diapering Asrai, who had decided to throw a fit of the wiggles. The infant would not stay in the middle of the clean pad, but as soon as her small bottom touched the cold desktop she let out a wail of protest. Dola took Asrai's ankles between her fingers and plumped her firmly down, and fastened the tapes before she could move again.

"I know." Pilton sighed. "But the boss-lady won't let you go yet."

"*Why?*" Dola demanded. With a flourish, she swaddled the baby in her blanket and sat down on the floor on her borrowed sleeping bag. Asrai was now willing to take formula from the bottle without the subterfuge of illusionary disguise, for which Dola was grateful. She took the warmed bottle out of the coffeemaker carafe, tested it, and offered the nipple to Asrai, who accepted it avidly.

"Dunno. Don't ask me any more. I can't tell you."

"You'll be here Sunday as well," Dola said warningly.

"Dammit to hell," Pilton swore, throwing up his hands. "Well, I can't do anything about it now. Hey, I brought you some egg salad sandwiches for lunch. Got some carrot sticks, too, and a slice of cake."

Dola nodded. She hunched over Asrai. The baby suckled, making happy noises deep in her throat. "I'm bored!" Dola announced. "At home I'd have games and toys, and tasks to do, and there'd be all my friends."

Pilton sat up. "Well, what do you want to do?"

The elf girl could stand it no longer. The imprisonment, the discomfort, the annoyance of not being able to wash her clothes, nor have any clean ones to change into, the lumpy sleeping bag that smelled as if it had been wet in a hundred times and washed in orange juice—the stupidity of her jailors. She burst into tears. "I want to go home."

Pilton dropped to his knees next to her. "Oh, come on, little girl, don't cry. Please. I'll do just about anything to keep you from feeling sad."

"She wants what?" Mona Gilbreth demanded. "Craft supplies? No. Simply no. I'm not running a nursery school. Tell her if she doesn't knock it off I'm shutting both of them in an empty tank."

"I can't do that, ma'am," Pilton said, shocked. "What would her folks say?"

Mona went white. H. Doyle again. "All right. But don't get too elaborate. I'm getting rid of her as soon as I can." She opened her desk drawer and took out the petty cash box. Resenting every last penny, she counted out ten dollars.

"Any more than this is on you," she said. "I didn't want them here, and I don't want to subsidize their entertainment."

Accepting the money happily, Pilton went off to find embroidery floss and the fixings that went with it for the little girl. He was evolving a kind of superstition in his own mind that he'd have good luck if he could make the fairy child happy. In spite of what Ms. Gilbreth and Jake said, he knew she was magical. He'd seen. If he won her good will and got her to put a blessing on him, he'd be a lucky man for the rest of his life. Maybe she would even invite him back to the land of fairies.

When he thought of it, it seemed strange that there were fairies right here in Illinois, when this had been Indian country for ten thousand years less the last two hundred. Never mind. That wasn't the kind of question you asked fairy people if you wanted to stay on their good side.

Tay eyed the Skyship Iris with clear distaste. It was only with an effort he brought himself to get out of the car with Holl and Keith to walk toward the seven-story-high ovoid.

"It isn't natural," he complained to Keith. "I don't feel safe about this floating around with a big silk handkerchief over my head. It'll spring a hole and run off with us, and we'll be shooting around the sky helpless while it deflates. Are you sure there's no other way?"

"Not if you want to be with us for the search," Keith said, patiently. "The sprites can't come down to our level, so if we want their help we have to go up to where they are. C'mon, it'll be fun." At his particular request the Iris's crew had helped set up the balloon, then backed off, accepting his explanation that he wanted to do some complicated photography, and needed the field clear of all other bodies. All it would take to launch the balloon was hitting the release on a series of clamps holding the ropes through steel-pegged loops hammered into the ground. The crew waved from the cab of the chase truck. Keith signaled back, holding up his camera. The engine of the truck revved and the headlights flashed, showing that Murphy and the others were ready to follow when the balloon lifted. Tay still hung back. "You want to stay behind, that's okay. We'll go," Keith said.

"No! I'd best come." Tay folded his arms firmly and tried not to look nervous.

"These your friends?" Frank asked, smiling down widely at Keith's diminutive companions. "Hi, kids," he said, then did a doubletake. He stared full-faced at the two elves with a kind of fascinated horror. "What *are* they?" he demanded of Keith. "Those ears!" The blond male he might have been able to explain away as a kid playing masquerade, but the silvery-haired fellow wore a beard that had to be his own.

Keith blinked at the pilot innocently. "Didn't I tell you the air sprites weren't the first supernatural beings I've met?"

"Supernatural?" Frank's voice squeaked on the last few syllables. Keith grinned.

"Pay no attention to this big fool. We're no more supernatural than he," Holl said, with an exasperated glance at Keith. He stepped forward and offered the shaken pilot his hand. "My name is Holl. This is Tay. It's our children you're helping us to find, and I promise you we appreciate it greatly."

Frank closed his own large hand around Holl's small fingers with the delicacy of someone handling breakable china. "How'd you do, uh . . . Shouldn't the Air Force or whoever's in charge of extraterrestrials know about them?" he asked Keith over Holl's head. The two elves looked alarmed, and Keith spoke quickly.

"Hey, they're not extraterrestrials," Keith said. "I know you can keep a secret, so they said I could tell you. If they don't want anyone else to know about them, wouldn't you say that was their choice?"

"Uh, you're right. Sorry," he said, glancing down at Holl, apology and wonder mixed on his face.

"No harm done," Holl said, with a smile. "Shall we go?"

Keith helped the two elves climb over the edge and into the basket. The Iris, tugging against a light wind, was eager to be off. When Frank nodded, Keith hit the release for the cables, and just to add verisimilitude for the chase truck, started snapping pictures.

The ascent was effortless, the finest Keith had yet experienced. The only sensation was the slight vibration the burners caused in the framework attached to the basket. Fascinated, Holl and Tay watched the ground fall away.

"Like watching a scene on the television," Tay said, with interest. "Zooming back to show the distance . . . uh, is that a house?" He pointed at the red roof of a distant barn. "A real house?"

"Yup," Keith said, following his finger. "We're about six hundred feet up already. Good cruising altitude."

"Six hundred feet!" Tay squeaked, staggering away from the edge. "I thought we'd be lifting thirty or forty feet to clear the trees!" He sat down in the bottom of the basket with his head between his knees and began to moan. Holl made a wry face.

"Leave him be," he suggested. "We live close to the ground," he explained to Frank, who was looking concerned. "We barely so much as climb trees."

Keith kept an eye on the altimeter as the balloon continued to rise. The Iris swept into a northeast wind and began to sail in the direction Holl said the girls' trace lay. He peered into the distance, hoping to spot landmarks.

"Well, where are they?" Frank asked, when they reached five thousand feet. He glanced around eagerly. "At this temperature I can go to fifteen thousand if need be."

"Please don't," Tay begged from the floor of the basket.

Keith grinned at the pilot. "I thought you didn't want to meet any more supernatural beings," he teased.

Frank squared his skinny shoulders. "Guess if they're up here, I ought to know."

"If it wasn't all your imagination in the first place," Holl said to Keith.

"Both of us saw it, right, Frank?" Keith said. The pilot nodded. "They'll be here, honest."

"I don't care if flying dragons appear," Tay said, miserably hunched among their feet, "so long as they're willing to help me find my daughter."

A vision of a sunrise interrupted the conversation. Holl stared at Keith. "What's wrong with my mind?" he asked.

"It's them," Keith said, and began looking around for his new acquaintances. The blue-white tail of a sprite looped swiftly past them around the balloon basket, until its delicate figure was level with them beyond the sheet cables.

"There it is!" Keith said, pointing. "Holl, Tay, look."

Tay glanced up briefly at the milk-colored creature, who blinked amiably at him, and went back to groaning with his head held in his hands. "Such things belong up here," Tay said. "All I wish is to get down to the ground where I belong."

Holl held his breath. He and the sprite stared at one another for a moment, and the young elf broke the silence with a sigh. He cocked his head at Keith. "Well, I owe you an apology, widdy. If anyone could find an imaginary being up here, it would have to be you."

The sprite, detecting that Keith was being teased, retaliated on his behalf with a clear image of Maura pushing Holl into the stream. In the vision, the elf landed on his rump in the mossy water. Keith laughed, and Holl shook his head.

"Oh, very well, then, friend, I submit," Holl said, good-naturedly. "You know all and see all. It really is too bad that your amazing discovery must take second place in importance to the rescue of our children, Keith Doyle, but you have my humble admiration.''

"Thanks.'' Keith grinned. "I'll spare you the 'I told you so,' and we can hold the scientific discussion later.'' He brought up his camera and showed it to the sprite. "Can I take your picture?'' he asked. "I'd sure like to show some other people that I met you.''

Take? Please do not take from our substance. The mental picture of a diminished sprite, looking woeful, appeared.

"Um, it doesn't actually take anything from your substance,'' Keith explained hurriedly. "It's only a reflection of you in my camera lens which hits a kind of light-reactive paper. Harmless. I promise.''

Timidly, the airborne creature inspected the camera, and its mental vista turned rose-colored. *All right.* It backed up, whipping its tail like a rudder.

"It'll make a noise,'' Keith warned, focusing the lens.

All right. The sprite held itself still, but showed its agitation in the way its extremities flapped as if caught in a light breeze. Keith pushed the shutter release, refocused, and took a second exposure. *That didn't hurt at all*, the sprite sent to him in surprise.

As if its approval was a signal, another and another winged being joined them, until the air was filled with sprites all signaling their image of sunrise to greet their fellows and the party in the balloon. Keith was busy taking pictures, asking the sprites to pose in groups, or to fly alongside one of the Folk to give him a scale of measure. Few were the same size as Keith's original acquaintance. Some were tiny enough to fly up his camera lens, if it had been hollow. One, of which they could see only a wingjoint or an eye in the shimmering, cloudlike mass, was nearly the size of the balloon. It looked like a friendly hurricane coming close to take a look. Most of the winged beings ranged in size somewhere in between. Frank goggled, but he kept control of his craft through sheer will power. Holl looked around and around in wonder.

"The Master will be glad of those snapshots,'' he said, with a sigh. "I hope we'll get to know these good folk better later on. How shall we begin this search, then? Will one guide us?''

There was a hasty conference among the air sprites, from which Keith got the fallout of images changing and shifting.

Most of the diaphanous beings swept away with a swift daydream of sunsets left behind as farewell. The party was left with Keith's friend, a larger one who pushed itself forward importantly, and a few of the smaller creatures.

Following the sprite's direction, Frank steered the Iris into a northward current.

"Full tanks, nice day, cool weather, last a long time," the pilot said, nodding.

"Then we will begin," Holl said.

Keith felt it on the edge of his mind when the two elves pooled together their strength and began the search for the children. Their sense spread out like a sensitive layer on the sky that could feel all the topography of the land below it, except that it sought mental touches, not physical. He connected with it a little, but couldn't follow it far. That kind of command of talent took years of practice, and a lot more magical oomph than he had. After a while Tay rubbed his eyes.

"It's the same trouble as before," Holl said. "There is something in the way that lifts and lowers between us like a heavy curtain. I sense them only part of the time, but this wispy friend of yours is indeed going toward the scent." He smiled at the hovering sprite, who made a rosy glow at him. The little ones danced around it like fireflies. The larger apparition narrowed its large pupils and twisted in the wind to point forward.

"Make sure you tell me when you want to land," Frank said. "No second chances here. Can't turn around."

"If we can," Holl said. "It depends greatly on what our friends tell us."

The large sprite stayed ahead of the balloon, glancing over its shoulder frequently to make eye contact with Keith or Frank. The gesture was for their benefit: Keith could tell it was able to see them in its mind's eye without turning around. When the winds wouldn't go where it led, the sprite hovered patiently, waiting for the shift in direction it wanted. It always knew, and made the image of a weather vane turning for Frank, so the pilot would be ready. The original sprite stayed back with the balloon, hovering companionably near.

Frank showed his big teeth. "My new best friends," he said, manipulating the cords to raise or lower the balloon. "You'll stay around?"

The sprite, its eyes alight, showed the Iris surrounded by itself and many others. Holl grabbed for Keith's arm.

"The trace is very strong ahead," Holl said. "No, I've lost it. I can't believe it winked out just like that." He looked at Tay hopefully, but the silver-haired elf shook his head.

"The interference is like clouds rolling in between us," Tay said.

"Or smoke?" suggested Keith.

Beneath them, the green cropfields had given way to a huge industrial center. Bare earth stained by greasy overflow supported corrugated tanks and pipelines. Trucks ran among them, and minute workers in khaki coveralls hooked up pipelines to the tank trailers. In the midst of the factory grounds was a broad, flat group of buildings: warehouses and the office center. At the same time the sprite broadcast the yellow-green sky image of warning, the occupants of the balloon were hit by a wave of stench that surrounded and stifled them.

"Ugh, horrors!" exclaimed Tay.

"That's Gilbreth Fertilizer down there," Keith said, coughing. "Look at all that leakage from the tanks. I bet there's half a dozen health violations right there. I didn't see those when I was there. I think the owner steered me away on purpose." He leaned over the edge and started taking pictures.

"What a smell!" Tay complained. "The very stink makes you itch."

"I know," Keith replied, from behind his viewfinder. "I kept sneezing the whole time."

Holl's expression changed from revulsion to enlightenment. "They're down there," he cried, grabbing Frank's elbow.

"The children?" Keith blinked. "At Gilbreth?"

"Yes! I felt them, just for a minute, safe and well. That chemical soup is what is blocking natural sense. Go back!"

"Can't!" Frank said, regretfully. "We can't change the wind."

The larger sprite whipped around the balloon, showing its agitation in snapshot-like images forced into their minds. The picture of the little girl forced to walk between two men repeated over and over. Frank waved a hand around his eyes, trying to clear his vision.

"Stop that!" Keith ordered. "We can't think." The pictures

stopped at once. The guide drew back, hovering tentatively just beyond the basket's edge, apology in its large eyes. They were passing over the buildings now. Shortly, they'd be beyond the property's edge.

Keith got a sudden inspiration. "Drop her!" he cried.

Frank, mentally weighing safety against the rescue of the children, nodded sharply once and yanked the parachute release. They heard the outrush of air, and saw a burst of sunlight up inside the dome as the great rainbow bag irised open on top. Swiftly, the balloon dropped toward the earth. Whipping its tail skyward, the sprite reversed and followed them downward head first. Keith gritted his teeth as the earth rushed toward them. Wind whistled in his ears.

"Ah, no!" Tay groaned, falling to his knees on the padding at the bottom of the basket. "I'll never leave solid ground again."

The balloon pilot slowed their descent as soon as he hit calm air closer to the ground. The craft jerked slightly, but all four men were well braced.

"Distraction's only good a short time," Frank said tersely. "Leave it to me. Truck's been tracking us. Take it home. Got it?"

"Got it," Keith said, crouching, ready for the impact of landing. Holl copied his posture, and clutched the edge of the basket with both hands.

The sprite shot upward and away, leaving behind a final image of Holl holding Asrai, and Tay with his arms around Dola.

"I think that means good luck," Keith said. He saw men on the ground running toward the descending balloon. "Get down!"

He and the two elves ducked farther below the edge of the rattan basket and held on. Frank landed the balloon with a hard thump. The gondola bounced and began to scoot along the ground, slowing as air rushed out of the balloon. When the deflating bag started to billow over them, he hissed, "Go!"

Keith slipped over the rear side and helped the elves climb out. They ran, crouched low, toward the industrial buildings, as the men closed in on Frank and the Iris, shouting for explanations.

"What are you doing here?" one man in guard uniform demanded.

"Hey, it's beautiful!" another cried. "Do you need help, fellah?"

Frank held up his cell phone. "It's okay! Chase car be here in a minute. Give a guy a hand?" He punched in the number of his truck's mobile phone.

The three ran around the corner of one of the brown brick buildings, avoiding the windows, and crouched out of sight of the crowd gathering around Frank and the balloon.

"Where to?" Keith whispered.

"I don't know," Holl said. "I've lost the trace again, but they must be in one of these buildings. The square footage is finite. We'll split up."

"I wish I'd been paying more attention to the floor plan when I was here," Keith said, glancing behind him. Their haven was surrounded by walls on three sides: a dead end. "I never dreamed they'd be *here*. I could've freed them days ago!"

"Never mind," Holl said. "Use your eyes and ears!"

Across the grounds, Frank was instructing an enthusiastic volunteer force in how to drag down the nylon canvas and lay it flat. Little breezes caught inside the lip of the bag made it billow upward. Laughing, the men grabbed for the fluttering edges and tried to make them stay on the ground. They called to others who came out of doors to come and help.

"He's keeping them busy," Holl said. "Go, then!"

Still hunched over, Holl slipped off to the left, signaling to Tay and Keith to go another way. Nodding, Tay went to the right. Keith followed him for a short time, then detoured down a narrow passage between two of the brick buildings.

Chapter
<u>ELEVEN</u>

In her prison at one end of the main building, Dola heard the commotion. She dragged the plastic chair to the window and stood on it to see what was occurring. In the narrow areaway outside, men were running and calling to one another. It didn't seem to be a disaster, such as a fire, for they seemed happy and excited. Something good, then, but unexpected. She pressed her cheek against the glass to see. Out of the corner of her eye she could see bright colors bobbing and billowing where there was normally only the marshy brown of the clay soil that underlay this place. While she watched, the colorful mass sagged and flattened out. She couldn't guess what it was.

In her arms, Asrai stirred, suddenly roused. Dola herself felt a mental touch, a nudge. Nothing physical intruded upon them: it was a push upon her aura, such as her mother might make, to check upon her well-being when she thought Dola to be asleep. This familiar touch was not her mother's but her father's! He had to be close by. The evilness of this place prevented her from being able to feel things far off. She sensed it getting closer. Dola became very excited, knowing she was about to be saved, then was overwhelmingly frightened. His presence here meant Tay was risking himself for her, risking discovery and capture. He hadn't been here before. He couldn't know that these terrible men and woman were intelligent, and would block any attempt he made to free her. In the meantime, she had to be ready to run away with him when he came.

Asrai wriggled and started to fuss. Dola pleaded with her. "Oh, not now, little one! For the love of all, please, please don't cry now!"

She willed the baby to hold in the shriek she could feel growing inside her like bread rising. A yell would bring Jake or Skinny on the hop, and she didn't want them near. Dola herself felt like screaming in frustration. Oh, if she never had to see them again, or spend another night in this smelly, cold room! Rescue was near. She could feel it.

At the end of the passageway, opposite to where all the men were running, Dola spotted a figure running, crouching, then running again, as if to avoid notice. When a knot of workers came around the corner, the figure threw itself among the dumpsters and burrowed behind the trash bags to avoid notice. It emerged again, moments after they passed, and resumed its furtive movement. Dola peered at it. Instead of the slim, muscular figure with silver hair she expected, the intruder was unexpectedly tall and lanky, with hair the color of autumn maple leaves. Keith Doyle! Keith had come to rescue her. Dola decided that she could just get through the window if she broke it out. She had one chance at freedom, and all the odds lay in the element of surprise. First, she had to find a way to delay the guard who would surely come when she started breaking the glass. She jumped off the chair and put the baby down in a hastily-arrayed nest of disposable diapers. Grabbing up her sleeping bag, Dola used the heavy cloth as a pad to shield her hands from the metal of the desk as she pushed it as far as she could toward the office door. Its feet groaned a protest that echoed up the corridor. Dola knew it would attract attention. Better to make double sure she had time to escape.

Using as much concentration as she dared, she enhanced the cohesion of one part of the metal door frame for another, willing them to stick together no matter what happened. She doubted it would hold together long on true metal, but it might earn her precious seconds. She grabbed Asrai in one arm, and picked up the body of the coffee maker in the other. Hefting it, she judged where the one strike she had would do the most good.

Dola sprang up onto the chair. Almost across from her now, Keith stared around at the darkened windows of the nearly empty office wing, searching. She wound up and smashed the coffeemaker's metal base into the window. The pane shattered outward, spraying fragments from a hole only the size of her head. Dola began beating on the remaining shards of glass, hammering them into powder.

"Keith Doyle!" she screamed.

He turned and saw her in the tiny window, waving the broken appliance through the hole. Her hand was bleeding and her face was pale, but she was alive and healthy.

"Dola!"

"Oh, hurry," she begged. She glanced hurriedly over her shoulder. There was shouting and pounding in the corridor behind her. She dropped the broken coffeemaker, turned back into the room, then held a bundle out to him. He rushed to take it from her.

"Hey, you!" a man's voice yelled. A tall, lanky man dressed like the others in khaki coveralls, but carrying a brown paper shopping bag, ran down the narrow passage toward Keith. "Who are you? What are you doing here?" He dropped the bag on the ground and made straight for Keith.

Keith reached for Dola's offering, but jumped back without it when the man came at him. He tried to dodge around, and was cut off by a feint from his opponent. Dola pulled back, watching in alarm as Skinny took a swing at Keith's head. Keith ducked, avoiding one punch, but taking the next squarely in the ribs. The breath was knocked out of him with a grunt, and he tripped backward. Dola cringed, holding the swaddled Asrai up out of the way of the fighters. On the ground, Keith kicked at his opponent's shins, making him dance backward. He scrambled back to his feet.

Suddenly, in the shadow of the trash cans, Tay was there. He saw his daughter, and beamed. He signaled encouragement to her, and Dola felt the warmth of his presence, something she had missed for days. It filled her heart, giving her hope. Holl was nearby, too. She could feel him but not see him.

"Open this damned door!"

Behind her, Jake was trying to get in, and had discovered the block she had set in the frame. By the muffled double-thump sound, he and another person were throwing themselves against it to break it in. It was not a strong door; they'd be through it in a moment.

"Hurry!" she called.

Skinny had trapped Keith Doyle in a wrestling hold, with one arm across his throat, and was slowly putting on pressure. The young man's face had gone red. He was not doing well at freeing himself. Skinny easily evaded his weakening kicks and backward-aimed punches. The factory worker shifted and increased the choke hold. Keith gasped and clawed at the other man's arm, trying to pry it loose.

In his hiding place, Tay flung his hands outward, throwing some kind of cantrip at Skinny.

"Kick free!" he shouted to Keith Doyle. "It'll be all right!" Keith nodded weakly, fought for a deep breath, and dropped limp. Skinny, puzzled, bent his head over Keith's shoulder to see what was wrong.

Behind Dola, the door splintered. Jake's meaty arm reached through and felt for the handle, encountering the top of the desk. There was a lot of swearing in the hallway, and Dola heard the boss-lady's voice.

"Break it down!" the woman shouted.

With a tremendous heave, Keith shifted all his weight forward to get his feet back on the ground. Caught off guard, Skinny bent with him. Keith lifted one heel and brought it solidly down on his attacker's instep, then, when Skinny's grip relaxed a fraction, stepped to one side and attempted to throw him over his hip. He struggled unsuccessfully for a moment, looking confused.

"He's fixed in place," Tay hissed. "Get away, then!"

Keith's face lit up as he realized his advantage. Making a knot of his hands, he shot one elbow backward into Skinny's stomach. The factory man doubled up for a moment, and lost his grip on Keith. The student danced away, and Skinny grabbed for him. With wildly flailing hands, Skinny toppled over forward, and hung there at a ridiculous forty-five-degree angle. His feet were fixed to the ground. Keith danced in, ready to paste Skinny another punch in the mouth, but Tay called out to him.

"It won't hold long in this mess. Hurry!"

Avoiding the man's grasp with an agility that would have done credit to a gymnast, Keith dashed to the window and reached up to help Dola out. She thrust the bundled-up infant into his hands and prepared to scramble out after it.

The door of the room burst apart, and Jake, carrying an axe, half-crawled, half-scrambled over the desk. Dola glanced back, and in so doing lost her advantage of surprise. She was partway out the casement when Jake grabbed her by the neck of her tunic and hauled her back.

"Go!" she cried to the others, almost sobbing in frustration. "Run!"

Keith gave her a startled glance, noticed the other faces in the window, and took to his heels, clutching Asrai. Tay and Holl were right behind him.

"It's that Doyle boy!" the boss-woman shrieked. "I knew he was tied up with that H. Doyle! He lied to me! How did they get in here? Where was security?" she demanded. "They should have stopped them at the gates." Jake shook his head, his lips pressed together.

She dropped to her knees beside Dola. "Look, she's bleeding." The angry brusqueness of her voice didn't mask the compassion underlying it, but it was small comfort to Dola. "Get some bandages. Move it!" The woman gripped Dola's shoulder and shook her gently, holding back from hurting her, but evidently frustrated. "I hope you realize you've just made things more complicated. Thanks a lot."

"I'll not apologize," Dola said, tears running down her face. She was too disappointed to act brave. "I'd do it again, too." *I wish them well away*, she thought.

Keith and the others pounded into the driveway just as the red pickup truck rolled onto the factory grounds. One handed, Keith scrabbled at the door handle, yanked it open, and threw himself inside. Tay and Holl all but jumped through the window after him into the truck cab. Together, they pulled the door to. The men in the back of the truck stared at them, and one pounded on the window for attention.

"What's going on?" Murphy asked, recoiling from contact with Keith's flailing elbows.

"Turn around," Keith panted. "Drive us out of here."

Across the field, Frank, free for a moment from expostulating with guards and factory workers as they squeezed the colorful envelope into a sausage and tucked it into its storage bag, gestured at them violently, *away*. Murphy didn't wait for further explanation. With his chin rammed into his shoulder, he spun the pickup in a wide arc, spraying gravel. He gunned the engine. The truck roared out of the compound.

"Who the hell was that?" one of the guards asked Frank.

"Hey, man, if you saw something this big floating around on the ground, you'd think there was a circus here, too. Happens all the time," Frank said, nonchalantly. "People come to look, just look. Ought to come up for a flight some time. Reasonable rates." He reached underneath the control panel for a handful of flyers and handed them to the bemused guard.

Strangers were trying to take his fairy woman away! Frantic, Pilton pulled at his trapped feet. The man who had broken the office window had somehow put a whammy on him while he reached in and took away the baby. Pilton's grabs for him fell yards short. Fortunately Jake and Ms. Gilbreth stopped the fairy child before she could climb out, too. It would have broken his luck.

He had to get the baby back. Yelling for help, he swung himself into a standing position, tugging at first one boot, then the other to pull it loose. No one paid any attention to him. Suddenly, he toppled over, his arms windmilling wildly, and fell with a thud to the dirt. His feet had been freed suddenly from their unexplained adhesion to the ground. Not stopping to wonder how or why, he scrambled up and ran yelling after the man and two boys. He saw them leap into the red truck.

"Hey, you guys!" he shouted at the crowd gathered around the balloonist and his gear. "Stop them!" He was just in time to see the truck disappear down the road in a cloud of dust. His shoulders drooped. Half his luck was gone.

He started walking back toward the building as Ms. Gilbreth and Jake came out of it. The boss-lady's face was white, and she looked mad enough to spit nails.

"They're gone," Pilton said unnecessarily.

The truck hurtled down the country road. Keith clasped the bundle closely. It was wriggling, but silent. As soon as he was sure they were out of danger, he relaxed a little, but kept an eye on the rear view mirror for anyone in pursuit.

"It's a shame we couldn't get Dola out of there," Tay said,

slamming his small fist against the side window. His pulse had started to slow down after the lightning raid on the factory complex.

"She's okay, though," Keith said.

"Aye, that's comfort," Tay agreed, slewing his gaze moodily around toward Keith. "What have you got there?"

Keith turned to Holl, whose eyes began shining when he realized they had not come away empty handed. "It's yours, I think," he said. He extended the bundle in his hands to Holl.

"Asrai," Holl said, hardly daring to believe it. "That brave, heroic girl saw her chance and used it to free one of them, at least." He took the small armful from Keith, and tenderly raised the fold of blanket over his daughter's face.

"Waaaaaaaaaaaaaaaaahh!" The moment she was exposed, Asrai let out a tremendous wail of protest. It packed such force and volume that it knocked the three men backward in the truck seat.

"My God!" exclaimed the driver, putting a finger in his right ear and wiggling it to restore his hearing. "What lungs that kid has!"

"Like taking the cork out of a bottle," Keith said, with respect. Asrai took another deep breath and broke into sobs, all but vibrating the truck's metal panels with each outburst. "Wow. She was saving that all up. Probably for days."

Holl looked shaken. "It's good to have her back again, and normal," he said, though he sounded doubtful. He lifted his hands out from underneath her one by one. "And she's wet."

Keith started laughing, half from relief and half from the expression on Holl's face. The others joined in, Holl reluctantly at first, then with greater heart.

"I feel better," Tay said, heaving a deep sigh and settling back in the seat. "Dola's well, and shrewd as ever, though her mother won't be best pleased we missed bringing her home as well."

"We'll get her out," Keith promised. "Soon."

"To think she was so close to home as this," Holl marveled, dandling the baby until she stopped crying. "I can't wait to see Maura's face."

Maura vacillated between joy, relief and tears when her daughter was restored to her. She wept, but gladly, tears glistening in the corners of her smile. All the Little Folk were gathered in the main room of the house, crowding around her, Tay, Holl, and Keith clucking over the baby and the handful of photographs Keith was passing around.

"You're a hero," Maura told Keith gratefully, clasping Asrai in her arms. The baby was all coos and gurgles now that she was reunited with her mother. Maura refused to turn her loose even to let her be held by adoring aunties and uncles.

"I only get a small part of the credit," Keith insisted. "It was Frank's balloon and his driver that got us in and out of there, and I wouldn't have been able to grab her at all if Tay hadn't glued that security man in place when he did."

"We all did our part," Tay said, grinning as Maura leaned across the chuckling baby in her arms to kiss him on the cheek. "We're all heroes."

"And we owe a lot to our new friends," Keith finished.

"A marvel," the Elf Master said, turning the instant photographs over and over again. "To think we haf nefer suspected their existence. Although since you say they cannot descend to our stratum, nor we easily ascend to theirs, it vill be difficult to establish close relations."

"They have a way of making themselves heard," Keith assured him. "I'm going back up as soon as I can to learn more about them."

"We ought to have a celebration," announced Dunn.

"No," Maura said, moving to Siobhan and putting an arm around her waist. "Not until we are all together again."

"Oh, that girl," Siobhan said, dabbing at the corner of her eye with the edge of her apron. "She'll be thinking it's all an adventure, I am sure."

"It's her Progressive upbringing," Keva said, glaring.

"And there they werre, in the center o' that polluter's factory?" Curran demanded, his eyes almost glowing with anger. "Look at tother snaps Keith Doyle made. That wooman has much ta answer fer."

But first, Mona Gilbreth's representative had something to say for himself. The telephone call came almost on the heels of the triumphant return of the rescue party. The man on the other end of the line was angry.

"We were willing to cooperate and do this peacefully," he snarled. "Now you've ruined it."

Holl had answered the call. "How? By bringing home an infant who was too young to be away from her mother in the first instance?" he asked. "You were doing her more harm by not giving her back right away. We'd have forgiven."

The bass voice nearly leaped out of the phone. Holl held the receiver a distance from his ear. "Yeah?" the man growled irritably. "Well, you don't make the schedule around here. I do. Since you can't be trusted not to play tricks, we'll do things my way when I'm good and ready." The bang as the other end was hung up resounded from the kitchen walls.

"They can't keep us from getting Dola back," Keith said, slamming his fist into his open hand. "We know where she is now."

The Master shook his head. "If someone found something I sought to conceal, I vould move it as soon as I could. This call vas evidently their vay of informing us that vas vhat they are doing."

"Oh," Keith said. "Otherwise they would have said 'we give up, come and get her'?"

"An ofer-simplification, but essentially correct," the Master granted, leaning back in his lecturer pose with his belly stuck out. "Her location is vun of their trump cards in order to force us to do as they wish. Ours is that she must do nothing more to antagonize us, or be reported to the authorities. It is much easier to hold on to a stolen child than to clean up spilled liquid. But still it is a standoff."

"Ve ought to haf let a spy," Aylmer said. "He could haf said vhere they take her."

"We don't have to," Keith said, grin widening until it threatened to consume his ears. "We know how to trace her now. And we've got friends in high places." He pointed up.

When darkness came, Mona oversaw the packing of all Dola's borrowed goods into Jake's pickup truck. There were more things to go: food supplies, and gear for a live-in guard. She intended Pilton to keep an eye on Dola until things were settled with Uncle H. Doyle. They couldn't keep the child in the office anymore, not when their adversary had the organization to pull off successful, lightning-fast, and virtually undetectable incursions as he had.

Mona wondered if he had had commando training, or something like it.

They'd never find the child where Mona was sending her now. And Mona was glad. She had other things she needed to do. With almost a week wasted, her campaign was suffering. Her campaign manager had called to complain she wasn't giving him enough opportunities for public appearances. But how could she have left, when at any moment someone might discover two kidnaped children incarcerated in an unused office of her factory? What she was doing now, she thought, she should have done a week ago.

As before, the two men escorted the child to the truck cab, put her in the front seat, and sat on either side to box her in. Dola glanced up at them distastefully. Williamson turned on the engine and revved it a couple of times to help warm it up. Mona stepped up and leaned in the window.

"You know where to go," Mona said, making the question a statement.

Jake nodded silently, staring straight ahead with his hands on the wheel. Skinny stared at the boss-lady. Neither of them looked at Dola. She felt like an inanimate parcel once again. She thought of kicking up a fuss and rebelling just to get the attention a living being deserved, then looked around her at the three solemn faces. Better not.

"Make sure you're not followed. And take care she doesn't learn the route in," the boss-lady said enigmatically. "I don't want any more surprise raids." She turned away. Dola wrinkled her forehead, trying to puzzle out what the Big woman meant. It became evident when Jake took a handkerchief out of his pocket and folded it diagonally. They were going to blindfold her so she couldn't see where they were driving. As if she could have told her relatives where to look. As if she had needed to, if the Big Folk had only known.

The cloth between his hands came toward her, an awful parody of Dola's vision-making ritual, and she shrank away, revolted.

"C'mere, dammit!" he growled.

Skinny seized her from behind, pinioning her arms. She twisted her head wildly, refusing to give in. Swiftly, Jake shot out a hand and caught her by the jaw, pinching in her cheeks with one gigantic thumb and forefinger. He brought his big face close to hers.

"You knock it off, or I'll tie you to the bumper. Got it?"

Terrified, Dola froze. Making no further resistance, she let him tie the cloth around her eyes, which he did swiftly and efficiently. Pilton let her go, then she felt a heavy strap drop across and tighten in her lap. The truck started to move forward. She sat, meekly quiescent, her face burning where the cloth rubbed.

She wondered what horrors awaited her at the next stop. Were they going to lock her into a tank, as Skinny reported the boss-lady had threatened? Or worse, were they taking her to some Big Folk fastness from which she would never emerge? Tay had found her once. She hoped he could locate her wherever she was going, and carry her off home.

Dola wondered how her father and Holl had located her at all in the smelly factory. She had felt nothing outside the confines of the cold office building. It must be something that Keith Doyle had done. He had so nearly gotten her out of there! She almost ached with the knowledge that she could have been free, if she had been just seconds quicker in climbing out of the window.

The road changed from smooth to rough. Dola was jostled and thrown against the restraint of her seatbelt, unable to guard against the acute turns she couldn't see coming. Jake swore under his breath.

After an interminable and bumpy drive, the truck swerved sharply to the left and stopped. Someone lifted her down and set her on the ground next to the warm-smelling truck. Her blindfold was removed.

Smoothing down her mussed hair, Dola looked around. It smelled green and wet around her, a relief after the week she had spent in the confines of the dusty factory. They were deep in the woods, far away from any other lights than moon and stars. In the almost-full darkness, a black shadow loomed before her, one with an angular, peaked top: a house. The walls were made of rough-hewn logs, chinked with grey material that picked up what little light the quarter moon provided. Jake stepped under the eaves and became a bulky shadow as he fumbled with the key in the lock. The door opened, creaking, and he reached in to switch on the lights. He motioned Dola inside. She felt

Skinny's hand in the middle of her back, urging her forward. She went.

Dola could tell that Skinny was uncomfortable in these surroundings, but she was delighted by them. The place, though it was musty, had an honest scent to it, of wood, stone, water, and growing things. She walked around, touching things. A huge tile and flagstone fireplace was built into the center of one wall, which bulged out above the mantel to show the girth of the chimney. Over the hearth itself she saw a heavy hook meant for holding a pot, and an iron door in the chimney beyond which lay a shelf for baking bread. There was no other stove, so this was where the little house's intimates cooked their meals. Her supposition was borne out by the fact that a small refrigerator in the cabinet of a Welsh dresser was plugged into the wall next to the hearthstone. Iron pans and pots, and a few lighter ones made of aluminum, were inside the upper cabinet alongside an array of mismatched plates, cups, and utensils. Dola hoped she would be allowed to cook. Since moving to the farm, cooking over open flame without worrying about the library cleaning staff calling the fire department over the smoke had been great fun for all those culinarily inclined. The novelty had not yet worn off.

Leading off from the main room were three doors. Beyond the nearest was a bathroom not unlike the one attached to the office in which she had been living, but with a rusty, white-enameled bathtub to one side. The other two doors swung open into bedrooms. Between them, a queer little hatch concealed the broom cupboard, containing cleaning supplies, broom, mop, dustpan, and pail. She ran a finger across the top of the hatch. It came up black with dust. If the next day was fine, Dola resolved to clean out the house and freshen it up. The cabinet also featured a horizontal bar, presumably for hanging up clothes, the fusebox, and a couple of painted wheels the size of her hand. Jake shouldered past her and turned both wheels clockwise, then went into the bathroom and to the small sink alcove next to the Welsh dresser, where he turned all the taps on full. Tortured groaning sounds came from beneath the floor, and rusty water gushed into the basins.

The furniture in the main room consisted of an elderly couch with scratchy tweed covering; two battered end tables bearing lamps; a deep, padded armchair as old, she was sure, as the

Master; a rug made of an endless, multicolored spiral; and two spindly-backed wooden chairs. It was all ancient but solid. Dola examined it with the experienced eye of a craftworker's daughter. The furniture had been so well made that, with a change of upholstery, it would be good for another lifetime. The rug just needed a thorough cleaning.

Jake and Skinny watched her explore for a while, then went out to get her things. They didn't speak in front of Dola, exchanging gestures instead. Jake put a heavy box of foodstuffs down beside the fireplace. Skinny threw her sleeping bag into one of the rooms, and more bedding into the other. He had evidently been assigned to stay with her. To judge by his mutters and sour glances, he was unhappy about it.

Skinny went outside after Jake, and Dola heard them talking at last.

"How come we can't just let her go, Jake? It's not right to keep her away from her folks like this."

"Do you want to go back to prison?" Jake's hard voice demanded. "If you don't let the boss-lady handle things her way, you're back in for ten years, and to hell with parole. You want that?"

"No . . ." Skinny said. "But it still ain't right." Dola felt grateful that at least one of them thought that way. Then she wondered why he had been in prison. The men's footsteps trudged away from the cabin, and back again.

On his next trip in, Skinny dumped the carton containing her borrowed books and magazines and new craft supplies next to the end table. Jake, carrying the last load, nodded briefly to Skinny. He pulled a shotgun out of the box, broke it to check the load, snapped it together and handed it over to the thin man.

"I'll be back to check on you tomorrow," Jake said, pointedly not looking at Dola. Skinny nodded back. Jake walked out the door, closing it firmly behind him.

Dola looked uncomfortably at the gun. She'd never been so close to one in her life. It was chilling. That thing, meant only to take lives, had no aura except the cold radiation of steel. She wondered suddenly if she was ever intended to go home again. Was Jake leaving so he didn't witness her murder? Holding her breath warily, she watched the man study the gun.

As soon as the sounds of the departing truck died away,

Skinny chucked the shotgun into a corner of the couch, and Dola breathed again.

"No television, no telephone, no video games, nothing, and the store's ten miles away," Skinny complained, dropping into the armchair. Dust flew out of the cushions. He coughed. "Ain't that the pits?"

"I'll miss none of those things," Dola said truthfully. "What is this place?"

"Hunting cabin, belonged to Ms. Gilbreth's father," Skinny said, offhandedly. "She comes here herself sometimes. Dead shot with a deer rifle." He looked around, discontented. "Got nothing but the bare bones here. I don't like sleeping in strange places. Too many creepy noises."

"Oh, I like it," Dola said, looking around herself and assessing the possibilities of the place, too curious to be haughty. "It's nice here. No humming things."

"Brr," Pilton said. The water was now running clear. He shut off the taps. A wind, autumn-cool, swept in under the door, across his feet, and set up a whirlwind in a cloud of dust on the floor. "No insulation, neither. I like a place that has things all set up for comfort, not a lonely cabin out in the middle of nowhere." Rustling and squeaking erupted outside. Skinny spun on his heel. "What's that?" he hissed.

Sitting on the hearthrug, Dola listened, her sensitive hearing picking up more detail than he could distinguish. The rustling became the movement of wings, the squeaking the voices of animals. "There are birds nesting in the eaves." She pointed. "Up on that side."

"Right," Skinny said at once. "I knew that. Nothing to worry about, right?" His voice went up half an octave on the last word.

"It's nice here," Dola said, in a soothing voice. Listen to me, she thought. I'll be telling him stories next.

"Uh-huh. You ought to get ready for bed, you know." Skinny walked into the room he'd designated as hers. She followed and watched him flatten out the sleeping bag on the bare, striped mattress, and plump up the thin pillow. He rummaged in the brown paper bags until he found the night-light, and plugged it into the wall next to the bed. Its soft yellow glow warmed the honey maple floor. "That'll do you."

"It will," Dola said, watching him. She smiled slightly, feeling the calm night beyond the cabin walls raising her spirits. "But you can take the night-light away. I won't need it in such natural surroundings." He bent to pull the unit out and headed for the door. Dola called out after him. "And thank you," she said.

It was the first time she had said it to him, and Pilton was charmed. "No problem," he said. He paused, as if he was going to say something, then seemed to change his mind. "You and I're gonna get along just fine here. G'night."

"Good night," Dola said. An owl hooted beyond the walls. Skinny went white around the eyes, then caught himself, and threw her a sheepish grin. He shut the door behind him.

In the middle of the night, Dola got up to go to the bathroom. When she passed Skinny's room, the glow of the night-light shone out from underneath his door.

Chapter
TWELVE

M ona Gilbreth, in full power suit, strode into the
PDQ offices with her head high, feeling as if the
beams of the brilliant Chicago sun were shining
just for her. People had paused on the street when
they saw her, standing back just a little in awe, the way they
would in the presence of a celebrity. She was *known*, and it made
her feel wonderful.

The taping at the television station had gone very well. The
television interviewer had been deferential, and stood strongly
behind all female candidates no matter what their affiliations.
The fact that she was a native daughter of Illinois made him
stress the fact that his state was sending more women to Washington this year than any other. Her campaign manager was delighted with the tape, which could raise her standing in the polls
still higher. Her rating was already at an all-time high. Not bad
for a campaign run strictly on the cheap. The station had given
her a high-quality copy of the interview. There were a few sound
bites in it that would make good ads.

Donations were still not pouring in, the curse of all smaller
candidates in a tough economic year. Her manager had hinted
that she should throw in more personal money to cover the bills
that were piling up. She pretended not to understand, and he let
the subject drop, saying that the creditors would undoubtedly
wait until after the election, especially if it was successful. Mona
knew he had hopes of becoming her aide in Washington—and

why not? He was a good organizer, great with people. He could get blood out of a stone, which it sounded like he was having to. He was definitely earning his place on her staff.

The telephone call from Jake the night before had reported that the child was giving no trouble, for which Mona was grateful. She was going to have to let the girl go sooner or later, but not until she elicited a promise from H. Doyle to let her alone in his turn. She sighed. Money would be nice, too. All that could be dealt with when she went home.

Paul Meier met her in the gray marble lobby, and escorted her personally up to the conference room. Mona looked down her nose at the hawk-faced man, then granted him a gracious smile. In the elevator, he complimented her on her suit, her hair, and her shoes, picking with unerring instinct the three items in which she had taken the most professional pride that morning. No question, he was good at his job. Whether or not the performance was put on, it still made her relax and feel expansive.

"We want to show you the spread of where your campaign ads are being placed," Paul said, walking beside her. "I've got a complete timetable, stations, programs, the works. We'd like to do more, but we've done the best we can with the budget."

Another hint for money. Mona, groaning inwardly, carefully put him off. "For now, let's do what we can with what's already on the table," she said, smiling sweetly. "Maybe around election time I'll authorize more."

"Maybe," Paul said practically, "but then you're competing for air time with the big boys and girls. No offense, but this is a presidential election year, too. Early name recognition can save you big bucks later. You don't want to be just one of the names in the pack."

"I'm depending on you to make me stand out," Mona said, confidently, and passed through the door he held open. She stopped in midstep, staring in shock.

Keith, rising as the guest arrived, stared. Mona Gilbreth stood in the doorway, gaping at him like a rabbit caught in a car's headlights. He probably looked as surprised as she did. Mentally, he cudgeled himself for forgetting that when he'd interviewed her she *had* said something about coming in this Monday. He'd even mentioned it himself when he left Gilbreth. He felt like an idiot. She wouldn't see him as an ally anymore, not after the last time she'd seen him, staring at her through a broken factory window, stealing back an elf baby.

On the tip of his tongue was a demand that she tell him where Dola was, and why she had kidnaped the children in the first place, but he quashed the impulse at once. He needed urgently to get her aside to talk.

"My latest crop of interns," Paul was saying, swinging a hand toward them. The supervisor pulled out the chair at the head of the table for his guest. She remained standing, so he moved away from her side to the foot. "Four of the brightest young minds ever to set foot in PDQ. I'd like to keep them on deck during our discussion, if you don't mind. Dorothy Scott, Brendan Martwick, Sean Lopez, and Keith Doyle." Each of the students nodded in turn.

"How do you do?" Ms. Gilbreth said, her voice weak at first but quickly recovered. "So you're Paul's next creative team?"

"They've been reviewing your accounts, Ms. Gilbreth," Paul said. "They've been eager to meet you. The rest of your team will be here in a moment. We're planning to cover both of your campaigns this morning, the political and the commercial. We shouldn't waste an opportunity while you're up here in our neck of the woods. Can I offer you coffee? Pastries?"

"Why, yes," Mona said. She was careful not to look back at Keith. "That would be lovely."

"I'll go," Keith volunteered at once. Paul nodded at him, and he shot out the door toward the cafeteria.

Thankful that Keith had removed himself, Mona took a few deep breaths. She had known he was connected not only with Hollow Tree Farm but with PDQ. Why had seeing him here struck her so hard? She ordered her pounding heart to slow down. The boy was not likely to blurt out in the middle of a meeting that she had kidnaped his young cousin, or whatever relation the girl was to him, and that she'd demanded money for her safe return. Or was he? Mona couldn't guess how he had figured out the child was concealed there. Was he working with the police? Had there been a tap on the phone line? Perhaps he had observed some trace of the children while he was visiting the factory, and arranged for the raid three days later. The thought made her uncomfortable. She realized that Paul and the young people were

staring at her. Mona shook off the uneasy sensation and, with
the air of a practiced stumper, set about getting to know the other
students.

It was more for practice than anything else, since none of the
young people lived in her constituency. Dorothy sat at the table
glancing up at her, and going back to her sketchpad, drawing
something. Mona watched for a moment as Dorothy swept long,
undefined lines onto the paper that suddenly took on the appearance of a handsome minimalist portrait, and began to add detail. Mona met her eyes and smiled. The black woman smiled
back, and opened her lips tentatively, as if she was about to
speak, but nothing came out. Mona smiled again, nodding.
Abandoning Dorothy for more interesting prospects, Mona
moved on to the two young men, who were still on their feet
beside their chairs.

"It's such a pleasure to meet you, Ms. Gilbreth," Brendan
Martwick said, enveloping her hand in both of his and pumping
it once as he looked deeply into her eyes. His own were a
compelling intense blue, something she always found attractive.
"I've been studying your product line, and I think we have
something new to say about fertilizer."

There was a muffled snicker from the girl at the table, and
Mona turned her back on her more firmly. She resented anyone
making fun of her product. It was hard enough to be taken
seriously by the people who actually bought it. "I'm looking
forward to it."

"Sean Lopez," the other youth introduced himself. His handshake was jerky and awkward, but his smile was more brilliant
even than Martwick's. She was struck by how handsome he was,
like a young Tyrone Power. "My grandfather is a wheat farmer
outside of Springfield. He uses your products."

"I'm very happy to hear that," Mona said. "I'd like to hear
more, but will you just excuse me a moment?" She parted
from her two admirers and took Meier aside. "That boy. Keith
Doyle."

Meier's forehead wrinkled. "Something wrong with him? I
know you met him last week."

"If you don't mind, Paul, I don't want him in here with us."

"Eh?" Paul asked, puzzled. "Keith is very creative. He's a

fine student, and has a real knack for ideation. He could be a real boon to this session."

"He looks . . . well," Mona struggled for an excuse, "like he might . . . vote Republican, if you know what I mean."

"You're the boss," Meier said, with a shrug.

Brendan Martwick came over to show her a handful of oversized art cards. She glimpsed the black-framed storyboard format on at least one of them. "Ms. Gilbreth, while we're waiting, perhaps we can show you some of the ideas we've been working on."

Meier, allowing Brendan a chance to prove himself, backed off a short distance. Mona smiled at Brendan as he turned over each card and looked up, seeking her approval. She liked the attentive attitude of this young man, and his dashing blue eyes.

"I know it's irregular to have input from college interns, but consider," Brendan said persuasively, "just consider the image of associating yourself with America the Beautiful. 'O Beautiful for spacious skies, for amber waves of grain,' your image appears, and then music under the ad copy, then the plug, 'Gilbreth Feed and Fertilizer, for a healthy future.' Wholesome, environmental, and appealing to patriotism, too. Can you picture it?"

Mona experienced a sense of exaltation. "Yes!" she said. "That's good! That's exactly the image I want. Did you come up with that? What a talented young man you are."

Brendan glanced back at the table to see if any of the others could overhear him. "Thank you, ma'am," he said, begging the question of whose idea it had been. "I thought you'd like it."

"Oh, I do. I like the idea of associating Gilbreth Feed with America the Beautiful." Mona looked at him, and wondered if she could consider him an ally. "In fact, I'd say you have a future in this business."

"I hope so," Brendan said sincerely. "PDQ is giving me a chance to prove myself. I hope I can."

"I've been a client for a long time," Mona informed him. "I know how the program works. Have you any idea whether you're being favored for the job offer?"

Brendan glanced over his shoulder at the young woman at the table, then at the door. Mona guessed that either Dorothy Scott or the young Doyle stood ahead of him. "As much as anyone," he answered at last.

"Well, the word of a client does have some weight around here," Mona said. "If I liked your work I could insist that you be the one given the job."

Brendan smiled, giving her that intense stare. "I'd be glad to put in extra time to please such an attractive client, ma'am."

"I'm sure you'd enjoy the work," Mona said. "That young man who left . . ."

"Keith?" Brendan asked. He glanced over his shoulder again to make sure no one had heard the surprised exclamation.

"Yes, Keith. You think he's a little ahead of you in the running?"

"Well, I wouldn't say that," Brendan demurred.

"If you helped me, I could see him removed entirely from the race."

"With pleasure," Brendan said, in a low voice, but never losing his edge of smooth persuasiveness. "He hasn't got his mind on his job right now, and I have no idea why. You know," he added conversationally, "there's no place for a scatterbrain in this business. The more on the ball we are, the better it is for you, our client."

Mona let Brendan babble on. Reminded of the child shut up in her summer cabin, Keith's 'niece', Mona felt a twinge of guilt but pushed it down again. She was here to help create a presence for her product and herself, but mostly herself, and to protect herself from Keith and his cronies at Hollow Tree Farm. The campaign was too important to let even worried environmentalists cause her grief. And money was becoming more scarce.

"I want this ad campaign to increase business," Mona insisted out loud, for the benefit of Paul and the others. "I'll be in favor of whatever it takes to raise my receivables."

"How's the bottom line been?" a man asked, coming into the room, and shaking hands with Mona. She remembered that his name was Benjamin Solanson, and he was her account executive. He'd clearly heard her last statement. "Will you be able to increase your budget slightly this season?" he asked. "The prices for all kinds of ads are going up, and television commercials are going off the scale. In an election year we have to compete for production house time. We could get better saturation of your voter spread with, say, fifteen thousand dollars more in the kitty."

Mona's heart sank. Not more talk about money, not when she was worrying about whether she was going to be hauled away to jail in the next half hour. Young Doyle had been gone a long time. Was he getting the police? Her worry must have shown on her face.

"Ssst, sst, sst," Paul said, with a concerned glance at her. He made damping down gestures. "Tact, Benjamin."

Solanson smiled his apology for being tactless. He pulled out Mona's chair for her. "Sorry," he said diplomatically. "I always want to do more. I forget not everyone shares my enthusiasm."

The door burst open, and Keith came in, a cardboard tray laden with small cakes and coffee cups balanced between his hands. There was a solid metal coffeepot hooked over his wrist. Gingerly, he set the bottom of the pot down on the table and worked his arm free without jostling the cups. "Sorry for the delay. We were out of doughnuts, so I ran down to the bakery." He started to approach Mona to offer her some, but Paul gestured to him to put the pastries on the table and to sit down. Keith complied promptly, and plunked into the only empty chair at the table, which lay at the end farthest from Mona. She was relieved that he hadn't come back with the police, but he'd attempted to get close to her, and that worried her.

"Very nice. Everyone help themselves. All right," Paul said, after a woman and another man had arrived and taken their places at the table. "We're all here. Mona Gilbreth, you know Suzy Lovett, our staff artist, and Jacob Fish, who's on your creative team." Mona nodded to them, and Meier beamed. "Ms. Gilbreth, it's getting crowded in here. Would it be all right with you to keep one of my students around? Teach them how it's done? They'll understand if you need your space."

It was a tactful lie. There was still plenty of room, but he was giving her an out to avoid having Keith present. The interns looked dejected but resigned.

"Well, I don't mind one. A single observer won't crowd things too much," Mona said, and the students brightened, each hoping to be chosen. "After all, voters are voters." She smiled at them, her gaze lingering longest on Martwick, who gave her an enthusiastic grin and nod. Meier didn't miss the silent exchange.

"Okay, Brendan, you stay." Keith goggled, and raised his

hand. "Nope. Room for only one. Everyone else, I've got assignments for you, too. Dorothy, you go help Ken Raito in Art with the prelim sketches on that first Judge Yeast layout. Sean, they're doing studio shots for Dunbar Tyres. I meant to tell you, they loved 'the Brain.' They want to talk to you." Meier nodded to Lopez, who looked suddenly jubilant, his big, dark eyes glowing. "Keith, Becky Sarter's going to be here pretty soon for a meeting. She especially requested you be in on the meeting. Go and wait in the lobby for her, will you?"

"Sure, Paul," the redhaired youth said, rising. He smiled at the table. The other two young people rose and followed him out. Mona let out a breath of pure relief when the door closed behind them.

Keith trotted down the hall toward the lobby, his head whirling. There was no point in lingering if Mona Gilbreth didn't want him there, but he wished he had some way to change her mind. He had sensed conspiracy when Paul suddenly sent the other interns away. Well, she had no reason to welcome his presence. He knew too much, and she didn't know what he was planning to do with his knowledge. Keith wasn't sure if he would trust himself if he was in Ms. Gilbreth's position. He was capable of embarrassing her, or worse.

All the way to the bakery and back, he had been trying to think how to approach her about Dola. He felt a little ashamed of himself for the subterfuge he'd used to get into the Gilbreth factory to get information on hidden scandals, but more ashamed that he had missed the most important thing there, the children, until the sprites had led him back. Now that he knew Gilbreth's secret, and she knew he knew, she was afraid of him. He didn't blame her, but he had to make her see reason. If she would let him act as an intermediary, maybe he could get her to release Dola in exchange for some consideration from the elves. She had let some man do the talking for her over the phone. The terms she had demanded through him were outrageous. Some middle ground had to be reached, and soon.

It was a good thing the baby had been returned to her mother. He'd seen how the elves were aroused when one of their own was threatened, and feared that delays on her part would only provoke a more serious response from them. Dola, if she wasn't in any real danger, could take care of herself pretty well. As her mother had said, it was possible the girl was even finding her captivity to be merely an adventure and an inconvenience, not life threatening.

He'd had a call from Frank, saying that the air sprites had gotten onto him while he was giving rides in the Skyship Iris. He'd gotten images that showed they'd found Dola's new hiding place. It had been too rough to balloon since, so the sprites were keeping an eye on her until he could get someone from the farm up there with him to track down the location.

"I guess this is what they meant in the song 'Someone to Watch Over Me,' " Keith had said impishly. Even if her family didn't know exactly where she was, Dola remained safe and well.

He wondered if the woman had any idea of the truth about Dola and her folk, and if she planned to expose them to the world. Keith swallowed. Having to hide ninety elves while he found them a new, safer haven, while being under observation himself, would be really tough.

Passing the receptionist's desk and noticing the interoffice mail on the ledge, Keith thought of sending a courier envelope in to Ms. Gilbreth during the meeting, asking to rendezvous later. But she'd probably show it to Paul, who would misunderstand, which would get Keith bounced out of the program.

The team was planning to talk to Gilbreth until 12:30, when they would take her to lunch. Keith saw that as his last window of opportunity to take her aside before she went away again. In the meantime, Paul had given him an assignment, and he didn't want to do anything else that would jeopardize his internship.

He had fun with Becky Sarter, who dressed in sloppy sweats but had a sharp mind and a cheerful disposition, a refreshing change from the business-suited executives who came to PDQ to be amused by their willing servants in the creative department. Becky, as she asked them to call her, had no unreasonable expectations, and got a visible kick out of humor and genuine creativity. The executive on her account sat back and listened most of the time, stepping in to interject current market data that she didn't have, and to make Keith go back to analyze the ads he had designed for the demographic range. They talked about limited markets and the frequencies of the ads needed to approach each of them. Keith learned a lot, and came back to the main conference room in a good mood. As he reached for the handle, the door was flung open, and Mona Gilbreth emerged. She met his eyes with panicked startlement, then turned away and headed down the hall, Meier and Brendan Martwick tagging behind her like puppies.

"I think the 'amber waves of grain' approach is very good," Ms. Gilbreth was saying. "Very clever of you to use it for the company ads, and then my November campaign spots. The tape brought together all the images I cherish about my company. *Very* good."

"They'll associate your good business values and integrity with your run for the House," Brendan said, almost gushing. "It's a natural. America the Beautiful, and Mona Gilbreth." Mona glowed, and Brendan looked very pleased with himself.

"Hey, that was my slogan," Keith said, standing in the doorway.

"It could mean real percentage points in the polls," the tall blond man walking with them said warmly. None of them appeared to have heard Keith. Heralded by its bell, the elevator arrived, and all of them piled into the car behind Ms. Gilbreth. The door slid shut.

"Brown-nosers," Keith muttered, giving up and turning back to the conference room.

"Don't you be talking down on brown noses," Dorothy said, pointing her own nose at the ceiling, with a disapproving eye on Keith.

"I'm sorry," he said, sighing. He slumped into a chair. "I didn't mean the kind you can smell with. I mean the kind Brendan has that's always stuck up someone's rear end." He glanced significantly toward the door, and Dorothy shook her head, smiling slyly.

She put down her pencil, and got up to close the door, after looking down the hall to either side. Keith watched her, curious.

"I don't want anyone to hear this," she said, coming back and sitting down close to Keith. "You've got trouble coming. That Gilbreth woman has something against you. I saw her conspiring with Brendan. He's up to something. What did you do to that woman?"

"It's nothing personal, honest," Keith said. "Purely . . . environmental."

"Uh-huh. You watch out for Brendan, you hear me?" the young woman warned. "He's a rat at heart, and now he's just been given a free-lance assignment to do what he'd like best, which is to bounce his competition out of this program."

Keith nodded. "Thanks, Dorothy, I'll be ready. I owe you."

"No way. We're partners," She gave him a thumbs up. "Judge Yeast, remember? And when are we going to work on that big ad spread that Paul wants us to come up with?"

Keith grinned. "How about now?"

"Good! I've got some ideas that beat your old ones hollow. What do you think of that?" Dorothy said, challenging him with her pencil raised like a rapier.

"Bring 'em on," Keith said with delight. "We'll see about that."

Refreshed from a good meeting, Keith felt his creative juices flowing. In no time, they had the beginnings of another good layout roughed out. Keith watched over her shoulder, and started to snicker at her final drawing.

"What's the matter with you?" she asked.

"If you put a loaf of French bread in that position, with that slogan, they won't be able to air this commercial before nine P.M. on weeknights," Keith said, composing his face with difficulty. Dorothy looked from him to her sketch, and laughed sheepishly.

"I just don't think in those terms," she said, her cheeks glowing. She swatted his hand with her art gum eraser. "All right, Einstein, what other kind of bread might be right for 'Getting off lightly'?"

"Brioches, maybe, or a regular loaf with a big round dome on the top. We'll make it bounce lightly across the screen, instead of lifting off at an angle."

When Brendan returned to the conference room, he had an angelic smile on his face. Keith and Dorothy glanced up at him, then went back to their work. He came around the table and sat down across from them.

"Nice. Have good meetings?" he asked them.

"Hot," Dorothy said. "They love me in Art."

"I was thinking about you during mine, Brendan," Keith said, deliberately taunting. "We were talking about desiccated prunes."

The other young man flushed. "You were all over our discussion, too, Keith. The subject was fertilizer."

"Oh, yeah," Keith said, nodding knowingly, one red brow lifted slightly. "The kind that feeds amber waves of grain."

"Hey," Brendan said, alarmed at the covert accusation of plagiarism, "we're supposed to be a team, right? Weren't you the one pushing for creative fission?"

"*I* give credit for ideas other people come up with."

"What's that about fission?" Sean asked, coming in and dropping into the chair at the end of the table. His notebook had loose pages hanging out at angles. He looked exhausted but happy.

"Keith's fishin' for a compliment," Dorothy said, with a wink. "Gilbreth liked one of his lines. Brendan sold it to her."

"Hey, pretty good, you two," Sean said encouragingly. "This is what the business should be like, huh?"

Paul appeared in the doorway and clapped his hands together like thunder. "Well, boys and girls, it's been a hell of a day, hasn't it? You've all done very well, and I'm proud of you. I'm gonna let you go early so I can go home and collapse, too. All right? Let's clean up, and free up the room."

While the others gathered their papers and cups from the table, Dorothy showed Paul the layout she and Keith had worked up.

"Good," he said, nodding. "Consistent. Marketable. Keeps the same idea in mind. As long as you make the punch line short, people will remember it." He handed it back with an encouraging smile. "Send it over to Bob, and let's see what he thinks, all right?"

"Sure, Paul," Dorothy said, then added shyly, "I think I'm getting the hang of this."

"I know you are," Paul said. "Good job. Send it over. I'm sure Bob will think the same as I do."

Keith slewed a glance over at Brendan. "No problem, Paul. I'll put it in interoffice mail at the desk."

Keith was lucidly aware of Brendan's eyes on his back as he picked up his drawings and layouts. They followed him to the file cabinet where each of them had a drawer for keeping things.

in the office. Paul had the master key, but the drawers were left open most of the day for easy access. Keith figured Brendan would strike at that first. He wasn't worried. There was little about physical practical jokes he didn't know, having had dozens played upon him in the dorm. He stuffed his notebook and papers into the drawer at the usual haphazard angles. Under cover of the rest, he crumpled one of them into a ball at the bottom of the drawer, putting his will into it, giving the fibers more strength, and *enhancing* the shape of the piece of paper, square and flat. Leaving the crushed paper concealed, he hastily slid the drawer shut.

"'Night, Paul. 'Night, Dorothy. I'll drop this at the desk for Bob." Keith left the room with a cheery farewell wave to the others, and whistled a little tune as he walked down the hall to the elevator.

He wished he could be there to enjoy the results when Brendan pulled the drawer open.

Chapter
THIRTEEN

Though he was impatient to know how the search was going, Keith waited until he got home that evening before calling the farm. Calla, Holl's mother, picked up the phone.

"They've moved her far away," Calla said, in answer to Keith's question, "but your friends are on the trail. The Big One and the Small Ones of the Air have sniffed out a hiding place they think to be hers."

"That's great!" Keith exclaimed.

"Aye. Holl and my great-grandson have gone out with them to see if the sighting was a true one."

"I can't believe Tay got back into a balloon on purpose," Keith said, laughing out loud. His brother and sister, watching television at the other end of the room, glanced back to see what was so funny, then went back to their program.

"Believe," Calla said, answering his chuckle with one of her own. "Love conquers even the greatest of fears. And did it not, he would still never dare to show the white feather. The Master has gone with them."

"You're kidding!"

She gave her warm laugh again. "No indeed. I wish I were a bird in the sky, to see what it is like."

"There'd be a flock of us up there," Keith said. "Keep me posted. I want to hear the moment they bring Dola home. And I've got to hear all about the Master in a balloon."

"I promise you, Keith Doyle," Calla said. "You shall."

174

* * *

"Your laconic discourse does nothing to enhance understanding," the Master said, disapprovingly. "Please try to use complete sentences. Ve haf plenty of time until the vind calms down and your craft may lift."

Frank took a deep breath and tried again to explain. Holl, leaning up against the balloon basket with his pipe between his teeth, exchanged sympathetic glances with Tay, and pushed the bill of his Cubs cap down over his eyes to hide his expression. Shaking his head, Tay copied his gesture. "Keith's air sprites came this morning while I was giving rides. Scared hell out of my passengers. They zoomed around like fireflies."

"The passengers?" the Master asked, peering at Frank over his glasses. For all that his inquisitor, fedora hat and all, came up no higher than his middle shirt button, Frank Winslow seemed to be thoroughly intimidated.

"N-no, the air sprites. They made pictures at me."

"Their means of communication, Master," Holl put in. "They can project images into your mind's eye."

"I see."

"Pretty but confusing," Winslow added. "Two pictures over and over again, one of that little blond girl in the dark in front of a—a striped house, and another where she was walking on a leash."

"Around her neck? Like a dog?" Tay asked, his face darkening.

Frank thought about it. "No, like a toddler." He sketched a body harness on his own frame with his hands.

"That gifs me a gut picture of her situation," the Master said. "And they vill help us to find the house vith stripes?"

The balloon pilot made an impatient gesture at the sky. "Yeah, if this wind ever dies down." The nearby treetops were leaning slightly to the northeast, and their uppermost twigs, whistling and crackling, swayed in an impatient dance.

At a small helium tank in the rear of the pickup truck, Frank filled a rubber balloon, tied it off, and let it go. It sped upward and out of sight into the eastern sky. There were already streaks of color at the horizon, reminding them that night was little more than an hour away. Frank watched it carefully, and shook his head. Holl tapped out his pipe and put it away.

"Pity we can't whistle down the wind, as Keith Doyle is always suggesting we can," Holl said, with a twinkle in his eye. Frank looked at him. "Oh, you've not been listening to his stories, have you?" Holl asked. "Do you think I can stick my fingers in my mouth like this," he put thumb and forefinger in his mouth and blew a piercing blast, "and the wind will die down as I will it to?"

At that moment, the treetops on the perimeter of the field straightened up and the swaying came to a standstill, their slight noise dying away. Frank turned to look at Holl, who returned his stare indignantly.

"Coincidence," he said. "Oh, come now, it was about to happen."

"Circus stunt," Murphy scoffed. "I saw the trees on the west calming down half a second before he did it."

"Uh-*huh*," Frank said, his eyes still on Holl. The other elves looked amused. He swallowed hard. "We better get moving, then." He and Murphy moved to pull the bag containing the balloon out of the truck bed.

"How may ve help you?" the Master asked.

Following the instructions of the humans, the Little Folk helped spread out the Iris's balloon, and helped raise its mouth to face the fan while Murphy and Frank fastened the steel loops of the cables to the burner assembly. Swiftly, the great rainbow filled out. Tay, the Master, and Holl helped hold it in place until the fan was replaced by the burners, and the balloon rose off the ground of its own accord.

"Sure are strong for midgets." Murphy offered a grudging compliment. Tay grinned.

"You should run away and join us at the circus," he shouted over the burners. "We've a place for giants like you."

Frank climbed into the basket and Murphy helped flip it upright. "Hop in!" Frank yelled. "She's ready to go!"

Tay and Holl hopped over the edge, and held out their hands to the Master. Murphy held on to the woven belt threaded through the basket, keeping it down until the little man was aboard.

Murphy let go, and the Skyship Iris once again performed her magic, as the earth dropped effortlessly and soundlessly away, and the trees came forward to meet them.

"Murphy thought you were from the circus," Frank said as

soon as they were aloft. "How come he didn't know what you are?"

"People see vhat they believe they see," the Master said. "He believes us to be vun thing, so for him that is vhat ve are. You see us as another thing, but efen you do not truly know."

"You must not be very much help at home," Dola complained to Skinny. He had spent nearly the whole of the first day, and half the second, reading magazines flat on his back on the old couch while Dola had cleaned around him. She decided she was not going to do all the work and leave him to sit about like an invalid.

"It's just gonna get dirty again," Skinny said, glancing around him. He pointed at the bottom of the door, which hung a thumb's breadth too high in its frame. "The wind comes right through here."

"Well, I can't live waiting for the dust to settle. Will you not help?"

Skinny seemed surprised she'd asked. "I thought you brownie things got all bent out of shape if anyone helped you with the housework," he said.

Dola put her hands on her hips. "I've told you, I'm a natural creature, not a fantastic thing like a brownie."

"Uh-huh, sure." Skinny went back to his magazine.

"Ugh!" Dola exclaimed, throwing up her hands. "I can't take the time to explain things over and over to you."

"Why not?" Skinny abruptly let loose all of the resentment he had saved up. His face turned red, and he waved his arms, advancing on her in fury. "We got nothing *but* time! All my days off, and I've gotta stay nights here, too! And then I'm stuck with a gal who yells more than my wife does. Go ahead, tell me again!"

Dola, big-eyed, dropped her broom and shrank back from Skinny. It was this new side of him Jake appealed to when he handed over the shotgun. She was reminded all over again that Big Folk were dangerous, and though he seemed as much a playful buffoon as Keith Doyle, Skinny was a stranger. She withdrew a half-step at a time toward her sleeping room, wondering if the iron lock on the door was enough to hold him off while she spelled the wood closed.

Skinny's fearsome mood ended as quickly as it had begun when he realized he'd frightened her. He extended a hand to her. "I'm sorry, little girl. I didn't mean to blow up at you. It . . . this is all wrong, I know it."

Dola nodded, not touching him, not prepared to trust him again so soon. She fought to regain her former confidence, but it sounded in her own ears like bravado. "All right, then," she said, looking up at him. "We're both shut up against our will. We will make the best of it, shall we?"

Skinny nodded slowly. He looked sidelong at her as if asking permission, then went back to the couch and picked up his magazine. She didn't protest. He sat down. Dola picked up the broom and went back to sweeping dust out of the corners. It was less trouble to work alone than to set off the Big One's unchancy temper, but she still resented his laziness.

Once the floor was reasonably clean, Dola sat down on the hearthrug with a frayed pillow slip taken from the store of tattered bed linens in the bedroom dresser. It was useless, having been washed and used until it was threadbare as gauze. But it would do to make light strips of the kind the Folk used at home, to supplement the sad light bulbs in the elderly lamps. She cut a small slit in the hem with her belt knife, gathered the edges in both hands, and tore.

Skinny's head popped up again. "What are you doing with that?" He leaned over the back of the couch and yanked the cloth out of her hands.

"Making a cleaning rag," Dola said reasonably. "This place is a terrible mess. Won't your boss-lady be pleased if it's in better order next time she comes?"

"I guess." Skinny tossed the cloth back at her. "All right. I'm being jumpy. You just scared heck out of me."

As long as he left her alone, she used the quiet time to concentrate on finding her folk in the great distance. The ride, two nights before, had taken so many twists and curves that she was all disoriented. Her mind swept slowly in a great arc, seeking and touching, until she found them. Strong as a beacon, the reassuring presence of the Folk reached out to her and gave her confidence. She wondered what it was that had stood between her and them before, and if they could see her now.

Now that she had a vector to follow, she might start out any time to find her way away from this place. But only the birds and cartographers knew what stood in the way between here and home. She'd bide her time until she knew more about the land in between. All the necessities were here for her comfort. The moment she was ready, she'd vanish. There wasn't enough metal in these walls to harm her. They were only wood, and felt so weak in some spots that she thought she could kick through with her bare foot. When she meant to escape, it would be no trouble.

In the depths of the old couch, Dola heard the rustle and sigh, as Skinny finished his magazine and put it down. She addressed him, pitching her voice so it was impossible for him to ignore her.

"Do you know why it is the boss-lady is keeping me here? I am sure she doesn't want me."

"Dunno," Skinny said. "I think it has something to do with Ms. Gilbreth running for election." He clapped his hand over his mouth.

"Oh, I already know her name," Dola said easily. "I know a lot about her. But why would anyone vote for her?"

"Well, 'cause she's for all the right things. Education. The environment. Farmers' rights."

"But it is only sensible to be for these things," Dola said. "Isn't her opponent in favor of them, too?"

"No," Skinny said, then added by way of amendment, "Well, he says he is, but he's lying."

"And how do you know that the boss-lady is not also lying?"

That flustered him. " 'Cause I work for her. I know she's for those things. She says so all the time."

"Saying is not doing," Dola said, thinking of the nasty-smelling sludge that had come out of the truck that took her away from Hollow Tree Farm. It was the same filth that the water-workers were complaining had to be cleaned out of the aquifer. It was proof that Gilbreth employees were the ones dumping, if only she could go home to tell the Master. "It does sound as if there is not much to choose between the candidates."

"You don't know about politics," Skinny said, but he didn't sound sure, either. He fell silent, staring at the window. Dola followed his eyes.

"It's a fine day. What about taking a walk in the woods?"

"No way," Pilton said, uneasily. "You'd just jump into a tree somewhere, and I'd never find you."

"Oh, would you stop?" Dola asked, exasperated. "I live neither in trees nor in little burrows under rocks. Walking's all I wish. Fresh air, and maybe some herbs for the cooking. We must eat, and I'd rather it be flavored with something other than the dusty preparations in those boxes." She shrugged toward the food supplies. "Unless you plan to cook."

"Uh-uh. I'm not so good at cooking. Usually my wife cooks."

"Never fear," Dola told him. "I will continue to make the meals. In exchange, you wash the dishes."

He eyed her. "Who's getting the short end of that deal, huh?"

"You needn't eat your own cooking. Isn't that worth a little trouble?" Dola asked.

Skinny stood up and stretched. "Oh, all right. It's better than being cooped up in here all day."

Dola went to the door to wait. Instead of following her, Skinny started looking around. His eye lit on the length of twine used to hold the food box shut. He lifted it, and yanked it between his hands to test its strength.

"And what is that for?" Dola asked, warily.

"For you," Skinny said. "I can't trust you. Jake and the boss-lady will be down my throat if I let you get away. Hold your arms out from your sides."

Patiently, Dola held up her arms and stood while Skinny tied a loop of rope around her waist. He took the free end in one hand and unlocked the door.

"*Now* we'll go."

It was well worth the inconvenience to get away from the musty-smelling cabin and into the fresh air. As soon as she was out from under the roof, she felt outward with all her strength for a sense of her family, hoping that her father and Holl would be able to trace her there.

She sensed nothing. Instead, she returned her attention to the world around her. The forest, rich with the rain that had fallen overnight, smelled green and healthy. Dola inhaled breath after breath, enjoying the fresh air.

Skinny stumped along behind her on the narrow dirt path, tugging on her tether from time to time as if to keep her in check.

After one annoyed glance over her shoulder to show him what she thought of such treatment, he stopped pulling back so hard. She needed her balance to keep from tripping over roots that rose up suddenly in the way. Her guess that it was a deerpath was confirmed when she spotted the narrow double-slotted hoofprints in the rain-softened earth.

And now to the question of herbs. The men had brought enough food with them to feed the village for two days. She had cooked something out of a box the night before, after choosing which one smelled the least antiquated. All the Big Folk packaged goods seemed as if they were years old. Nothing could make generic macaroni and cheese or dehydrated beans and sauce *delicious*. If she added something fresh, it at least might make them palatable. She spotted a handful of wild mustard growing in the midst of a rough patch of ground. She started toward it, thoughts of cooked greens and spice making her mouth water. She was jerked back harshly, and uttered a wordless protest.

"Where are you going?" Skinny demanded, as she straightened up with the help of a tree branch.

"Only to pick herbs," she said. "Look there."

"Weeds?" he asked scornfully.

"No, food! Look about you! Tender young dandelion greens, a few late fiddlehead ferns, a few early mushrooms here and there. It's a cornucopia of good things to eat, all fresh and all free."

"Well," Pilton thought about it, "if you want to eat them, I guess you can. Maybe your diet's different than mine."

"Healthier, I'm sure," Dola said, ironically. With Skinny in close attendance, holding her leash tightly, she picked a huge elephant-ear leaf and began to fill it with young plants. She dropped to her knees beside the lushest bed of plants and began to tell them over. The quick-growing mustard was in all three stages: green, flowering, and past gone to seed. Some was even young enough to yield the tender greens that were the tastiest. Judging Skinny's appetite to be three times hers, she picked enough to feed them both.

None of the oldest mustard plants had any seed left. All the pods were dried to brown husks and split open. Well, that wouldn't stop the cooks at home who wanted mustard to cook with, and she had the skills to follow their example. She glanced behind her to see what Skinny was doing. He looked down at her from time to time, but he was bored, and was paying little attention to what she was doing. All the better, she thought.

With a little smile, she put two fingers on either side of the nearest sulphur-colored blossom and pulled at it, *enhancing* the growth process. Behind the blossom, which began to wilt, the seed pod lengthened into a tube of green as long as her finger and as thick as a pencil lead. It filled out slowly. The petals dropped off, leaving the pistil, and the pod began to turn golden, then sere. She moved on to the next one, until she had plenty of ripe seed, and uprooted the weed into her makeshift basket. Her attentions had aged the plant before its time, but she took care to drop a pod's-worth of seed where the roots had been, to start the next generation of plants growing. No sense in robbing the forest that had been so generous to her.

"What's all that?" he asked.

Dola described everything in the leaf-basket.

"My mama makes good greens," Pilton said, hopefully. Maybe this walk wasn't the wild-goose chase it first seemed.

"So does mine." Dola felt a pang as she thought of Siobhan and Tay.

"Come on, let's go back," Pilton said, with an impatient tug at her leash. Dola straightened up, her treasures in her hands.

Skinny seemed much more cheerful on the way back to the cabin. He even filled a pan with water so she could soak the sand out of the greens. Dola turned them over, yanked out the tough inner veins, and went looking through the foodstuffs to find things to cook with.

Many of the supplies were packet mixes, which claimed to be complete meals. Dola read them all, and discarded anything that had more than three ingredients she couldn't recognize. Soon, there was an aluminum Dutch oven swinging from the pot hook, filled with a savory, bubbling mixture smelling delightfully of mustard seed, wild chives, and wild marjoram. There was a can of bacon in the box, a traditional American addition to greens. She handed the package to Pilton to open. Using a hooked attachment in his pocket knife, he ratcheted the lid off. Recalling as much as she could of her mother's recipe, Dola fried a chunk of bacon until there was a film of grease in the bottom of the pan, then added the greens to wilt.

"You oughta use the cast iron pot," Pilton said.

"I don't like those," she said, eyeing the iron cookware uneasily.

"Well, aluminum causes Alzheimer's disease, you know."

"This is lighter," Dola said sharply, not wanting to talk about her Folk's sensitivity to iron. "If you cook, you may cook in what you please."

"Well, all right," Skinny said, and went back to his magazines. Dola was glad to have the peace and quiet to think.

It was satisfying to be in such a good place. The logs were well-aged hardwoods, providing a steady, hot flame. Swiftly, she tended the fire under the pot, and mixed a simple dough to make flattened breads on the pot lid while the meal was cooking.

"You're good at that, you know?" Pilton said suddenly from behind her. He was impressed by the little girl's adaptation to her surroundings, and her knowledge of woodcraft and housekeeping. Whoever had taught the little fairy woman how to do it all ought to be proud of their pupil.

She nodded politely at his compliment, and went back to tending the cooking.

It was a pity he'd had to go and have a temper tantrum like that earlier, because the girl had shied away from him ever since. She had every reason to be aloof, because she was a prisoner. He wished she would like him, because she was really something different. He wondered when he could get her to grant a wish for him.

Not far above three hundred feet, a couple of air sprites swooped in upon the Skyship Iris, circling and circling it, their tails whipping past their eyes at amazing speed. Holl saw the traditional image of sunrise in his mind, and tried to picture a slightly different one in response. They seemed to be happy with his efforts, for they slowed down and stared, the pupils of their huge eyes widening joyfully at him.

"Sunrise is their greeting," he explained to the Master, "and sunset their farewell."

"So Meester Doyle has told me," the Master said tersely. He had said little during the ascent. Holl wondered if he was as nervous as Tay, who had retired to his usual spot on the floor of the basket. Likely not: he seemed to have no difficulty looking down at the ground, but that could be because he was forcing himself. It was also impossible to tell if he was enjoying the flight.

The Master, knowing in advance from Keith Doyle what to expect, was able to communicate immediately in the sprites' pictorial style without needing to verbalize at the same time. Holl knew that there was a conversation going on between them only because he could see the sprites' replies to the Master's queries. He was asking about their origins, their numbers, and what they subsisted on. The images were colorful, but confused, as if they didn't understand why he was asking those questions.

"They seem to haf very limited intelligence," the Master said at last. "Each does not haf much on its own. I belief they haf more of a hive consciousness, like bees."

The sprites protested at once, showing a beehive from which sprites swarmed out and in that burst apart into individual clouds.

"They say no," Holl translated. In their typically feisty and mischievous response to a challenge, the sprites' next image was one of the Master in the basket of the balloon, smiling broadly and looking around him with wonder in his eyes. Even though the situation was serious, and he didn't show any outward signs of enjoyment, the Master had apparently found there was much to take pleasure in. Holl smiled. "They also say you are having a good time."

The Master peered disapprovingly over his glasses at the nearest sprite. The creature's pupils swelled, giving it an innocent, puppylike expression. It gazed back.

"It's no use." Tay laughed. "They can read your thoughts."

"Then let them see these," the Master said, his brow furrowing. The creatures of the air soared up and back in agitation, then revealed the images Frank had told them about: Dola in front of a log cabin chinked with concrete, and Dola walking on a rope lead before a tall man with brown hair.

"They vill now lead us to her," he said, folding his arms with an air of finality. The sprites swirled away from the basket and took their places ahead of the balloon.

Night was falling. Dola scraped the last of the food out the door onto a pile Skinny had designated for edible garbage. She took the pots back inside and washed them out, then banked the cookfire so it would keep them warm until bedtime. She was getting bored with her imprisonment. Skinny was not worth talking to. There were no friends to play with, no lessons, no books to read, no music, and, she sighed, no Asrai. She felt it was time to formulate her escape.

Skinny was her chief obstacle, but she felt she could get around him, with care. He'd been so suggestible while she was incarcerated in the office. If they hadn't been interrupted by Jake, she and Asrai would have been long gone.

It wasn't too late to prepare the ground again. Besides, Dola chided herself, she ought to practice her lessons. Just because she was away from home didn't mean she could be allowed to get rusty. Dola quivered to think what the Master would say if she was saved, and had neglected her education. She glanced up. Skinny was in the bathroom. When not there he always lay at one end of the couch, reading by the light of the lamp over his head, with his feet up on the other armrest. She studied the lamps. Both had woven cloth shades that reached almost all the way to their earthenware bases. She got up to touch one. The illusions almost leaped from her fingers to the rough fabric. It would hold pictures well. She made a face appear to grin conspiratorially at her.

Normally she had had to hold on to a cloth to keep the illusion alive. She yanked her hands back from the shade, seeing how long the face would remain without contact. She was able to count to sixty before the illusion faded. That was a good long time, she told herself. But how to extend the effect? More concentration might be the answer, lending a little of her will to the tooth of the cloth. The face laughed at her for twice sixty and longer. Dola was jubilant. She made the whole thing seem to vanish. All that remained visible was the toelike shape of the protruding base and the tip of the brass bulb holder on top.

She heard water running, and fled back to her seat on the hearthrug. Skinny emerged, wiping his hands on his pantslegs. She looked up innocently at him. He flopped down on the couch and picked up his magazine.

"Where'd the lamp go?" he asked.

"I've not taken it away," Dola said, turning a page in her book. "It's a big heavy thing. I'd not lift it."

"But it's gone," Skinny said, pointing. The earthenware base, much the same color as the table on which it sat, blended with its surroundings.

"No, it is right there," she insisted. With a sigh for the obtuseness of Big Folk, she rose and went over to the lamp. At the same time that she turned it on, she dropped the illusion. "There. You see? But we don't need it; it is not dark out yet." She turned it off. Skinny gave it an uneasy glance and picked up his magazine.

Dola left a fading charm on the lampshade, so that it vanished slowly away again. Over the edge of his periodical, Skinny checked again, and jumped.

"You stop that!" he demanded. Dola raised her hands.

"I've done nothing," she said, but she was secretly pleased.

During the next few hours, Dola played with the shadows in the room, practicing making faces appear amidst the hanging curtains and long arms of darkness reach forth from the sides of the chimney. The thin man kept looking up from the page he seemed to have read a dozen times, becoming more and more nervous. The shadows looming about the fireplace grasped for him, and withdrew into the dancing of the firelight.

"I dunno what's going on in here," he said.

"All houses have an aura, did you know?" Dola said, matter-of-factly. "A personality of their own. It may be that this one doesn't like you, holding an innocent child prisoner as you are."

He looked around suspiciously, refusing to acknowledge that he more than half believed her. "It ain't as if I'm hurting you," he said, projecting his voice to the corners of the room. "Besides, you aren't an innocent child. Well, you aren't an ordinary one anyhow."

"Then beware, lest my presence stir up the household spirits to haunt you," Dola said, in the sepulchral voice she used for telling ghost stories to the smaller village children. Skinny blanched.

A light breeze came in under the door and whistled in the chimney. Dola played with the shadows, making pictures on the floor in the firelight. Left to themselves, they crept across the rag rug, spiraled up the leg of the couch like snakes, and waited for the human to notice them. Catching a peripheral glimpse of his stalkers, Skinny's head jerked first one way, then the other. He whimpered. The shadows melted. Dola saw the whites of his eyes show all the way around his irises and decided it was time to stop teasing him. He was really frightened. Maybe one more vision, but something harmless and colorful, as she might make for the baby. In the fabric of the rug, she began to craft her illusion.

"I don't want the house to hate me," Skinny said. "Ms. Gilbreth would be real sore if I let you go. But maybe I'd do it anyway, if you do some real magic for me."

"What do you want, a chest of jewels?" she asked, with heavy sarcasm.

"Can you do that?" he asked, surprised, then greedy. Dola was disgusted.

"No! We can barely cover the mortgage payment of a month. Of all the foolish questions. I'm an ordinary girl. All the things I do are ordinary."

"I know better," the man said, leaning back with his arms folded over his chest. "I saw you vanish the other day, and you know it. Do some big magic for me."

She started to stir the influence she was drawing from the rag rug. No illusion was beyond her power, but what if he wanted to touch what she conjured up? It was all very well, having him promise to set her free, but she couldn't pay his price. Maybe she should use this vision to scare him again. A dragon! No, a rainbow. Dola thought of her father, and Holl, and the Master, out looking for her, standing in a wicker basket high in the air, suspended underneath a rainbow. Keith Doyle had visited more than once in such a conveyance. She attempted to thrust the vision away, putting it down as an unlikely fantasy. Besides, rainbows weren't scary.

At the same time, she felt that someone was looking at her. Something white bobbed past the window of the cabin. Dola bent her head and glanced sideways to watch it. Pictures appeared in her mind: of Tay smiling, Holl falling in a river, Keith Doyle with his camera. She tilted her head further, and saw kindly blue eyes looking in at her through the glass. The face itself made her gasp. It was featureless, the blue-white of cirrus clouds. The head and body were grotesquely distorted, and kept changing shape as she watched. She had no idea what kind of being it was, only that it was friendly and intelligent. It was trying to tell her that her folk were seeking her.

Behind it, far away in the sky, she saw a colorful dome shape, the same thing she'd seen the day Keith and her father had rescued Asrai. All at once she realized it was the great balloon that belonged to Keith Doyle's friend. Taking the bobbing creature's appearance as an omen of good fortune, she decided it was time to escape. The white thing would serve as a proper distraction.

"I can't fetch money for you, but I can make visible the spirit of the house so you can atone. Look there!" She pointed out the window. The white shape floated past again, its body stretching and re-forming. "See!"

"A ghost!" Pilton yelled. "This place is haunted!"

Dola leaped to her feet. While he was frozen, Dola meant to make a dash for the door and let herself out. Skinny cut her off in his dive for the shotgun. He pushed her down into the shadow of a chair. She realized too late what Skinny was doing.

"Go away!" she cried to the creature. But the man, rolling over like a commando, drew a bead, aimed, and fired.

The crash of the glass pane blowing out of the window was drowned out by Dola's scream. The white creature, caught in a shape with a grossly inflated head and puny, wasted body and wings, seemed to explode soundlessly. It spread out across the sky, becoming more and more misshapen until it dissipated like oil on the surface of a pond. Before it vanished, Dola saw an image in her mind of the kindly eyes going wide in fear and pain. She sank to the floor where she crouched, rocking, tears racing down her cheeks.

"It was a live thing! You've killed a lively, intelligent creature." Dola wept. "I can't sense it anymore. It's gone."

Skinny gawked at the shards of glass hanging in the window frame, went over to look down, around, then up. "No, you made it up. There ain't nobody out there. I bet there's nothing in the house, either," he accused her. "You're trying to make me feel bad because you're stuck here with me. It was just an illusion, wasn't it?" He didn't sound convinced, and he was getting worried, watching her cry. "You did the magic."

"I didn't, I didn't," Dola insisted. "It was real. It came to look after me, and now it's dead."

* * *

The small sprite fluttering about the balloon cables gave them the picture it received: Dola sitting on the floor of a small building with something white in her hands. Then, abruptly, the air creature became agitated, zooming back and forth like a hysterical firefly.

"Vhat ails this being?" the Master asked. "All it shows us is empty sky." The tiny sprites flying alongside swirled together like dust-storms and broke apart, their huge eyes wide with fear.

"It's gone," Frank said, his voice rough and dry. "They don't know where. What happened?"

"Frightened by something into fleeing out of range?" Tay guessed.

Holl watched the terrified antics of the remaining sprites and shook his head. What he felt from them chilled his heart. "Farther away than that," he said. "They communicate over great distances. It probably can't find its friend because its friend isn't there to find any longer. Something terrible has happened."

All four of them fell silent for a long time. The Little Folk were upset because the missing sprite had assumed great personal risk to go into the lower atmosphere to help them find Dola. Whatever had befallen it was partly their fault. Frank's eyes and nose were red with suppressed grief and anger. Holl guessed that the sprites were to him a representation of a kind of benevolent force of the skies. They meant something more to the pilot than just new acquaintances. Holl was very sorry for him.

Turning his face away from the Little Folk, Frank flicked a careless finger at the gauge. It showed that the propane tanks were nearly empty. "Going down," he pronounced shortly.

Almost automatically, he searched out a safe place to land the balloon, and dialed the number for the chase truck, directing it to the right field. The other sprites surrounding the balloon flew in mournful circles, until the Iris dropped below their safe limit, and went away.

Pilton took Jake aside on the porch that evening when he came by to check on them. He told the whole story of the afternoon: herbs, disappearing furniture and all, ending with the story of the ghost and the child's bursting into hysterics.

"This ain't right," he said over and over. "We can't just keep her here forever. The spirits are mad at us. Something awful's gonna happen if we don't let her go home."

"Take it easy, Grant," Jake said. "You saw a wood pigeon or a lost lake gull, not a ghost."

"If I shot a gull, then where is it?" Pilton demanded. "You shoot something dead, there's a body. I know I killed it. You gotta send this kid home, Jake." He was shaken. Jake couldn't understand. He hadn't seen the thing fly apart into a million pieces, and he didn't have to sit with the fairy woman as she cried her eyes out over something that died but didn't bleed.

"She won't talk to me no more," Grant added. "And she locked herself in her room. She's been there for hours."

Jake went away and then came back to keep watch with him while the boss-lady drove up to meet them.

Mona came out of the cottage, feeling as if she'd just gone twenty rounds in the ring with the heavyweight champion. It had taken all her skill at persuasion to talk her way into the barricaded bedroom to talk to the child, who had then stared at her sullenly and given only single-syllable replies to her questions.

"You scared the hell out of me with your phone call, Grant," Mona said, shutting the door quietly. "She's all right. You don't understand how important she is to us. She is our only guarantee of H. Doyle's good behavior. He's got too much on us. You've just got to keep her from getting hurt. You're not to scare her anymore. You're not even to talk loud. Understand?"

"Yes, Ms. Gilbreth," Pilton said, apologetically.

Mona leaned against the cabin wall. "I don't like this. The whole situation is escalating. I feel threatened, and I don't know what to do. Since her people have proof that it's us, why haven't they called in the police?"

"Probably afraid the kid'll wind up dead," Jake said, standing just beyond the cabin's light. Mona stared at him, shocked, then realized he was right. That would be what *she'd* think.

"They can't call the police," Pilton corrected them scornfully. "They're fairies. As far as the police are concerned, they don't exist."

"No," Jake said, thoughtfully, "but maybe the place is full of illegals. There's a company running from that location, called Hollow Tree Industries. Makes woodcrafts for gift stores. Isolated—perfect place for illegals to hide out. I checked on the census. The place is owned by Keith Doyle."

Mona exclaimed wordlessly.

Williamson continued. "But there's no one else. No voters registered, no driver's licenses at that address, nothing. Just Keith Doyle."

"Course not," Pilton said scornfully, though the others were ignoring him. "No one believes they exist. 'Cept me, of course."

"So neither of us wants the cops involved," Mona said thoughtfully. "I didn't think anyone could be so squeaky clean. That evens things out a little. But they *know* it's us. That's the part that worries me. They gave up a little too easily. I want to know what they're up to."

Chapter
FOURTEEN

"**A**t least we know now that she is safe," Siobhan said, shaking her head. She had joined the vigil in the kitchen that evening, sitting up through the next morning, waiting for more communication from their Big Folk helpers or the kidnapers. They had called Keith Doyle to tell him about the disappearance of the air sprite. Their friend was devastated, but was as helpless as they to do anything. Holl begged him not to cut another day out of his work schedule, but to work on their behalf from where he was. Keith swore that was what he would do. Diane had phoned a few minutes later, saying she had talked to Keith. She volunteered to take the next trip up with Frank Winslow as a proxy for Keith. The Little Folk were not yet certain when they would hear again from the pilot. After the balloon had landed, he had packed up his craft, driven them home, and driven away again, all in complete and bitter silence. His grief was deeper than any of theirs.

The sun had been up for an hour, and there was still no call. Siobhan had passed beyond tears, and into a kind of exhausted resignation. "A pity the little one could not tell you where to find her."

"It may have tried," Holl said, gently, "but its fellows were too upset at its disappearance—I dare not call it death, for we don't know—to tell us of its last sendings. The area where it flew is forested and hilly. We could explore it, but we would have to do so on foot. And our bumbling around would likely alert Dola's guardians."

"If this was our Library," Curran said, peevishly, "we'd hae no trouble at a'. We knew every nook of th' place. This big world belongs to Big People, and has noothing to do wi' us."

"Our hands remain tied," the Master said.

"I'd shut the gates on the lot of them in a twinklin'," Curran finished. "We can do f'r oursel', have done and still can."

"Now, father, you know ve may not do that," Rose said, taking his arm. "Ve haf taken on responsibilities, and those ve may not lay down." The crotchety old elf seemed ready to continue the argument when the telephone rang.

Catra jumped up to take the call. She picked up the receiver to listen. Turning to the others, she put her hand over the mouthpiece and nodded her head. Holl strode over and took the handset from her.

"Hello?" the man's voice said.

"Put on your mistress," Holl said. "I will not talk to you any longer. We know you're not alone."

Ignoring the look of desperation on his employer's face, Jake extended the phone to Mona. She was shaking too much at first to take it, and had to hold the receiver in both hands to keep from dropping it on the desktop. Jake leaned in close to listen.

"What do you want?" Mona whispered.

The hated voice of H. Doyle spoke. "Give us your final condition so that we can have our child back again."

"Is this being taped?" Mona asked.

"You'd not believe me if I said no, so does it matter? Tell me your condition."

"I want you to stop pestering me in the paper," Mona said, her voice growing stronger as she felt herself getting angry. "No more letters. No more complaints. You're ruining my campaign, my business—my whole life. I never want to see or hear from Hollow Tree or you as long as I live. Leave me alone!"

"I see," the voice said. "I must consider this. I will call you back." There was a click on the line, and a dial tone.

"He hung up on me," Mona said, aggrieved.

* * *

"It's a stupid woman," Tay's wife declared, bitterly. "A
we have to do was make a promise we would bother her no mor
and she would give back our girl."

"I dinna believe it," Keva said. "Nor should ye."

"It vould not be enough now," the Master said. "The griev
ance does not end vith us. She has been responsible for damagin
the land with her poisons. She vould still be liable for her crime
against nature. She must stop. If for no other reason than those
we could claim injury from her. It is our land upon vhich sh
has been pouring out the trucks full of vaste, and the harm
done. There has been no promise from her that she vould nefe
again commit the same deed. She vill haf her punishment, an
it vill be appropriate. As in *The Mikado*, let the punishment
the crime. Keith Doyle has said not to antagonize, but not to g
in. I agree vith his suggestion." There was a protest. He signe
to the others to be silent. Out of respect, they sat down to lister
The Master continued.

"Let us appear to be cooperating for the moment. When th
time comes, we will have our vengeance. She has commande
us under threat to refrain from criticizing her. It is a small thing
Ve shall appear to do as she asks. In the meantime, let
undermine her. Others vill seem to write the diatribes. Ve vi
influence those vith whom ve come in contact."

Holl's lips smiled, but his eyes were hard. Tay, beside him
nodded. "Good thinking, Master."

Holl dialed the number for Gilbreth Farm and Feed. The swe
voice of the receptionist answered, and offered to transfer th
call. The other end was snatched up on the first ring.

"We promise we will make no more direct attacks upon you.

"Good," Mona Gilbreth said. Holl thought she sounded r
lieved.

"What about the girl?"

Gilbreth paused. "I'm too busy today. I'll be in touch wi
you later." She cradled the phone hastily, but didn't bang
down.

"She retains overt control," the Master said, nodding, "b
the real power is still ours. Now ve vill make her nervou
In time, she may gif up Dola vithout asking us to fulfill h
demands."

Following the Master's instructions, Catra and Marcy s

down at the human woman's personal computer and composed
a handbill about clean environment and honesty in government.
Marcy supervised the printing out of a hundred or so copies and
handed them over to the Little Folk who enhanced the sense of
reasonableness of the text.

"It vill haf the underlying effect of making the reader question
the potential polluter in their midst," the Master explained. "The
seeds vill be planted. Efery day she delays returning Dola to us,
the effect vill be stronger."

At Midwestern University, the administration and the Voters
of the Future Program had set up a platform for the local candidates to use. Both Mona, and the incumbent seeking reelection
to the House seat she wanted, were going to be allowed equal
opportunity to address the students and faculty. On the advice of
her campaign manager and some of her volunteer workers who
were of college age, Mona had tailored her speech, leaving out
references to farm subsidies and retirement benefits, in favor of
stressing the environment, education, and rights for the disabled.
Her workers, visible in their pressed-foam skimmer hats with
rose-colored bands, worked the crowd, handing out buttons and
balloons. The campaign staff for the other side countered, handing out blue impedimenta to those who wouldn't take "Gilbreth
for Congresswoman" literature.

Her adversary, an older man with grizzled hair and distinguished-
looking white sideburns, whose once athletic shoulders were slip-
ping gradually into his midsection, approached her and offered her
a firm handshake. She returned it with a dignified nod.

"Ladies first?" he suggested, gesturing at the podium.

"Oh, no," Mona countered, with an artful smile. "Please go
ahead, Congressman. *Seniority* ought to count for something."

She hadn't actually said, 'Age before beauty,' but the Congressman couldn't have missed the inference, and she didn't
want him to. The heavy folds of fat under his chin shook with
annoyance, but he bowed to her and mounted the steps of the
platform. His force of bodyguards and volunteers separated from
her bodyguards and volunteers, and arrayed themselves around
the stage. The Congressman cleared his throat into the microphone, and the crowd quieted down.

His speech was predictable, enumerating his successes over

the years on behalf of his district. Mona covered her mouth with her hand but still yawned visibly enough to be seen by half the attending student population. A couple of her campaign workers grinned openly. At length, the incumbent descended, and disappeared into a circle of voters and reporters shouting questions at him.

Mona waited to be introduced by her campaign manager, then took the podium as if it was the dais of her throne.

"Ladies and gentlemen, we've heard from the distinguished gentleman from Washington. I now present to you the Environmental Candidate, Ms. Mona Gilbreth!"

There was applause, and some scattered cheering. Mona smiled down on her audience. She found that to be effective, the formula that the younger the listeners, the shorter the speech always worked best, even if it meant letting the other candidate have more 'air time' than she had. 'Leave them wanting more,' she thought. People in the audience showed real interest as she outlined her specific causes and enumerated what she would do to support them once she took office. A blond girl, a black man and a bunch of children were handing out flyers at the perimeter of the crowd. There must be some kind of protest going on. But then, this was a college campus. There was always a protest going on somewhere. It couldn't have anything to do with her. She gave her audience about five minutes less than the Congressman had, then came down to shake hands and kiss a few babies, so to speak.

As with her opponent, Mona was mobbed as she got off the platform. "Ms. Gilbreth!" one young man called out. He rushed up and pumped her hand to the accompaniment of the flashing and clicking of cameras. "I'm glad you're a woman candidate. I'm voting for you."

"Thank you," Mona said, smiling for the reporters. "I'm going to Washington for *you*." The student drew away, beaming. Another took his place.

More followed with similar comments and well-wishes. She shook hands with all of them, posed for pictures, with her campaign manager standing about ten feet away, beaming at her. The session was going very well. This was not the group from which she could expect much in the way of donations, but enough of them were residents of the district that if she earned their respect and kept it, they'd continue to send her back to Washington for the next generation to come.

A few of the students asked earnest, complicated questions, and she fielded them with the answers that were becoming so pat in her mind they were almost sound bites.

A short, heavyset young woman came forward clutching a flyer. "Ms. Gilbreth, I'd like to know if in your business you follow safe procedures in getting rid of toxic waste. Are you using licensed haulers and disposal systems?"

"Why, yes," Mona said, the smile freezing on her face. Thankfully, her noncommittal answer was at the ready. "As you know, the Environmental Protection Agency has approved very specific and stringent processes for disposing of toxic waste. My technicians have all of them at their fingertips."

"What's in the waste you dump?" a young man asked. He was thin, with red hair. Mona looked sharply at him, thinking at first it was Keith Doyle. When she saw he was a stranger, she relaxed and smiled.

"Mostly nitrogen-based by-products. A complete list of the chemicals is available from my office. Thank you." She turned ostentatiously to the next querent. The young man retired, obviously dissatisfied, but he was crowded away from her by well-wishers and other people who wanted to talk to her or just shake hands. As the crowd began to thin, her campaign manager came over to stand beside her. There were scattered flyers on the ground. He picked one up and began to read it while Mona dealt with the last questions and some unwelcome comments, and posed for just a few more pictures. Mona glanced over at her manager. His face seemed almost to change visibly while he read. Tucking the paper into his jacket pocket without seeming to think about it, he sidled up to her.

"You are following environmentally safe waste procedures, aren't you?" he whispered, in a brief lull between questions.

She got exasperated with him. Maybe his post on her staff wasn't so secure after all. "Of course I am," she hissed.

The crowd dissipated at last, and she stalked off the Campus Common to the waiting limousine. Her campaign manager trailed behind in her wake, wondering what he'd just done wrong.

* * *

Nine-year-old Borget arrived in the barn panting. "Master, there's a police car in the drive!" he cried. "Rose wants to know what to do!"

The Master set his pointer tip down on the floor. "It has begun. She moves against us using the techniques of harassment. If ve do not show the face she expects, she vill expose us."

Catra and Candlepat stood up from behind the archives desk. "Should we flee?" Candlepat asked. "We can hide in the cornfields."

"A mass exodus should not be necessary." The Master turned to Marcy, who stood with Enoch at the sawyer's table. He made her a little bow. "Mees Collier, may I ask a favor?"

The county officer leaned on the bell again. Nice house, set in pretty lands, but kind of isolated among all these trees. He peered through the gauzy curtains hanging behind the glass panel in the door, at the big, wood-paneled room. Empty. He had no idea what the Gilbreth woman wanted him to investigate. She'd handed the sheriff a line about illegal aliens running a factory out of this place. There was one car in the driveway. It had a city sticker for one of the Chicago suburbs. That didn't really suggest a flood of immigrant workers. Well, one more ring, then he'd go around the house to the barn, see if anyone was out there. He pushed the buzzer, and leaned up against the glass with his hand shading his eyes. "No one here, dispatch. No, wait a minute. Here comes somebody."

A pretty girl with very pale skin and black hair came running out of one of the doors leading off the big, wood-paneled room. She pulled the front door open.

"Can I help you?" she asked, smoothing a wisp of hair off her face.

"Sheriff's police, ma'am. Is there a Mr. Doyle here?" He checked his notes. "The owner of this place, Mr. Keith Doyle?"

"He's not here right now," Marcy said, trying to stay calm. "He's working in Chicago this semester. Is there something I can do for you?"

"Who are you, miss?" the officer asked.

"My name's Marcy Collier," she said. "I, uh, live with Keith." She could almost sense Enoch glowering at her from his hiding place, and felt her cheeks burn. The officer probably thought she was embarrassed because of the irregularity of the arrangement, not because she was lying.

"Well, Miss Collier, you've got to answer to your own conscience for that. I understand there's a business run off this farm?"

"Why, yes, but that's not illegal, is it?" Marcy asked.

"No, ma'am. This property is zoned for certain commercial operations. Are you involved in this business?"

Marcy could hear whispering from the Folk conferring in the kitchen. Maura was there, too, with Asrai. She prayed the baby wouldn't cry. It would be impossible to ignore Asrai's air-raid siren voice, and she didn't want the officer thinking she was concealing an illegitimate baby, as well. If the rumor got back to her parents, she was dead. "Only peripherally. I help out sometimes, packing boxes and things. Keith and I go to the same college. The workshop is a cooperative. We have lots of friends who come in and use the tools. Um." Greatly daring, she added, "Would you like to see it?"

"I'd like that just fine," the officer said, still serious. He holstered his radio in a square pouch on his belt. She escorted him through the great room and into the kitchen. The red barn was visible through the window at the far end of the room.

Marcy picked up a hastily discarded dishrag one of the Little Folk had dropped on their flight from the house. She tossed it casually onto the drainboard. She hoped he thought she had been interrupted doing dishes when he rang. The officer seemed to be looking at everything in the room, counting the stacks of small benches and kindergarten-sized chairs.

"There's just one phone line here, isn't there?" the officer asked, pausing in the middle of the room.

"That's right," Marcy said. "Right there." She pointed, then held open the back door, wishing he'd follow her out. He glanced at the waist-level wall phone and did a doubletake.

"What's it doing down there?"

She tried to think of an excuse and wondered what Keith would say. "Oh, my aunt's in a wheelchair," Marcy said, at last, swallowing. "She can't reach it if it's at eye level for us."

"She visit a lot?" the officer said, squinting at her.

"Oh, yes."

"Any other extensions in the house?"

"Well, no," Marcy said. "I mean, why? There's just two of us. The workshop is this way."

The September grass was too dry to take footprints, so there were no traces from the Little Folk who had fled for cover in the barn or the fields beyond it. Out of the corner of her eye, she spotted Enoch slip out of the house behind them. He was keeping watch on her, in case the officer became unfriendly. She smiled affectionately, then hid the expression, not wanting to have to explain herself to her visitor.

The barn almost echoed, so devoid it was of living things. Even the cat who'd been asleep on the Archivist's desk was gone. Lonely dust filmed the usually shining power tools and tables. Marcy, after more than a year of living among the Little Folk, knew that all the signs of disuse were illusionary, and that there were many pairs of eyes watching.

There must have been more than adequate time to empty the workshop. Most of the supplies were put away on the shelves and in the open-faced cabinets. The Master had even had time to erase the equations on his chalkboard before concealing himself. The pointer lay casually placed across the easel tray.

"Nice, huh?" the sheriff asked, going around the room. He ran a finger through the sawdust on the floor next to the drill press. His were the only footprints marring the scattered wood shavings. "What do they make here?"

"Oh, Christmas ornaments, cooky cutters, necklaces," Marcy said. She showed him the elaborate chain of wooden beads and stones she was wearing. Enoch had given it to her for her birthday. The officer seemed impressed.

"Pretty good. I like the design," he said, nodding. "Creative. My wife'd like it." He picked up one of the small lanterns that stood on a worktable, waiting to have the filigree screens dropped into the slotted sides before the small roof and ring was fixed on. He put it down and lifted the power drill. "You make some of this stuff, too?"

"Goodness, no!" Marcy exclaimed, her voice squeaking a little. She aimed a hand at the power tools. "I don't know how to use these things. I'm just an Arts and Sciences major. I hardly do anything practical."

There was a nearly-inaudible, high-pitched giggle in the loft.

Marcy almost gasped. She wondered if the policeman could hear the breathing and low whispers that followed, or if she was just being too sensitive. He looked at the numbers of chairs and benches set out in rows before the Master's easel.

"Everything's so small," he said, jokingly. "Are you sure you're not violating the child labor laws?"

"Oh, no!" Marcy said, horrified. "We—we have a lot of children who come in for demonstrations. You know," she said, reaching back in her memory for something Keith had once said, "Junior Achievement?"

The officer nodded. "Oh, yeah, belonged to one of them myself when I was twelve," he said, fondly. "Well, okay. Sorry to bother you, miss. I can find my own way back to my car."

He sketched a small salute to the young woman and climbed the slight slope up the house. Ms. G. just had a bee in her bonnet, he thought. She was probably looking for another cause to back for her campaign, and decided to pick on what sounded like a hippie commune workshop smack in the middle of her constituency. Turned out to be nothing, and he'd tell her so. Her daddy had been a big man in the county when he was alive. His daughter ought to just tend to her business before she tried to take his place. By all accounts the fertilizer factory was suffering from neglect. He wasn't planning to vote for her anyhow. The county officer climbed back into the car and lifted the radio to report in. Politicians were all alike. You couldn't trust a one of them.

Not long after the officer disappeared around the corner of the house, Rose appeared at the back door and waved a dish towel. All clear. Marcy sank down onto one of the benches with her shoulders slumped, and just breathed.

Enoch emerged from beneath the workbench and came over to sit beside her. He seized her hand and kissed it fiercely.

"I don't even like to hear you say things like that," he said. "Living with Keith Doyle!"

"I'm sorry," Marcy said, helplessly. "That was all I could think of."

"Never mind," Enoch said, softening his scowl to a tender smile. He moved closer and put an arm around her. "It was . . . expedient. Do you feel all right?" Marcy nodded.

The Master seemed to appear out of thin air. He patted her on the shoulder.

"Vell done, Mees Collier. The first attack has been repulsed. Our own counterattack goes on, to continue the military metaphor. There vill be more sallies by our foe, of that I am certain. Ve vill be ready."

"Keith Doyle?" the secretary said into the microphone of her headset. She checked the office clipboard and reached for a pad of pink forms. "I'm sorry, he's not in right now. May I take a message?"

"No, wait!" Brendan, passing by the desk in the reception hall, jumped in front of the secretary and signaled until he got her attention. "I'll take it."

"Hold, please." The woman pushed a few buttons that transferred the call to the phone on the desk.

Brendan picked up the receiver. "Hello?"

"Keith?" a woman's voice asked. The tinny quality of the sound told Brendan it was long distance.

"No, sorry. I just work with him. I'll be seeing him this afternoon. Can I give him a message?"

"No, I guess I can call back. Do you know when he'll be in?"

"Uh, no," Brendan said. "He's off with another one of our co-workers, Dorothy. They could be a while, you know what I mean?" He gave the phrase all the lascivious glee he could muster.

"No, I do not know what you mean," the woman said, with asperity. Brendan was delighted.

"Well, you know, they call 'em 'nooners' but they can last longer than the noon hour—oops," Brendan interrupted himself and continued in a horrified whisper. "Is this his girlfriend? It's nothing. I'm gossiping. Rumors can be so malicious. Forget I said anything. Sorry. I'll tell him you called. Bye." He hung up the phone and sauntered away from the desk. The receptionist barely spared him a glance as he went by.

Only a few moments later, Keith and Dorothy, their arms full of paper bags from the bakery, came in together through the glass doors. They were laughing at some private joke. Keith held the door open by leaning against it as Dorothy passed through.

Every time she glanced up at him, he wiggled his eyebrows, and she burst into a fresh attack of giggles.

"Hey, Keith," Brendan said, coming over and helping himself to a jelly doughnut from one of the bags. "Your girlfriend called."

"Hey, thanks, Brendan," Keith said.

"Don't mention it." Brendan smiled.

It was only late afternoon when Mona returned to the plant, but she felt as if she had been out hiking forever. It had been a tiring and irritating day. Her feet nearly sighed with relief when they sank into the meager padding under the carpet in the reception area.

"Ms. Gilbreth," the receptionist said as she passed by, going toward her office to put her legs up. The girl held out a stack of pink slips. "I've got a whole bunch of messages for you. Here's your mail, too. Oh, and there's a couple of men around here somewhere. They said they were from the EPA."

"The EPA?" Mona asked, her heart sinking as she thought of the dumping she had authorized in forest preserves all over the county, not only in the one behind Hollow Tree Farm. Had someone spilled the beans? "As in Environmental Protection Agency?"

"Yes'm. They showed me their badges, so I called Mr. Williamson. I guess he took them around."

"Thank you," Mona said, hobbling down the gray hallway. She stuffed the handful of messages into her purse. "Could you find me some coffee, Beryl? A whole pot."

"Sure, ma'am," the receptionist called after her.

All the whistle stops after her early-morning speech at Midwestern had been horrible reruns of the first. People Mona had never met before came up to complain to her about her policy of waste disposal and ask pointed questions concerning her support of open-land greenways. Siccing the EPA on her factory was the crowning insult. She wondered if there had been time to shovel dirt over the leaks in the number eight tank, or to take the suppurating truckloads of overdue waste off the grounds.

Jake arrived at the same time as the coffee. Mona, her shoes discarded under the table, poured her mug a quarter full, swirled it around to cool it a little, gulped it down, and refilled the mug to the lip.

"All right," she said, settling down behind her desk with a sigh. "What's this about the EPA?"

The foreman shook his head. "It's nothing, ma'am. They got a call from some indignant female claiming Gilbreth is full of violations. She was such a pest the inspectors promised to look into it right away. I cooled it with them. They'll come back for a spot check next week, after we've had a chance to clean up."

"My God, if we can find the money between now and then. What lit a fire under them?" Mona asked, feeling personally put upon. "Normally it takes months to set up an investigation."

Jake shrugged. "Who knows? Who cares? They're gone."

She started to turn over each of the messages. "What's going on here?" she asked, astonished. "These are all complaints about the plant. Air pollution, air pollution, runoff, the smell, dumping, runoff, the smell—was there a letter in the paper yesterday that I missed? The day before?"

"No, ma'am, I've been keeping an eye on things. There's been nothing from *them* for the last week, since you've had the kids." He let his words trail off and raised his eyebrows significantly.

"Small mercy," she said, but she didn't feel consoled. The letters, some of which had been delivered by hand, were full of the same kinds of complaints she'd been fielding all day long. One letter was printed in a juvenile hand and full of exclamation points and underlining. "Even kids think I'm the incarnation of Satan. How could that be? I'm running on a pro-environment package. What set these people off?"

"How about the guy you're running against?" Jake asked.

"Not a chance," Mona said, waving a hand. "He hasn't got the imagination to stir up this kind of hate mail. Who are all these people who are complaining?"

Jake glanced at the phone. "You know who to ask."

"They wouldn't dare!" Mona said. But she was worried. D-Day for the election was getting closer and closer. Any questions about her integrity now would make it harder for her to continue, especially when money remained so scarce. The rest of her mail was bills. Some of them—*most* of them—said "Second Notice" or "Final Notice." She couldn't hold the creditors off forever, and she didn't dare kite checks, not with the last House banking scandal still fresh in everyone's memory. She had to get money somewhere, not only to cover general business expenses, but also haulage fees, or she was ruined. Under the circumstances, any hope of borrowing cash discreetly from the election funds was out of the question. So was dumping any more waste on Hollow Tree Farm, dearly as she would have loved to. Nobody deserved it more. "I've got to stay clean."

"Maybe, but if it was me, I'd let the kid go, take the money and run." Jake had a disconcerting trick of reading her mind when she was thinking about money.

"I can't," she said, taking another healthy swig of coffee. It was still too hot, and she gasped. "Everyone's watching me too closely right now."

"Here's the sheriff's report," Jake said, taking an envelope out of his pocket. "There's nothing out of the ordinary at that farm. No one was there but a girl who says she's Doyle's live-in. She said she's a student at Midwestern. That checks. She couldn't have had a baby in the spring, and she's not old enough to be the mother of the kid at the cabin unless she started in grade school. You also got a call from your little pal at PDQ. Keith Doyle reported for work this morning right on time. Except for an hour for lunch he's been there every minute."

"So Keith Doyle and H. Doyle aren't the same person," Mona said. "Who is it that's answering that phone?"

Chapter
FIFTEEN

The morning papers were full of eloquent letters complaining about Gilbreth Feed and Fertilizer. None of them was signed H. Doyle, but they voiced similar questions and concerns. Some were written to provoke the most severe reactions in their readers. The Folk felt their flyer had met with wonderful success, and it was only a matter of time before responses appeared in print, provoking an outcry from the ostensibly wounded party.

Holl was clutching the editorial section in one hand and drinking his morning tea when the telephone rang. He put the cup down to pick up the handset.

"Back off!" Mona Gilbreth's voice blasted from the receiver. Holl held the handset at nearly arm's length to save his ears. The echo bounced off the kitchen walls. "You promised no more letters to the press. The girl's all right, and she'll remain all right, but get off my back! You know what I could do if I find you're trying to thwart me."

"It was not I," Holl said, drawing the mouthpiece close enough to speak. "I gave you my word, and I am keeping it. Not one of those letters was written by me."

He thrust it away, wincing, when she began to shout again. All the Little Folk in the room could hear her next demand perfectly. "What about the rest of the people who work at Hollow Tree Industries? Did they write them?"

"I swear that no one who works for Hollow Tree sent a single letter to the editor," Holl said carefully. "Call any of the people who signed the letters. Would I endanger my own flesh and blood?"

"If you're smart you won't," Gilbreth snarled.

"You can't keep her forever," Holl reminded her. There was a very long pause.

"If you don't back off and leave me alone," the woman at the other end said in a careful, deliberate voice, "I will tell the *National Informer* that your little girl is really a pixie, and you'll never get her back. She'll spend the rest of her life in freak shows or laboratories."

"No!" Holl exclaimed involuntarily. He stared up at the others, knowing that they had heard every word.

Tay looked shocked. Holl knew his face only echoed his nephew's expression of horror. It was the nightmare that had haunted them from the time they set foot onto the Midwestern campus more than four decades ago: freak shows, experiments, the end of privacy and integrity. The last year and a half in comparative safety on their own lands only made Gilbreth's threat that much more terrifying. Such an outcome had to be prevented at any cost. Tay backed away from the phone and began to converse in a low voice with the others. There were startled exclamations, and Siobhan began to cry. Maura broke away from the crowd and came to Holl, twisting at the ring on her finger. She offered it to him in both hands. Holl looked from the winking blue stone to his lifemate's eyes, and she gave him a helpless but brave smile. Regretfully, he nodded. It was the only really valuable thing they owned. A love token to redeem a loved one seemed only right.

"No," he repeated into the phone, in a quieter voice. "We'll send you a token of our good faith to prove that we will stand by your conditions."

"All right," Gilbreth said. "I'll wait for it."

Mona sat with her hand on the phone for a moment, feeling strangely triumphant.

"Inspiration?" Jake wanted to know.

"No," Mona said, tiredly. "I got the idea from Grant. He's still going on about those deformed ears the girl has—he thinks it means that she's the will-o'-the-wisp or Tinkerbell. Sounds like they've heard something like it before. It got one hell of a strong response, didn't it?"

"Sure did." Jake stretched back in his chair with his hands behind his head. "I wonder what this token'll be like."

"They must be illegal aliens," Mona said, looking thoughtful. "That H. Doyle has got to be an illegal, or else why would they stay so cagey even while I'm threatening to give his niece away to the circus? That has got to be why they're always hiding. Hmm. His name sounds Irish."

"So what?" Jake asked. "So does Gilbreth."

"Yes, but I was born here. I bet he wasn't, him or his family. Maybe I can get them deported," she said, picking up a pencil and tapping it against her teeth. The thought made her happy. "After he pays the ransom and I give him back his kid."

"How could she know?" Tay asked, wringing his hands.

"I don't know if she does," Holl said. "It could have been a shot in the dark. In her case, we've stooped to bribery to ensure Dola's safety. Keith Doyle will not be pleased, nor will the Master, but what else could we do?" He held up the ring and drew his small carving knife from the sheath on his belt. "I swear I'll replace this with something as good or better one day," he said to Maura.

"Never mind," she replied, shaking her head ruefully. "If it will save Dola from the Big Folk you could take my finger with it."

"Sticks and stones," Tiron said, peevishly. "You'll not have to give it up that easily. Send it to the woman, do, but I'll have it back in your hands before long. You have my word on it."

With a deft motion, Holl prized the sapphire from the setting and handed the ring back to Maura. He held the gem steady while Tiron laid a charm of finding on it. "We'll mail this stone today. She must soon set a time and place for the exchange of ransom. We'll be ready for it when the time comes."

Wednesday morning, Paul Meier had assigned his interns to work together on a series of ads for a regional cleaning service, but inspiration was not coming easily. "Come To Dust" should have provoked something clever out of the students, and Paul was showing his disappointment. He was particularly unhappy with his star 'ideator.' Keith's mind seemed to be everywhere except right there with him in the conference room.

"Come on," Meier urged them. "It's Shakespeare. Shakespeare?" He leaned over his cup, half-full of dilute coffee and congealing non-dairy creamer, and appealed to the four interns. Dorothy was deep in her inner world, making little sketches of faces and fashion designs. Sean was earnest but empty. Brendan was bored, and didn't care who knew. Meier slammed his hands down on the table and rose behind it. "All right. Give it a rest. Someone go read *Cymbeline* and meet me back here after lunch." He headed for the door, and Sean and Brendan trailed listlessly behind him.

The bang of the door closing behind them seemed to have aroused Keith out of his reverie. He looked around for the others, and ended up meeting Dorothy's gaze.

"*Cymbeline*?" Dorothy asked.

"Shakespeare play," he said, forcing a worried grin. "What about it?"

" 'Come to dust' is a quote from Shakespeare," she said patiently. "That's the name of our product line here. Got no images for the ads. That's what we've been doing all morning. Where's your brain, the moon?"

"Maybe," Keith said apologetically. He picked up the data sheet PDQ had received from the parent company. "Uh, it's a clever line, like it was meant to mean something about cleaning. You have any idea what *Cymbeline* is about?" Dorothy shook her head. "Me, neither. Well, how about young men and women in *Midsummer Night's Dream* costumes pirouetting around a living room dusting and vacuuming?"

"Yes, why not? I can do that," Dorothy said. The lines flew out from under her pencil. With a few deft touches, she created lively figures in floating draperies wielding feather dusters and mops.

"Cute," Keith said, watching her enviously. "I wish I could do that."

"All it takes is practice," Dorothy said, self-deprecatingly. "I bet you'd be good."

"My, my, what have we here?" Brendan asked, coming in and looking over Dorothy's shoulder. "Very nice."

"Good enough to steal?" Keith asked. Dorothy's eyes widened, but she said nothing.

"Temper, Keith," Brendan said, wagging a finger at him. "See you after lunch."

"What's he done?" Dorothy asked as their *bete noir* disappeared out the door again.

"Nothing much," Keith mumbled. "Forget it."

"Well, why don't you tell Paul about it?"

"I don't want to bring him into it," Keith said. "It's personal."

"Uh-huh," Dorothy said. "Everything gets personal with Mr. Smug out there. Sorry I asked. Want to get something to eat?"

"I'm not really hungry."

"Hey, come and watch me eat, then," she said.

"Sure," Keith said, forcing a modicum of good humor into his voice. With an effort, he stood up and followed her. His legs and arms, as well as his brain, seemed to have been encased in lead. Nothing was moving today.

"Keith?" the secretary called, as they appeared in the reception hall.

"Yes?"

"Telephone call for you. I can put it through to the conference room if you don't want to take it out here."

Keith hoped it was Diane. "I'll take it back there. Thanks." He shrugged regret at Dorothy. "Sorry. It's important."

"Win some, lose some," she said. "See you later."

Keith dashed back to the room and punched the blinking light on the telephone. "Hello?"

"Keith Doyle?"

"Holl? What's wrong?" Keith suddenly had a mental picture of the elves besieged, and remembered what he was supposed to have been doing before he became so preoccupied.

"Nothing more, be reassured. We've had an interesting conversation with the woman, and I wanted to bring you up to date." Holl repeated the exchange he had had that morning with Mona Gilbreth, and what they planned to do.

"You shouldn't send her anything, Holl," Keith said, pacing up and down in the empty conference room. "She's responsible for kidnaping your baby, killing a being we hardly knew anything about, and she's still refusing to say when she'll let your other kid come home. You'll have her on your back forever if she can get you to start paying blackmail because you think she knows you're elves."

"We're not," Holl said firmly, "and it ends the moment we have Dola back," he promised.

"Well, yeah, she's what's important," Keith agreed. "What are you sending to Kill-breath as this token?"

"The stone from Maura's ring," Holl said. "It's a small thing, truly."

"Oh, Holl," Keith said, sympathetically, then suddenly stopped pacing. "Oh, God, where are you going to get anything like that for the rest of the ransom?"

"We will not. The rest need not resemble the first offering. We will substitute something appropriate."

"You keeping up with orders? Is there anything coming in?"

"Now that we have come to terms with shock, loss, and violation, we are functioning. All is well on that end."

"Well, you can't miss the house payment," Keith said practically, walking around and around the conference table and playing out the phone cord between his fingers as he thought. "We'll find a way to raise it." He wished once again they could call in some kind of authority. It would solve the problem long before it got to the ransom stage. He started to plan out loud a lightning raid on the gift shops in the Midwestern area to collect orders, but none of it really added up to the amount Gilbreth's henchman had demanded. "I don't think even Ms. Voordman would have an order that would amount to more than a fortieth . . ." Holl stopped him in midsentence.

"We'll manage," the elf said in a soothing tone. "The solution needn't be thought of in this same minute."

Keith stopped pacing and leaned his head against a wall. "Sorry. I'm under pressure. One of my fellow interns is making a total pest of himself. He follows me all over the place. He poured coffee on one of my layouts. It took forever to reproduce." Holl murmured sympathy. "Thanks, but that's not the worst of it. He fielded a call from Diane and told her I was out with Dorothy, one of the other interns. We were only having lunch, but he made it sound like we were having a quickie affair. Now Diane's not speaking to me. I called her back, and she kept hanging up on me. He convinced her that within one month out of her sight I've turned into a Casanova with my coworkers. I wish I had something to rub his face in, say wet concrete studded with live scorpions. I haven't been able to concentrate on anything all day long. Dorothy warned me Gilbreth had sicced him on me, but I never imagined he'd stoop to sabotaging my love life.''

Holl sounded sympathetic but amused. ''You sound as if you're under siege in that great fastness where you work. All will be resolved in time.''

''Yeah,'' Keith said. ''I know. We just have to live through it. There are more important things to worry about, like Dola.''

''Aye. But for pity's sake, Keith Doyle, if you want to assuage Diane's concerns, why do you not declare yourself to her?''

''Aw, come on, Holl— Gotta go,'' Keith said suddenly, hearing the doorknob turning and seeing an unwelcome face appear. ''Brendan's coming,'' he whispered in a breath that only an elf would be able to hear.

''Ready for the next round, Keith?'' Martwick asked brightly, slapping his briefcase on the tabletop.

''Looking forward to it, Brendan,'' Keith said, hanging up the phone. Sean came in and put his jacket into the closet.

''Have a good lunch?'' he asked them. They glared at each other and smiled at him.

Dorothy came in with Paul Meier. ''So where is it, Keith?'' Paul asked, slapping his hands together and rubbing them. ''Dorothy tells me you got something together on 'Come To Dust' just before lunch time. Let's see.''

Keith sifted through the papers on the tabletop, growing more frantic as he reached successive layers without seeing the sketch.

''What's the matter?'' Meier asked.

''The sketch isn't here,'' Keith said.

''Did you take it somewhere?'' Dorothy asked.

''No. I was only out of the room for a minute,'' Keith said. ''I've been in here on the phone almost the whole time.'' He looked at Brendan, who raised his hands innocently.

''I didn't see it. I left before you guys, remember?''

It didn't mean he hadn't come back. Keith opened his mouth, planning to deliver a sour retort when Paul interrupted him.

''Well, come on, kids. If it's a good idea, I want to see it. If the sketch is missing, do another one.''

Keith turned appealing eyes toward Dorothy. The artist hated

to do things over again, but she reproduced the drawing with
admirable skill, and showed it to Paul. He nodded over it and
stroked his chin.

"Kind of predictable, but I bet the client had an idea like that
anyway. I don't know why they didn't just suggest it when we
first met with them. Not bad."

"I'd rather you said it stunk than you thought it was *predictable*," Keith said, feeling discontented.

"That's the attitude you want for advertising," Paul said,
approvingly. "All or nothing. Well, work on it if you're not
happy. Look, it's better than nothing. Okay, everyone, we'll
give it a rest. Here are your missions for this afternoon."

Keith hardly listened as he was assigned to go run coffee and
doughnuts for the Appalachi-Cola account vice president. He
hated to be thought of as mediocre, and was now completely
annoyed with the world. Brendan was just the biggest part of
what was wrong with it all. Keith realized with dismay how
much he had come to dislike Brendan over the space of only a
few days. The smug youth had been a minor annoyance in the
first weeks of their internship, but he was now a downright pain
in the ass. He heard Paul call on Brendan.

"You're going to work with Ben Solanson on the Gilbreth
campaign," the supervisor said. "She likes you. Ben likes you.
It's a good situation." Brendan looked even more self-satisfied
than usual, and patted his leather-bound notebook. "Good. We'll
meet back here at the end of the day to count noses." He held
up his coffee cup for a sip and noticed it was empty.

"I'll get you some," Brendan offered, keeping up with his
new role as fair-haired boy. He took Meier's cup over to the side
table. While his back was turned and the others were watching
him perform the small task of pouring coffee, Keith tipped up
the cover of the notebook with a pencil, and read some of the
notes jotted down about Gilbreth on the top page under the
heading "Pamphlet."

I didn't know she was a Rhodes scholar, Keith thought with
interest.

"Say, Paul," he asked, as Brendan came back with the coffee,
"is PDQ responsible if we disseminate false information?"

Meier's black brows drew down over his long nose. "Sometimes. Why?"

"No reason, Paul," Keith said, rising from the table to get his notes. "Thanks."

He was fairly sure the jottings he had done on the Appalachi-Cola account the week before were in the back of his file drawer. As he opened it, he checked the charm-alarms on his files. One of them had been triggered.

Carefully, making sure no one else was watching him, he flicked the file folders forward with the edge of a storyboard card, and felt his way to the violated envelope. Nothing had been taken out; in fact there was something there that shouldn't have been: Dorothy's first sketch for "Come To Dust."

"I should have known," he muttered.

Keith asked the secretary in reception for an outgoing telephone line, and called the Chicago Public Library from the remote phone.

"Reference information hot line? Yeah. Is there some kind of list of Rhodes scholars?" he asked, being careful to keep his voice down. "Uh huh. Could you check a name for me?" Messengers, agency employees, and clients passed around him while he waited, all immersed in their own business. Keith smiled at the ones who met his eyes. "Uh huh, that's great. Yeah, thanks."

He walked away from the phone whistling.

Mona couldn't understand how her nemesis could avoid detection so neatly. H. Doyle was *always* there when she called, but never there when anyone else visited. The police hadn't seen a trace of him on the first or subsequent visits. The phone company representative reported seeing only the one young woman. When she left for the afternoon, no one answered the door, and no signs of life were apparent either in the barn or the house. The INS officer went over within minutes after Mona hung up after speaking with H. Doyle, but he was already gone and no one on the surveillance team had seen him leave. It was like magic. The line check confirmed there was only one line into the house, and only one phone inside, and that one was at half-height on the kitchen wall. She wondered if, as the young woman's comments had suggested, he might be in a wheelchair, but no wheelchair-bound person could move so fast when the investigators dropped by. And he wasn't Keith Doyle, because Brendan Martwick reported that Keith was in Chicago at work at the times she called. There was something very weird going on at Hollow Tree Farm.

In the meantime, the harassment continued. Mona got more carping phone calls and letters of complaint, and suffered confrontations in the street and at rallies. She called up the farm and accused H. Doyle, who gave her his word that he wasn't responsible. He continued to push for a date to have the girl returned to him.

Mona was waiting to see the 'token' he had promised before she would make any commitment. She wasn't about to sell out cheaply, not with accounts receivable barely covering the in-plant expenses. Gilbreth Feed was pushed to its credit limits. She put off paying some other bills to get money to cover the haulage account to please the EPA inspectors on their return visit, and used charm on her other creditors so they would wait a little longer for their money. They were not pleased, but her promise that they would receive the very next available funds ensured they'd keep supplies and services running satisfactorily.

The EPA surprise inspection had set off another firecracker. Mona, returning from more campaigning Wednesday afternoon, found an urgent message from the office of the Democratic National Committee waiting for her. With her heart hammering in her throat, she dialed the number and asked for Jack Harriman, the assistant to the state chairman.

"Mona!" the hearty voice greeted her. "Glad to hear from you. So glad you called back."

"Jack," she said, equally heartily. "To what do I owe this pleasure?"

"Well, lady, it's like this. There's a rumor floating around up here that you're having a few problems with EPA standards— some overspill from your tanks?"

"Well, perhaps a little—it's fertilizer, of course," Mona replied, in the sweetest voice she could muster. "There are nothing but farm fields on all sides of the plant. It doesn't hurt corn to feed it more fixed nitrogen, especially in this season. You ought to come down and see for yourself. Very green."

"Uh, no, thanks, lady," Jack said. "I'm an urban cowboy,

myself. What we want to know is, if there was a chemical spill, why didn't you report it to the EPA or the county yourself? We're getting flak up here."

Mona swallowed. "I'm sorry you're being harassed, Jack. It happens to me all the time."

"That's not good in this kind of messy election year," the assistant said. Mona could sense the veil coming off the threat. "We're too vulnerable. If it goes on, it could turn into a media circus. Your viability comes into question, Mona. The party might have to pull back on endorsing you, out of pure survival instinct."

"What?" Mona cried. "But we're almost there! It's September. What about my position in the community? My platform?"

"We can't go on calling you the Environmental Candidate if you're . . . misleading us all about your environmental standards," Jack said reasonably. "I'll be frank with you, lady. If the Committee—not to include myself in that group, but we've all got to kowtow to them—starts to feel you're an embarrassment, they're going to cut their losses and run with the candidates they think can go the distance." He sounded apologetic. "We've got to keep the Democratic majority in the House. Unless you've got something substantial to add to the Committee?"

Mona knew what that meant. The higher-ups were taking her public humiliation as a chance to ask for a donation. Her perceived wealth as a property and business owner was once again working against her. Only she knew how bare the cupboard was, but she had little choice. They were forcing her to cough up or concede.

"Of course," she said, keeping her voice level. "I'll have something substantial to funnel toward the party very soon."

Jack offered effusive thanks, and hung up. Mona cradled the phone feeling flustered and angry. She was certain that the continued annoyances—culminating in a threat to discontinue her dearly-won candidacy—could be laid at the feet of Hollow Tree Farm and the Doyles, in spite of their promises. She knew there was no way to prove her suspicion. They kept saying they would never do anything to jeopardize the safety of the child. It was hard to argue with that kind of logic, but equally hard to disagree with the gut feeling she had about them.

The blond child was still holed up in the cabin bedroom, emerging only for the necessities. Williamson reported that Grant Pilton was upset because she had been doing the cooking, and now he had to rely on his own meager skills. The child was becoming more of a nuisance with every day that passed. Mona resolved to get rid of her as soon as she had a good, financial reason to do so.

Chapter
SIXTEEN

A little discreet questioning by Keith around the office
on Thursday gleaned the information that publishing
false data was regarded as the advertising industry's
equivalent of insider trading: it was okay as long as the
perpetrator didn't get caught. Keith fully intended that Brendan
would get caught.

The vice president in charge of Mona Gilbreth's accounts was
very pleased with Brendan, a fact that the young man announced
to anyone who would listen, or anyone who didn't move away
too quickly. He dropped first names with alacrity, something
Keith and Dorothy, at least, found funny.

Keith thought the V.P. would have been happy with anybody
willing to do all the gruntwork on a project but leave most of the
credit for him. He was trusting Brendan to do everything right,
so he hadn't been checking on what was going into those press
releases that he approved. Brendan bragged at length about having the vice president's trust when he returned to the conference
room at the end of the day. Keith, sitting next to him, rolled his
eyes toward heaven as the paean of self-praise went on and on.
Sean, across from Keith, grinned.

"So you think it's all in the bag for you, huh, Brendan?"
Sean asked, uneasily. In spite of the fact that the creative team
for Dunbar professed undying love for Sean's ideas, Dunbar was
kicking up a fuss with the PDQ administration. Sean was afraid
that if Dunbar went shopping for another agency, PDQ would
to vanish.

Mona grabbed for the arm to the storekeel and immed until

consider it his fault and drop him from the program. He'd been nervous all week. "The job and all?"

"Surely, my man, surely," Brendan said, delivering a loving pat to a sheet of paper sitting on top of his notebook. "Ben loves my touch with a press release." He rose. " 'Scuse me."

He left the room, leaving the press release temporarily unguarded. Keith couldn't resist temptation like that.

"Immortal words," he said, spreading a clean sheet of paper on top of Brendan's draft. "Rest in peace." He signed the cross over it. Sean laughed and went back to his tire ads.

Staring hard enough at the paper to burn holes in it with his eyes, Keith willed the blank sheet to take on an image of the print below. As Brendan returned to the room, Keith snatched back his sheet of paper, curious why no print had appeared. In a moment of inspiration he glanced at the back, then wondered what part of Catra's instructions he had gotten wrong. The copy had been reproduced in perfect mirror image on the side that had touched the original.

He secreted the page in his notebook and carried it into the hall to peruse. Backward or forward, the release made interesting reading. Brendan had decided, either on his own or after prompting by Mona Gilbreth, to pad her credentials to make her sound much more impressive than she was. Keith intended that Brendan would get caught with his factual pants down, but not right away. He didn't want to jeopardize Dola's life by retaliating against Gilbreth's student stooge. Once Dola was safe, all bets for Brendan's future sanity, career, or peace of mind were off. Brendan was going to pay for making trouble between him and Diane. It was especially irritating when there was no time to go down to Midwestern in person to straighten things out. Keith was delighted Brendan himself had provided him with the proof that he was indulging in unapproved business practices. As long as Keith kept his eyes open for attacks by Brendan and kept a step and a half ahead, he could wait until the correct opportunity came along to help Brendan get what he deserved.

Thankfully, there was nothing else going on down at the farm to which he needed to give his attention. At least at present, Gilbreth was holding the line on letting Dola go. The harassment of the Folk on the farm made Keith furious, but they assured him they were handling it.

Ground searches by the Little Folk with Big Folk drivers had been curtailed because all the college students had classes. He wasn't forgetting, as Diane had accused him hurtfully over the phone, that other people had their own responsibilities. He winced at the memory of her angry voice. Brendan had a lot to answer for.

It had been too windy downstate to fly, grounding the balloon surveillance team, and besides, Frank Winslow hadn't exactly been in the mood since the air sprite popped out. Keith couldn't blame him. He knew the way he would feel if anything serious ever did happen to one of the elves. All in all, it seemed there was no way to find Dola until Gilbreth was ready to give her up. That meant Keith could only worry until the weekend, when he could finally go down to supervise the hunt himself, and make up with Diane.

Keith stuffed the paper back into his notebook and went back in to join the others. Where one indiscretion lay, there would undoubtedly be more. He suspected that Brendan was also pushing the envelope on the budget for the Gilbreth double account. He had seen an order for "Amber Waves Of Grain" posters sitting on the secretary's desk in the foyer. There was an additional request appended in Brendan's handwriting for a hundred single-sheets. Chances were good that neither Paul nor Solanson had authorized them. Keith saved up the fact to tell Paul when next he needed ammunition. It was a chance to get back at both of them. Gilbreth had enlisted Brendan to make life tough for him, and he intended to return that favor with interest.

Maybe if he could get ahold of the single-sheets when they arrived, he could infuse them with a sense of revulsion. He'd laughed out loud when the Master had told him about Diane, Dunn, and the enhanced flyers at Gilbreth's rallies. It was too good an idea not to repeat. Just to make certain, he took a copy of the print order.

The weekend was only two days away. Keith wondered how he could hold on forty-eight hours more. Saturday morning, wind, rain, or shine, he was going down to Hollow Tree Farm, and he was determined that they would get Dola back that day, or bust.

* * *

Mona Gilbreth received her mail with trepidation. On top, her receptionist had placed the increasing stack of overdue bills and dunning memos from her creditors. The very sight of them depressed her. There were more letters, too, she noted with dismay. Unable to stomach answering even one more, she tossed them unopened into the wastebasket. That left only one more item, a small box.

"What's this?" she asked.

"I don't know, ma'am," the receptionist said. "It was in the mailbag."

Mona turned over the small cardboard carton, and nearly dropped it. On the back, the return address was Hollow Tree Farm. She retrieved the pile of mail, carried them and the tiny box into her office, and locked the door.

Inside the box was a round blue jewel. Mona picked it up and let it rest in her palm, admiring the lights that shone through it onto her skin. The sapphire looked almost *too* perfect, but it had an aura of genuineness that impressed her into deep and silent respect.

The jeweler, an old friend of the family, came at her request to have a look at the stone. After making a careful examination of it, first through his spectacles, then through a loupe and a small microscope that he carried in a case, he looked up at her.

"You're right, Mona dear. It's real, and worth a pot of money. It's an antique cut, absolutely flawless. *Perfect*. I haven't seen anything like this outside of a museum, even the Smithsonian. May I ask where you got it?"

"It's a family heirloom," Mona said. "I just inherited it." She held up the box it had arrived in, but carefully kept the address out of sight.

"Wonderful," he said, shaking his head.

"Could you sell it for me?"

"Without any trouble, dear. You leave it to me. Shall I take it with me now?" He seemed to be as reluctant as she had been to put it down.

"Um . . . what's it worth?"

For answer, the jeweler took a pad of paper and pen, and wrote a number on it. He pushed it toward her. "Not a penny less than that, and maybe more."

Mona gazed at the figure. For the first time in two weeks she started to think that things were looking up. The jeweler packed the sapphire into a padded, plastic pillbox, and placed it carefully into the box with the microscope.

"I'll call you. If nothing else, *I'll* buy the stone from you. As an investment. I'll call you by the end of the day."

"Thank you!" Mona remembered to say as the old man left. She picked up the phone and dialed out. As soon as the other end was answered, she said, "That's quite an interesting package I received today. I wouldn't mind hearing there was more where that one came from."

"There is," H. Doyle said. "We'll give you two pounds of the same if you return our child." Two pounds of fabulous jewels, each stone worth a fortune! Mona was elated. She must have punched exactly the right button to make these people squirm. "When can we meet?"

"Wait a minute," Mona said. "It has to be exactly the right place. I'm not going to let you bully me into someplace I feel vulnerable. I want the least exposure possible. I'll be in touch with you," she said.

Without waiting for H. Doyle to protest, she briskly slapped down the phone and strode out of the room, pausing long enough to grab her purse.

"Hold all my calls," she said to the receptionist on her way out the door. "I'm going shopping!"

Dorothy came into the conference room, looking panic-stricken. Brendan smiled up at her, but her gaze went past him and lit upon Keith.

"Hey, I thought you sent the storyboard for 'Getting Off Lightly' over to Bob," she said accusingly. "I just met him in the hall. He says he's been waiting three days for it."

"I did send it," Keith said, his mouth dropping open. "I put it in interoffice mail on Monday."

"Well, it didn't get there," Dorothy said warningly. "I'm not going to do it all over again."

"It'll be okay," Keith said. "I'll go and explain to the team what happened."

"They won't be happy," Dorothy said, following him out the door.

Brendan was delighted. It was the first trick he had played on Keith that had really paid off. He'd had the most incredible run of bad luck trying to set Keith up. File drawers Keith used wouldn't open to anyone else's touch. Some wouldn't close after Brendan pried them open. Sprays of paper exploded out of pigeonholes and notebooks, without any visible mechanism propelling them. He was dying to ask Keith how the trick worked, but he didn't dare. Keith would want to know, and reasonably, too, what Brendan was doing in his files.

The weird thing was that Keith always seemed to know what stuff had been messed with. Brendan didn't know how he did that, either. Maybe there were spycams in the ceiling? He checked the room's corners, looking for surveillance equipment. It wouldn't surprise him if he did find them. There was no trust whatsoever in this place; he ought to know.

He gloated, wondering just what Keith was planning to say to the creative director about the missing storyboard, which only he, Brendan, knew was floating in the Chicago River under the Michigan Avenue bridge.

"What are we going to say to them?" Dorothy demanded, as they strode down to the media coordinator's office.

"Nothing but 'I'm sorry this is late,' " Keith told her. "We have to stop here, first." Keith pushed open a door, and held it for her to pass through in front of him.

"Research?" Dorothy asked, recognizing the department.

"Mrs. Bell, hi there!" Keith said. "How's my favorite investigator?"

"Can the crap, sonny," Mrs. Bell said. She was a short, plump woman with a cigarette perpetually stuck in the corner of her mouth. Her desk was the only untidy spot in the room. She was legendary for her organization, and Dorothy had learned to revere her in the short time the interns had spent in her department. "What do you want?"

"Can I have my file?" Keith asked, bowing on one knee to the research librarian.

The woman reached into a deep drawer and pulled out a brown cardboard portfolio. She brushed cigarette ash off its surface. "Taking it with you?"

"Nope," Keith said, untying it and fishing through its contents. Over his arm, Dorothy could see dozens of storyboards and sketches.

"What is this?" she asked.

"Security," Keith said. "Since my stuff started disappearing, and getting sent to the wrong offices, or getting things spilled on them, I've been making color Xeroxes of everything and hiding them down here. That way I never lose any more work. There we go." He pulled out a copy of the Judge Yeast layout and handed it to her. Deftly, he retied the folder and returned it to Mrs. Bell. "Come on," he said cheerfully. "The team won't wait forever."

Brendan slipped into Paul Meier's office in the afternoon. Paul glanced up from his work. "Hi, Brendan. All done with the Gilbreth campaign?"

"Coffee break," Brendan said, managing to make it sound amusing and beneath his notice.

The subtlety was not lost on Meier. He raised an eyebrow. "So what can I do for you? Sit down." He gestured at a couple of chairs against the wall.

Brendan pulled a chair up to Meier's desk. "Paul, I wanted to bring something up. I feel kind of hesitant about saying anything."

"Well, that's a first," Meier said dryly.

"What?"

"Nothing. What is it?"

Brendan leaned forward confidingly. "Well, in the last week or so, something seems to have been bugging Keith. Oh, he's here, most of the time," Brendan said, laying slight stress on the last phrase, "but his *mind* isn't here."

"I noticed, but he seems to be doing the work," Paul said. "What's the problem?"

"Part of our grade is based on attendance, right? Well, he's been taking days off. The rest of us all come every day. It isn't right, when we're expected to show up. Take last Wednesday. He wasn't here because he had to run downstate because of a personal matter. You sent him to see Ms. Gilbreth while he was there. When she came in on Monday, she wouldn't talk to him. What do you think he must have done?"

"I can't imagine. So what are you suggesting? That he

shouldn't get the same grade as you because he's got poor attendance and he enrages the clients?''

"If he's upsetting clients, should he even be in the program?" Brendan asked delicately. "If his personal life affects the way he treats clients?"

Paul tilted his head back and looked down his long nose at Brendan. "You raise some interesting points, Brendan. You think maybe I should talk to Keith?" he asked, his voice expressionless. "Find out if he made an ass of himself downstate?"

"Oh, yes," Brendan said, then added hastily, "but I'd appreciate it if you wouldn't mention me, okay? I'm just trying to keep the program running at its best."

"I'm sure you are," Paul said, standing up. "Thanks for coming to me."

Brendan left the office at a quick trot. He was halfway down the hall before he gave vent to his joy. Ms. Gilbreth was going to be so pleased with him. The job was absolutely his—in the bag, signed, sealed and delivered. He bent, fist clenched, into a convulsive gesture of glee. "Yes!"

The executives and employees passing by him in the corridor shot half-curious looks at him, and kept going.

Meier caught up with Keith as the redheaded student was carrying a veiled storyboard from a conference room down to the art department.

"How's it going, Keith?" Meier asked, falling into step beside him.

"Great," Keith said. He was cheerful. "The vice president for the Dunbar account just pitched 'The Brain,' and the client loves it."

"That's not your slogan," Meier said. "It's Sean's."

"Nope, but Sean is part of our group," Keith explained. "Every time one of us succeeds, there's less resistance among the account executives for listening to student-generated ideas."

"Don't be so sure." Meier shook his head. "Remember the delicate balance between someone being overjoyed at getting ideas he didn't pay for and someone worried about preserving his job. But I'm glad you're an optimist. Keith, it's come to my attention that you and Ms. Gilbreth didn't exactly hit it off. Now, she's not PDQ's biggest client, but she's important to us. We don't want to lose her. Is there something going on between you that I don't know about?''

"Nothing to do with me, Paul," Keith said, picking his words carefully. "It turns out she knows one of my cousins. They don't get along. They have . . . different views."

"On politics?"

"Yeah, among other things. They've had a couple of run-ins recently, and I'm just catching the flak."

Meier was mollified but not fully convinced. "Well, all right, but get some work done, huh? I've got another new product that needs some hot ideas, and you're my idea man. Fairy Footwear, kids' wear from American Footwear. Fantasy stuff for little girls, on up to teenagers, but orthopedically correct."

"Hmmm," Keith said. " 'The most comfortable thing on two feet'? 'The lightest thing on two feet'?"

"Keep going," Meier said, pushing the door of the art department open for him. "I think you're onto something there. By the way, are you and Brendan having problems? I caught him stuffing papers into your file drawer Tuesday morning. He said they all fell out."

"Fairy Footwear," Keith mused, sitting in the students' borrowed conference room with a pen and legal pad. He tapped his upper lip. "What do fairies and shoes have in common?" He started doodling. "Shoemakers? No way. Little girls aren't interested in making shoes. Dancing?"

Dorothy came in. "Hey, sketching is my act."

Keith grinned up at her. "Sorry."

"What's that?" Dorothy asked, pointing a red-tipped finger at his drawing.

"They're dancers," he said. Keith hastily moved his hand to cover up the illusion of a real dancer he had cast on the edge of the pad to give him the pose he wanted, and let her look at the rough sketch. By their postures, his stick figures seemed to be afflicted by fleas, nervous tics, or live fish down their shorts. They were ranged in a circle around a hemispherical lump covered with jagged lines that were meant to indicate grass and flowers. Dorothy shook her head and clicked her tongue at them. Keith flushed.

"Come on, I know drawing isn't my long suit. I'm working

on something for Fairy Footwear. This is a fairy ring," he said. He started to explain about fairy mounds, rings, and the associations people in olden times had had with certain kinds of geological and biological features. In a few minutes, his explanation had developed into a full-scale lecture.

Dorothy found herself getting interested, and settled in with her elbows propped up at the table. "You know a lot about this legendary stuff, don't you?"

"My life's work," Keith threw off lightly. "I'm a research mythologist when I'm not coming up with hit slogans and ad layouts." He drew stick figures of creatures with wings. Without intending to, he started filling in the features of the air sprites, then changed his mind. Sprites didn't have feet to wear shoes on. "The old storytellers used to say that fairies danced in these rings, and where they stepped, things like mushrooms grew up. They're really caused by the natural outward progression of a multi-generation fungus colony."

Dorothy wrinkled her nose. "Ugh. I didn't need to know that." His hand had slipped away from the edge of the pad. She grabbed his fingers and moved them to see what was under them.

"How come you draw your roughs in stick figures when you can do drawings like that?" she asked, pointing to the beautifully realized image of a dancer.

Keith hastily covered the illusion again, and scrubbed at it with his eraser to make it look like he was wiping it out as he dispelled it. "I think better in stick figures, I guess," he said. "The fancy stuff takes too long."

Dorothy flung back the cover of her sketch pad. "So you're thinking of fairies dancing, huh? What do your fairies look like? Besides white, I mean. That much I can guess."

Keith thought about what fairies did look like. He thought of the last time he had seen Dola, and had a sudden, overpowering inspiration.

"You know, I know a little girl who would be perfect for a commercial like this," he said. "Dancing in the moonlight, with little wings on her shoulders. She looks like one of the, uh," he searched his memory for the name of the artist, "Kate Greenaway watercolors of fairies."

"Oh, I know those. I know the style. Describe her," Dorothy said, her pencil poised. "Sounds like you've got an idea. You tell me, and I'll draw it. You're not gonna get the executive excited about a lot of stick figures.''

Keith pictured Dola as best he could. "Well, she's about three feet tall, with long blond hair. Her eyes are blue. Her nose is little, and tilts up at the tip, yeah," he said, watching Dorothy draw. "Like that. And she has a pointed chin, but it's not a sharp point, more like a little ball. Her face is thin in the jaw, but it gets wide over her cheekbones, and there's a shadow underneath them that goes up to meet the line of her ears."

"Which are pointed, right?"

"Yeah," Keith said, surprised.

Dorothy sighed. "I should have guessed."

At length, Dorothy had a gorgeous representation of one small winged girl dancing in a moonlit glade, holding hands with other beings whose features were only suggested by shadows.

"That is absolutely fabulous," Keith said. He stood up. "It gives me all sorts of great ideas. I've got to go tell Paul." He tore the drawing from the pad and made for the door. "Thank you!" he called over his shoulder.

"No problem," Dorothy said, shaking her head.

"It's pretty," Paul said, after listening to Keith's enthusiastic ravings about the drawing, "but really, I don't quite see it."

"A spokeswoman," Keith said. "A . . . a mascot for Fairy Footwear. They could have the Fairy Footwear Fairy. Kids would learn to recognize her, like grown women look for Paulina Porizkova or Cindy Crawford. We could have a whole search to find The Fairy Footwear Fairy. Statewide!"

"Well, yeah," Paul said, starting to look more interested. "Yes, good. You need more realization for this. Why don't you get Dorothy to do a whole storyboard for you. You've got to really sell this to the customer. I think it's great, but I'm only the V.P., I don't buy campaigns *for* the customer."

"Okay," Keith said, rolling the drawing into a tube. "Tomorrow I'll have something that'll knock their eyes out!"

"It'll get the ball rolling," Keith expostulated into the phone, waving one hand in the air as he paced up and back in the family kitchen. "If I can get PDQ to cooperate, they'll have a casting call to find the right little girl to fill Fairy Footwear. That'll be Dola. It'll be a way for us to get Ms. Gilbreth to bring Dola up here to Chicago.''

"All very well to speculate," Holl said, trying to get Keith to calm down, "but how do you convince them to spend the time and money seeking all the way down here for their model?"

"The illustration in the ad is going to look just like her," Keith said. "By the time I get through with them, they won't be satisfied with any other model. They'll want *her*. All we need to do is get the brass to agree to put out a casting call right away. As Paul said, I've got to sell it to them, and I don't think any old storyboard will do the job. But if we can get Gilbreth to bring her up here, pow! We've got her!"

"The best of luck to you, Keith Doyle," Holl said. "We'll be ready to go whenever you say."

Making sure Jeff wasn't in the house, Keith pushed both beds in their room as close against the walls as they would go. In the space, he set up a card table and draped it with a white sheet. Using Dorothy's illustration as a model, Keith started to work on his sample commercial.

"If you can see an illusion," he reasoned out loud, "you can film an illusion."

From a locked suitcase hidden under his bed, he unearthed a wooden 'magic lantern' given to him by the Little Folk. Its particular virtue was that it was able to record about a minute's worth of sight and sound of anything it was pointed at. He peered at it, and blew dust off its gauze 'screen.' It hadn't been used in a couple of years. He tested it, making faces into the screen, then directed it to play back. His face, shrunk down to an inch across, confronted him, grimacing horribly. Keith grinned, and began to construct his illusion.

On a cassette tape recorder, he excerpted about a minute of the "Dance of the Sugar Plum Fairies," and played it over and over, listening to the rhythm. In the center of the table, he raised an image of the fairy mound he had seen in Scotland.

It was easier to draw an illusory ring above it and affix more illusions to it, carousel style, than to try and make independent figures dance in a circle. He didn't think it was necessary to really define the others with more detail than cartoons of fairies, but the figure of Dola had to be absolutely exact. He dug out photographs he had of her, and even played back the videotape of Holl's wedding to make sure he got the image right. The child had been wearing a wreath in her hair that day. Keith fashioned his Dola wearing the simple green tunic he'd last seen her in, and the flower circlet. With an indulgent hand, he added lacy wings, and made her smile. It was almost as if she was really there. He wished he could touch her.

"We'll spring you, I promise," Keith told the simulacrum.

Using Paul's product photos, he added shoes to Dola's feet. They were an incredible lime green with purple, pink, and teal accents. Maybe it was because the combination of colors blunted the senses, but they looked good against the green grass of the mound.

"Now, come on. Let's dance."

It was exhausting work getting the figures to move and caper the way he wanted them to. He was grateful the magic lantern worked by itself. He felt it was very appropriate, using illusions to help free Dola, whose special talent was making illusions.

On the twentieth try, he got the movements to correspond to the beat of the music, and was looking forward to calling it a wrap when Jeff barged in.

Keith looked up in horror. The little figures froze in place. Keith fought to hold on to his concentration. There was no way he'd be able to conjure them back the way he wanted them before morning. He cursed his brother's timing.

"Hi," he said weakly.

Jeff stared down at the table. "What's this?" he asked.

"Computer holographs," Keith said, desperately. "You know. Puppet figures, entered into computer memory banks. Then we shoot them through a special split lens, and when you project it, it makes a holographic image. See? Pretty good?"

"Bullshit," Jeff pronounced. "There's no computer, no projector, and I don't see any strings." He shook his head, showing the first respect he had had for Keith since they were kids, and it was tainted with a modicum of fear. "Is it . . . magic?"

Keith said nothing. Jeff dropped down on the bed across from him.

"There's been weird stuff going on with you ever since you

went away to college, and Mom and Dad won't talk about it,'' Jeff said, warily. "You aren't in one of those *cults*, are you?"

"No. Honest to God," Keith said. "I swear. All natural. One hundred percent organic."

"Well," Jeff said after a long pause, "then can I watch?"

Chapter
SEVENTEEN

The 'holograph' session went on a lot longer than Keith had originally envisioned. Having broken the ice, Jeff demanded further demonstrations. He wanted to know everything about magic, the Little Folk, and all of Keith's studies, and kept him talking almost 'til dawn. He even weaseled a loan of some of Keith's most precious books on mythology. But the most important upshot was that, by morning, they were friends again.

"I don't get it," Keith told his father privately after breakfast. "I thought he'd be scared into freaking out, but instead he spent the night asking questions."

"What's so strange about that?" Mr. Doyle asked, his grin a twin of his eldest son's. He patted Keith on the back. "He is a Doyle, after all."

In the conference room that morning, Keith ran the demo commercial for Paul and the others. Hiding the magic lantern against the back of the videotape recorder under the television, he pretended to roll a tape cassette. The interns and their supervisor watched spellbound, and broke into loud applause at the end.

"Again!" Paul called from the head of the table. "Run it again! This is absolutely amazing. You did this in one night?"

"Yup," Keith said. "You know you only gave me the assignment yesterday."

"Colossal! God, you must be exhausted."

"Computer animation?" Sean asked.

"Something like that," Keith admitted.

"The setup must have cost a fortune," Brendan said in a sour voice. He was jealous of the admiration Keith was getting.

No one paid attention to him. "This is just great," Paul said, watching the circle of cartoon fairies whisking the figure of Dola around and around to the tinkling music. The closeups cut in, first of Dola's twinkling feet, clad in the gaudy sneakers, followed by one of her glowing face. The American Footwear logo appeared over the next long shot. "You know, this is close enough to pro quality that they might just air it like it is."

"Oh, no! Uh, they can't!" Keith said, frantic.

"Why not?"

Keith swallowed. If they did take his perfect images, where was the need for searching for the right performer that would thereby rescue a little girl who'd been kidnaped? But he couldn't say that. "Uh, I'm not union," he choked out. It was lame, but effective. Paul snapped his fingers.

"Damn, you're right. That would skunk us for sure with the networks. Come on. We'll take it to Scott right now. This is brilliant! He's got to see it. He'll wet his pants."

The media director for the American Footwear account, a man with a broad and silky mustache, agreed that Keith's commercial was everything that the shoe company was looking for.

"It's got legs, pardon the pun," the director said, with an apologetic grin. "Just like this it could run—sorry, that was irresistible—*last* a long time. *Years*. Search for the Fairy Footwear girl? We'll have to. A great idea. Good publicity, too. I'll put it to the company this afternoon. You've saved me a ton of work, making a sample ad to show. The idea is always to leave as little to the client's imagination as possible, and this more than does the job. We could have a cattle call by the end of this week. The search for the Footwear Fairy." He drew a banner in the air.

"The end of this week?" Keith asked excitedly. "Tomorrow?"

"Sure, why not?" Scott said, showing his teeth under his mustache. "Things happen fast in the advertising business. Hot stuff, Paul. They'll love us. We've only had the product two days, and we're already in production. This could be worth a million."

"They might not take it," Paul said.

"Oh, they'll take it," Scott said.

His prediction was correct. By afternoon, Keith was asked to join the meeting with the representatives from American Footwear. He showed the ad over and over again, to the growing delight of the executives.

"God, it's perfect," said the director of public relations, a slender and balding man in his forties. "I *hated* the name when the designers came up with it, but you've made me love it. I'm behind you a hundred percent."

"It's a go," the finance director said. He was broad, bald, and pot-bellied. "I cannot believe how fast you came through, Paul, Scott. Absolutely cannot believe it." He chuckled.

"Brilliant," said the vice president of American Footwear, a middle-sized woman with carefully styled blond hair. She beamed at all of them. "I knew we were right to hire PDQ."

Keith sat beside the video ensemble, happy as a clam who had just won the Irish Sweepstakes. At the end of the meeting he reclaimed his magic lantern and stuck it into his briefcase. The executives drifted out toward the lobby, escorted by Paul, still talking about market share, frequency, and the search for just the right model.

"Uh, Scott?" he said, "can I take the press release down to the P.R. department?"

"Take it down?" Scott said. "You can write it if you want, Keith." He looked at his watch. "If you get your butt in gear and turn it in in the next half hour, we'll make the Saturday morning papers with time to spare." He sighed. "Even short notice like this will mean we'll be mobbed," he said sadly. "Every stage mother in the city will have her kid here before we open in the morning."

"How about statewide?" Keith suggested. "You only want to do this once, right?"

"You *are* a glutton for punishment. Sure. Statewide. Alert the troops. You'd better take the rest of the day off after you turn out the Press release. You'll need your strength tomorrow."

"Me?"

"Sure, kid. It's your idea," the director said. "You get to suffer the consequences along with the rest of us."

"Great!" Keith exclaimed.

Elated, he ran up to use a typewriter in one of the copywriters' offices. The words for the press release ran out easily under his fingers, and in no time, he had a notice of the correct length, in the correct format, ready to be signed off. He included a frame from his mockup commercial to illustrate the report.

Paul gave the text his approval. "A little flowery, but so what? It's your first time. Get out of here, and I'll see you in the morning. You look shot to pieces. Get some sleep. I'm sending the others home as soon as they finish today's assignments."

"Thanks, Paul!" Keith said.

On the way out, he took a small package addressed to Paul out of his file drawer. He thought of leaving it in Paul's mailbox, but elected not to, in case things didn't go as he hoped Saturday. Better to make sure, instead of jinxing the procedures ahead of time by being too cocky. He decided he'd rather wait and see.

Saturday morning, Jake Williamson and Mona Gilbreth paid a visit to Pilton at the cottage in the woods. Jake gave Pilton the daily paper and a carton of fresh milk, while Mona talked her way into the back room to see how her bankroll—she stopped herself in mid-thought—her *guest* was doing.

The girl looked at her sullenly from the corner of the room, her cheeks sunken and unhealthy looking. It seemed that she had been in that position for days. Mona only had Grant's word that the girl had even set foot out of the room.

"Are you sure she's eating?" Mona demanded, coming out of the bedroom. Behind her, the door lock snapped shut. The child must have flown to latch it as soon as Mona was out again.

"Yes'm, peanut butter and jelly sandwiches," Pilton confirmed, glancing up from the gossip column. "She eats about one a day. She never talks to me anymore, even though I said I'm sorry."

"You've got to stop apologizing for shooting her imaginary friend," Jake told him severely.

"It wasn't imaginary, Jake," Grant insisted. "I saw it too! And I thought maybe she'd be my lucky charm."

"Well, she's certainly been mine," Mona said. Her jeweler friend had come through with an offer for the antique sapphire, and the enormous sum was being transferred directly to her account. She had called each one of her creditors to say that the bills were being paid in full. She hadn't felt so wonderful in ages. Taking care of the outstanding invoices hadn't left a lot for the Democrats, but the ransom the child's folks had promised to pay would take care of that. She was just waiting for the right moment, the right place, to claim it.

"Hey. Look at this," Grant said, holding up a framed notice at the end of the gossip column for the others to read. "Isn't that funny? They're running a contest to find a fairy. We got us a *real* fairy right here. Matter of fact, the picture's a ringer for her."

"Aw, shut up, Grant," Jake said, impatiently.

Mona took the page away from him and read it carefully. Light dawned on her face. The fairy in the illustration *was* almost a perfect likeness of the little girl. Jake and Mona exchanged glances. Both of them knew it was deliberate, beckoning to them. The next move was theirs.

"Well, well," she told her foreman. "I don't think the resemblance is accidental. See? This contest is being run by PDQ. That Doyle boy must have set it up so we can exchange the kid for the cash quietly, where no one will notice. If this contest is real, it'll be the perfect cover. It's today. We can make it to Chicago if we start out right away. Her folks can have her back, if they have the money, and good riddance to her."

"If it's real," Williamson said.

"Get the girl ready," Mona said. "I'll be back in fifteen minutes."

She found a roadside phone booth and woke up Brendan Martwick at his home. Casually, she asked him about the contest in the newspaper. He didn't seem to think it was extraordinary that a state candidate would get him out of bed to ask him about a shoe commercial.

"Yes, ma'am," Brendan said sleepily. "I think Keith set it up, but it's real, all right. The media director's expecting five hundred kids. Are you coming up? It would be great to see you."

Mona said something noncommittal and hung up. She took a few deep breaths before dialing the next number.

"All right," she said into the phone. "We saw the ad. This is it. We'll meet you there. You bring the ransom. I'll bring the girl. We'll trade, er, packages, and get it over with. Yes, there. No police, or press, or any funny stuff."

"The ransom will be there," H. Doyle promised.

The jeweler was very pleased to meet the visiting gentleman from Ireland who was hunting for quality gemstones.

"Price is no object," Mr. Tyrone O'Wicklow said, expansively. He sat with his elbows propped on the low chair back. He seemed to have difficulty reaching up toward it, which puzzled the old man. Still, he reasoned, arthritis could happen to anyone. The Irishman hadn't even reached up to doff his hat.

"And you're specifically interested in a sapphire?" he asked.

"It's my sister's favorite stone," O'Wicklow said.

"Well," the jeweler said, temptingly, "if you're sure price is no object, let me show you something very special I just acquired." From his safe, he took the Gilbreth sapphire, and placed it carefully upon a black velvet board. Gently, reverently, he placed it before his visitor.

"Very nice," O'Wicklow said. "Ah, how lovely a color. You'd almost say the sky was trapped in glass, wouldn't you?" The jeweler picked up the gem between his fingers and turned it underneath the high-intensity lamp. The crown facet caught the light, which blazed into the old man's eyes.

Borrowing a loupe from his host, the Irishman leaned in to have a good look at the stone. The jeweler laid it in his palm and watched anxiously as he peered through the glass.

"What's this?" O'Wicklow demanded. "Do you take me for a child, then? Do I look like a great fool, for you to try and pass me a stone of paste?"

"Paste?" the old man asked, picking the sapphire off the man's outstretched palm. "This is real. I tested it myself." He took back the loupe and examined the stone. It still looked all right to him. Every facet had the right refractive value. "It couldn't be paste."

"There's a type you don't know, poor man," Mr. O'Wicklow said, calming down again. He sounded almost kindly. "Ah, you were a fool to take this without submitting it to the G.F. test." He pushed back from the desk and made a little bow. "If this is all that this poor town has to offer, I'll be taking myself away, then. I thank you for your time."

* * *

By ten A.M., the hall outside of the PDQ media director's office resembled back stage of a winter performance of *Nutcracker Suite* sharing a dressing room with a production of *The Wizard of Oz*. There were hundreds of little girls in gauzy costumes, some accompanied by their mothers, a few their fathers, and a few in the company of agents. They stood or sat against the walls of the corridor. A couple, in undisguised ballet garb, did stretches with hands on chairbacks for stability. Most of them were wearing makeup. A handful had gigantic, commercial rubber pixie ears stuck on.

The parents all had portfolios in their laps or against their knees, from notebook-sized up to leather zip cases that would hold theatrical posters flat. Keith, Dorothy, Sean, and Brendan had been given stacks of applications and a quick lesson in how to process the talent through to the media director.

"Just be polite and keep them happy while they're waiting," Scott said. "They'll be on good behavior right up until the time I turn them down for the part. Every one of them knows there's only one winner in this game, and they want to be it."

"I know you'll be fine," Paul said. "If there's a real problem you can't handle, come and get me." He added his blessings, and disappeared with Scott and the American Footwear executives into the inner sanctum.

Keith threaded his way between the shrill-voiced children, fielded the questions of a couple who wanted to know where the bathroom was, and helped the woman in charge of an entire Brownie troop in Halloween princess costumes fill out her application forms, all the time searching the faces for the ones he knew. Holl, Tay, Enoch, and the Master were coming up with Marcy. Dunn was already there, sitting close enough to an African-American child and her father to seem as if he was with them. Lee, interviewing a simpering mother and her precocious child, winked at Keith over their heads. He was there to do a human-interest story on the shoot for his newspaper, and run interference where and if needed.

A couple of the creative staff and the receptionist had come in to help out, too. The only stranger was Scott's assistant, a thin, intense young woman with pixie-cut brown hair and huge

glasses that dominated her small face. She flashed lightning-
quick smiles at everyone, and kept the queue moving smoothly
with charm and the implied threat of expulsion.

Diane had arrived by herself. She had taken charge of a clipboard, listened silently as Keith explained how to fill out applications, and was running completed forms up to the end of the hall,
to the media director's office. No one questioned her assured,
confident presence. Each of the executives in the audition room
thought she belonged to a different one of them. She ushered a
set of Japanese twins, aged about eight, into the office, sweeping
right by Keith without seeming to notice that he was there. She
passed him again, her eyes focused straight forward. He tried to
stop her and talk to her, but she shook his hand off her arm
without looking at him.

From the time she had arrived, she had refused to speak to
Keith. Whenever he had tried to talk about anything but Dola or
the auditions, she had turned him out and started a conversation
with one of the others from Midwestern. Frustrated and upset,
Keith watched her go by.

Dorothy came up to him after seeing the performance repeated
more than once. "You look like one of Little Bo Peep's lost
sheep. What's wrong with her?" she asked, in an undertone. "I
thought she was your girlfriend."

"Brendan," Keith said, his face red. "He told her you and I
were, well, having a thing, and she won't believe it's not true.
Well, we have had dinner together a couple of times. I didn't
deny that. I wouldn't. But she took it all wrong. You know how
persuasive Brendan is."

"Yeah. He wants to be in advertising," Dorothy said, wryly.
"Hang loose."

Diane, with cool efficiency, helped one of the children fill out
her application, and attached the portfolio photograph to the back
with a plastic paper clip.

"Just sit here for a moment, and we'll call you," she said.
She favored the little girl and her parent with a polite smile, and
moved on to the next one. Dorothy moved in on her and, paying
no attention to her protests, pushed her up the hall and into the
empty lunchroom. Diane tried to break free, but Dorothy kept
her arm in a solid grip.

"You and I have got to talk," Dorothy said. She planted her back against the door, blocking Diane's attempts to pull it open.

Diane retreated a few feet, tossed her head back and stared down her nose in mock hauteur. "You're extremely pretty. I can see why Keith's attracted to you. Let me go. I'm leaving." She made as if to force her way past, but retreated before actually laying hands on the other young woman.

Dorothy sighed and put her hands on her hips. "Listen, honey, I've got a man of my own. I don't need yours, and believe me, that man is *all* yours. You know it, too, or you wouldn't be here right now helping him. Why make life tougher for him than you need to?" The blond girl was staring at her as if Dorothy was speaking a language that she could just barely understand, but enlightenment was dawning. "You poor child," Dorothy said, with sincere sympathy, "I can tell you're so much in love with him that you'd believe any stupid thing you heard about him, right?"

"Yes," Diane said, in a whimper. "You're absolutely right."

Dorothy shook her head. "Tch, tch, tch. Don't you know he's shown your picture to everybody in this building? He talks about you nonstop. I've known about you from Day One. You've got to consider the source, you know. You go ahead and tidy up, then come out again. It is Crazyville out there. We need you. You're being a big help."

Kindness from one she had thought was a rival was too much for Diane. Her eyes filled up with tears, and she fumbled in her pocket for a tissue. Dorothy walked over to the sink and yanked a couple of paper towels off the roll.

"You know, your boyfriend sat and listened to me cry in this very room not too long ago," Dorothy said, handing them to her. "What goes around, comes around." She slipped out of the room and left Diane alone.

Feeling as if she had misunderstood everyone horribly, Diane sat and snuffled miserably until the paper towels grew soggy in her hands. Poor Keith, with so much on his mind. And she had refused to listen to him when he was telling her the truth.

She felt her way blindly out of the lunchroom and found the nearest lavatory. Staring at her red-eyed reflection in the mirror, she resolved to go tell Keith she had been wrong. After dousing her face in cold water, she went out to find him.

* * *

Keith spotted Marcy standing on her tiptoes at the end of the hall. She waved at him, then lowered her hand. He nodded, to let her know he understood. The Little Folk were in the building. He glanced around to find Holl, and came face to face with Diane. He goggled at her.

"Diane, I . . ."

"I need to talk to you," she said. Her eyes were red.

"This way," he said, taking her by the hand. He led her toward the conference room, afraid to let go in case she changed her mind about talking to him.

On a Saturday, that part of the hallway was deserted. None of the children, eager to cooperate and act like professionals, had defied the arrow sign in the foyer and gone down to investigate the opposite corridor. Keith started to reach for the handle of the conference room door. Diane suddenly pulled back against his grasp.

"I don't want to go in there," she said.

Suddenly, Keith felt he didn't either. It took him a moment to recognize the force of an avoidance charm. The Master and the other Little Folk must be inside. Keith pushed at the substance of the charm. He braced himself against the curtain of repulsion, pushing through by main force of will.

"I don't want to go in there," Diane repeated, trying to pull away.

"Yes. You. Do," Keith gritted out, and they were through. He shoved the door closed behind him, and the two of them were suddenly face to face with the four elves. Politely, the Little Folk drew back to the extreme end of the room, to give the couple privacy.

Keith reddened. "Excuse us," he said. He dragged Diane across the conference chamber to the closet, pulled open the door, pushed her inside before him, and closed the door. The only light was a thread that peeked in past the doorjamb. It drew a glimmering line down one side of Diane's face, illuminating a tear drifting onto her cheek from her lashes. Keith pulled his handkerchief out of his pocket and dabbed at it. She took the small cloth from him and clutched it between her hands.

"Everyone's pushing me around today," she said, miserably.

Keith waited for her to blow her nose.

"Now," he said in a low voice. "I'm sorry you misunderstood what was happening up here. I tried to explain, really. I'm sorry you were upset with me. It wasn't my fault."

"I know," Diane said. She snuffled. "I hung up on you. I'm sorry, too, but I was so hurt thinking you could go off with anyone else. I've been under such a strain, worrying about the children. And then there was that poor air sprite getting killed, and I had a Chemistry exam I thought I blew, and then *he* said you were in bed with somebody else, and well," she finished in a burst of woe, "I *missed* you down there and it hurt thinking you didn't miss me as much."

"But I love *you*," Keith said, genuinely surprised, "and someday I want to marry you, when we're both out of school and I can explain to your parents why it wouldn't be a detriment to have me in the family."

Abandoning the handkerchief, Diane laughed. She threw her arms around him and squeezed him in a rib-cracking hug. Keith took the opportunity to express the devotion that had been building up over the past weeks of separation, kissing her with increasing ardor.

"Oh, Keith, my parents already like you," Diane said, managing to get a few syllables out between kisses. "And I love you, too."

"Ah!" the Maven said, clear across the room from the closet. His sharp hearing had picked up every word of the whispered conversation. He settled back in his chair with his hands behind his head. "*Finally.*" The Master, Enoch, and Tay added their indulgent smiles.

"But, Mommy," a shrill voice announced from the hallway, "that girl butted right in front of me!"

The child's voice was clearly audible in the closet. Keith and Diane broke apart and looked at each other, feeling guilty.

"Dola," they said together. They fled out of the conference room and into the hall to separate the two ten-year-olds, who were circling each other like prizefighters. The parents, each behind their own child, clutched applications and portfolios like cut and patch kits. One girl, round-faced and freckled, confronted the other, smaller and slimmer, but with a long, hollow-cheeked face.

"She pushed in ahead of me first!"

"Ladies, please!" Keith said. "Hey, both of you look absolutely pixielike, don't you think so, Miss Londen?"

"Oh, yes!" Diane exclaimed, not knowing exactly where Keith was going, but following valiantly.

"There's hardly any way to choose between you," he said, in a confidential whisper, hunkering down on his heels beside them and holding both girls' hands, "so we're going to turn you over to Mr. Martwick, who's going to take you right inside for your interview. All right?"

The girls glared at one another, but both recognized the benefits of getting in ahead of the rest of the crowd, even in a joint audition, so they nodded. The horsefaced child beamed determinedly, and turned back to her mother to have her rouge reapplied.

As soon as they were ready, Keith marched both children over to Brendan, who was just emerging from the office at the end of the hall. "Mr. Martwick, in the interest of fairness, both of these amazingly fairylike youngsters have got to be taken in to see our media director *next*, don't you agree?"

Brendan, uncertainly, grinned at the girls and yanked Keith aside. "What's going on, Keith? Relatives of yours? One of them's Gloria Swanson reincarnated and the other one's the Pillsbury Dough Girl. They haven't got a chance."

"They were fighting," Keith said under his breath. "If you want to keep it from becoming a mob in here, get them in and out as fast as you can. Picture it: five hundred little girls all screaming and crying . . ."

"Say no more," Brendan said, blanching at the mere idea. He took the girls' hands and escorted them into the office. "Right this way, please." The parents followed, bestowing smug glances on the other mothers who were still waiting. The door closed behind them.

"Whew!" Diane breathed. Dorothy came up behind them, and winked at Keith.

"Nice work. Nice work on Brendan, too."

"Thanks for straightening things out for us, Dorothy," Keith said.

"I'm so sorry for thinking there was something wrong," Diane said, her cheeks reddening.

"Hey, no charge," Dorothy said. She floated away from them to take on the next group of new arrivals.

Taking a moment for a breather, Keith went back to the conference room to check in with the Little Folk. They knew now to expect him, so the spell's substance pushed back before him like a curtain.

The elves sitting around the boardroom table grinned up at him as he came in. He realized that they must have heard his whole conversation with Diane. Feeling foolish, he ignored their expressions. Business was business.

"I'm glad you got here," he said. "Now we're ready. You sure she said she'll be here?"

"I do. I think she'll be as glad of it as we are," Holl said.

"The situvation has passed beyond her management," the Master said, regally upright at the head of the table. "She must resolf it, for she cannot continue to lif vith it for any measureable period of time."

"Good," Keith said. He retrieved his packet of papers from a spell-jammed file drawer where he'd placed it early that morning. "As soon as she turns Dola over to us, I'm giving this to Paul Meier."

"What is it?" Enoch asked.

Keith grinned wickedly. "The rope to hang friend Brendan up by his ankles."

"Oh, give it to me," Enoch said, holding out a hand. His dark eyes glowed like embers. "I'd be pleased to help any of that woman's collaborators to hang by any parts that would give them the most pain, after all she's done to us. I'll make sure Paul Meier does not read it until the correct moment."

Keith was alarmed. "Don't put any compulsions on him, okay? He's a good guy."

"I will not," the elf said, slightly affronted. There was a flash of the old, sullen Enoch Blackhair of the days before he fell in love with Marcy. "It will be on the papers. Your friend will find them irresistible when the woman has passed in and out of the building once."

Keith breathed relief. "That'll be perfect." Another wail erupted in the hallway. "Oops, gotta go!"

* * *

"I'm scared," Diane told Keith on one of her increasingly frequent passes by. "What if they don't come?"

"They'll come," Keith said, exuding a confidence he didn't feel. He glanced around to see if any of the other interns were looking, leaned over and gave her a quick peck on the cheek. She smiled. Things were back to normal between them—or better. Keith was relieved.

"Hey, Keith," Brendan called to him, coming out of the office. "They want coffee in there. You want to get some?"

"What's the problem?" Keith asked, closing the distance. "Forget how to boil water?"

"Hey, they need me in there," Brendan said. He decided not to argue with Keith. Looking around, he found another potential sucker. "Hey, Sean, you want to get some coffee for the media director? Two with one sugar, one with cream and no sugar. And maybe you could see if there's some doughnuts."

"Sure, Brendan," Lopez said, always willing to help. He strode off toward the lunchroom.

Keith let Brendan go back into the inner sanctum. He didn't dare leave the corridor again, out of concern that Mona Gilbreth would come while he was away, and he preferred that Brendan wasn't in the way. He passed, and smiled at, a little blond girl wearing a belted tunic, soft shoes, and a Peter Pan hat. Her shining hair hung down over her knees in braids tied with big bows of ribbon at the ends, and she had huge rouge spots over her sharp, high cheekbones. Her elf ears looked pretty good, very realistic. He got three steps beyond her, did a full double take, and turned around on his heel for a full stare. It was Candlepat. She came up and shyly tugged on his shirttail, and he stooped down to speak to her.

"I'll never forgive you for not knowing me," she said mischievously, "but look around you."

Two benches away, her sister Catra sat, dressed in an oversized tent of gauze and crepe, looking very fairy-like but too sophisticated for this kind of thing. Rose's granddaughter, Delana, with her massed tresses of red, drew eyes to the far end of the corridor from the media director's office. With a little more careful scrutiny, Keith made out Pat Morgan, wearing a false mustache, pretending to be the girl's father. Why not? he thought, realizing that he had asked Pat for advice on casting calls, but forgotten in his haste to ask for his help.

"Lee brought us," Candlepat said, as if reading his mind. "All of us wanted to help bring Dola home, but the ones who look too old," she preened, knowing she herself looked like an advertisement for the fountain of youth, "stay home and await our success."

Keith, looking around him and realizing how much of the cavalry was behind him, laughed. The stage, as far as it was ever going to be set, was set.

One by one, the line snaked forward. Some emerged from the Media office with tears in their eyes, others hopeful but bemused. The parents were invariably indignant that they had to wait so long, and scornful that their precious infants were being rejected.

The children, used to lengthy casting calls, were incredibly well-behaved during the ordeal. No one acted out by running up and down the hall, but a few took out their boredom and frustration on the other children, rivals for the single part to be had. Keith wasn't quite in time to save the child who pulled Candlepat's long, golden braids. The girl spent the next several minutes chasing an imaginary bee that buzzed around her head. No one but Keith and the other Little Folk could see the enhanced dust mote. The girl was near tears before Keith came up behind Candlepat and gave her a meaningful poke in the shoulder blade. Her response was to turn huge, innocent, blue eyes up to him, but the bee vanished immediately.

"C'mon," he said. "I've got to watch the door. I can't keep an eye on you all the time."

"I do wish you would," she said, with a hopeful expression, not missing a chance to vamp him. Keith grinned.

"Go away, little girl, you bother me," he said, in his best W. C. Fields voice.

More children came in as the line moved up to make room for them.

Dola did not really understand where they were taking her when they rousted her out of the little room in the cottage. For a change, she was not made to ride in the bumpy truck, but instead in a plush-padded automobile seat with Skinny beside her.

They had been driving for hours. Dola was worried, because she was moving ever farther away from the comforting trace of her people. Boss-lady spared her only the briefest glances over the back of the front seat. Jake didn't talk to her. And Dola could not understand what Skinny was talking about, with his ravings of a contest to find a real shoe fairy.

Her last word on the subject was "I do not make shoes." Since then, she had sat, with her arms folded across her chest, ignoring Skinny's attempts to make conversation.

The scenery they were driving through was very different from anything she had seen outside of television. She could see for a long way ahead of her. The city was taking over the landscape, brown and gray overwhelming green. Gigantic buildings thrust up out of the ground, getting more and more imposing as the car approached them.

Inside, she was feeling terrified and small, but she kept a cool exterior, as if she visited Chicago every day of her life. She had listened to the low exchanges between Jake and Mona Gilbreth, but none of them had made her any wiser as to her coming fate. Would she be left alone in this cold city?

The car turned onto a street entirely lined with skyscrapers, veered sharply around a corner, and plunged down into the darkness of a curved ramp. At the bottom of this terrifying ride was nothing more than a parking lot, but strangely secreted underground. Dola was made to alight from the car and walk between Jake and Skinny. She felt like a military prisoner marching between guards.

The only noise in the corridor they walked was their footsteps and breathing. They passed briefly up onto the surface of the city street, up a flight of three stairs, and into a building fronted with gray glass panels and gray glass doors. Jake pushed one of these open.

Massed voices of countless, shrill-voiced children all talking at once struck her ears like the clash of cymbals. The Big Folk hustled Dola through one more door, and she stood at the end of an informal line consisting of a hundred little girls and their hundred mothers and fathers. In the midst of the crowd, she saw Keith Doyle.

She wanted to call out to him to get his attention, to help get her away from her captors. Jake saw her take a deep breath and jammed his huge hand over her face. "You keep quiet until we tell you to talk." Keith disappeared, and Dola's heart sank.

The four of them pushed forward through the crowd. Dola tried to struggle free, to run and find Keith. Skinny kept a firm grasp on her arm and tugged her back into line. One father, whom they all but pushed out of the way, looked at her and up at the men. "Listen, guys," he said, "if she doesn't want to audition, don't make her. Sheesh."

"She could get lost in here if she gets loose," the boss-lady said to Skinny. "Hang on tight."

Keith popped his head in the conference room door. Tay, by the window, was pacing up and down. The Master sat at the head of the room, his eyes fixed on nothing. Enoch kept looking around, sighing impatiently. Holl was at the table with a large bag between his hands. They all looked up at Keith.

"They're here," he said.

Holl tied up the bag, but not before Keith got a look at the contents. He was dumbstruck.

"My God, where did you get all those jewels?"

"Go on," Holl said, urgently. "Hurry."

The two men kept Dola at one end of the room. She looked up at Diane, who hurried over to hand both of them forms and pencils. The blond woman smiled down on her, but her expression showed she thought Dola was a stranger. Not comprehending, the child felt more lost and alone than she had before. Skinny let go to fill in his sheet of paper, but Jake kept his grip.

Thankfully, Keith reappeared. The boss-lady bustled up to him, and her voice was still audible to Dola half a room away.

"Well?"

"Ms. Gilbreth, what a pleasure to see you!" Keith said out loud, turning from side to side to see if he could attract anyone's attention. None of the parents or children in the room had any time for anyone else's concerns.

Mona turned pale.

"Shh," she begged him, covering the side of her face with one hand. "No names, *please*! I'm ready to make the exchange."

Keith looked over her shoulder at Dola, and winked. "How

do I know that you'll let her go when we give you the ran—the package?"

"Don't be a fool! This has all gone on too long. Now, come on. Give me . . . what I asked for."

Keith peered sideways and nodded. A boy with blond hair came out of an alcove where he had been waiting, concealed. He showed her a bag. He hefted it, and it shifted with a sound like clattering dice.

Mona's eyes widened with greed. "Good!" She reached for it. The boy drew back.

"We want the girl released first," Keith explained.

"No!" Mona said. "I want to be out of here first. I don't want anyone to associate me with you, or anything else. And I'm holding you to your word—no persecution in the press, now or ever!"

"Sure," Keith said, ostentatiously raising his hands to shoulder level. "Whatever you want." Seeing his signal, Lee advanced upon her with his notebook in hand, camera slung over arm.

"Ms. Gilbreth? Ms. Mona Gilbreth! I'm Lee Eisley with the *Indiana Daily Star*. Can I have a word with you?"

"You lied!" Mona shrieked at Keith. "You promised no press!"

"I've got nothing to do with him," Keith said, giving Lee a puzzled look. "He's here covering the human-interest story."

She spun on her heel, and drew a sharp vector with a red fingernail toward the door. The muscle-man grabbed Dola and started to hustle her outside. The Master and the others flew out of their hiding places.

"Hey," said one mother, watching them run past, "they're not auditioning boys, too, are they?"

With a sweet, regretful smile, Candlepat abandoned her interview with the casting director's assistant and ran toward the others, rolling up her sleeves. The assistant ran after her.

"Wait!" she cried.

Brendan, emerging from the media director's office, ran up to Keith. "Wasn't that Ms. Gilbreth?"

"Uh, no!" Keith said, not wanting Brendan in the middle of things. "Hey, there's Paul in the doorway. I think he's looking for you."

"He is?" Brendan turned around. The door had drifted shut. "I'd better get in there."

Keith waded through the dozens of children who were wondering what was going on, and out into the foyer where a peculiar kind of fight was going on.

The skinny man who'd beaten up on him at Gilbreth's factory was under attack by Holl, Candlepat, and Enoch. Marcy and Diane were flailing at the bigger man with their clipboards, while Tay wound up a handful of air and flung it straight into the man's solar plexus.

"That's for being greedy!" he cried. "And that! That's for keeping my girl."

Battered and groaning, the big man doubled over in pain.

"What'd you do to him?" Keith demanded in a frantic whisper.

"Gripes," Tay said, in satisfaction. "He'll be no use the rest of today, tonight, and as long as it'll hold."

"That," Holl said, gumming together Pilton's back teeth, fingers, and toes, "is for the air sprite, and for Frank Winslow, whose heart you broke."

The skinny man promptly fell over onto the floor and tried to help himself up, with his fingers glued together into flippers.

Mona saw that she was getting the worst of the disagreement. Children, little children, were beating up her two bodyguards. It was time to get out. No more easy cooperation, she vowed, hustling the children toward the doors. She would take the girl to the backwoods of Montana and chain her up with mountain lions, and move her from place to place so those lying Doyles would never find her again. She dodged past the two black men. The dark-haired girl tried to get in her way. Like a linebacker with the ball, Mona held on to Dola and made for the gray glass doors.

"She's getting away!" Candlepat shrilled.

"No!" Keith yelled.

He grabbed Holl's shoulder and threw an illusion with all his strength and will onto the nearest gray glass panel. A door handle shimmered into existence, and the handles on the doors seemed to vanish.

Mona grabbed for the sole visible doorknob and threw herself against the door to get it open. Nothing happened. She hammered on the panel, wondering if it was stuck. In the momentary delay, the small woman with the big glasses advanced upon Mona and Dola.

The others were closing in around the three of them. Mona was cornered. She would be exposed. She'd go to prison.

"She's perfect!" the casting assistant cried, dropping to her knees beside the little girl. "How could you *think* of leaving before we saw this absolutely enchanting child? I think that Scott would love to see you. Wouldn't you like to stay for an interview, miss?" she asked the blond child.

The little girl looked to Keith Doyle for guidance. He nodded violently. The little girl nodded violently, too.

"Oh, yes!" she said. "Wouldn't that be nice, Ms. Gilbreth?"

"Ms. Gilbreth, how about an interview?" Lee said, raising his camera, and focusing for a picture.

"Take it and go, Ms. Gilbreth," said a low voice behind her. She felt something shoved into her fist.

Wide-eyed, Mona recognized the voice of H. Doyle, and looked down at the child-sized being behind her. The family resemblance was there, including the strangely deformed ears. But he was so small. . . . Her mind refused to accept any more conflicting data. He pushed open one of the real doors for her. Panic-stricken and overwhelmed, she clutched the bag and shot out of the room. As soon as they could, the two men followed her.

The casting assistant took charge of Dola and led her back into the main hall, chatting in enthusiastic tones about her coming audition.

"You look like a real fairy," the young woman told her.

Diane whispered in Keith's ear. "Do you know, she's been zinged, and she doesn't even know it?" He caught her sly grin and returned it.

As they returned to the hall, Keith watched as slowly, inexorably, Paul Meier reached for the packet of papers left on a chair, and started to read them. Enoch's spell was effective, and right on target. Brendan came up to confront Keith.

"That *was* Ms. Gilbreth I saw!" Brendan said. "I'd better go to her. She'll think I didn't notice she was here. She was expecting to see me."

"She just left, Brendan," Keith said, shaking his head.

"Well, I'll catch her. Be back in a moment." He started to follow her, but Paul Meier came up behind him and took his arm in a firm grip.

"Brendan, can I talk to you? It's about these pamphlets you wrote up on the Gilbreth campaign. Ms. Gilbreth wasn't a Rhodes scholar, was she? And I didn't know she was president of Greenpeace. And this stuff about her Ph.D. in chemistry—don't you know anything about ethics? Or research? Do you know what putting out false information does to PDQ's reputation? I want to have a little word with you in the conference room. Do you have a moment?"

Blanching, Brendan let himself be led away.

Still talking, the casting assistant came up to Keith. "Was Dola here with Ms. Gilbreth? Who's her guardian?"

Tay started forward, but Keith pushed in front of him. "I am. I'm her . . . cousin."

The young woman beamed. "Keeping it all in the family, eh? Well, come on. Scott has got to see this girl." She went on at length about how perfect Dola would be for the layout, and how perfect the makeup job was that someone had done on her. Keith Doyle agreed with everything she said.

"And the Tinkerbell outfit, just adorable," the assistant gushed, escorting them past the crowd and into the office.

"This old thing?" Dola said, astonished. "I've been wearing it for two weeks!"

"Well, it's got such authenticity, doesn't it?"

Scott, by contrast, had only one sentence to say to Dola.

"Do you want the job?"

Dola, having gone from incarceration in a lonely cabin, to having the world make a fuss over her, was delighted to agree to anything Keith Doyle was so happy about. "Oh, yes! But what is it?"

"Great," said the tall man with the mustache. "Shooting begins Monday. You come here. Contracts. Here. We want you to sign right away. You have an agent?"

"No. Do I need one?" Dola asked, looking up at Keith, who looked it over.

"Between you and me, Scott," Keith said, "is this an honest contract?"

"It's okay," Scott said. "It's fair. Standard form. How about it?"

"It's okay," Keith said, handing a pen to Dola. In careful, Palmer penmanship, Dola signed 'Dola Doyle' on the line.

"Pretty name," Scott said, accepting the document. "Eupipinous."

"I think you mean 'euphonious,' " Dola corrected him gently.

"Hey, smart little kid."

"It runs in the family," Dola said, with a sly upward glance at Keith. He put his arm around her shoulders and squeezed.

"Well, the part's filled," Scott said, leaning back in his chair and smoothing his mustache, "although I think the artist had someone particular in mind all along, didn't you, Keith?"

"Well, yes," Keith admitted.

"That's all right. It worked out perfectly. You've got just one more dirty job to do."

"What's that?" Keith asked.

"You've got to tell all those kids out there to go home."

Chapter
EIGHTEEN

When the hall was cleared out, Keith took Dola back to the conference room, where all of the allies, Big and Little, were waiting. Marcy and Diane set up a cheer as soon as Dola appeared. As soon as she saw her father, Dola ran across the room and jumped into his arms to give him a big hug and kiss. She all but danced from person to person, giving them enthusiastic embraces. Even the Master unbent when she hopped up to kiss him on the cheek.

"I want a bath, and I want to eat something that tastes like food," Dola said, reaching Keith and Holl at the end of the line, "and oh, how is Asrai?"

"She misses you," Holl said gravely. "You'll see her soon."

"Thank you," Dola said. "And thank you, Keith Doyle." She tried to jump up into his arms. He caught her up and swung her in a circle. Diane spun Keith around and hugged Dola at the same time, making an affectionate sandwich out of the little girl.

"I'm *so* glad to see you safe," Diane said, fiercely. "Are you all right?"

"Oh, yes, I'm fine. Skinny was kind to me. I almost liked him, up until the time he shot the ghost—oh, Keith Doyle!" Dola cried, twisting to face him. "I've remembered what I was going to tell you! When I was in the house in the woods, we were visited by a creature. I've never seen one like it. It looked like a ghost, and it made pictures in my head. It was friendly. I think it was looking for me. And then the skinny man shot it, and oh, Keith Doyle, I think it was my fault! It was another kind of being, not like us or like you, but intelligent! I grieved when it was killed, but I guessed that where one existed, there must be more. You must go looking for them, right away!"

Keith exchanged solemn glances with the Master and Holl. "I think I know who you're talking about."

"You know? You've seen it?"

"Yup."

"Can that not wait?" the Master said. "Ve must leaf here before they close up the building."

"Right. Sorry, Master," Keith said. "Congrats, everyone. Are you all going home now?"

"Certainly not," Catra said.

"No, indeed," said her sister. "Lee has promised to take us to the amusement park. I think we well deserve the treat, and no old Conservatives to say no—uh, er, unless you disapprove, Master?" she amended humbly, noticing the village headman's half-lidded gaze upon her and suddenly remembering they were not as devoid of authority figures as she thought.

The Master lifted the corner of his mouth, which for him was a mark of great good humor. "No, in fact I agree. You deserf a reward. It is Big Folk culture, but vun afternoon vill not spoil you. Go."

Delighted and grateful, they started talking about the wonders they were going to see. "I hear there is also a shopping center nearby!" Candlepat exclaimed excitedly.

"Oh, yes," Marcy said, drawn into the conversation. "Right across the street. It's *enormous*."

"Oh, no," Lee said. "I'm not going to take a bunch of women all around no shopping mall."

"Me, neither," Dunn added, shaking his head. Enoch, looking disgusted, folded his arms and shook his head once. Dunn took that as support for his side. "Yeah. The park. That's it. Okay?"

The young women surrendered with disappointed nods. "All right. We agree," Catra said, a little dejected. "The park it is." The party, consisting of everyone but Holl, the Master, Tay, Dola, Diane and Keith, divided itself into carloads, and prepared to go.

Keith reached into a pocket. "Wait!" he called. "It's on me." He took money out of his pocket and handed it to Lee. "Have a good time."

"Thanks, Dad," Lee said, with a wink and a grin. "We'll see." He shepherded the others out the door.

"Do you want me to take you home now?" Keith asked the Master. Tay and Dola, who had been talking together a mile a minute and heard nothing, glanced up at the mention of home. "Dola's been away a long time. I know everyone will want to see she's okay."

"Not at all," the Master said, wagging a finger at Keith. "A telephone call vill do for now. You haf promised to take me to see Professor Parker and his display. I hold you to it. I vish to go. And also this brave child deserfs indulgence after her ordeal. You shall take her somewhere special of her choosing aftervards."

"With pleasure," Keith said, bowing him out of the room. "I never mind spoiling Dola. Your chariot awaits. You old softy," he muttered under his breath.

The Master glanced back at him, clearly having heard every syllable. He gave a frosty look through his glasses, which quickly changed to an amused twinkle.

A thought struck Keith as they were leaving PDQ.

"Holl," he said, taking the elf aside, "you don't have twenty thousand dollars. You hardly have cab fare. Where did you get all those jewels you gave Mona Gilbreth?"

"We gave her what she expected to see," Holl said, reaching into a pocket. He handed Keith a faceted ruby an inch across. Keith handled it with awe.

"My God, that's beautiful! Did you find a mine or something?"

"Oh, no," Holl said. "We found a box in the pantry." From his pocket he took another gem of fabulous size, put it in his mouth and chewed it. It broke apart into fragments, then melted away. Keith watched, thunderstruck. "They're made of Jell-O. Remember? We had some at our wedding. Maura reminded me. And by the bye, she's got her ring back again."

Leaving her assistants to deal with their peculiar and sudden ailments, Mona hurried to keep her appointment at the national party headquarters. Jack Harriman met her at the door.

"I've got something really special to show you," she said, brandishing the bag. "Call everyone. They have to see, too."

With such a tantalizing mystery at hand, all activity in the central office came to a swift halt. Telephones rang unattended, as Mona Gilbreth prepared to unveil her great secret. Even the state party chairman was present in the crowd around a table in the middle of the big office.

"Okay, lady," Jack said, giving her a big smile. "We're ready. Lay it on us!"

Quivering with anticipation, Mona held out the bag of jewels. It was worth far more than the twenty grand she had demanded from H. Doyle. With this treasure trove, she would reinstate herself as the Environmental Candidate. It would rocket her in popularity among the party. She could sponsor committees. People would look up to her. She could almost feel the chair in her upcoming Washington office under her tailbone.

"Here's my donation to the Democratic Party for this election year!" With a flick of her wrist, she sent the jewels scattering across a tabletop.

There were gasps and cries of wonder. People picked up the gems and played with them, tried them on their fingers. In the strong lights overhead, the blues, greens, and reds glimmered like a fantastic stained glass window.

"It's a fortune," the state chairman said, seizing Mona's hand and shaking it. "What a windfall! Thank you, Ms. Gilbreth— or should we say, Congresswoman?"

Mona beamed. "Just Mona, please," she said. *Noblesse oblige*, she thought, enjoying the adulation.

"Hey, what's the matter with this one?" one of the volunteers said. She held out an emerald. Something was wrong with one of the facets. It looked as if it was chipped, but when the young woman flicked it with her fingernail, it quivered.

All around her, the same thing was happening to all of the other gems. Gradually, they became sticky and started to melt. People drifted away from Mona's side, leaving the lumps of colored goo on the table. After a short time, there was nothing left but brightly colored puddles. Mona looked up at Jack and the state chairman.

"I'm afraid," Jack said, with regret, "this isn't going to earn you any election-year goody accounts, lady."

The chairman walked away from the table and stalked back to his office. "Tell her to get out of here, Jack," he said. The door slammed behind him. Mona stood staring at the puddles of goop.

"If you're smart," Jack said, raising his shoulders apologetically, "you'll give the reason for your concession as being too busy keeping your business environmentally sound. People will buy that." He patted her on the shoulder. "Good luck, lady."

Mona tottered toward the door, wondering desperately if the first stone she had received would have turned to goo as well. If so, she was ruined, forever. She glanced back at party headquarters, already back to business as usual. No one paid attention to her. Unhappily, she slipped out of the door and hurried to find the nearest phone.

"How dare you slip me a fake gem?" the jeweler demanded, almost snarling. He didn't let her get a word of explanation in. "The damned thing *melted* on the table when I took it in for analysis. My reputation is ruined, and all because of you! I want every dime back today, and if I don't get it, I'm suing you for every single thing you own, my girl. I respected your father. He'd be ashamed to admit he knows you, Mona Gilbreth. . . ."

Mona hung up the phone in the midst of the tirade, and slunk dejectedly back to her car.

The guard at the Field Museum recognized Keith on sight. He was ready to pitch him out the door at once, until Professor Parker came barrelling out of the office to meet his guests.

"Dr. Alfheim, how wonderful to see you!" The little professor's kind face was beaming. "I am so delighted to see you all. And who is this delightful child?"

"My sister, Dola," Holl said, at once. "We're in town to have a tour."

"And this youngster?" Parker asked. "A friend of yours?"

Tay started forward to protest that he was not a child, and that Dola was his daughter. Keith waved madly behind Parker's back to shut Tay up. Holl had to use a charm on him speedily that locked together his jaws so he couldn't speak.

Through gritted teeth Tay grumbled. "You didn't have to do that. I'll play along. I thought he was one of us."

"In the search for the truth, yes," Holl whispered as they followed the small professor into the heart of the museum, "but there's a divergence in our family trees a good deal farther back than between you and me."

"Yes, my tenure here has been very interesting," Parker said, talking rapidly to the Master. "Very interesting indeed. A pity you didn't see my lecture, but I'll be happy to lend you the notes."

"I vould be fery grateful to haf them," the Master replied.

"What did you do to that guard?" Diane asked Keith as they trailed behind the Master and his friend. She noticed that the uniformed man was still behind them at a distance.

"Nothing," Keith said. His face was red to the ears.

As they made their way down through the main floor, the elves began to twitch uncomfortably because of the many magical presences in the museum, but were visibly discomfited when they got to the basement. Dola stuck her fingers in her ears and kept them there. Parker escorted them to his little cubbyhole and excused himself.

"I think my notes are in the secretary's desk. I will be right back."

"It's the charm on the left," Keith said, unnecessarily, as the Master and the other Little Folk crowded around the glass case to see. "What is it?"

"Most interesting," the Master said. "It is a charm for finding—a location beacon. It is designed as a toy for children, as you see. It may be sewn to the clothes, or carried in the hand like a doll. This one might haf been used as either, as you may see by the loop. It sends out a compelling signal to let you know where the child is, especially if the child is lost or too small to call out for help by itself. After many centuries, the signal has simply become louder and louder when no one answered."

"Oh," Keith said, and paused thoughtfully. "That would have shortened up our hunt for Dola by a whole lot. How come your kids don't have them?"

"Vhy?" the Master asked, rhetorically. "They haf not been able to go out of eye's distance in decades. This is the first time ve haf had room to range, when any could get lost."

"I'm making one for Asrai the moment we get home," Holl

vowed. He noted the design, and began to figure out the mechanics of the spell that made it work.

"And I one for Dola," Tay said. He smiled down at Dola.

"Interesting," the Master said, turning away from the case.

"Well, don't you want to get it out of there?" Keith asked in an undertone, worried. "Anyone who can hear it, *you* know . . . I'm sure I'm not the only one."

"No. You are surely not the only one. But all you haf to do is turn it off." Master laid a hand over the front of the case, closed his eyes, concentrated. Gradually, the low, bloodchilling wail for attention died away and stopped. Keith could feel his ears uncurling. Holl and Tay similarly relaxed, and Dola took her fingers out of her ears.

"That's only the worst of the unheard noises," Holl said, epigrammatically. "We must get out of here."

"I do agree," the Master said. "The ambience of this place is becoming most painful. But I do not vish to cut short my fisit vith my friend."

Parker returned at that moment with a bundle of papers, which he handed to the Master. "Wonderful thing, the high-speed photocopy machine," he said, smiling. "Americans have so many marvelous machines. Here are copies of all my data from the dig. I'd appreciate your feedback, having seen the site. For example, read this . . ."

"Yes, indeed," the Master said, hastily. "Perhaps not now."

"Professor Parker," Keith interrupted. "You're a stranger in these parts, too. I'm taking Dr. Alfheim around on a tour of the city. You want to come along?"

"Well, bless me, I think I'm free this afternoon. Why not? I'd be delighted. I'd love to get out of here for a while."

"Moved and seconded," Holl said, with relief.

"Oh, Keith Doyle," Dola asked in a hushed whisper as they left the museum. He had to lean close to hear her, and she pulled his ear down to her mouth. "You promised to show me—you know—how to find the ghostly beings."

Keith exchanged glances with Diane and Holl. "Okay. I think I know just exactly where to look."

"You do?" Diane asked, skeptically.

"Sure I do," Keith said, cheerfully. "Come on." He gave

one hand to Dola, and the other to Diane. The two of them skipped alongside him down the steps.

". . . so the man goes all over Europe with his camera," Keith said, pantomiming taking pictures in every direction, "shooting hundreds of rolls of film." He stood in the corner of the observation deck on the ninety-fifth floor of the John Hancock Center, telling jokes out loud and translating them simultaneously into mental images for both halves of his appreciative audience. Inside were Holl, Tay, Diane, and Dola, watching with fascination as the other half of his listeners gathered outside the window. Dola pressed herself against the glass, exchanging winks and blinks with the friendly 'ghosts,' no longer distorted by the pressures of heavy atmosphere. More and more of them gathered as his story progressed, sharing images of sunrise and rosy hues.

The Master, together with Professor Parker, sat talking together on chairs against inner building walls, discussing archaeology, and paying no attention to the entertainment.

"The man takes pictures of everything he sees—everything! Children, scenery, interesting garbage cans, cats, you name it. He has to get a separate suitcase for all of his film. The customs agents ask him if he bought stock in a foreign branch of Kodak. When he gets home, his best friend calls him up and asks, so, did you have a good time?

" 'I can't tell,' the man said." Keith visualized his tourist shrugging. " 'The pictures haven't come back yet!' "

Dola laughed delightedly, and the sprites outside the window showed their approval by swooping to and fro in a complicated knotlike dance like happy Japanese kites.

Keith chuckled. "You're my kind of audience. Oh, and have you heard the one about the man who went door to door selling mud packs . . ."

"Keith Doyle," Holl said, tapping him in the right kidney, "your audience is growing beyond my ability to fend off the attentions of the crowd around us."

Keith looked up, aware for the first time how the crowd of air sprites had grown, and how numerous the Big Folk tourists were becoming. "Ooops, sorry," he said sheepishly. "That's the end of the show, folks. Hey, look, the balloon racers are getting closer."

"Which one is Frank's?" Diane asked. Keith pointed to the

Skyship Iris, well back among the pack, but moving toward them in a frisky air current.

"Oh, it's so pretty!" Dola said.

The flock of sprites broke up, most of them flying up into the clouds, where they instantly blended in and disappeared. One came close to the window, winked at Dola, and fled out over the lake toward the balloons, leaving thoughts of sunset behind it. She stared after it, starry-eyed.

"They're so nice," she said, turning her face up to Tay. "Father, I wonder if we might build a tower on the farm so I can visit with them. Or can I go up in the balloon, like Keith Doyle did?"

"We'll see what your mother says," Tay said, diplomatically, putting an arm across his daughter's shoulders.

The Master came up to join the group admiring the cluster of colorful balloons. Only a few of the sprites remained, including Keith's first friend, who hovered at eye level.

"The professor had to leaf us. I am fery interested in our new friends here," the Master said, looking up at the sprites with interest. "I vould know more about them."

"Well, to me, the most important thing is you know you're not the only ones out there, I mean right here," Keith said, pointing this way and that. "One day, there ought to be a mass conclave of all the Little Folk in the world, so you can all get to know each other."

The air sprites responded to this idea with a mindnumbing display of creatures of all shapes and descriptions.

"You mean these all exist?" Keith said. "Yeah, if I can get them all interested, we could have one fabulous party."

"You organize it," the Master said, after a disbelieving stare at Keith, "and ve vill come."

"You bet," Keith said, dreamily. "Maybe we can even find the real *bodach* of Jura." An idea struck him. "Say, Master, I wanted to ask. After seeing how the advertising business works, are you sure you don't want me to make up an ad campaign for Hollow Tree Industries? It'd be a prizewinner."

"No, thank you," the Master said, fixing him with a disapproving stare calculated to drive the idea right out of his mind. "After vhat I haf seen I belief ve vould much rather be a vord-of-mouth success."

Epilogue

"I have this incredible compulsion to go shopping," Diane said, looking up at the great screen. "I don't know why."

Keith plastered innocent fingertips to his chest. "Don't look at me. Must be something in the air."

He smoothed the front of his rented tuxedo and looked around at the crowd. It was easy to tell who at the Clio Award banquet was in the business, and who were guests. The advertisers were paying no attention to the commercials being shown on the big screen over the dais, and the visitors couldn't keep their eyes off it. Too bad, when there were so many more interesting things to look at.

Diane, for example. She looked absolutely incredible in her drop-dead evening gown of black satin and lace, with a cluster of pink-tipped ivory roses clipped to the bosom. Beside her were Dorothy and her boyfriend, Jerome, who had medium brown skin, but startling green-hazel eyes that picked up lights from his date's metallic lamé gown that was green one way you looked at it, and pewter-black the other. Dorothy looked drop-dead gorgeous, too. She was celebrating getting the offer from PDQ. Her selection, she pointed out, was partly due to Doug Constance, suffering an attack of conscience and throwing his weight behind her.

"I'm happy for you," Keith said, raising his glass to her. "I really am."

"Even though you didn't get it?" Dorothy asked. "We were neck and neck there."

"It really doesn't matter to me," Keith promised. "It never did. And I'm planning to get my Master's degree, so I couldn't come to work right away anyhow."

"He means it," Diane said.

"If you ever come on the market, I may take you up on your application as a copywriter," Dorothy said. "No one at PDQ's as crazy as you. You hear from Sean?"

"Yup," Keith said. Dunbar Tyres had, as he feared, picked up and moved to a rival agency, but on their recommendation, the new agency had hired Sean on the strength of The Brain. "It's too bad about the shift, but I'm glad he got credit."

"Okay," Meier said, "but you and Brendan get credit, too, because Goodling Tyres UK like The English Channel, so nothing's wasted. You'll be seeing the commercials over the winter. I'll call and tell him, but I'm not so sure he'll be glad to hear my voice."

"Where is he?" Diane asked.

"Oh, he went back to Daddy's stockbroker firm," Meier said, with a wink. "We didn't charge him for the extra billing for Gilbreth, although we could have. Accounting is working it out with her. Her account has been . . . er, temporarily downsized. She'll be on her feet again one day. Still, PDQ got the best of the deal." He leaned over and patted Dorothy's hand. "We got this talented young lady on our staff, and someday she's gonna knock 'em dead."

"Maybe you'll hire me next year, huh?" Keith asked, playfully.

"I may be forced into it," Paul said.

"Why?" Keith asked. "Because of working with Dorothy?"

Paul shook his head, his usual wry smile on his face. "No, but you never know."

There were network cameras set up all over the room, gathering what Paul described as 'pick-up shots.' Keith concentrated on eating neatly to avoid looking like a slob when the camera panned their table. The technicians running the equipment became more energetic, and started passing hand signals to each other.

"It's starting," Paul said, turning around in his chair.

A tall man with gleaming white teeth stood up behind the podium and raised his hand. Everyone stopped talking to listen to him. He made a short speech and went straight to the nominations. Another man in evening wear handed award after award to a gowned woman, who passed them to the happy recipients. Speeches of thanks were short and frequently witty. Keith enjoyed the spectacle.

". . . Winner of the honorable mention, Judge Yeast, 'All Rise,' Perkins, Delaney, Queen," the master of ceremonies said. Bob, the account executive, accepted the statuette as the big screen showed the Judge Yeast commercial.

"I'm proud of the two of you," Paul said, leaning over the table. "First crack out of the box," he said when Bob sat down, "and you got an honorable mention. You can hope for better in the future."

"I hope so," Keith said.

"Count on it," said Paul.

The account executive was effusive. "This young lady," he said, framing Dorothy with his hands, "this brilliant young woman had the vision. The client was crazy about it, and you can always tell when a team really loves their product." Dorothy and Keith exchanged glowing glances. Diane squeezed Keith's arm, sharing their triumph.

"I hope that means a raise, Bob," Dorothy said, slyly.

"Praise is free," Paul said, shaking his head. "You gotta do better than an honorable mention for a raise."

The announcer went on with his presentations. Paul stopped the conversation at the table with a wave of his hand as the American Footwear commercial featuring Dola appeared over the announcer's head.

Keith admired the way the production team had taken his idea and run with it. In the aired commercial, Dola sat in a field of tall grass with a wreath of flowers on her head until the music began. The whole thing had been shot with a soft-focus filter. She sprang up and ran lightly down a path of short-cropped grass, to join an animated circle of dancers on a fairy mound. The camera followed the motions of her feet, then cut to the delight on her face.

"What a cute little girl she was," Dorothy whispered. "You were right. She was absolutely perfect for the campaign. Relative of yours?"

"Sort of a cousin," Keith whispered back. "She loved acting. I think we've created a monster."

Dorothy shook her head. "She's going to break hearts when she grows up, you know."

He exchanged wry glances with Diane. "She nearly broke mine already."

Diane leaned over to whisper to him. "I forgot to tell you, Holl says the water is pure again."

"Great!" Keith whispered back.

"Shh!" Paul hissed.

The announcer's voice interrupted him. "And the award goes to American Footwear, Fairy Footwear, Paul Meier, Scott Milliard, Dorothy Scott, and Keith Doyle."

"Go on, go get it," Keith urged Paul.

"Nope, you do it," Paul said, the half smile becoming a full grin. "You deserve it. Here's to this one and many more." He raised his glass.

"Huh?" Keith said.

"Accepting this award," the announcer said, "will be Keith Doyle."

Keith looked at Paul, who winked. "You knew about it."

"I set it up! Everything's on purpose in advertising, kid. I told you. Now, go. Enjoy."

Flushed, Keith made his way to the podium, shook hands with the announcer and the award presenter, and accepted the small statuette. He leaned over the mike and cleared his throat. The room became silent. Diane held up her hands and blew him a kiss.

Keith smiled at the audience and looked into the lens of the television camera. I sure hope this is being televised downstate, he thought.

"I don't have a prepared speech, so I'd just like to thank my team, Paul Meier, Scott Milliard, Dorothy Scott, Sean Lopez . . . and," his eyes twinkled mischievously, "all the Little People who made this possible. Thank you."